THE RABBIT HUNTER

Lars Kepler is a No.1 bestselling international sensation, whose Joona Linna thrillers have sold more than 12 million copies in 40 languages. The first book in the series, *The Hypnotist*, was selected for the 2012 Richard and Judy Book Club. *The Rabbit Hunter* is the sixth novel in the series and went straight to No.1 in Sweden, Denmark, Norway, Holland, Finland, the Czech Republic and Estonia.

Lars Kepler is the pseudonym for writing duo, Alexander and Alexandra Ahndoril. They live with their family in Sweden.

f Facebook.com/larskepler
www.larskepler.com

Also by Lars Kepler

The Hypnotist
The Nightmare
The Fire Witness
The Sandman
Stalker

THE RABBIT HUNTER

LARS KEPLER

Translated from the Swedish by Neil Smith

HarperCollins*Publishers*

HarperCollins*Publishers*
1 London Bridge Street
London SE1 9GF

Published by HarperCollins*Publishers* 2018
1

Originally published in 2016 by Albert Bonniers Förlag, Sweden, as *Kaninjägaren*

Lars Kepler asserts the moral right to
be identified as the author of this work

A catalogue record for this book
is available from the British Library

ISBN: 978-0-00-820590-4 (HB)
ISBN: 978-0-00-820591-1 (TPB)

Typeset in Electra LT Std by Palimpsest Book Production Ltd,
Falkirk, Stirlingshire

Printed and bound in Great Britain by
CPI Group (UK) Ltd, Croydon, CR0 4YY

MIX
Paper from
responsible sources

FSC
www.fsc.org
FSC™ C007454

It's early morning, and the still water of the inlet is shimmering like brushed steel. The luxurious villas are asleep, but outdoor lights glint behind tall fences and hedges.

A drunk man is walking along the road by the shore, a bottle of wine in his hand. He stops in front of a white house whose elongated façade faces the water. Very carefully, he puts the bottle down in the middle of the road, steps across the ditch, and climbs the black metal railing.

The man weaves his way across the lawn, then stops and sways as he stares at the big windows, the reflections of the patio lights, the indistinct outline of the furniture inside.

He heads towards the house, waving at a large, porcelain garden gnome, and then stumbles out onto the wooden deck. He manages to hit one knee, but keeps his balance.

The water of the pool shines like a blue sheet of glass.

The man stands unsteadily on the edge, unzips his trousers and starts to urinate into the pool, then weaves his way over to the navy-blue garden furniture and proceeds to soak the cushions, chairs and round table.

Steam rises from his urine in the chill air.

He zips up his trousers and watches a white rabbit as it hops across the lawn and disappears under a bush.

Smiling, he walks back towards the house, leaning against the fence. He makes his way down to the lawn, then stops and turns around.

His befuddled brain tries to make sense of what he just saw.

A black-clad figure with a strange face was staring at him.

Either the person was standing inside the dark house, or was outside, watching him in the reflection.

1

Summer

Drizzle is falling from the dark sky. The city lights glow high above the rooftops. There's no wind, and the illuminated drops form a misty dome that covers Djursholm.

Beside the still waters of Germaniaviken lies a sprawling villa.

Inside a young woman walks across the polished floor and Persian carpet as warily as an animal.

Her name is Sofia Stefansson.

Her anxiety makes her register tiny details about the room.

There's a black remote control on the arm of the sofa, its battery cover taped in place. There are water rings on the table. An old plaster is stuck to the long fringe of the carpet.

The floor creaks, as if someone is creeping through the rooms behind Sofia.

There are splashes of mud from the wet stone path on her high heels and toned calves. Her legs are still muscular even though she stopped playing football two years ago.

Sofia keeps the pepper spray in her hand hidden from the man waiting for her. She keeps telling herself that she has chosen this situation. She's in control and she wants to be here.

The man is standing by an armchair, watching her move with unabashed frankness.

Sofia's features are symmetrical, but she has a youthful plumpness in her cheeks. She is wearing a blue dress that shows off her bare shoulders. A row of small, fabric-covered buttons stretches from her neck down between her breasts. The little gold heart on her necklace bobs up and down at the base of her throat in time with her increased heart-rate.

She could say she's not feeling well, that she needs to go home. It would probably annoy him, but he'd accept it.

The man is looking at her with a hunger that makes her stomach flutter with fear.

She is seized by the feeling that she has met him before – could he have been a senior manager somewhere she worked, the father of a classmate a long time ago?

Sofia stops a short distance away from him, smiles, and feels the rapid beat of her heart. She's planning to keep her distance until she's figured out his tone and gestures.

His hands don't look like they belong to a violent man: his nails are neatly trimmed and his plain wedding ring is scratched from years of marriage.

'Nice house,' she says, tucking a stray lock of hair away from her face.

'Thanks,' he replies.

He can't be much more than fifty, but he still moves ponderously, like an old man in his old home.

'You took a taxi here?' he asks, and swallows hard.

'Yes,' she replies.

They fall silent again. The clock in the next room strikes twice with a brittle clang.

Some saffron-coloured pollen falls silently from a lily in a vase.

Sofia realised at an early age that she found sexually charged situations exciting. She enjoyed being appreciated, the sense of being chosen.

'Have we met before?' she asks.

'I wouldn't have forgotten something like that,' he replies.

The man's grey-blond hair is thin, combed back over his head. His slack face is shiny, and his brow is deeply furrowed.

'Do you collect art?' she asks, nodding towards the wall.

'I'm interested in art,' he says.

His pale eyes look at her through horn-rimmed glasses. She turns away and slides the pepper spray into her bag, then walks over to a large painting in a gilded frame.

He follows her and stands slightly too close, breathing through his nose. Sofia startles when he raises his right hand to point.

'Nineteenth century . . . Carl Gustaf Hellqvist,' he lectures. 'He died young. He had a troubled life, full of pain. He got electric shock therapy, but he was a wonderful artist.'

'Fascinating,' she replies quietly.

'I think so,' the man says, then walks towards the dining room.

Sofia follows him even though she feels like she is being lured into a trap. It's as if the way out is closing behind her with sluggish slowness, cutting off her escape route little by little.

The huge room is furnished with upholstered chairs and highly polished cupboards. There are rows of leaded windows looking out across the water.

She sees two glasses of red wine on the edge of the oval dining table.

'Can I offer you a glass of wine?' he asks, turning back towards her.

'I'd prefer white, if you have any,' she replies, worried that he might try to drug her.

'Champagne?' he says, without taking his eyes off her.

'That would be lovely,' she replies.

'Then we shall have champagne,' he declares.

When you visit the home of a complete stranger every room could be a trap, every object a weapon.

Sofia prefers hotels, because at least there's a chance that someone would hear her if she had to call for help.

She's following him towards the kitchen when she hears a peculiar, high-pitched sound. She can't figure out where it's coming from. The man doesn't seem to have noticed it, but she stops, and turns to look at the dark windows. She's about to say something when there's a very distinct sound, like an ice-cube cracking in a glass.

'Are you sure there's no one else here?' she asks.

She could slip her shoes off and run towards the front door

if anything happened. She's more agile than him, and if she were to run, leaving her coat hanging where it is, she'd be able to get out.

She stands in the kitchen door as he takes a bottle of Bollinger from a wine fridge. He opens it and fills two slender glasses, waits for the bubbles to settle and then tops them up before walking over to her.

2

Sofia sips the champagne. She lets the taste spread through her mouth, hears the bubbles burst in the glass. Something makes her look over towards the windows again. A deer, maybe, she thinks. It's dark outside. In the reflection she can see the sharp outline of the kitchen and the man's back.

The man raises his glass again and drinks. His hand is shaking ever so slightly as he gestures towards her.

'Unbutton your dress a little,' he says weakly.

Sofia empties her glass, sees the mark of her lipstick on the rim, and puts it down on the table before gently teasing the top button open.

'You're wearing a bra,' he says.

'Yes,' she replies, and undoes the second button.

'What size?'

'Sixty C.'

The man stays where he is and watches her with a smile, and Sofia feels her armpits prickle as she starts to sweat.

'What panties are you wearing?'

'Pale blue, silk.'

'Can I see?'

She hesitates, and he notices.

'Sorry,' he says quickly. 'Am I being too direct? Is that it?'

'We should probably handle payment first,' she says, trying to sound simultaneously firm and casual.

'I understand,' he says tersely.

'It's best to get it out of the—'

'You'll get your money,' he interrupts with a hint of irritation in his voice.

When she sees her regulars things are usually very straightforward – pleasant, even – but new clients always make her nervous. She worries about things she's experienced in the past, like the father of two in Täby who bit her on the neck and locked her in his garage.

She advertises on *Pink Pages* and *Stockholmgirls*. Almost all the people who contact her are a waste of time. Lots of crude language, promises of wonderful sex, threats of violence and punishment.

She always trusts her gut instinct when she starts to correspond with someone new. This particular message was well-written. It was fairly direct, but not disrespectful. He said his name was Wille, his phone number was blocked, and he lived in a nice area.

In his third email he explained what he wanted to do to her, and how much he was willing to pay.

She took that as a warning.

If it sounds too good to be true, then there's something wrong. There are no free meal-tickets in this world, and it's better to miss out on a generous deal than put yourself in danger.

Still, she's here now.

The man returns and hands her an envelope. She counts the money quickly and puts it in her bag.

'Is that enough for you to show me your underwear?' he says.

She smiles warmly, gently takes hold of both sides of her dress and slowly lifts it above her knees. The hem rubs against her nylon tights. She pauses and looks at him.

He doesn't meet her gaze, just stares down between her legs as she gradually raises the dress to her waist. Her silk underwear shimmers like mother-of-pearl beneath her pale tights.

'Are you shaved?' he asks in a slightly hoarser voice.

'Waxed.'

'Completely?'

'Yes,' she replies.

'That must hurt?' he says, sounding genuinely interested.

'You get used to it,' she says with a nod.

'Like a lot of things in life,' he whispers.

She lets her dress drop again and takes the opportunity to wipe the sweat from her palms as she smooths the fabric over her thighs.

Even though she has the money she's starting to feel nervous again.

Possibly because he paid so much, five times more than any previous client.

In one of his emails he explained that he was prepared to pay extra for her discretion, and for his specific wishes, but this is way above her normal rate.

When he wrote to tell her what he wanted to do, she didn't think it sounded that bad.

She remembers one man with worried eyes who dressed up in his mother's underwear and wanted her to kick him in the crotch. He paid for her to pee on him as he lay on the floor crying in pain, but she couldn't do it. She just grabbed the money and ran.

'People get turned on by all sorts of things,' Wille says with an embarrassed smile. 'Obviously you can't force anyone . . . I mean, you have to pay for some things. I'm not expecting you to actually enjoy what you do.'

'It depends, but I do sometimes enjoy it if the man's gentle,' she lies.

Naturally Sofia promises full discretion in her ad, but she still has one safety measure as a precaution. She keeps a diary at home, where she makes a note of the names and addresses of people she's arranged to meet, so that someone will be able to find her if she ever goes missing.

Besides, Tamara saw Wille once, just before she stopped working as an escort, got married and moved to Gothenburg. Sofia knows that Tamara would have posted a warning on the sex-workers' forum if he'd behaved inappropriately.

'As long as you don't find me revolting and repulsive,' the

man says, taking a step closer to her. 'I mean, you're so beautiful, and I'm . . . well, I know what I look like. I was OK when I was your age, but . . .'

'You look good now,' she assures him.

Sofia thinks of all the times she's heard people say that escorts have to be like psychologists, but most of the men she sees never say anything personal.

'Shall we go up to the bedroom?' Wille asks lightly.

3

Sofia follows him up the broad wooden staircase thinking about how badly she needs to pee. The soft carpet is held in place on each step by thin brass rods. The light from the large chandelier reflects off the varnished banister.

Sofia's initial plan had been to concentrate on exclusive clients, the ones who were prepared to pay more for an entire night, ones who wanted company at a party or on a trip.

In the three years she's been working as an escort she's had maybe a couple of dozen jobs like that, but most of her clients just want a blow-job after work before they go home to their families.

The master bedroom is well-lit, dominated by an imposing double bed with beautiful grey silk sheets.

On the wife's side there's a Lena Andersson novel and a jar of fancy hand cream, and on Wille's side there's an iPad with finger-marks on the dark glass.

He shows her the black leather straps he's already tied around the bedposts. She notes that they're not new, the creases are slightly cracked and the colour has begun to flake off.

The room suddenly shudders and spins around a couple of times. She looks at the man, but he seems unconcerned.

He has white marks at the corners of his mouth, from tooth-paste.

The staircase creaks and he glances towards the hallway before looking back at her.

'I have to be able to trust you to release me when I say so,' he says as he unbuttons his shirt. 'I have to be sure that you won't try to rob me or just run off now that you have your money.'

'Of course,' she replies.

His chest is covered with fair hair, and he's making an effort to suck in his stomach while she looks at him.

Sofia thinks that she can ask to go to the bathroom once he's tied up. There's an en-suite. The door is open and she can see the shower and a patch of gold mosaic wall in the mirror.

'I want you to tie me up, and take your time with it – I don't like violence or force,' he says.

Sofia nods and takes her shoes off. She feels dizzy again as she straightens up. She looks him in the eye before lifting her dress up to her navel. It crackles with static. She slips her thumbs beneath the top of her tights and starts to pull them down. The feeling of constriction eases as the thin fabric puddles around her calves.

'Perhaps you'd rather be tied up instead?' he asks, smiling at his suggestion.

'No, thanks,' she replies as she starts to unbutton her dress.

'It's actually pretty comfortable,' he jokes, tugging gently at one of the straps.

'I don't do that sort of thing,' she explains breezily.

'I've never tried it the other way around . . . I'd be prepared to double your fee if you did it,' he says with a laugh, as if the thought surprises and delights him.

What he's now offering is more money than she earns in two months, but having to lie there tied up is much too dangerous.

'What do you say?' he smiles.

'No,' she replies.

'OK,' he says quickly, and lets go of the strap.

The buckle makes a tinkling sound as it hits the bedpost.

'Do you want me to take all of my clothes off?'

'Wait a while,' he replies, giving her an oddly searching look. 'Is it OK if I use the bathroom?'

'Soon,' he says. He sounds like he's trying to control his breathing.

Sofia's lips feel strangely cool. When she raises one hand to her mouth she sees his face break into a wide smile.

He walks over to her, takes hold of her chin tightly, and then spits straight in her face.

'What are you doing?' she asks, as a rush of giddiness sweeps through her head.

Her legs suddenly give out and she lands so heavily on the floor that she bites her tongue. She sinks onto her side as her mouth fills with blood, and she sees him standing over her, unbuttoning his corduroy trousers.

Sofia doesn't have the strength to crawl away. She rests her cheek on the floor and sees a dead fly in the dust under the bed. Her heart is beating so hard that she can hear it thudding in her ears. She realises that she must have been drugged.

'Don't. Don't do it,' she gasps, before closing her eyes.

Before Sofia loses consciousness it occurs to her that he might be about to murder her, and that this might be the last thing she ever experiences.

4

Sofia wakes up coughing. She suddenly remembers where she is. She is tied to Wille's bed. She's on her back, held in place by the leather straps. He's tied her so tightly that the muscles in her legs and arms are straining. Her wrists are burning and her fingers are ice-cold.

Her mouth is bone-dry, her tongue feels swollen and sore.

Her thighs have been spread, pushing her dress up around her waist.

This can't be happening, she thinks.

He must have drugged one of the champagne glasses while it was still in the cabinet.

Sofia hears a business-like conversation from the next room. Someone used to being in charge is talking.

She tries to lift her head up to look out of the window, to see if it's night or morning, but she can't. It hurts her arms too much.

It has just occurred to her that she has no idea how long she's been lying there when he comes into the room.

Fear fills Sofia's heart. She feels her throat constrict and her pulse race.

What definitely mustn't happen has happened.

She tries to calm herself, thinks that she needs to get a conversation going. She has to make him realise that he's picked the wrong girl, but that she won't say anything if he lets her go right away.

Sofia promises herself that she's going to quit being an escort, she's been doing it for too long, and she wastes the money on things she doesn't need.

The man is looking at her with the same hunger as before. She tries to adopt a relaxed expression. She knew right from the start there was something wrong here. But instead of turning around and walking away she ignored her gut instinct. She's made a catastrophic mistake.

'I said no to this,' she says in a composed voice.

'Yes,' he replies with a slow smile, and lets his eyes roam all over her body.

'I know girls who think this is OK. I can put you in touch with them if you'd like.'

He doesn't answer, just breathes heavily through his nose and steps to the end of the bed, between her legs. She feels sweat break out all over her body, and tries to prepare herself for what's to come.

'This is assault, you do realise that, don't you?'

He doesn't respond, just pushes his glasses up his nose and looks at her with great interest.

'This is making me feel very uncomfortable and violated,' Sofia begins to say, but stops when her voice starts to tremble.

She forces herself to breathe more slowly, to try not to seem scared, not to beg. What would Tamara have done? She can see her friend's freckled face in front of her, that slightly mocking smile, the hardness in her eyes.

'I've got your information written down in a book in my flat,' she says, looking him in the eye.

'What details?' he asks casually.

'Your name, which is presumably made up, but the address here, your email, the time of our meeting . . .'

'So now I know that,' he nods.

The mattress rocks as he starts to crawl up the bed towards her. He stops between her thighs, swaying, then grabs her underwear and pulls. The seams don't break, and her shoulder aches as if it's been dislocated.

15

The man tugs again, with both hands. It stings as the underwear cuts into her hips, but the reinforced seams won't tear.

He whispers something to himself, then leaves her on the bed.

The mattress sways again, and Sofia can feel her thighs starting to cramp.

She has a fleeting memory of football practice, the way she could tell when a cramp was on its way, the tightening of her calves as she tried to pick out lumps of mud from her cleats.

Her friends' hot red faces. The noisy locker room, the smell of sweat, liniment and deodorant.

How has it come to this? How did she end up here?

Sofia tries not to cry. She feels like she's finished if she shows fear.

The man returns with a small pair of scissors and cuts through her underwear on both sides, then pulls them off.

'There are plenty of people willing to do bondage,' Sofia says. 'I know—'

'I don't want girls who are willing to do it,' he interrupts, tossing her underwear onto the bed beside her.

'I mean, there are girls who get turned on by being tied up,' she says.

'You shouldn't have come here,' he declares bluntly.

Sofia can't hold her tears back any longer and starts to cry. She arches her back and tugs at the straps so hard that her skin tears and blood starts to trickle down the bottom of her right arm.

'Don't do it,' she sobs.

The man pulls off his shirt, throws it on the floor, pushes his trousers down and rolls a condom onto his half-erect penis.

He kneels down on the bed and she can smell the rubber on his fingers as he pushes her shredded underwear into her mouth. She starts to retch and comes close to throwing up. Her tongue is completely dry and tears are streaming down her cheeks. The man squeezes one of her breasts through the dress, then lies down heavily on top of her.

Sofia wets herself with fear, and a hot pool of urine spreads out beneath her.

When he tries to push into her, she twists to the side quickly and shoves him with her hip.

A drop of sweat falls from his nose onto her forehead.

He grabs her throat with one hand, looks at her, tightens his grip and lies on top of her again. His weight makes her sink into the mattress, which pulls her thighs further apart. Her ankles sting as the bedposts creak.

She struggles to breathe, tossing her head until she manages to get some air into her lungs.

He tightens his grip on her throat, and her vision starts to flicker. The room fades away as she feels him trying to force his way inside her. Sofia struggles to twist aside, but it's impossible, this is going to happen anyway. She can't stay inside her body, she has to think about something else. Flashes of memory dart past, cool evenings on the big football field, ragged breathing, clouds in front of her mouth, the silence down by the lake, the old school in Bollstanäs.

The coach points at the ball, blows the whistle, and then silence.

The grip on her throat disappears, Sofia spits out her underwear and gasps for air as she blinks.

Someone's ringing the doorbell downstairs.

He grabs her chin and forces her mouth open, then shoves the underwear back in, and she starts to retch again, breathing through her nose, unable to swallow.

The doorbell rings again.

The man spits on her and gets off the bed, pulls his trousers up and grabs his shirt before leaving the room.

As soon as he's gone Sofia pulls her right hand as hard as she can, without thinking of the consequences.

She feels excruciating pain, but her hand comes out of the strap.

Only the underwear in her mouth stops her from screaming out loud.

Her head is thudding. She's on the brink of passing out, and her whole body is shaking with pain. Her thumb could be broken, and the ligament feels torn. Her skin looks like an old glove and blood is coursing down her arm. She pulls the underwear from her mouth.

She whimpers out loud as she tries to loosen the strap around her left wrist. Her fingers keep slipping, but eventually she manages to pick the buckle open. She quickly tugs the strap through the catch, then sits up and removes the restraints from her ankles.

She gets up on unsteady legs, clutching her wounded hand to her stomach, and starts to walk across the thick carpet. Her head is pounding with shock and pain. Her feet feel numb and her dress is wet and cold over her backside.

Carefully she makes her way out of the bedroom and creeps along the hallway where the man has just disappeared.

Sofia stops before she reaches the staircase. She can hear another voice downstairs, and decides to shout for help. She can't hear what the other man is saying, and tentatively moves closer. There are clothes from the dry-cleaners hanging over the banister. Through the thin plastic she can see bundles of identical white shirts.

She clears her throat carefully, ready to shout for help, when she realises that the other man isn't inside the house. His voice is coming from the intercom. A messenger, asking to be let through the gate. Wille says that he'll have to come back, then puts the phone down and walks back towards the staircase again.

She staggers but manages to keep her balance. She has pins and needles in her feet as the blood flow returns.

Sofia moves backwards. The floor creaks beneath her and she looks around and sees a larger room further down the hall, with painted portraits on the walls. She thinks about running in and opening a window to call for help, but realises that she doesn't have time.

5

Sofia makes her way quickly along the wall and past the stairs, until she reaches a narrow cupboard door. She grabs the handle and pulls.

Locked.

Through the prisms of the chandelier, she watches the man walk up the stairs.

He'll reach her soon.

She walks back towards the stairs and crouches down on the floor, hidden by the dry-cleaned shirts. If he looks directly at her he'll see her, but if he just walks past she'll have a few seconds' headstart.

Her hand hurts so much that she's shaking, and her neck and throat are swollen.

The steps are old and worn, and the staircase creaks. She sees him between the banisters and shrinks back cautiously.

Wille reaches the top and walks down the hallway.

He walks towards the bedroom without noticing the blood she's left on the carpet.

Carefully she gets to her feet, watching his back and suntanned neck as he walks into the bedroom.

She walks silently around the railing and starts to run down the stairs.

She realises that he's turned around, and is already coming after her.

The thudding footsteps speed up.

She clutches the throbbing, bleeding fingers of her injured hand with her good one.

All she knows is that she has to get out of the house. She rushes through the large hallway, hearing the harsh creak of the stairs as the man comes after her.

'I don't have time for this!' he yells.

Sofia runs across a narrow rug towards the door. She trips over a pair of shoes but keeps her balance.

The alarm system is glowing on one side of the front door.

Her fingers are so wet with blood that the catch slips out of her hand. She wipes her hand on her dress and tries again, but it won't budge. She pushes the handle down and shoves the door with her shoulder, but it's locked. Her eyes dart around, looking for the keys as she tries twisting the catch again. She gives up and runs through the double doors leading to the living room.

Something metallic hits the floor in another room.

She moves away from the large windows, her own reflection a silhouette against the pale wall behind her.

She hears him coming from the other direction, retraces her steps and hides behind one of the doors.

'Every door is locked,' he says loudly as he enters the living room.

She holds her breath, her heart pounding in her chest, and the door creaks gently. He stops in the doorway. She can see him through the crack between the hinges, his mouth half-open, his cheeks flushed.

Her legs start to shake again.

He walks a few more steps, then stops to listen. She tries to keep quiet, but her frightened breathing is loud.

'I'm tired of this game now,' he says as he walks past her.

She hears him searching for her, opening doors and closing them again. He says loudly that he just wants to talk to her.

Furniture scrapes the floor, then silence.

She listens. She hears her own breathing, the ominous ticking of a clock, but nothing else.

Just silence.

She waits a little longer, listening for creeping footsteps, knowing this could be a trap, but still chooses to leave her hiding place, because this could be the only chance she gets.

She creeps further into the living room. Everything is quiet, as if enveloped in a hundred-year sleep.

Sofia goes over to one of the chairs around the polished table and tries to lift it, but it's too heavy. Instead she drags it by its back with her one good hand, pulling it towards the windowed patio doors, groaning with pain when she has to use both hands. She runs two steps, spins her body, and yelps as she swings the heavy chair against the glass.

The chair hits the window and falls back into the room. The inner pane shatters and crashes to the floor, scattering splinters of glass everywhere. Larger pieces slide down and are left leaning against the intact outer glass.

The burglar alarm starts howling at an ear-splitting volume.

Sofia grabs the chair again, ignoring the fact that the splinters are cutting her feet, and is just about to swing it against the window when she sees the man coming towards her.

She lets go of the chair and walks straight into the big kitchen, her eyes darting across the white floorboards and stainless steel countertops.

He follows with measured steps.

She remembers being chased as part of a game when she was little: the feeling of impotence when she realised her pursuer was so close that there was no chance of escape.

Sofia leans against the countertop for support and manages to knock a pair of glasses and an unusual-looking bracelet to the floor.

She doesn't know what to do. She looks over at the closed patio doors, then goes over to the island unit which has two sparkling saucepans standing on top of it, and yanks the drawers open with shaking hands, panting hard. She finds herself staring at a row of knives.

The man comes into the kitchen and she picks up one of the knives and turns to face him, backing away slowly. He stares at her, clutching a soot-stained poker from the fireplace in both hands.

She holds the broad-bladed kitchen knife up at him, but realises immediately that she doesn't stand a chance.

He could easily kill her. His weapon is much heavier.

The alarm is still shrieking. The soles of her feet are stinging from where she's cut them, and her injured hand feels numb.

'Please, stop,' she gasps, backing into the island unit. 'Let's go back to bed, I promise, I won't give you any trouble.'

She shows him the knife, then puts it down on the stainless steel countertop and tries to smile at him.

'I'm still going to hit you,' he says.

'You don't have to do that,' she pleads. She feels like she's losing control of her face.

'I'm going to hurt you badly,' he says, raising the improvised weapon above his head.

'Please, I give up, I—'

'You only have yourself to blame,' he interrupts, then unexpectedly lets go of the poker.

It falls heavily to the floor with a clatter, then lies still. Ash flies up from the prongs.

The man smiles in surprise, then looks down at the circle of blood spreading out from his chest.

'What the hell?' he whispers. He fumbles for support with one hand, but misses the countertop and staggers.

Another bloodstain appears in the middle of his white shirt. The red wounds on his body blossom like stigmata.

The man presses one hand to his chest and starts to stumble towards the dining room, but stops and turns his blood-smeared palm over. He looks like a frightened child. He tries to say something before sinking to his knees.

Blood squirts out onto the floor in front of him.

The alarm is still blaring.

Sofia sees a man with a very oddly-shaped head over by the pale curtains.

He is standing with his feet wide apart, and he's holding a pistol with both hands.

His face is completely covered by a black balaclava apart for his mouth and eyes. What look like strands of hair or stiff scraps of fabric hang down one cheek.

Wille presses his hand to his chest again, but the blood seeps through his fingers and down his arm.

Sofia turns unsteadily and looks straight at the man with the gun. Without taking his eyes from Wille, he takes one hand off the pistol and quickly snatches up the two spent shells from the floor.

He runs forward, passing her as if she doesn't exist. He kicks the poker away with his military boot, grabs Wille by the hair, yanks his head back, and presses the barrel of the pistol against his right eye.

This is an execution, Sofia thinks, and walks towards the living room as if in a dream. She hits her hip against the edge of the counter, and slides her hand along it. As she passes the two men, a shiver runs down her spine and she starts to run but slips in the blood. Her feet slide away from her, and she falls back and hits her head hard on the floor.

Her vision blurs and goes black for a moment, then she opens her eyes again.

She sees that he hasn't pulled the trigger yet, the barrel is still pressing softly against Wille's closed eyelid.

The back of Sofia's head is burning and throbbing.

Her vision is unfocused, everything is spinning. What she had thought were rough leather strips hanging down the man's cheek now look more like wet feathers or matted hair.

She shuts her eyes as dizziness clutches at her, then hears voices above the loud wail of the alarm.

'Wait, wait,' Wille pleads, breathing fast. 'You think you know what's going on, but you don't.'

'I know that Ratjen opened the door and now . . .'

'Who's Ratjen?' Wille gasps.

'And now hell is going to devour you all,' the masked man concludes.

They stop talking and Sofia opens her eyes again. A peculiar slow motion seems to have taken hold of the house. The masked man looks at his watch, then whispers something to Wille.

He doesn't answer, but looks like he understands. Blood is welling from his stomach, pouring down to his crotch. It forms a puddle on the floor.

Sofia sees that his glasses are lying beside her on the floor, next to the object she initially thought was a bracelet.

Now she realises that it's a personal alarm.

A small steel gadget with two buttons, attached to a watch-strap.

The masked man is standing perfectly still, looking at his victim.

Sofia carefully moves her hand sideways towards the alarm, tucks it against her body and presses the buttons several times.

Nothing happens.

The man lets go of Wille's hair but continues to press the barrel of the pistol to his right eye. He waits a few seconds, then squeezes the trigger.

There's a loud click as the bolt hits home. Wille's head is thrown back and blood cascades from his skull. Fragments of bone and grey matter spray across the kitchen floor, all the way to the dining room.

Sofia feels warm drops spatter her lips as she sees the empty cartridge fall and bounce across the floor.

A cloud of grey powder hangs in the air, and the dead body falls like a sack of wet clothes to the floor and lies there motionless.

The masked man bends over to pick up the shell and his watch slips down towards the back of his hand.

He stands with his legs on either side of the dead body, leans forward and presses the barrel of the pistol to the corpse's other eye. Then he flicks his head to shake what looks like matted hair away from his face before squeezing the trigger again.

6

Her work phone's ringtone becomes part of a dream about a stream running through dense vegetation. A moment later Saga Bauer is wrenched from sleep and gets out of bed so fast that she drags the covers onto the floor.

She hurries over to the gun-cabinet in her underwear as she dials the number she knows by heart. The glow of the streetlights filters through the slats of the blind, illuminating her sinuous legs and naked back.

She quickly unlocks the heavy steel door and listens to the instructions on the phone as she pulls out a black bag, and tucks a holstered Glock 21, along with five spare magazines, into it.

Saga Bauer works as an operative with the Security Police, specialising in counter-terrorism.

The ringtone that woke her means that a Code Platinum has been declared.

She runs to the hall as she listens to the final instructions, then drops the phone in her bag.

There's no time to lose.

She pulls her black leather bodysuit over her naked body, feeling the cool fabric against her back and breasts, then pushes her bare feet into her boots and grabs her helmet, heavy bullet-proof vest and gloves from the rack.

Without wasting time locking the door she leaves her flat,

tugging her zipper up to her chin. She pulls her helmet on, tucking in a few stray strands of blonde hair.

There's a filthy Triumph motorcycle out on Tavast Street. It has a shoddy muffler, frame sliders that have been repaired a number of times, and a broken transmission. She runs over to it, and lets the lock fall to the tarmac with its heavy chain.

She straddles the motorcycle, kicks the engine into gear and sets off as fast as she can.

Ignoring traffic lights and stop signs, she accelerates to pass a taxi.

The engine vibrates against the inside of her knees and thighs, and the noise in her helmet sounds like a creature bellowing underwater.

Officer Saga Bauer is five foot six, with muscles like a ballet dancer. She was once one of the best boxers in northern Europe, but stopped fighting competitively a couple of years ago.

She's twenty-nine years old, and still breathtakingly beautiful with her pale skin, slender neck and clear blue eyes.

She doesn't think about her appearance much, and never notices that people tend to smile and blush in her presence.

A plastic bag swirls into the air in front of the motorcycle and she is dragged from her thoughts.

When she reaches Söder Mälarstrand she turns sharply left. The pedal scrapes the road but she manages to hold the line as she passes beneath the Central Bridge and up the access ramp.

This is the first time she's been involved with a Code Platinum. It's the alert reserved for the highest threats to national security.

She feels like she's flying as she passes the spires and narrow alleyways of Gamla stan and Riddarholmen.

Saga has trained for scenarios like this. She is expected to act independently and not be swayed by anything, even the law.

She can see the gloomy brick buildings of Karolinska Hospital ahead, and pulls onto the E4, pushing the three-cylinder, 900cc engine to its limits and hitting two hundred and twenty kilometres an hour. She passes Roslagstull and turns left towards the university.

The cold air helps her stay calm as she thinks through the

information she has been given and formulates an initial operational strategy.

Saga gets off the highway and speeds along Vendevägen towards Djursholm with its lush greenery and sprawling villas. The turquoise glow of swimming pools shimmers between fruit trees and bushes.

She pulls onto a roundabout too quickly, and takes the first exit to the right. Before her brain has time to notice the parked car her muscles instinctively react and the bike swerves sharply. She almost falls, but manages to counteract the momentum using her bodyweight. The rear wheel slides across the road. There's a muffled thud as she hits a large plastic dustbin before she regains control of the bike and accelerates hard.

Her heart is pumping.

Fortunately, her motorcycle has a low centre of gravity and extremely responsive steering.

That's probably what saved her.

Saga sees big yachts out on the water as she follows the wide curve of the road through the imposing houses. She's already leaning hard to her left, but accelerates further as she reaches the shore.

7

Saga slows down as she approaches the address she was given.

She lets the bike fall sideways onto the grass beside the road, drops her helmet and pulls on her bulletproof vest and holster.

Thirteen minutes have passed since her phone woke her up.

The alarm is shrieking inside the house.

For a moment, she wishes Detective Joona Linna was there. She has worked alongside him in all her biggest cases so far. He's the best police officer she's ever met.

She let him down once, but will never do it again.

They lost touch after he received his prison sentence. She would have liked to visit him, but she knows he needs to construct a new life for himself. It's going to take a lot to win the trust of the other prisoners.

Now a Code Platinum has been declared, and Saga is on her own.

No one else from the Security Police has arrived yet.

She climbs over the gate and runs up to the main entrance of the villa. She inserts an opener into the lock, then the thin end of her lock-pick. She moves the pick slightly to the right inside the mechanism until the catch releases.

The lock opens with a dull click.

Dropping her tools on the ground she draws her Glock, releases the safety and opens the door. The sound of the howling alarm drowns out everything else.

Saga quickly checks the entrance and large hallway beyond it, then hurries back to the alarm control panel and taps in the code she memorised.

Silence sweeps through the house. It feels foreboding.

With her pistol raised and her finger on the trigger she goes through the hallway, past the staircase, and reaches a large living room. She checks behind the doors and along the wall to the right, then continues in a crouch.

One of the big windows at the back of the house has been broken. A chair is lying overturned on the floor, surrounded by sparkling fragments of glass.

Saga moves on, towards the door to the kitchen, and sees herself reflected in the glass surfaces.

Blood and fragments of skull are splattered across the floor, sofa and coffee table.

She sweeps the room with her pistol then keeps moving slowly as more and more of the kitchen comes into view. She sees white cupboards and stainless steel countertops.

She stops and listens.

She can hear a low ticking, as if someone is tapping a fingernail on a tabletop.

Aiming her gun at the door to the kitchen, Saga moves silently to one side of it, and sees a man lying on his back on the floor.

He's been shot through his chest and both eyes.

The back of his head is gone.

A dark puddle has spread out beneath him.

His hands are lying by his sides, as if he's sunbathing.

Saga raises her pistol again and checks the rest of the kitchen.

The curtains in front of the patio doors are swaying, billowing into the room. The rings on the curtain rod are tapping against each other.

Blood from the first shot to the man's head has sprayed far across the floor, and been trodden about by bare feet.

The prints lead directly towards Saga.

She quickly turns and sweeps her pistol around the room

before walking back towards the double doors leading to the living room.

Saga startles when, from the corner of her eye, she sees a person crawling out from their hiding place behind one of the sofas.

She spins around just as the person stands up. It's a woman in a blue dress. Saga points her pistol between the woman's breasts as she takes an unsteady step.

'Hands behind your head!' Saga calls out. 'Get on your knees, get down on your knees!'

Keeping the pistol raised, Saga runs forward.

'Please,' the woman whispers, dropping the personal alarm on the floor.

She barely has time to show that her hands are empty before Saga kicks her from the side, just below her knee, so hard that both her legs are knocked out from under her and she falls to the floor with a thud, hip first, then her cheek and temple.

Saga is on her instantly. She punches her in her left kidney, then presses the pistol to the back of her head, holding her down with her right knee as she scans the room again.

'Is there anyone else in the house?'

'Only the gunman, he went into the kitchen,' the woman replies, gasping for breath. 'He fired and then went—'

'Quiet!' Saga interrupts.

Saga quickly rolls her onto her stomach and pulls her arms behind her. The woman submits to everything in a disconcertingly calm way. Saga handcuffs her with a zip tie, then gets to her feet and hurries into the kitchen, past the dead man.

The curtains are still billowing, blown by the wind.

Aiming the pistol ahead of her, she steps over a soot-smeared poker, checks the left-hand side of the kitchen, then moves behind the island unit towards the sliding doors.

There's a round hole in the glass, made by a diamond cutter, and the door is open. Saga goes out onto the deck, and sweeps the lawn and flowerbeds with her pistol.

The water is still, the night silent.

Someone who broke into a house and carried out such a clean execution would never stay at the scene of the crime.

Saga goes back inside to the woman. She ties her ankles with more zip ties, but keeps one knee on the small of her back.

'I need some answers,' she says quietly.

'I have nothing to do with this, I just happened to be here, I didn't see anything,' the woman whispers.

Saga pulls the woman's dress down to cover her bare backside before she gets up. Soon five SUVs will pull up outside and the Security Police will pour into the house.

'How many gunmen?'

'Just one, I only saw one.'

'Can you describe him?'

'I don't know. He had a mask over his face, I didn't see anything, black clothes, gloves, it all happened so quickly. I thought he was going to kill me too, I thought—'

'OK, just wait,' Saga interrupts.

She goes over to the dead body. The man's round face is intact enough that she has no trouble identifying him. She pulls out her phone, moves a short distance away and calls the head of the Security Police. It's the middle of the night, but he's been waiting for the call and answers immediately.

'The Foreign Minister's dead,' she says.

8

Seven minutes later the house and grounds are swarming with members of the Security Police's specialist unit.

For the past two years the Security Police has dramatically increased the level of protection for members of the government, with bodyguards and modern personal alarms. There are different levels of alert, but because the terrified woman managed to press both buttons on the alarm simultaneously for longer than three seconds, a Code Platinum was declared.

The crime scene has been cordoned off, three separate zones around the Greater Stockholm area are being closely monitored, and roadblocks have been set up.

Janus Mickelsen comes in and shakes Saga's hand. He's taking over command of the operation inside the house, and she quickly briefs him on the situation.

Janus has an almost hippie-like charm, with his strawberry-blond hair and pale ginger stubble. Saga always thinks he looks all peace and love, but she knows he used to be a professional soldier before he ended up in the Security Police. He took part in Operation Atalanta, and was stationed in the waters off Somalia.

Janus positions one agent at the door, even though they won't be keeping the usual list of people visiting the crime scene. Under Code Platinum regulations, no one can know who is informed or aware of events and who isn't.

Two Security Police officers walk over to the young woman Saga handcuffed. Her eyes are red from crying and her mascara has run down her temple.

One of the two men kneels down beside her and takes out a syringe. She becomes so scared that she starts to shake, but the other officer holds her tightly as the sedative is injected directly into her vein.

The woman's cheeks turn red, she cranes her neck, her body tenses and then goes limp.

Saga watches them cut the zip ties, put an oxygen-mask over her nose and mouth, then lift the sedated woman into a body-bag and zip it closed. They carry the inert form outside to a waiting van.

The four other teams are already busy with their examination of the crime scene, scrupulously documenting everything. They're recording finger- and shoe-prints, mapping splatter patterns, bullet-holes and firing angles, gathering biological evidence, textile fibres, strands of hair, bodily fluids, fragments of bone and brain, as well as pieces of glass and splinters of wood.

'The minister's wife and children are on their way home,' Janus says. 'Their plane lands at Arlanda at 08.15, and everything needs to be cleaned up here by then.'

The members of the unit have to gather information in one search. They won't get another chance.

Saga goes up the creaking staircase and into the Foreign Minister's bedroom. The room smells like sweat and urine. Leather straps hang from the four bedposts. There are bloodstains on the sheets.

A riding crop is visible on top of a chest of drawers, in the glow of a watch-winding case. Behind the glass a Rolex ticks silently next to a Breguet.

Saga wonders if the minister's wife knew about the prostitutes.

Probably not.

Maybe she just didn't ask.

Over the years you realise that you can put up with all sorts of cracks in your self-image and still cling to security.

Saga herself spent years in a relationship with a jazz pianist, Stefan Johansson, before he walked out on her.

He's moved to Paris now. He plays in a band and he's engaged.

When Stefan is on tour in Sweden, he calls her late at night and she lets him come over. She knows there's no chance he'll leave his fiancée for her, but has nothing against sleeping with him.

Saga knows she isn't easy to live with. She has a fiery temper and a tendency to overreact in certain situations.

She goes back downstairs to the bullet-riddled body in the kitchen.

The glare from the lights reflects off the ridged aluminium floor. It feels like she's standing on a silver bridge above a scene of bloodstained chaos.

Saga spends a long time looking at the dead man's upturned palms, the yellow callus beneath his wedding ring, the sweat-stains under the arms of his shirt.

The team around her are working quickly and silently. They're filming and cataloguing everything on an iPad using three-dimensional coordinates. Strands of hair and fabric are taped to transparent film, while tissue and skull-fragments are placed in test-tubes which are then immediately chilled.

Saga walks over to the patio door and examines the circular hole in the three layers of glass.

The alarm didn't go off until the chair was thrown at the window, when the acoustic detectors and magnetic contacts reacted.

So the chair wasn't thrown by the killer.

Saga thinks back to the look of terror on the woman's face, her wounded wrists, the smell of urine.

Was she being held captive here?

Two men are covering the floor with large expanses of chilled foil, pressing it down using a wide rubber roller.

One IT specialist wraps the hard-drive from the security-camera controller in bubble-wrap, then puts it in a cool-box.

Janus is stressed. His jaw is clenched, and his freckled brow almost white and beaded with sweat.

'OK . . . what do you think?' he asks, coming over to stand beside Saga.

'I don't know,' she replies. 'The first shot to his abdomen was fired from a distance, and from a slightly strange angle.'

Blood has been oozing from the Foreign Minister's stomach onto the floor.

A bullet leaves a ring of dirt around its entrance hole. There are two circles of powder dust on the man's shirt.

The first two shots were from a distance, then there were two at extremely close range.

Saga bends over the body and looks at the entrance wounds in the eye-sockets, noting that there is none of the usual cratering around the openings.

'He used a silencer,' she whispers.

The killer must have used the kind of silencer that also muffles the flare, because there is no evidence of the percussive gases igniting. Otherwise the gas would have forced its way under the skin and left an obvious depression around the wound.

She straightens up and steps aside to make room for a forensics officer, who spreads a sheet of plastic over the dead man's face. He presses it against the bullet-holes in an effort to gather particles from the ring of dirt, then marks the centre of the entrance holes on the plastic with a marker.

'He was rolled onto his stomach after his death, then over onto his back again,' Saga says.

'What for?' the forensics officer asks. 'Why would—'

'Shut up,' Janus interrupts.

'I want to see his back,' Saga says.

'Do what she says.'

They all feel like time is starting to run out. They anxiously fasten bags around the Foreign Minister's hands, and lay out a body-bag beside him. They lift him up carefully and lay him down on his stomach in the bag. Saga looks at the wide exit wounds in his back and the messy void at the back of his head.

She stares at the floor where he was lying and sees the bullet-holes from the two final shots, then realises why the body had been rolled aside.

'The gunman took the bullets with him.'

'No one does that,' Janus mutters.

'He used a semiautomatic pistol with a silencer . . . Four shots fired, two of which were clearly lethal,' she says.

A heavyset man is going around the dark-toned furniture in the living room, spraying luminol over the fabric as another forensics officer puts an armchair back into place over the depressions in the rug.

'Get ready to pack up, everyone,' Janus shouts, clapping his hands. 'We're cleaning the house in ten minutes, and the glazier and painter will be here within an hour.'

The heavyset man removes the forensic team's floor-tiles behind them as they leave. As soon as they exit the door a team enters the house to clean it.

The killer not only took the spent cartridges with him, but also dug the bullets out of the floor and walls while the alarm was howling and the police were on their way. Not even the very best hit men do that.

They're dealing with a perfectly executed murder, yet he left a witness. He could hardly have failed to notice someone watching him at the crime scene.

'I'll go and talk to the witness,' Saga says. The woman must be involved somehow.

'You know we've already got our experts there,' Janus says.

'I need to ask my own questions,' Saga replies, and sets off towards her motorbike.

9

The bomb-shelter beneath Katarinaberget in Stockholm was the biggest nuclear shelter in the world when it was built at the start of the Cold War. Today the whole place, other than the section that used to house the backup generators and ventilation units, is used as a parking garage.

The machine house is a separate building, blasted into the bedrock alongside the actual shelter.

These days it is used by the Security Police.

It's the site of the secret prison known as the Spinnhuset. The most highly classified interrogations take place deep in the bowels of the old ice pools.

It's still early in the morning when Saga passes the Slussen junction on her motorcycle. Her sweaty leather bodysuit feels cold against her breasts. She drives in through the arched entrance next to the petrol station, and heads down into the garage. The shift in acoustics amplifies the sound of the engine.

Rubbish has gathered beneath the peeling yellow railings, and loose cables hang from the loudspeakers.

The panels covering the wide groove in the floor rumble beneath the tyres as Saga passes the shelter's immense sliding doors, designed to protect against a pressure wave.

As she heads down the concrete ramp, her mind ponders the unsolved riddle.

Why would the woman activate the security alarm and then stay at the crime scene if she was involved in the murder?

Why would the killer leave a witness if she wasn't involved in the murder?

The Security Police see her as a security risk whether she was involved or just happened to be in the wrong place at the wrong time.

Saga brakes carefully as she circles deeper and deeper inside the parking garage.

The woman's identity has been verified. Her name is Sofia Stefansson, and she appears to work part-time as a prostitute, though that hasn't been confirmed.

So far they're relying on what she said, and the very limited documentation they've found in her flat.

Saga can't rule out the possibility that Sofia has been recruited by a terrorist organisation.

Maybe she was the bait; maybe she filmed what happened in bed in order to blackmail the Foreign Minister?

But in that case, why was he killed?

Saga lets go of the brakes and swings into the lowest level.

She drives past a few parked cars, tyres squealing. Red dust swirls up around the motorcycle. She parks and walks over to a blue blast-proof door.

She swipes her ID, taps in the nine-digit code and waits a few seconds. The door opens onto an airlock.

She shows her ID again and is signed in by a guard who takes her pistol and keys. After passing through the full-body scanner she is let through the inner door of the airlock.

Jeanette Fleming sits inside the staffroom. She's a psychologist, and one of the Security Police's specialist interviewers. She's a beautiful middle-aged woman, with ash-blonde hair cut in a boyish style.

Jeanette is elegantly dressed as usual. She's eating salad from a plastic container. 'You know I'm not hitting on you, but you really are ridiculously attractive,' she says, pushing her plastic fork into the salad. 'I somehow forget about it every time . . . some sort of self-preservation instinct, I assume.'

38

Jeanette puts the rest of the salad in the fridge. They walk towards the lifts.

'How's your appeal going?' Saga asks.

'I've been turned down.'

'Sorry to hear that.'

Jeanette waited eight years for her husband to decide he was ready to have children, and then he left her. She then spent three years trying Internet dating before applying for artificial insemination from the Swedish health service.

'I don't know, if they say no, I might go down to Denmark to do it . . . but I still want the child to speak Swedish,' Jeanette jokes as she gets into the lift with Saga.

She presses the button for the lowest level.

'I've only read the initial report on my phone,' Saga says.

'They were too rough on the girl. She got scared and clammed up,' Jeanette says. 'They had orders to go in hard.'

'Who gave the orders?'

'I don't know,' Jeanette replies.

The lift descends quickly. The light from the cage reflects off the rough rock walls, and the counterweight shimmers briefly as it glides up past them.

'Sofia's afraid of being hurt again. She needs someone who'll listen to her, protect her.'

'Who doesn't need that?' Saga smiles.

They reach the bottom and walk quickly down the hallway. At this depth everything seems still and grey.

Sofia Stefansson's story has been corroborated by the discovery of a high dose of the fast-acting sedative flunitrazepam in her blood. Her wrists and ankles are wounded and there's bruising on the inside of her thighs. Her fingerprints have been found on the chair that smashed the window.

If her story is true, then she's a victim according to the law prohibiting the purchase of sexual services: she was assaulted and exploited by her customer, and should be allowed to speak to both the police and a psychologist.

But since she could also be involved in a serious act of terrorism, the law doesn't matter.

'I think it's best if I wait in the control room to start,' Jeanette says.

Saga taps in the code and opens the door to the former ice-store.

The lighting in the windowless room is very bright. A security camera is recording at all times.

The store was built to fit two hundred tons of ice to keep the shelter cool in case of nuclear war.

Sofia Stefansson is standing uncomfortably in the middle of the floor on a plastic sheet. Her shoulders are pulled back tightly, and her hands are tied behind her back. Her weight is held by the cable she's hooked to, which stretches up to a plank beneath one of the beams. Her head is lowered and her lank hair hides her face.

10

Saga walks straight over to Sofia. She makes sure she's still alive and then explains that she's going to lower her to the ground.

Saga starts to turn the winch. Sofia gradually sinks to the floor. One of her legs starts to buckle.

'Put your heels on the floor and take the strain,' Saga calls.

The skin on Sofia's ankles is torn, and Saga thinks of the bloody straps around the bedposts upstairs in the house.

First she was there, and now she's down here.

Sofia is lying on her side on the plastic sheet. Her breathing is laboured. She looks even younger without makeup. She could be very young. Her eyelids are swollen and the bruising around her neck is more pronounced.

When Saga loosens the straps on her arms she starts to tremble and her body tenses up.

'Don't hurt me,' she gasps. 'Please, I don't know anything.'

Saga winches the empty cable back up towards the ceiling, then pulls a chair over to Sofia.

'My name is Saga Bauer. I'm an officer with the Security Police.'

'No more,' she whispers. 'Please, I can't bear it.'

'Sofia, listen to me . . . I didn't know they were treating you like this. I'm sorry about that, and I will be bringing it to my boss this afternoon,' Saga says.

Sofia lifts her head off the floor. Her cheeks are smeared with tears. All her jewellery has been removed, and her brown hair is plastered to her pale face with sweat.

Saga has experienced waterboarding. It formed part of her advanced training, but she doesn't consider it particularly effective.

She looks over at a bucket of bloody water with a towel floating in it, and thinks to herself that the only thing torture reveals is the torturer's own secrets.

Saga gets a bottle of water and helps Sofia drink some, then gives her a piece of chocolate.

'When can I go home?' Sofia whispers.

'I don't know. We need answers to a few questions first,' Saga says apologetically.

'I already told you all I know. I haven't done anything wrong. I don't understand why I'm here,' Sofia sobs.

'I believe you, but I still need to know what you were doing in that house.'

'I already told them everything,' she whimpers.

'Tell me,' Saga says gently.

Sofia slowly raises her stiff arms to wipe the tears from her eyes.

'I work as an escort, and he contacted me,' she replies in a thin voice.

'How did he contact you?'

'I advertise, and he wrote an email explaining what he was interested in.'

The young woman sits up slowly, and accepts another piece of chocolate.

'You had pepper spray with you. Do you usually have that?'

'Yes, usually, although most people are pretty kind and considerate . . . I actually have more trouble with people falling in love with me than people getting violent.'

'Is there anyone who knows where you're going, who can come if you need help?'

'I write the names and addresses in a book . . . and Tamara, she's my best friend, she'd already had him as a client and didn't have any trouble.'

'What's Tamara's last name?'

'Jensen.'

'Where does she live?'

'She moved to Gothenburg.'

'Do you have a phone number?'

'Yes, but I don't know if it works.'

'Do you have other friends working as escorts?'

'No.'

Saga takes a few steps back and looks at Sofia. She thinks she's telling the truth about her work.

There's nothing that contradicts her story, even though there's little that backs it up.

'What do you know about your client?'

'Nothing. He was just prepared to pay a lot of money to be tied up in bed,' Sofia replies.

'And did you tie him to the bed?'

'Why do you all keep asking the same thing? I don't get it. I'm not lying. Why would I lie?'

'Just tell me what really happened, Sofia,' Saga says, trying to catch her eye.

'He drugged me and tied me to the bed.'

'What did the bed look like?'

'It was big. I don't remember much about it. Why does that matter?'

'What did you talk about?'

'Nothing.'

Forensics have been through her computer, mobile phone and the notebook with the addresses – there's nothing that suggests Sofia realised her client was Sweden's Foreign Minister.

Saga looks at the young woman's drained face. It occurs to her that Sofia could be sticking to her original story a little too well. It's almost as if she's avoiding certain details in order not to be found out telling lies.

'Was there a car parked outside the gate when you arrived?'

'No.'

'What did he say on the intercom when you rang the bell?' Saga asks.

'I don't know who he is,' Sofia says, her voice close to breaking.

'I get that he's rich and important, but I don't know anything about him, just that he said his name was Wille. But it's normal for men to use fake names.'

Saga knows that if Sofia is part of some radicalised group and sympathises with their goals, she's not going to confess anything. But if she has been tricked or forced to participate, there's a chance she might open up.

'Sofia, I'm listening, if there's anything you want to tell me . . . You haven't murdered anyone, I already know that, and that's why I think I can help you,' Saga says. 'But to be able to do that, I need to know the truth.'

'Am I being charged with anything?' Sofia asks blankly.

'You were present when the Swedish Foreign Minister was murdered, you lay tied up in his bed, you threw a chair to break his window, and you stepped in his blood.'

'I didn't know,' Sofia whispers, and her face turns white.

'So I need some answers . . . I understand you might have been tricked or coerced, but I'd like you to tell me what your mission was yesterday evening.'

'I didn't have a mission. I don't know what you mean.'

'If you're not prepared to cooperate with me then there's nothing I can do for you,' Saga says firmly, and gets up from her chair.

'Please, don't go,' the young woman says desperately. 'I'll try to help you, I promise.'

11

Saga lets Sofia beg her not to leave as she walks over to the door.

'If anyone's threatening you or your family, we can help,' Saga says, opening the door. 'We can organise a safe-house, new identities, you'd be all right.'

'I don't understand, I . . . Who's threatening us? Why would . . .? This is crazy.'

Saga wonders once again if Sofia really was simply in the wrong place at the wrong time. But that still begs the question: why would a professional killer leave a witness behind?

If she really is a witness, she must have seen something that could help the investigation. When she was questioned before, she wasn't able to give a description of the killer. She just kept repeating that his face was hidden, that the whole thing happened so quickly.

Saga needs her to start remembering genuine details. The tiniest thing could open up memories she's blocked out due to shock.

'You saw the murderer,' Saga says, turning around.

'But he was wearing a hood. I already said that.'

'What colour were his eyes?' she asks, closing the door again.

'I don't know.'

'What was his nose like?'

Sofia shakes her head, and a crack in her lip starts to bleed.

'The Foreign Minister was shot. You turned around and saw the killer standing there with the gun in his hand.'

'I just wanted to get away. I started to run but I fell, and then I found that alarm, which . . .'

'You need to tell me what the perpetrator looked like when you turned around,' Saga says.

'He was holding the pistol with both hands.'

'Like this?' Saga asks, demonstrating a two-handed grip.

'Yes. He was staring straight ahead, past me . . . He didn't care that I was there. I don't even know if he saw me. Everything happened in a matter of seconds. He was behind me, but he ran past and grabbed hold of . . .'

She stops speaking and frowns, staring ahead of her as if seeing events unfold in her mind's eye.

'He grabbed him by his hair?' Saga asks gently.

'Wille fell to his knees after the second shot . . . The murderer was holding him by his hair, and he pressed the pistol against one of his eyes. It was all so unreal.'

'He was bleeding a lot, wasn't he?'

'Yes.'

'Was he scared?' Saga asks.

'He seemed terrified,' Sofia whispers. 'He was trying to buy time, saying the whole thing was a mistake. He had blood in his throat and it was hard to hear, but he was trying to say it was a mistake, that he should let him live.'

'What were his exact words?'

'He said . . . "You think you know everything, but you don't . . ." and then the murderer said . . . really calmly, that . . . that "Ratjen opened the door". No, hold on, he said: "Ratjen opened the door" . . . and "hell will devour you all", that's what he said.'

'Ratjen?'

'Yes.'

'Could it have been any other name?'

'No . . . well . . . I mean, that's what it sounded like.'

'Did it seem like the Foreign Minister knew who Ratjen was?'

'No,' Sofia replies, closing her eyes.

'Come on, what else did he say?' Saga asks.

'Nothing. I didn't hear anything else.'

'What did he mean about Ratjen opening the door?'

'I don't know.'

'Is Ratjen the one doing this? Is he responsible for unleashing hell?' Saga asks loudly.

'Please . . .'

'What do you think?' Saga asks.

'I don't know,' Sofia replies, and wipes tears from her cheeks.

Saga walks quickly towards the door. She hears Sofia calling after her.

12

The driver's face is immobile as he glances in the rear-view mirror to check that the vehicle behind him is still following closely.

The sound of the engine runs through the Prime Minister's custom-made Volvo like a comforting purr.

A year ago the Security Police decided that the Swedish Prime Minister needed an armoured, reinforced vehicle. It has twelve cylinders and 453 horsepower, and can do one hundred kilometres an hour in reverse. Its windows are designed to stop bullets from high-velocity weapons.

The Prime Minister is sitting on the spacious leather seat in the back of the car with the finger and thumb of his left hand gently massaging his closed eyelids. His dark-blue suit is unbuttoned, and his red tie hangs crookedly across the front of his shirt.

Saga sits beside him, still in her leather bodysuit. She hasn't had time to change, and she's hot. She feels like unzipping the bodysuit down to her waist, but doesn't because she's still naked underneath.

The head of the Security Police, Verner Sandén, sits in the front seat. His hand is curved over the back of the seat, and his long frame is twisted so that he can look at the Prime Minister while he briefs him on the situation.

He runs through the chronology in his deep voice, from the time the Code Platinum was declared, to the accelerated examination of the crime scene and the ongoing reports from the forensics team.

'The house is back to its original state. There's nothing to indicate what happened there last night,' Verner concludes.

'My thoughts are with the family,' the Prime Minister says in a low voice, turning to look out of the window.

'We're keeping them out of this. Naturally, we're maintaining the highest level of secrecy.'

'You say the situation is dire?' the Prime Minister asks as he replies to a text.

'Yes, there are specific circumstances that led us to request an urgent meeting with you,' Verner replies.

'Well, as you know I'm travelling to Brussels this evening. I really don't have time for this,' the Prime Minister explains.

Saga can feel her butt cheeks sticking to her leather bodysuit.

'We're dealing with a professional or semi-professional killer who sticks within the framework of his brief,' she says, trying to raise her butt a little.

'The Security Police are always prone to grand conspiracy theories,' the Prime Minister says, looking down at his phone again.

'The killer used a semiautomatic pistol with a silencer that cools the percussive gas,' she says. 'He killed the Foreign Minister with one shot through his right eye. Then he picked up the empty shell, leaned over the dead body, put the pistol to the left eye, fired again, picked up the shell, then turned—'

'What the hell?' the Prime Minister says, looking up at her.

'The killer didn't trigger any of the alarms himself,' Saga goes on. 'But even though the alarms were blaring loudly enough to wake the entire neighbourhood, and even though the police were on their way, he stayed to dig the bullets out of the wall and wooden floor before leaving the villa. He knew where all the security cameras were, so there's no footage of him anywhere . . . And I can tell you now that forensics aren't going to find anything that could lead us any closer to him.'

She stops speaking and looks at the Prime Minister, who

takes a swig of water, puts the heavy glass back down and wipes his mouth.

The car glides towards north Djurgården. To their left is the great grass expanse of Gärdet. In the seventeenth century the area was used for military exercises, but today the only people around are a few joggers and dog-walkers.

'So it was an execution?' he asks in a hoarse voice.

'Yes. We don't know why yet, but it could be blackmail. The killer could have been trying to get classified information,' Verner explains. 'The Foreign Minister could have been forced to make some sort of statement on film.'

'That doesn't sound good,' the Prime Minister whispers.

'No. We're convinced this is an act of political terrorism, even though no one has claimed responsibility overnight,' Verner replies.

'Terrorism?'

'There was a prostitute in the Foreign Minister's home,' Saga says.

'He has his problems,' the Prime Minister says, wrinkling his long nose slightly.

'Yes, but—'

'Drop it,' he interrupts.

Saga glances at the Prime Minister. There's a distant look in his eyes, and he's clenching his jaw. She wonders if he's trying to come to terms with what's happened. His government's Foreign Minister has been murdered. Maybe he's thinking back to the last time that happened.

On a grey autumn day in 2003, then Foreign Minister Anna Lindh was out shopping with a friend when she was attacked by a man who stabbed her in the arms and chest.

The Foreign Minister had no bodyguard with her, no personal protection. She was badly wounded and died in the operating room.

Sweden was different back then. It was a country where politicians still believed they had the right to proclaim socialist ideals of international decency.

'The woman who was being used by the Foreign Minister,' Saga goes on, looking the Prime Minister in the eye. 'She heard a fragment of conversation which leads us to believe that this is the first in a number of planned murders.'

'Murders? What sort of damn murders?' the Prime Minister asks, raising his voice.

13

The Prime Minister's Volvo rolls across Djurgårdsbrunn's narrow stone bridge, then turns left alongside the canal. The grit on the road crunches beneath the tyres. Two ducks wade into the water and swim away from the shore.

'The killer mentioned Ratjen as some sort of key figure,' Verner says.

'Ratjen?' the Prime Minister repeats questioningly.

'We believe we might have identified him. His name is Salim Ratjen, and he's serving a long prison sentence for narcotics offences,' Saga explains, leaning forward to free her damp back from her leather bodysuit.

'We see strong links between last night's events and a Sheikh Ayad al-Jahiz, who leads a terrorist group in Syria,' Verner adds.

'These are the only images we have of Ayad al-Jahiz,' Saga says, holding up her phone.

A short film clip shows a man with a pleasant, mature face. He has a grey-flecked beard and glasses. He is looking into the camera as he speaks. It sounds like he's addressing a group of attentive schoolchildren.

'He has drops of blood on his glasses,' the Prime Minister whispers.

Sheikh Ayad al-Jahiz concludes his short speech and throws his arms out in a benevolent gesture.

'What was he saying?'

'He said . . . "We have dragged unbelievers behind trucks and troop carriers until the ropes came loose . . . Our task now is to find the leaders who support the bombing and shoot them until their faces are gone",' Saga replies.

The Prime Minister's hand is shaking as he wipes his mouth.

They drive across another bridge and up towards the marina.

'The security service at Hall Prison recorded a call that Salim Ratjen made to an unregistered mobile phone,' Verner says. 'They discuss three big celebrations in Arabic. The first party coincides with the date the Foreign Minister was killed . . . the second is supposed to take place on Wednesday, and the third on October seventh.'

'Dear God,' the Prime Minister mutters.

'We have four days,' Verner says.

Branches brush the roof of the car as they turn abruptly and start to head back towards the Kaknäs Tower.

'Why the hell weren't you keeping this Ratjen under closer surveillance?' the Prime Minister asks, pulling a paper napkin from the box in the car door.

'He has no previous connections to any terrorist networks,' Verner replies.

'So he was radicalised in prison,' the Prime Minister says, wiping his neck.

'That's what we believe.'

The rain is getting heavier and the driver turns on the windshield-wipers. The blades sweep the tiny droplets from the glass.

'And you think that I might be . . . one of these celebrations?'

'We have to consider that possibility,' Saga replies.

'So you're sitting here telling me that someone might murder me on Wednesday,' the Prime Minister says, unable to conceal his agitation.

'We need to get Ratjen to talk . . . we need to know what his plans are before it's too late,' Verner replies.

'So what the hell are you waiting for?'

'We don't believe Salim Ratjen can be questioned in a conventional way,' Saga tries to explain. 'He didn't respond when he was questioned five years ago, and didn't say a single word during his trial.'

'You have ways and means – don't you?'

'Breaking someone down can take many months,' she replies.

'I have a fairly important job,' the Prime Minister says as he scrunches up the napkin. 'I'm married, I have two children, and . . .'

'We're very sorry about this,' Verner says.

'This is the first time you've really been needed – so don't tell me there's nothing you can do.'

'Ask me what we should do,' Saga says.

The Prime Minister looks at her in surprise, then loosens his tie slightly.

'What should we do?' he repeats.

'Tell the driver to stop the car and get out.'

They've reached Loudden, and the gloomy oil depot. The long spine of the pier is almost invisible in the grey rain.

Although the Prime Minister still looks uncertain, he leans forward and talks to the driver.

It's raining harder, a chill rain that splashes the puddles. The Security Police driver stops right in front of one of the oil tanks.

The driver gets out and stands a couple of metres from the car. The rain darkens his pale beige uniform jacket in a matter of seconds.

'So what should we do?' the Prime Minister asks once more, looking at Saga.

14

Work is over for the day in Unit T of the high-security prison at Kumla, and fifteen inmates are jostling for space in the cramped gym.

No kettlebells, dumbbells, bars or any other equipment that could be used as a weapon is permitted.

The inmates move aside when Reiner Kronlid and his body-guards from the Brotherhood come in. Reiner's power is based on the fact that he controls the flow of all narcotics in the unit, and he guards his position like a jealous god.

Without him saying a word, a skinny man gets off his exercise bike and quickly wipes the saddle and handlebars with paper towels.

The static fluorescent strip-lights reveal the shabby walls. The air is heavy with the smell of sweat and tiger balm.

As usual, the group of old junkies is standing outside the dividing Plexiglas wall, and two Albanians from the Malmö gang are loitering by the folded table-tennis table.

Joona Linna finishes a set of pull-ups, lets go of the bar and lands softly on the floor. He looks over at the window. Dusty sunlight fills the gym again. His grey eyes look like molten lead for a few seconds.

Joona is clean-shaven, and his blond hair is cut short, almost in a crew-cut. His brow is furrowed, his mouth set firm. He's wearing a pale blue T-shirt, its seams stretching over his bulging muscles.

'One more set before we switch to a wider grip,' Marko says to him.

Marko is a wiry older prisoner who has taken it upon himself to act as Joona's bodyguard.

A new inmate with a thin, birdlike face is approaching the gym. He's hiding something against his hip. His cheekbones are sharp, his lips pale, and his thinning hair is pulled up in a ponytail.

He isn't dressed for the gym. He's wearing an open rust-red fleece jacket that reveals the tattoos on his chest and neck.

The thin man passes beneath the last security camera mounted in the ceiling and enters the gym, then stops in front of Joona.

One of the prison guards outside the Plexiglas turns, and the baton hanging by his hip swings against the glass.

A few of the inmates have turned their backs on Joona and Marko.

The atmosphere becomes tense, everyone moves with a new wariness.

The only sound is a high-frequency hum from the ventilation.

Joona stands underneath the pull-up bar again, jumps, and pulls himself up.

Marko stands behind him with his sinuous tattooed arms hanging by his sides.

The veins in Joona's temples throb as he pulls himself up again and again, raising his chin above the bar.

'Are you the cop?' the man with the thin face asks.

Small motes of dust drift gently through the still air. The guard on the other side of the Plexiglas exchanges a few words with an inmate, then starts to walk back towards the control room.

Joona pulls himself up again.

'Thirty more,' Marko says.

The man with the thin face is staring at Joona. Sweat glistens on his top lip, and is dripping down his cheeks.

'I'm going to get you, you bastard,' he says with a strained smile.

'*Nyt pelkään*,' Joona replies calmly in Finnish, and pulls himself up again.

'Understand?' the man grins. 'Do you understand what the fuck I'm saying?'

Joona notices that the new arrival is clutching a dagger by his hip, a homemade weapon made from a long, thin shard of glass bound with duct-tape.

He'll aim low, Joona thinks. He'll try to get below my ribs. It's almost impossible to stab someone with glass, but if it's held by splints under the tape it can still penetrate the body before it snaps off.

A few other inmates have gathered on the other side of the Plexiglas, looking into the gym with curiosity. Their body language betrays a restrained eagerness. They just happen to stand in the way of the cameras.

'You're a cop,' the man hisses, then looks at the others. 'You know he's a cop?'

'Is that true?' one of the onlookers says with a smile, then takes a swig from a plastic bottle.

A crucifix swings on a chain around the neck of a man with haggard features. The scars on the insides of his arms are frayed from the ascorbic acid he's used to dissolve the heroin.

'It is, I fucking swear,' the prisoner with the thin face goes on. 'He's from National Crime, he's a fucking pig, a dirty cop.'

'That probably explains why everyone calls him "the Cop",' the man with the plastic bottle says sarcastically, and chuckles silently to himself.

Joona keeps doing pull-ups.

Reiner Kronlid is sitting on the exercise bike with a blank look on his face. His eyes are perfectly still, like a reptile's, as he watches the scene play out.

One of the men from Malmö comes in and starts to run on the treadmill. The thud of his feet and the whine of the belt fill the cramped room.

Joona lets go of the bar, lands softly on his feet and looks at the man with the weapon.

'Can I give you something to think about?' Joona says in his

Finnish-accented Swedish. 'Feigned ignorance is born of confidence, illusory weakness is born of—'

'What the fuck are you talking about?' the man interrupts.

After his time in the Paratroop Unit Joona received enhanced training in unconventional close combat and innovative weaponry in the Netherlands.

Lieutenant Rinus Advocaat trained him for situations very similar to this. Joona knows exactly how to deflect the man's arm, how to crush his throat and windpipe with repeated blows, how to twist the glass knife from his grasp, how to jam it into his neck and break off its point.

'Stab the cop,' a member of the Brotherhood snarls, then laughs. 'You don't have the nerve . . .'

'Shut up,' a younger man says.

'Stab him,' the other man laughs.

The prisoner with the thin face squeezes the makeshift knife and Joona looks him in the eye as he comes closer.

If Joona is attacked now, he knows he's going to have to stop himself from following through with the sequence of movements that are imprinted in his body.

During his almost two years in prison he's managed to steer clear of serious fights. His only aim has been to serve his time and start a new life.

He just needs to deflect the arm, twist the weapon from the man's hand and knock him to the floor.

Joona turns his back on the newcomer with the knife. As he exchanges a few words with Marko, he can see the man's reflection in the window looking onto the yard.

'I could have killed the cop,' the man says, breathing hard through his thin nose.

'No, you couldn't,' Marko replies over Joona's shoulder.

15

Twenty-three months have passed since Joona was found guilty of using violence to help a convicted felon escape custody. He was taken away to the risk assessment unit at Kumla Prison.

The prison service transportation unit took his few possessions, custody documents and ID. Joona was led into the reception centre, where he was stripped, made to give a urine sample for a drug test, and given new clothes, sheets and a toothbrush.

After five weeks of evaluation he was placed in Unit T instead of the secure unit in Saltvik where convicted police officers are usually sent. He would spend the next few years in a cell measuring six square metres, with a plastic floor, a sink and a small, barred Plexiglas window.

For the first eight months Joona worked in the laundry with the rest of the inmates. He got to know a lot of the men on the second floor, and told each of them about his work with the National Police and his conviction. He knew it would be impossible to keep his past a secret. Whenever a new prisoner arrives in the unit, the others are quick to ask a relative on the outside to find out what they were sentenced for.

He has a relaxed relationship with most of the groups in the unit, but keeps his distance from the Brotherhood and its leader,

Reiner Kronlid. The Brotherhood has links to extreme right-wing groups, and is involved in drug-trafficking and protection rackets in all the big prisons.

By the end of the summer Joona had encouraged nineteen prisoners to start studying, at various levels. They formed a support group, and so far only two of them have dropped out.

The monotonous routines make the whole establishment run very slowly. All the cell doors are opened at eight o'clock in the morning and locked at eight o'clock in the evening.

As soon as the automatic lock clicks open each morning, Joona leaves his cell to shower and have breakfast before the entire unit heads down into the ice-cold tunnels that link the different parts of the prison like a sewage system.

The men pass the junction where the commissary used to be before it was shut down. They wait for the doors to open, allowing them further along the tunnel.

The guys from Malmö run their fingertips superstitiously over the mural of Zlatan Ibrahimović before heading to the powder-coating workshop.

The study group head for the library instead. Joona is halfway through a course in horticulture, and Marko has finally got his GCSEs. His chin trembled when he said he was thinking of studying science.

This could have been yet another identical day in prison. But it won't be for Joona, because his life is about to take an unexpected turn.

Joona sets the table in the visitors' room with coffee cups and saucers, smooths the tablecloth that he's spread out, and switches on the coffee-maker in the little kitchen.

When he hears keys rattling outside the door he stands up and feels his heart beat faster.

Valeria is wearing a navy-blue blouse with white polka dots, and black jeans. Her dark-brown hair is tied back and hangs in soft coils.

She comes in, stops in front of him and looks up.

The door closes and the lock clicks.

They stand and look at each other for a long time before whispering hello.

'It still feels so strange every time I see you,' Valeria says shyly.

She looks at Joona with sparkling eyes, taking in the slippers with the prison service logo, the grey-blue T-shirt with sand-coloured sleeves, the worn knees of the baggy trousers.

'I can't offer much,' he says. 'Just sandwich biscuits and coffee.'

'Sandwich biscuits,' she nods, and pulls her trousers up slightly before sitting down on one of the chairs.

'They're not bad,' he says, and smiles in a way that makes the dimples in his cheeks deepen.

'How can anyone be so cute?'

'It's just these clothes,' Joona jokes.

'Of course,' she laughs.

'Thanks for your letter. I got it yesterday,' he says, sitting down on the other side of the table.

'Sorry if I was a bit forward,' she mumbles, and blushes.

Joona smiles, and she does the same as she looks down, before raising her eyes again.

'Speaking of which, it's a shame they turned down your application for leave,' Valeria says, suppressing another smile in a way that makes her chin wrinkle.

'I'll try again in three months . . . I can always apply for re-acclimatisation leave,' Joona says.

'It'll be OK,' she nods, feeling for his hand across the table.

'I spoke to Lumi yesterday,' he goes on. 'She'd just finished reading *Crime and Punishment* in French . . . It was good, we just talked about books, and I forgot I was here . . . until the line went dead.'

'I don't remember you talking this much before.'

'If you spread it out over two weeks, it's only a couple of words an hour.'

A lock of hair falls across her cheek and she tosses her head to move it. Her skin is like brass, and she has deep laugh-lines at the corners of her eyes. The thin skin beneath her eyes is grey, and she has traces of dirt under her short nails.

'You used to be able to order pastries from a bakery outside,' Joona says, pouring coffee.

'I need to start thinking about my figure for when you get out,' she replies, with one hand on her stomach.

'You're more beautiful than ever,' Joona says.

'You should have seen me yesterday,' she laughs, her long fingers touching an enamel daisy hanging from a chain around her neck. 'I was out at the open-air pool in Saltsjöbaden, crawling around in the rain preparing the beds.'

'Yoshino cherry trees, right?'

'I picked a variety with white flowers, thousands of them. They're amazing . . . every year in May it looks like a snowstorm has hit just those little trees.'

Joona looks at the cups and the pale blue napkins. The light from outside is falling in broad stripes across the table.

'How are your studies going?' she asks.

'It's exciting.'

'Does it feel weird to be training for something new?' she asks, folding her napkin.

'Yes, but in a good way.'

'You're still sure you don't want to go back to police work?'

He nods and looks over towards the window. The dirty glass is visible between the horizontal bars. His chair creaks as he leans back, disappearing into the memory of his last night in Nattavaara.

'What are you thinking?' she asks in a serious voice.

'Nothing,' he replies quietly.

'You're thinking about Summa,' she says simply.

'No.'

'Because of what I said about a snowstorm.'

He looks into her amber-coloured eyes and nods. She has the peculiar ability to almost read his mind.

'There's nothing as quiet as snow after the wind has dropped,' he says. 'You know . . . Lumi and I sat with her, holding her hands . . .'

Joona thinks back to the strange calmness that settled on his wife before she died, and the absolute silence that followed.

Valeria leans across the table and puts her hand to his cheek without saying anything. He can see the tattoo on her right shoulder through the thin fabric of her blouse.

'We're going to get through this – aren't we?' she asks quietly.
'We're going to get through this,' he nods.
'You're not going to break my heart, are you, Joona?'
'No.'

16

Joona feels a lingering joy after Valeria has left. It's as if she brings him a small portion of life every time she visits.

He has almost no space in his cell, but if he stands between the desk and the sink he has just enough room to do some shadow-boxing and hone his military fighting techniques. He moves slowly and systematically, thinking of the endless flatlands in the Netherlands where he received his training.

Joona doesn't know how long he's been practising, but the sky is so dark that the yellow wall that encloses the prison is no longer visible through the barred window when the lock clicks and the cell door opens.

Two guards he hasn't seen before are standing in the doorway, looking at him rather anxiously.

He thinks it must be a search. Something's happened, maybe an attempted escape that they suspect he's involved in.

'You're going to see a defence lawyer,' one of the guards says.

'What for?'

Without answering they cuff his hands and lead him out of the cell.

'I haven't requested a meeting,' Joona says.

They walk down the stairs together and on down the long hallway. A prison guard passes them silently and disappears.

Joona wonders if they've realised that Valeria has been using her sister's ID when she visits him. She has a criminal record of her own, and wouldn't be allowed to see him if she used her own name.

The colour and style of the pictures along the walls change. The harsh lighting shows up the shabbiness of the concrete floor.

The guards lead Joona through security doors and airlocks. They have to show the warrant authorising the transfer several times. More locks whirr, and they head deeper into a section Joona isn't familiar with. At the far end of the hallway two men are standing guard outside a door.

Joona immediately recognises that they're Security Police officers. Without looking at him they open the door.

The dimly lit room is completely bare apart from two plastic chairs. Someone is sitting in one of them.

Joona stops in the middle of the floor.

The light from the low-hanging ceiling lamp doesn't reach the man's face. It stops at the pressed creases of his trousers and the black shoes, wet mud visible beneath their soles.

Something is glinting in his right hand.

When the door closes behind Joona the man stands up, takes a step forward into the light and tucks his reading glasses in his breast pocket.

Only then does Joona see his face.

It's Sweden's Prime Minister.

His eyes are cast in darkness, and the shadow of his sharp nose lies like a stroke of black ink across his mouth.

'This meeting has never taken place,' the Prime Minister says in his characteristic hoarse voice. 'I haven't met you, and you haven't met me. No matter what happens you'll tell people you had a meeting with your defence lawyer.'

'Your driver doesn't smoke,' Joona says.

'No,' he replies in surprise.

The Prime Minister's right hand moves aimlessly towards the knot of his tie before he continues.

'Last night my government's Foreign Minister was murdered in his home. The official story is that he died after a short illness, but we're actually dealing with an act of terrorism.'

The Prime Minister's nose is shiny with sweat, and the bags under his eyes are dark. The leather bracelet carrying the emergency alarm slips down his wrist as he pulls the other plastic chair forward for Joona.

'Joona Linna,' he says. 'I'm going to make you a highly unorthodox offer, an offer that is only valid here and now.'

'I'm listening.'

'An inmate from Hall Prison is going to be transferred and placed in your unit. His name is Salim Ratjen. He was convicted of drug offences, but found not guilty of murder . . . The evidence suggests that he occupies a central position in a terrorist organisation, and that he may even be directing whoever carried out the murder of the Foreign Minister.'

'Background information?'

'Here,' the Prime Minister replies, handing over a thin folder.

Joona sits down on the chair and takes the file with his cuffed hands. The plastic creaks as he leans back. As he reads he notices that the Prime Minister keeps checking his phone.

Joona skims the report from the crime scene, the lab results and the interview with the female witness in which she says she heard the killer say that Ratjen had opened the door to hell. The report concludes with graphs of telecom traffic and Sheikh Ayad al-Jahiz's command that western leaders should be tracked down and their faces blown off.

'There are plenty of holes,' Joona says, handing the folder back.

'This is just a preliminary report. A lot of test results are still missing, and—'

'Holes that were left on purpose,' Joona interrupts.

'I don't know anything about that,' the Prime Minister says, slipping his phone back in the inside pocket of his jacket.

'Have there been any other victims?'

'No.'

'Is there anything to suggest that more attacks are planned?'

'I don't think so.'

'Why the Foreign Minister?' Joona asks.

'He was pushing for coordinated European action against terrorism.'

'What do they achieve by killing him?'

'This is a clear attack against the very heart of democracy,' the Prime Minister goes on. 'And I want the heads of these terrorists on a fucking plate, if you'll pardon the expression. This is about justice, about putting our foot down. They cannot and will not frighten us. That's why I'm here, to ask if you're prepared to infiltrate Salim Ratjen's organisation from inside prison.'

'I assumed that. I appreciate your faith in me, but you have to understand that I've built up a life in here. It wasn't easy, because people are aware of my background, but over time they've learned that they can trust me.'

'We're talking about national security here.'

'I'm no longer a police officer.'

'The Security Police will have your conviction quashed and you'll get conditional parole if you do this.'

'I'm not interested.'

'That's how she said you'd react,' the Prime Minister says.

'Saga Bauer?'

'She said you wouldn't listen to any offer from the Security Police . . . That's why I decided to come in person.'

'I'd be more inclined to consider the job if I didn't think you were withholding vital information from me.'

'What is there to conceal? The Security Police think you can help them identify Salim Ratjen's contact on the outside.'

'I'm sorry you wasted your time,' Joona says, then gets to his feet and starts walking towards the door.

'I can get you pardoned,' the Prime Minister says to his back.

'That would require government approval,' Joona says, turning around.

'I'm the Prime Minister.'

'As long as I feel I'm not being given all available information, I'm going to have to say no,' Joona repeats.

'How can you claim to be unaware of what you don't know?' the Prime Minister asks, obviously irritated.

'I know you're sitting here even though you should be in Brussels for a meeting of the European Council,' Joona says. 'I know that you gave up smoking eight years ago, but now you've suffered a relapse, judging by the smell on your clothes and the mud on your shoes.'

'Mud on my shoes?'

'You're a considerate man, and because your driver doesn't smoke you got out of the car to have a cigarette.'

'But . . .'

'I've noticed you checked your phone eleven times, but you haven't answered any messages, so I know there's something missing, because there was nothing in that report I read that indicates there's any real urgency.'

For the first time, the Prime Minister looks lost for words. He rubs his chin and seems to be thinking hard.

'We believe we're dealing with a number of planned murders,' he says eventually.

'A number?' Joona repeats.

'The Security Police removed that from the report, but there seem to be three murders planned, at least to start, and the next one is believed to be planned for Wednesday. That's why it's urgent.'

'Who are the likely targets for these attacks?'

'We don't know for sure, but the information we do have suggests precise and well-planned executions.'

'Politicians?'

'Probably.'

'And you think one of them might be you?' Joona asks.

'It could be anyone,' the Prime Minister replies quickly. 'But I've been led to believe that you're our best option, and I'm hoping you'll accept the job. And if you do actually manage to discover information that helps stop these terrorists, I'll see to it that you get your old life back.'

'You can't do that,' Joona replies.

'Listen, you have to do this,' the Prime Minister says. Joona can tell that he's really scared.

'If you can get the Security Police to cooperate fully with me, then I promise to identify the people responsible.'

'And you understand that it has to happen before Wednesday . . .? That's when they kill their next target,' the Prime Minister says.

17

The Rabbit Hunter is walking restlessly around the large shipping container in the crooked glare of the fluorescent ceiling light.

He stops in front of a few open crates and a large petrol can. He presses his fingers to his left temple and tries to calm his breathing.

He looks at his phone.

No messages.

As he walks back to his equipment he steps on a laminated map of Djursholm lying on the floor.

He's put his pistols, knives and rifles in a pile on a battered desk. Some of the weapons are dirty and worn, while others are still in their original packaging.

There's a pile of rusty tools and old mason jars full of springs and firing pins, extra cartridges, rolls of black bin bags, duct-tape, bags of zip ties, axes and a broad-bladed Emerson knife, its tip honed as sharp as an arrowhead.

He's stacked boxes containing different types of ammunition against the wall. On top of three of them are photographs of three people.

A lot of the boxes are still closed, but the lid has been torn off one box of 5.56x45mm ammunition, and there are bloody fingerprints on another.

The Rabbit Hunter puts a box of 9mm pistol bullets in a

crumpled plastic bag. He examines a short-handled axe and adds it to the bag, then drops the whole thing on the floor with a loud clang.

He reaches out his hand and picks up one of the small photographs. He moves it to the edge of one of the container's metal ribs, but it falls off.

He puts it back carefully and looks at the face with a smile: the cheery set of the mouth, the unruly hair. He leans forward and looks into the man's eyes, and decides that he's going to cut his legs off and watch him crawl like a snail through his own blood.

And he'll watch the man's son's desperate attempts to tie tourniquets around his father's legs in an effort to save his life, and maybe he'll let him stem the flow of blood before going over and slicing his stomach open.

The photograph falls again and sails down amongst the weapons.

He lets out a roar and overturns the entire desk, sending pistols, knives and ammunition clattering across the floor.

The glass jars shatter in a cascade of splinters and spare parts.

The Rabbit Hunter leans against the wall, gasping for breath. He remembers the old industrial area that used to be between the highway and the sewage plant. The printing works and warehouses had burned down, and beneath the foundations of an old cottage was a vast rabbit warren.

The first time he checked the trap, there were ten small rabbits in the snares, all exhausted but still alive when he skinned them.

He regains control of himself. He's calm and focused again. He knows he can't give in to his rage, can't show its hideous face, not even when he's alone.

It's time to go.

He licks his lips, then picks a knife up off the floor, along with two pistols, a Springfield Operator and a grimy Glock 19. He adds another carton of ammunition and four extra magazines to the plastic bag.

The Rabbit Hunter goes out into the cool night air. He closes the door of the container, pulls the bar across it and fastens the padlock, then walks to the car through the tall weeds. When he opens the boot a cloud of flies emerges. He tosses the bag of weapons in beside the bin-bag of rotting flesh, closes the boot and turns towards the forest.

He looks at the tall trees, conjures up the face in the photograph, and tries to force the rhyme out of his head.

18

In the Salvation Army's offices at 69 Östermalms Street, a private lunch meeting is underway. Twelve people have made one long table out of three smaller ones, and are now sitting so close that they can see the tiredness and sadness in each other's faces. The daylight shines in on the pale wooden furniture and the tapestry of the apostles fishing.

At one end sits Rex Müller, in his tailored jacket and black leather trousers. He's fifty-two years old, still good-looking despite his frown and the swollen bags under his eyes.

Everyone looks at him as he puts his coffee cup back down on the saucer and runs a hand through his hair.

'My name is Rex, and I usually don't say anything, I just sit and listen,' he begins, then gives an awkward little smile. 'I don't really know what you want me to say.'

'Tell us why you're here,' says a woman with sad wrinkles around her mouth.

'I'm a pretty good chef,' he goes on, and clears his throat. 'And in my line of work you need to know about wine, beer, fortified wine, spirits, liqueurs and so on . . . I'm not an alcoholic. I maybe drink a little too much. I do stupid things sometimes, even though you shouldn't believe everything the papers say.'

He pauses and peers at them with a smile, but they just wait for him to go on.

'I'm here because my employer insisted, otherwise I'll lose my job . . . and I like my job.'

Rex had been hoping for laughter, but they're all looking at him in silence.

'I have a son. He's practically grown up now, in his last year at high school . . . And one of the things I probably ought to regret about my life is not being a good dad. I haven't been a dad at all. I've been there for birthdays and so on, but . . . I didn't really want children, I wasn't mature enough to . . .'

His voice cracks in the middle of the sentence, and to his surprise he feels tears welling up in his eyes.

'OK, I'm an idiot, you might have realised that already,' he says quietly, then takes a deep breath. 'It's like this . . . My ex, she's wonderful, there aren't many people who can say that about their ex, but Veronica is great . . . And now she's been hand-picked to launch a big project about free healthcare in Sierra Leone, but she's thinking of turning it down.'

Rex smiles wryly at the others.

'She's perfect for the job . . . so I told her I was trying to stay sober these days, and that Sammy can live with me when she's away. Since I've been coming to these meetings she believes I've started to show more responsibility . . . and now she's actually going on her first trip to Freetown.'

He runs his fingers through his messy black hair and leans forward.

'Sammy's had a pretty tough time. It's probably my fault, I don't know, his life is very different to mine . . . I'm not for a minute thinking I can repair our relationship, but I am actually looking forward to getting to know him a little better.'

'Thanks for sharing,' one of the women says quietly.

Rex Müller has spent the past two years as the resident chef on a popular morning programme on TV4. He's won silver in the Bocuse d'Or contest, has worked with Magnus Nilsson at Fäviken Magasinet, has published three cookbooks, and last autumn he signed a lucrative contract with the Grupp F12 restaurant company, making him head chef at Smak.

After three hours in the new restaurant he hands things over to Eliza, the sous chef, changes into a blue shirt and suit, and heads over to the inauguration of a new hotel at Hötorget. He gets photographed with Avicii, then takes a taxi out to Dalarö to meet his associates.

David Jordan Andersen – or DJ, as everyone calls him – is thirty-three years old, and set up the production and branded content company that bought the rights to Rex's cooking. In three years he has taken Rex from one of the country's foremost chefs to genuine celebrity status.

Now Rex sweeps into the restaurant of the Dalarö Strand Hotel, shakes DJ's hand and sits down across from him.

'I thought Lyra was thinking of coming?' Rex says.

'She's meeting her art school friends.'

DJ resembles a modern-day Viking with his full blond beard and blue eyes.

'Did Lyra think I was difficult last time?' Rex asks with a frown.

'You *were* difficult last time,' DJ replies frankly. 'You don't have to give the cook a lecture every time you go to a restaurant.'

'It was supposed to be a joke.'

The waiter arrives with their appetisers. He lingers a little too long, then blushes as he asks if Rex would mind giving the gang in the kitchen his autograph.

'That depends on the food,' Rex replies seriously. 'I can't stand it when a lemon emulsion tastes like sweets.'

The waiter stands beside the table, smiling awkwardly, as Rex picks up his knife and fork and cuts a piece of chargrilled asparagus.

'Take it easy,' DJ cajoles, rubbing his blond beard.

Rex dips a piece of smoked salmon in the lemon sauce, smells it, then tastes it, chewing with a look of intense concentration. He finally takes out a pen and writes on the back of the menu: *My congratulations to the master chefs at Dalarö Strand Hotel. Warm regards, Rex.*

The waiter thanks him and hurries back to the kitchen with a look of unfeigned delight on his face.

'Is it really that good?' DJ asks quietly.

'It's OK,' Rex replies.

DJ leans across the table, fills Rex's glass with water, then nudges the bread-basket towards him. Rex takes a sip and looks out at a large yacht heading out to sea from the harbour.

Their plates of fried herring, charred red onion and mashed potatoes arrive.

'Have you checked to see if you can make it next weekend?' DJ asks tentatively.

'Is that when we're meeting the investors?' Rex asks.

Rex and his team have spent over a year developing the first items in a set of kitchen equipment with Rex's name on them.

They're very good quality, sleek design at a reasonable price, and intended to be for 'kitchen royalty'. *Rex of Kitchen.*

'I thought we could spend some time with them, have a decent meal. It's really important that they feel special,' he explains.

Rex nods and cuts a piece of herring, then reaches across the table for DJ's glass of chilled beer.

'Rex?'

'No one needs to know,' he says with a wink.

'Don't do it,' DJ says calmly.

'Are you going to start too?' Rex says, smiling, and puts the glass down. 'I'm sober, but it's pretty ridiculous. Everyone's just decided that I have a problem without asking me.'

They finish their meal, pay, and walk down to the hotel jetty, where DJ's motorboat, a Sea Ray Sundancer that's seen better days, is moored.

It's a warm evening, almost impossibly beautiful. The water is still, the sun is setting slowly, and the clouds are lit with golden light.

They cast off and slowly pull away from the jetty, rocking through the wake of another boat. They head carefully into the main waterway. The hillside on the port side is strewn with ornate wooden houses.

'How's your mum these days?' Rex asks, sitting down beside DJ on the white leather seat.

'A little better, actually,' he replies, accelerating slightly. 'The doctors have switched her medication and she's not feeling too bad now.'

His voice is drowned out by the roar of the engine when they reach open water. White foam whips up behind them, the bow lifts up and the hull strikes the waves. They keep accelerating, and the boat starts to plane and shoots off across the water.

Rex stands up unsteadily and starts to pull on the water-skis that are tucked behind the seats.

'Aren't you going to take your suit off?' DJ shouts.

'What?'

'It'll get soaked.'

'I'm not going to fall in!' Rex shouts back.

He starts unrolling the line, then feels his phone buzz in his inside pocket. It's Sammy, and Rex gestures at DJ to slow down.

'Hello?'

He can hear music and voices in the background.

'Hi, Dad,' Sammy says, with his phone very close to his mouth. 'I just thought I'd check what you're doing tonight.'

'Where are you?'

'At a party, but . . .'

The swell from a large yacht makes Rex sway. He loses his balance and sits down on the white leather cushion.

'Are you having a good time?' he asks.

'What?'

'I'm out at Dalarö with DJ, but there's some of last night's sole in the fridge . . . You can have it cold, or heat it up in the oven for a few minutes.'

'I can't hear you,' Sammy says.

'I won't be late,' Rex tries to shout.

He can hear loud music over the phone, the thud of a heavy bassline, and a woman shouting something.

'See you later,' Rex says, but the line has already gone dead.

19

It's late at night when the taxi rolls down Rehns Street and stops in front of an ornate wooden door. Rex has borrowed some dry clothes from DJ, and has his wet suit in a black bin-bag. He's supposed to appear on television early the next morning, and should really have been asleep hours ago.

Rex makes his way inside, shivering as he presses the button for the lift. It doesn't move. He steps forward and peers up into the lift shaft. The cabin is standing motionless on the fifth floor. There's a creaking, scraping sound. The cables are swaying and he wonders idly if someone is moving out in the middle of the night.

He waits a little longer, then starts to walk up the stairs, the bag of wet clothes over his shoulder like he's Santa Claus.

When he gets halfway up he hears the lift creak as it starts to move. It passes him on the third floor, and through the grille he can see that it's empty.

Rex reaches the top floor, sets the bag down and catches his breath. As he puts the key in the lock he hears the lift come back up and stop at his floor.

'Sammy?'

The doors slide open, but the lift is empty. Someone must have pressed the button for the sixth floor, then got out.

Rex walks through the flat without turning the lights on,

wondering if it's worth checking to see if Sammy has left any of the sole before he goes to bed. The floor glints silver in the gloom, and through the glass door to the deck he can see the city's carpet of lights spread out below.

Rex opens the fridge and has time to register that Sammy hasn't touched the fish when his phone rings.

'Rex here,' he answers hoarsely.

The receiver crackles. He can hear heavy music in the background, and someone whimpering.

'Dad?' a voice whispers.

'Sammy? I thought you'd be home by now.'

'I'm not feeling too good,' his son slurs.

'What happened?'

'I lost my stuff, and Nico's pissed off at me . . . I don't know. For fuck's sake, just stop it, will you?' he says to someone at the other end.

'Sammy, what's going on?'

Rex can't hear what his son says, his voice is swallowed up by the noise, then there's the sound of dishes breaking, and a man starts shouting.

'Sammy?' he says. 'Tell me where you are and I'll come and get you.'

'You don't have to . . .'

There's a loud noise, as if Sammy has dropped his phone on the floor.

'Sammy?' Rex shouts. 'Tell me where you are!'

A lot of crackling, then Rex hears someone pick up the phone again.

'Come and get him before I get really sick of him,' a woman with a deep voice says.

With his heart pounding, Rex makes a note of the address, calls a taxi and runs downstairs. When he gets outside in the cool air he tries calling Sammy again, but there's no answer. He tries at least ten more times before the taxi pulls up in front of the building.

The address the woman gave him is on Östermalm, the wealthiest part of Stockholm, but the building on Kommendörs Street turns out to be public housing from the 1980s.

Loud music is streaming from a door on the ground floor. There is a strip of tape across the letterbox that says 'More ads, please'.

Rex rings the doorbell, then tries the handle, opens the door and stares into a small hallway full of shoes. Loud music reverberates off the walls. The flat smells like cigarette smoke and red wine. There's a pile of coats on the worn hardwood floor in the hall. Rex goes into the dimly lit kitchen and looks around. The counter is littered with empty beer bottles. The remains of a bean stew have dried onto a pan, and the sink is overflowing with plates and improvised ashtrays.

A man dressed in black wearing heavy makeup is sitting on the kitchen floor drinking from a plastic bottle. A young woman in denim shorts and a bright pink bra stumbles over to the counter, opens one of the cabinets and takes out a glass. The cigarette between her lips wobbles as she concentrates on filling her glass from a box of wine.

She taps her ash onto the pile of dirty plates as Rex pushes past her. She slowly exhales a plume of smoke, following him with her eyes.

'Hey, chef, could you fix up an omelette?' she says with a smile. 'I'd love a fucking omelette right now.'

'Do you know where Sammy is?' he asks.

'I think I know pretty much everything,' she replies, handing him the glass of wine.

'Is he still here?'

She nods and gets another glass from the cabinet. A black cat jumps up onto the counter and starts to lick bits of food from a kitchen knife.

'I want to sleep with a celebrity,' she jokes, and starts giggling to herself.

He moves a chair so he can get past the kitchen table, and feels the young woman wrap her arms around his waist. The weight of her body makes Rex lurch forward.

'Let's go in and wake Lena up, then we can have a threesome,' the woman mumbles, pressing her chin against his back.

Rex puts the glass down on the table, removes her hands, turns around and looks at her drunk, smiling face.

'I'm just here to pick up my son,' he explains, and turns to look at the living room.

'I was only joking anyway. I don't really want sex, I just want *lurve*,' she says, and lets go of him.

'You should go home.'

Rex squeezes between a highchair and a folded cot. Two glasses clink against each other in time to the music.

'I want a daddy,' he hears her mutter as he goes into the living room.

On a checked sofa a man with long grey hair is helping a younger man snort cocaine. Someone's brought out a box of Christmas decorations. There are mattresses on the floor around the walls. A heavyset man with his trousers unzipped is sitting with his back to the wall, picking at an acoustic guitar.

Rex walks through a narrow hallway with deep scratches in the floor. He glances into a bedroom where a woman is sleeping in just her underwear, her tattooed arm across her face.

Back in the kitchen a man laughs, and calls out in a loud voice.

Rex stops and listens. He can hear thuds and sighing from nearby. He looks into the bedroom again and finds himself staring between the woman's legs. He turns away.

The door to the bathroom is ajar, its weak light spilling out into the hallway.

Moving sideways, Rex catches sight of a mop and bucket in front of a washing machine.

He hears the sighing again as he approaches the bathroom. He reaches out his hand and gently pushes the door open, and sees his son kneeling in front of a man with a large nose and deep lines around his half-open mouth. Sammy's face is sweaty and his mascara has run. He's holding the man's erect penis with one hand as he guides it into his mouth. A black pearl earring is bouncing against his cheek.

Rex steps back as he sees the man run his fingers through Sammy's bleached hair and grab hold of it.

He hears crying from the hall.

Rex turns away and goes back into the living room, trying to catch his breath as waves of conflicting emotions crash through him.

'Oh, God,' he sighs, and tries to smile at his own reaction.

Sammy is an adult, and Rex knows he doesn't want to be defined by his sexuality. Still, he's extremely embarrassed that he stumbled upon such an intimate situation.

On the checked sofa the man with long grey hair has tucked his hand under the younger man's T-shirt.

Rex needs to go home and get some sleep. He waits a few seconds, wipes his mouth, then heads towards the bathroom again.

'Sammy?' Rex calls out before he gets there. 'Are you in there?'

Something topples over in the bathroom, clattering against the sink. He waits a few seconds before calling his son's name again.

Shortly after that the door opens and Sammy comes out, dressed in a pair of tight jeans and an unbuttoned floral shirt. He's leaning against the wall with one hand. His eyelids are drooping, and his gaze is unfocused.

'What are you doing here?' he slurs.

'You called me.'

Sammy looks up but doesn't seem to understand what Rex is saying. His eyes are lined in kohl, and his pupils are dilated.

'What the hell's going on?' the man in the bathroom calls out.

'I'm coming, I just . . . just . . .'

Sammy loses his footing and almost falls.

'We're going home,' Rex says.

'I have to get back to Nico. He'll get angry if—'

'Talk to him tomorrow,' Rex interrupts.

'What? What did you say?'

'I know you have your own life, I'm not trying to play at being your dad. I can give you money for a taxi if you want to stay,' Rex says, trying to make his voice gentler.

'I . . . I should probably get some sleep.'

Rex takes his jacket off and wraps it around his son's shoulders. He starts to lead him out of the block of flats.

When they reach the street the sky is starting to brighten and the birds are singing loudly. Sammy is moving slowly. He's alarmingly weak.

'Can you stay on your feet while I call a taxi?' Rex asks.

His son nods and leans heavily against the wall. His face is extremely pale. He sticks his finger in his mouth and leans his head forward.

'I . . . I'm . . .'

'Can't we just try to get through these three weeks together?' Rex suggests.

'What?'

Sammy swallows, sticks his finger in his mouth again and looks like he's about to throw up.

'What's going on, Sammy?'

His son looks up, breathing in laboriously. His eyes roll back and he collapses on the pavement, hitting his head against an electricity box.

'Sammy!' Rex yells, and tries to help him up.

The boy's head is bleeding and his eyes are swimming behind half-closed eyelids.

'Look at me!' Rex shouts, but his son is unresponsive. His body is completely limp.

Rex puts him down again and listens to his chest. His heart is beating fast, but his breathing is far too slow.

'Fuck,' Rex mutters as he fumbles for his phone.

His hands are shaking as he tries to call an ambulance.

'Don't die, you can't die,' he whispers as the call goes through.

20

His mobile phone rings, making Rex jump so hard that his arm jerks and he hits his hand against the back of the couch. He stands up and wipes his mouth. The sky outside the hospital window is as pale as parchment. He must have dozed off.

He isn't sure how many times they pumped Sammy's stomach. Over and over again they poured water through a tube down his throat, and sucked it out again using a huge syringe. Sammy kept flailing his arms weakly in an attempt to remove the tube, and whimpered as the remains of the red wine and pills poured out of him.

Rex's mobile phone is still ringing, and when he picks the jacket up his phone slips out of the pocket and bounces onto the floor.

He crawls after it and answers on all fours:

'Hello?' he whispers.

'Please, Rex,' the programme's producer says, sounding stressed and angry. 'Tell me you're sitting in a taxi.'

'It hasn't arrived yet,' Rex manages to say.

It's Sunday. He cooks live on TV4 every Sunday. He can't possibly have missed it, but he has no idea what time it is.

The lino floor and electric lights fade into darkness as Rex stands up. Leaning against the couch, he tries to explain that he wants a picture of the raw ingredients on the Barco wall, and a close-up when he stir-fries the shrimp.

'You should be in make-up right now,' the producer says.

'I know,' Rex agrees. 'But what can I do if the taxi doesn't show up?'

'Call another taxi,' she sighs, and hangs up.

A nurse gives him an inscrutable look as she passes him in the hallway. Rex leans against the wall, looks at his phone to see what time it is, then calls a taxi.

He thinks about the look on Sammy's face when he drank the charcoal solution that breaks down toxic substances in the intestines. Rex sat with him, wiping his clammy forehead with a damp towel, telling him the whole time that everything would be OK. Around six o'clock in the morning they put Sammy on a drip, tucked him into bed, and assured Rex that he was out of danger. He went and sat down on a couch in the hallway so that he'd hear Sammy if he called for him.

He woke up forty minutes later when his phone rang.

Rex walks quickly to the door and looks in at his son, who's still fast asleep. His make-up has washed off, and his face is very pale. The bandage over the cannula in his arm has folded over. The tube and the half-full infusion bag are glinting in the morning sun. His stomach is rising and falling with his breathing.

Rex jogs to the lifts and presses the green button as the purchasing manager of the TV4 group calls.

'I'm sitting in the taxi now,' he replies, just as the lift machinery whirrs into action.

'Should I be worried?' Sylvia Lund says.

'No need – they just got their bookings mixed up.'

'You were due in make-up twenty minutes ago,' she says warily.

'I'm coming. I'm on my way now. We're already on Valhallavägen.'

He leans his forehead against the mirror and feels jagged exhaustion catch up with him.

The taxi is waiting outside the entrance to the emergency department. Rex gets in the back seat and closes his eyes. He tries to have a quick nap during the short drive, but can't stop thinking about what's happened. He's going to have to call Sammy's mother, Veronica.

As Rex understands it, Sammy will be referred to a psychologist, who will evaluate him for signs of substance abuse and suicidal tendencies.

The car turns and pulls up in front of the TV4 building. Rex pays, not bothering to wait for a receipt. He hurries in through the glass door.

Sylvia hurries over to him. Her face is neatly made-up, her hair blow-dried so that it curls in towards her neck and jawline.

'You haven't shaved,' she says.

'Haven't I? I forgot,' he lies, feeling his chin.

'Let me look at you.'

She studies his crumpled jacket, messy hair and bloodshot eyes.

'You're hungover,' she says. 'This can't be happening.'

'Leave it, I can handle this,' Rex says tersely.

'Breathe on me,' she snaps.

'No,' he says with a smile.

'You may be having a hard time, but that won't make any difference . . . TV4 will walk away from their contract with you if you make a fool of yourself again.'

'Yes, so you said.'

'I'm not letting you into that studio unless you breathe on me.'

Rex blushes as he breathes into his boss's face, looks her in the eye and then walks away.

A young woman comes running over to hold the door open for Rex and Sylvia.

'We've still got time,' she says breathlessly.

Rex starts walking towards the dressing rooms, but feels sick on the steep metal steps. He has to stop and cling onto the handrail before moving on.

He passes the green room where this week's guests are waiting and quickly goes into his dressing room. He hurries over to the sink and rinses his face and mouth with cold water, spits and then wipes himself with a paper towel.

His hands shake as he changes into his pressed suit, then the chef apron.

The young woman is waiting in the hallway and follows him as he half-runs towards make-up.

He sits down on the chair in front of the mirror and tries to get a grip on his stress by watching the news. One make-up assistant shaves him and a second blends two types of foundation on a palette.

At regular intervals the presenters announce that 'superstar chef Rex will be here soon to share some of his best hangover tips'.

'I didn't get any sleep last night,' he manages to say.

'That's OK, we can fix that,' one of the make-up assistants assures him, holding a damp sponge to his swollen eyes.

He thinks about when Sammy was little and said his first words. It was a frosty autumn day, and his son was playing in the sandpit when he suddenly looked up, patted the ground beside him, and said 'Daddy sit'.

He never wanted children. Veronica's pregnancy wasn't planned. All he wanted was to drink, cook and fuck.

The make-up artist runs her fingers through his hair one last time to get it to lie flat.

'Why are people so crazy about chefs?' she asks rhetorically.

He just laughs, thanks her for making him look human again, and hurries off to the studio.

21

The soundproof door closes behind Rex. He creeps into the studio and sees that the host, Mia Edwards, is sitting on the sofa talking to a writer with pink hair.

Rex steps carefully over the cables and takes his place in the kitchen on one side of the group of sofas. A sound technician fixes his microphone while he checks that all the ingredients for his pasta dish are in place, that the water is simmering and the butter is melted.

He watches the large monitor as the author being interviewed laughs and throws her hands up. The ticker along the bottom of the screen talks about growing criticism of the UN Security Council.

'Are you hungry?' Mia asks the author after getting a prompt through her earpiece. 'I hope so, because today Rex has prepared something extra special.'

The lights come up and as the black lenses of the cameras swing towards him he's drizzling oil into the beaten-copper pan.

Rex increases the heat of the gas burner, starts picking basil leaves from a large pot, and smiles straight into the camera:

'Some of you may be feeling a little worse for wear today . . . so this morning we're focusing on the perfect hangover food. Tagliatelle with fried shrimp, melted butter and garlic, red peppers, olive oil and fresh herbs. Imagine a really lazy morning

. . . waking up next to someone you hopefully recognise . . . and maybe you don't really want to remember what happened last night, because all you need right now is food.'

'Forget all about dieting,' Mia says expectantly.

'But only for this morning,' Rex chuckles, and runs his hand through his hair, messing it up. 'It's worth it though, I promise.'

'We believe you, Rex.'

Mia comes over and watches as he chops a chilli pepper and garlic with lightning-fast flicks of the knife.

'Take extra care if you're feeling fragile . . .'

'I can do that just as fast,' Mia jokes.

'Let's see!'

He throws the knife in the air, and it spins twice before he catches it again and puts it down next to the chopping board.

'No,' she laughs.

'My ex always called me a *schmuck* . . . I'm still not quite sure what she meant,' he grins, and stirs the deep-rimmed frying pan.

'So you've dried the shrimp on paper towels?'

'And because they're not pre-cooked, you may need to add a little more salt than usual,' Rex says as he lowers the fresh pasta into the simmering water.

Through the cloud of steam his eyes take in the latest news on the ticker at the bottom of the monitor: *Swedish Foreign Minister William Fock has died after a short illness.*

His stomach lurches with angst and his head suddenly goes empty. He forgets where he is and what he's supposed to be doing.

'You can get organic shrimp these days, can't you?' Mia asks.

He looks at her and nods, without actually understanding what she's saying. His hands are shaking as he picks up the tea-towel from the counter. He dabs slowly at his forehead so as not to spoil the make-up.

It's a live broadcast. Rex knows he has to get through this, but all he can think about is what he did three weeks ago.

This can't be true.

He holds onto the edge of the counter with one hand as he feels sweat trickling between his shoulder-blades.

'In the past you've talked about saving some of the pasta water to pour on the cooked pasta afterwards if you want to cut down on the amount of oil,' Mia says.

'Yes, but . . .'

'But not today, eh?' she says with a smile.

Rex looks down at his hands, sees that they're still working. They've just turned up the heat beneath the frying pan, and are now squeezing lemon juice on the shrimp. As he squeezes the fruit, a few drops of juice end up on the edge of the pan. They look like a string of tiny glass pearls.

'OK,' he whispers. His brain keeps repeating the news: the Foreign Minister has died after a short illness.

He was sick, and nothing I did made any difference, Rex thinks as he picks up the bowl of shrimp.

'The last thing you do is fry the shrimp,' he says, watching as the hot oil swirls in dreamlike patterns. 'Are you ready? *Um, dois, três . . .*'

The dolly-mounted camera films the big copper pan as he empties the bowl with a theatrical gesture and the shrimp tumble into the oil with a noisy hiss.

'High heat! Keep watching the colour, and listen . . . you can hear the moisture evaporating,' Rex says, turning the shrimp.

The pan sizzles as he sprinkles a pinch of salt over it. The second camera is filming him head-on.

'Give it a few seconds. Your beloved can stay in bed because the food's all ready now,' he smiles, lifting the pink shrimp from the pan.

'It smells fantastic. I can feel myself going weak at the knees,' Mia says, leaning over the dish.

Rex drains the pasta, quickly tips it into a bowl, stirs in the garlic butter and peppers, then adds the oiled shrimp, adds a splash of white wine and balsamic vinegar, then plenty of chopped parsley, marjoram and basil.

'Then you can take the bowls back into the bedroom with you,' Rex says directly to the camera. 'Open a bottle of wine if you want to stay under the covers, but otherwise water goes very well.'

22

The Foreign Minister is dead, Rex repeats to himself as he leaves the studio where the guests are eating his pasta dish. He hears them praise the food as he pushes the soundproof door open.

Rex runs along the hallway to his dressing room, locks the door behind him, staggers into the bathroom and throws up in the toilet.

Exhausted, he rinses his mouth and face, lies down on the narrow bed and closes his eyes.

'Fuck me,' he whispers, releasing the hazy memories of that night three weeks ago.

He had been at a party at Matbaren, and he had a little too much to drink. He decided that he was in love with a woman who worked for some investment company with a stupid name.

Almost every time he got drunk, the night ended with him in bed with a woman. If he was lucky, she wasn't a production assistant at TV4 or the ex-wife of a colleague. On this occasion, she was a complete stranger.

They got a taxi back to her villa out in Djursholm. She was divorced and her only child was on an exchange trip to the USA. He kissed the back of her neck as she switched the alarm off and let them in. An old golden retriever came padding through the rooms.

They both knew what they wanted, and didn't talk much. He

selected a bottle of wine from the large wine fridge, and remembers swaying as he tried to open it.

She got out some cheese and crackers which they never touched.

With an air of inevitability, he had followed her through the carpeted hallway towards the master bedroom.

She dimmed the wall lights and disappeared into the bathroom.

When she came back she was wearing a silver nightgown and kimono. She opened the drawer of the bedside table and handed him a condom.

He remembers that she wanted to be taken from behind, maybe because she didn't want to look at his face. She got on all fours, with her pale backside uncovered, the nightgown pulled up, bunched around her waist, and her mid-length hair hanging over her cheeks.

The antique bed creaked and a framed embroidered angel wobbled on the wall.

They were both too tired, too drunk. She didn't orgasm, didn't even pretend to, just muttered that she needed to sleep when he was finished, sank onto her stomach and fell asleep with her legs wide apart.

He had gone back to the kitchen, helped himself to a glass of cognac, and leafed through the morning paper, which had just been delivered. The Foreign Minister had made some stupid comment about how there were extreme feminist forces that wanted to destroy the age-old relationship between men and women.

Rex had swept the paper onto the floor and left the house.

He had one thing in mind. He had walked straight down to Germaniaviken and followed the shore all the way to the Foreign Minister's villa.

He was too drunk to care about any alarms or security cameras. Driven on by a very clear sense of justice, he clambered over the fence, walked right across the grass and up onto the deck. Anyone could have seen him there. The Foreign Minister's wife could have been standing at the window, or a neighbour could have driven past. Rex didn't care. One thought was running through his mind: he had to piss in the Foreign Minister's floodlit swimming pool. It felt like the right thing to do at the time, and he smiled like a prize-fighter as his urine splashed into the turquoise water.

23

Rex ignores the taxi that's waiting outside the TV4 building and starts walking instead. He needs space to breathe, needs to collect his thoughts.

A few months ago he would have calmed his nerves with a large glass of whisky, followed by another three.

Now he walks along beside the busy Lidingövägen instead, and is trying to figure out what the cost of his behaviour might be when DJ calls.

'Did you see me?'

'Yes, really good,' DJ says. 'You looked almost hungover for real.'

'Sylvia thought so too. She asked if I'd been drinking.'

'Did she? I can come and swear that you only drank water yesterday . . . even if a fair bit of it was seawater.'

'I don't know . . . it's just so ridiculous that I have to pretend to be an alcoholic so I don't lose my job.'

'But it can't be a bad idea for you to take it a bit—'

'Stop that. I don't want to hear it,' Rex interrupts.

'I didn't mean it in a bad way,' DJ says quietly.

Rex sighs and looks through the railing at the entrance to the big sports stadium that was built for the 1912 Olympics.

'Have you heard that the Foreign Minister is dead?' he asks.

'Of course.'

'We had a complicated relationship,' Rex says.

'In what way?'

'I didn't like him,' he replies, and walks through the stadium entrance and out onto the red track.

'OK, but you shouldn't talk about that just after his death,' DJ says calmly.

'It isn't just that . . .'

David Jordan says nothing as Rex admits what he did. He says that he had a little too much to drink three weeks ago and just happened·to urinate in the Foreign Minister's swimming pool.

He concludes the confession by saying that he got all the garden gnomes and threw them into the pool as well.

Rex walks out onto the football field and stops at the centre circle.

The empty stands surround him. He remembers that some of the gnomes floated while others sank onto the bottom, surrounded by little air-bubbles.

'OK,' DJ says after a long silence. 'Does anyone else know what you did?'

'The security cameras.'

'If there's a scandal, the investors will pull out – you know that. You do realise that, don't you?'

'What should I do?' Rex asks pathetically.

'Go to the funeral,' DJ says slowly. 'I'll make sure you get invited. Talk about it on social media, say you lost your best friend. Talk about him and his political achievements with the greatest respect.'

'That'll look bad if the security footage gets out,' Rex says.

'Yes, I know. But pre-empt it by getting in first and talking about your jokey relationship and the silly pranks you used to play on each other. Say that you sometimes went too far, but that was just what you were both like. Don't admit to anything specific, because with any luck the recording has already been deleted.'

'Thanks.'

'What did you have against the Foreign Minister, anyway?' DJ asks with interest.

'He was always a slippery bastard, and a bully. I'm going to piss on his grave – one last prank.'

'As long as no one films you,' David Jordan laughs, and ends the conversation.

Sammy is sitting on the bed drying his hair with a towel when Rex walks into his hospital room.

'Nice make-up, Dad,' he says in a hoarse voice.

'Oh, yeah,' Rex says. 'I came straight from the studio.'

He takes a step towards the bed. Chaotic images of the stomach pump and his own angst at the Foreign Minister's death fight for space in his head.

He reminds himself the only option right now is to stay calm, not to be judgemental.

'How are you feeling?' he asks tentatively.

'OK, I guess,' Sammy replies. 'My neck hurts. Like someone pushed a tube down my throat.'

'I'll make some soup when we get home,' Rex says.

'You just missed the doctor. Apparently I need to talk to a counsellor before I'm allowed to leave.'

'Do you have an appointment?'

'She's coming at one o'clock.'

'I have time to see DJ before then,' Rex says when he realises that he has an AA meeting in half an hour. 'But I'll come straight back after that . . . we can get a taxi home.'

'Thanks.'

'Sammy, we need to talk.'

'OK,' his son says, clamming up instantly.

'I don't ever want to have to go through this again,' Rex begins.

'It can't have been much fun,' Sammy says, turning his head away.

'No,' Rex replies.

'Dad's a celebrity,' Sammy says with a crooked smile. 'Dad's a superstar TV chef, and he doesn't want a failure for a son, a faggot who wears make-up and . . .'

'I don't give a damn about that,' Rex interrupts.

'You don't have to put up with me for long, just a few weeks,' his son says.

'I hope we can still have a reasonable time together – but you have to promise to try.'

Sammy raises his eyebrows.

'What? How am I supposed to try? Is this about Nico?'

'This isn't some kind of moral debate,' Rex explains. 'I don't have an opinion, I believe that love just happens between people.'

'Who's talking about love?' Sammy mutters.

'Sex, then.'

'Did you love Mum?' Sammy asks.

'I don't know. I was very immature,' Rex replies honestly. 'But now, in hindsight, I can see that she was the person I should have stayed with . . . I would have liked to have lived my life with the two of you.'

'Look, Dad, I'm nineteen years old. I don't get it. What do you want from me?'

'No more stomach pumps, for a start.'

Sammy gets slowly to his feet and goes to hang the towel up.

'I thought Nico was counting the pills he was giving me,' he says when he comes back. 'But there were too many.'

'Count for yourself in the future.'

'I'm weak-willed. And it's actually OK for me to be weak,' he replies quickly.

'Then you won't make it. There's no place for weakness in this world.'

'OK, Dad.'

'Sammy, it's not like I'm making this up – that's just the way it is.'

His son is leaning against the doorframe with his arms folded. His cheeks are flushed and he swallows hard.

'Promise me you won't do anything dangerous,' Rex says.

'Why not?' Sammy whispers.

24

No terrorist organisation has claimed responsibility for the murder, but the Security Police don't think that's strange given the specific nature of the attack. The underlying reason for shooting the Foreign Minister is to frighten a small group of high-ranking politicians rather than terrify the general population.

On Sunday they continue evaluating the forensic evidence and the thousands of lab results. Everything points to the fact that they're dealing with a highly professional killer. He didn't leave any fingerprints or biological evidence, he didn't leave any bullets or cartridges, and he doesn't appear in any security-camera footage.

They have several of his boot imprints, but they're a type that are sold all over the world, and analysis of the dirt on them hasn't come up with anything.

Saga is sitting with Janus, who's the head of the investigation, and a few colleagues in one of the conference rooms of the Security Police Headquarters. Janus is wearing a pale green, tie-dye T-shirt. His almost white eyebrows take on a pinkish tone when he gets agitated.

Security around government buildings has been tightened and key individuals have more bodyguards, but they're all aware that this might not be enough.

Stress levels in the conference room are high.

Salim has been isolated at Hall Prison in preparation for his transfer to Joona's unit. No one believes that isolating him will prevent more murders, because even if he can't give any further orders it's possible that the first three have already been arranged.

Right now almost all of their hopes are pinned on Joona gaining his confidence inside the prison. If he fails, their only real option is to wait and see what happens on Wednesday.

'We're dealing with a meticulous killer. He doesn't make any mistakes, doesn't get carried away, doesn't get scared,' one of the men says.

'Then he shouldn't have left a witness alive,' Saga says.

'This is all assuming he isn't just a pimp who thought the Foreign Minister had gone too far this time,' Janus smiles, blowing his red hair away from his face.

Jeanette and Saga have conducted three more interviews with the witness, but nothing new has emerged. She's sticking to her story, and there's nothing to suggest that she's lying. But they haven't been able to verify the fact that she's a prostitute.

No one else in the business knows Sofia, but the investigators have managed to trace Tamara Jensen, who now appears to be the only person who might be able to confirm her story.

Tamara's number was in Sofia's mobile phone, and by using three base-stations to trace her phone they've managed to identify an exact location: Tamara's movements are restricted to a small area just southwest of Nyköping.

She isn't married, and she hasn't moved to Gothenburg, as Sofia claimed.

She's still advertising on a website that says it offers an exclusive escort service in the Stockholm area. The photograph shows a woman in her mid-twenties, with lively eyes and shiny hair. Her presentation promises cultured company for social events and trips, nights and weekend packages.

Saga is navigating while Jeanette drives the dark grey BMW. The two women always enjoy each other's company even though they're very different in both personality and appearance.

Jeanette's hair is held in place by a silver clasp, and she's wearing a light grey skirt and white jacket, thick tights and pumps with a low heel.

They're talking and eating liquorice from a bag in the centre console.

Saga is telling Jeanette how her ex-boyfriend, Stefan, sent her lots of drunken texts from Copenhagen yesterday, wanting her to go to his hotel.

'Well, why not?' Jeanette says, helping herself to another piece of liquorice.

Saga laughs, then looks thoughtfully out of the side-window at the industrial buildings flashing past.

'He's an idiot, and I can't believe I'm still sleeping with him,' she says quietly.

'Seriously, though,' Jeanette says, drumming the steering wheel lightly with one hand. 'Who cares about principles? This is your life, the only one you've got, and you're not seeing anyone else.'

'Is that your advice as a psychologist?' Saga smiles.

'I really believe that,' she replies, looking at Saga.

It's late evening by the time they reach Nyköpingsbro, an all-night restaurant situated on a bridge over the highway.

Jeanette drives around the car park until they find Tamara's old Saab. They block it in with the BMW, then go into the restaurant.

The restaurant is almost empty. Saga and Jeanette walk around the tables anyway, but there's no sign of Tamara. They pass a deserted ballpit trapped behind a smeared glass screen, next to a green sign with tourist information.

'OK, let's go outside,' Jeanette says in a low voice.

It's dark in the car park. The air is cold and Saga zips up her leather jacket as they walk past the tables and benches. A few magpies are scrambling around on top of the overflowing dustbins.

Saga and Jeanette walk towards the lorry park as a blue articulated lorry pulls up in front of them. The vehicle's weight makes the ground shake. It turns and parks wheezily beside the furthest lorry.

There are nineteen lorries parked on this side of the bridge. Beyond them the murky darkness of the forest takes over. The roar of the highway comes in waves, like exhausted surf on a beach.

It's dark and strangely warm between the vehicles. The smell of diesel mixes with urine and cigarette smoke. The hot metal clicks. Dirty water drips from a mud flap.

Someone tosses a bag of rubbish under a trailer and clambers back up into the cab.

Cigarettes glow in various places in the darkness.

Saga and Jeanette walk around the huge vehicles. The tarmac is covered with oil-stains, empty chewing-tobacco tubs, Burger King wrappers, cigarette butts, and a tatty porn magazine.

Saga crouches down and looks under one of the trailers. She sees people moving around between the lorries further away. One man is peeing against a tyre. They can hear a muted conversation, and somewhere a dog is barking.

One lorry, smeared with dirt, starts up beside them and idles for a while to get the engine warmed up. Its red tail-lights illuminate a pile of empty bottles at the edge of the forest.

Saga crouches down again to look under the rusty vehicle frame, and sees a woman climb out of one of the cabs. Saga's gaze follows her thin legs as she totters away on platform boots.

25

Saga and Jeanette hurry towards the woman in high heels just as the articulated lorry rumbles out from the lorry park. It turns heavily on its axis and passes so close that they have to press up against another lorry to avoid getting crushed.

The huge tyres crunch past.

A hot cloud of exhaust fumes in the air and Jeanette coughs quietly.

Some distance away a man calls out, then wolf-whistles.

They walk around the other lorry and catch sight of the woman in platform boots. She's standing with her hands cupped around a cigarette, the glow of the lighter reflected on her face. It isn't Tamara. The woman's eyes are red-rimmed, and she has deep lines running from her nose to the corners of her mouth.

Her thin hair has been bleached, but the roots are completely grey.

She's wearing a low-cut top and a suede skirt.

The woman is standing next to a Polish lorry and saying something to the men in the cab. She takes a deep drag on the cigarette and suddenly teeters backwards, almost falling between the cab and trailer. Saga and Jeanette hear the men in the lorry explain in English that they aren't interested in paying for sex. They're trying to be polite, saying that all they want to do is call their children to say goodnight, then get some sleep.

The woman waves them aside dismissively and moves on. She's just knocked on the door of another cab when Saga and Jeanette catch up with her.

'Excuse me, but do you know where Tamara Jensen is?' Saga asks.

The woman turns stiffly towards them and brushes her hair from her face.

'Tamara?' she repeats hoarsely.

'I owe her some money,' Jeanette says.

'I can give it to her for you,' the woman says, unable to hold back a smile.

Saga laughs.

'Is she here?'

The woman points towards the back of the restaurant.

'I'll check,' Saga says.

Jeanette stays by the lorries and watches Saga walk between the big vehicles, a thin silhouette against the light from the restaurant.

'Can I ask you something?' she says, turning back towards the prostitute.

'Listen, I've already found salvation,' the woman replies automatically, tottering once more.

The engine of the lorry beside them roars into life. It wheezes and then slowly starts to move forward, spreading hot diesel fumes. The back tyre rolls straight over a glass bottle. There's a crash as pieces of glass fly out with considerable force. Jeanette feels her calf sting. She touches her torn tights with her fingers, then looks at them and sees that they're covered in blood. When she straightens up again the woman has vanished.

Saga walks past the restaurant and around the public toilets and showers. The glow from the yellow petrol station sign is visible through the trees. The rear of the restaurant is littered with rubbish: old milk cartons, strips of toilet paper, and the remains of scattered food.

Tamara is sitting on the ground leaning against the wall, holding a freezer-bag over her nose and mouth.

'Tamara?'

The woman crumples the bag and slowly lowers it. Her eyes roll backwards and a deep sigh emerges from her lips.

'My name is Saga Bauer, and I'd like to talk to you about your best friend, Sofia Stefansson.'

Tamara looks at Saga as a string of saliva runs down her chin. Her hair is greasy and her face is grey and shut-off, like someone who's unconscious.

'This is my best friend,' she says, raising the plastic bag.

'I know you know Sofia.'

Tamara coughs. She almost topples sideways, but puts her hand down to steady herself and inhales deeply from the bag again.

'Sofia,' she mumbles, and nods vaguely.

'Is she an escort?'

'She thinks she's better than other people, but she's just a stupid cow who doesn't understand anything.'

Her eyes close and her head sinks onto her chest.

'What is it she doesn't understand?'

'The perks of the job,' she whispers.

'Have you ever seen her when she's with clients?'

Tamara sighs and opens her eyes again. She realises that she's got a tied condom stuck to her wrist, grabs it and throws it on the ground.

'I've got a really weird taste in my mouth,' she says, looking up at Saga. 'If you want to get me something to drink, we can talk.'

'OK.'

Tamara coughs again, struggles to her feet and squints at Saga.

She's very thin. Her hands and cheeks are covered in tiny scabs, and her lips are cracked and dry. A hair slide that's lost its ornament is hanging down over her forehead.

There's very little about her that resembles the smiling woman on the website.

Tamara starts to move, hunched over, her head drooping. When they get inside the restaurant she stands still for a moment, swaying, as if she's forgotten where she's going, then walks towards the counter.

'I want a chocolate milkshake . . . and French fries with ketchup . . . and a large Pepsi . . . and this,' she says, putting a big bag of car-shaped sweets on the counter.

Jeanette Fleming is walking along close to the trucks in the direction she thinks the prostitute went. Closer to the edge of the forest it's so dark between the vehicles that she has to hold her hands up to feel her way. The air reeks of diesel, and the lorries are radiating heat like sweating horses. She passes one cab with check-patterned blinds over the windows.

Jeanette suddenly sees the woman. She's standing a short distance away, spitting on the ground as she knocks on one of the driver's cabs. She leans heavily on the huge front wheel.

'Where else have you worked?' Jeanette asks when she catches up to her.

'I used to work in really fancy places.'

'Have you ever had any clients in Djursholm?'

'I only take the best,' the woman mumbles.

The cab door opens and a heavy man with glasses and a beard looks at them. He blows Jeanette a kiss, then looks impatiently at the other woman.

'What do you want?' he asks.

'I was just wondering if you'd like some company,' she replies.

'You're too ugly,' the man says, but doesn't close the door.

'No, I'm not,' she replies. It's obvious that the man is enjoying being cruel to her.

'So what part of you isn't ugly?'

The woman pulls her top up, showing her pale breasts.

'And you expect to get paid for those?' he says, but still beckons her into the cab with his head.

26

Jeanette watches the woman clamber up into the cab and close the door behind her. She waits for a while in the darkness, listening to the creak of the springs in the seats.

Headlights sweep the ground and the shadows quickly slide away. Laughter and muffled music reach her from the other end of the lorry park.

A drunk woman shrieks somewhere, her voice angry and hoarse.

Jeanette peers under the trailer. In the distance a cigarette falls to the ground in a cascade of sparks before someone stamps it out. She detects a movement from the other direction. It looks like someone's crawling on all fours under the lorries, heading towards her. A shiver runs down her spine. Jeanette starts to walk towards the restaurant.

Another lorry is on its way into the car park, but stops with a squeal to let her pass. The brakes wheeze. A chain clanks as it sways beneath the vehicle. Jeanette can't see the driver, but still walks across the road through the dazzling glare of its headlights.

She looks around as she gets close to the restaurant, but there's no one following her.

Jeanette slows down a little and decides to take her torn tights off and wash the cut on her leg before she calls Saga.

She goes over to the bathroom, but all the cubicles are occupied. The blood has congealed around the wound and run down her calf.

The thin metal door of one of the toilets swings open and a woman with bleached blonde hair emerges. She's clutching her phone to her ear and is yelling that she had a client, and that she can't do everything at once.

The woman disappears down the hall, waving her arms angrily.

A handwritten sign saying 'Out of order' has been taped to the door, but Jeanette goes in anyway and locks it behind her.

It's a disabled toilet, with thin metal walls. The white armrest is folded up, and there's an illuminated red alarm button close to the floor.

She takes off her torn tights and throws them away. There are lots of used condoms in the bin. There's wet toilet paper all over the floor and the walls are covered with graffiti.

Jeanette looks at herself in the mirror, takes her powder out of her purse and leans over the sink. She can hear someone in the cubicle next to her, moving around in the confined space.

She powders her face and notices that there's a round hole in the wall between her and the next cubicle. Maybe that's where the toilet-roll dispenser used to be. She puts her powder away again and turns around to see that the wall is moving slightly.

Someone is leaning against it from the other side.

There's a rustling sound and a folded banknote falls onto the floor from the hole. The wall creaks. Jeanette is about to say something when a large penis appears, dangling through the hole in front of her.

The situation is so absurd that she can't help smiling.

A memory of something she once read about a swingers' club in France flashes into her head, about them having rooms like this.

The man on the other side thinks she's a prostitute.

She stands there for a moment, and swallows hard. She stares at the penis, feeling her heart beating fast in her chest, then looks at the door to make sure it's definitely locked.

Slowly she reaches out and takes hold of the warm, thick member.

Jeanette squeezes it gently and feels it stiffen and start to rise. She gently strokes back and forth, and then lets go of it.

She has no idea why she does it, but she leans forward and takes the penis in her mouth, sucks it tentatively, feeling it swell and get stiffer. She pauses for breath, puts her hand between her thighs, pulls her underwear down and steps out of it as she massages the erect penis.

She tries to breathe quietly. She thinks she's going to stop. She can't do something like this. She's crazy. Her pulse is throbbing. She turns around and holds onto the cistern with one hand. Her legs are trembling as she stands on tiptoe, bends the penis down and lets it slide into her from behind. She gasps and looks over at the lock again. The metal wall creaks as Jeanette is pushed forward, and she clings onto the cistern and pushes her backside against the cool metal.

Saga is sitting opposite Tamara in one of the booths in the restaurant, waiting while she eats a plate of French fries with ketchup on the side. A streak of snot shimmers under her nose. Beneath them traffic passes by on the highway, white lights in one direction, red in the other.

'How well do you know Sofia Stefansson?' Saga asks.

Tamara shrugs, and drinks some of her milkshake through the straw, sucking her cheeks in. Her forehead turns white.

'Brain-freeze,' she gasps when she finally lets go of the straw.

She carefully dips the fries in the ketchup and eats, smiling softly to herself.

'Who did you say you were again?' she asks.

'I'm a friend of Sofia's,' Saga says.

'Oh yeah.'

'Could she have faked working as a prostitute?'

'Faked it? What the hell do you mean? We did a job together in a building's rubbish collection room once . . . she got fucked up the ass . . . I don't know if that counts as faking?'

Tamara's face suddenly goes slack again, as if she were lost in some absorbing memory.

'Why did you stop working as an escort in Stockholm?' Saga asks.

'You could go a long way too . . . I've got contacts, I used to be a lingerie model . . . just without the lingerie,' Tamara says, and shakes with soundless laughter.

'You once had a client out in Djursholm, a big house facing the water. He may have said his name was Wille,' Saga says calmly.

'Maybe,' Tamara says, eating the fries with her mouth open.

'Do you remember him?' Saga asks.

'No,' Tamara yawns, then wipes her hands on her skirt and tips the contents of her bag onto the table.

A hairbrush, a roll of plastic bags, a stump of mascara, condoms and perfume from Victoria's Secret roll out across the wax tablecloth. Saga notes that Tamara has three dark-brown glass ampules of Demerol, an extremely addictive opioid. Tamara presses a Valium from a blister-pack of ten pale blue pills, and washes it down with Pepsi.

Saga waits patiently until she has swept everything back into her bag again, then takes out a photograph of the Foreign Minister.

'I don't give a shit about him,' Tamara says, then purses her lips.

'Did he speak to anyone on the phone while you were there?'

'Seriously. He was really stressed and drank a lot. He kept going on about how the cops ought to stand to attention . . . he said it, like, a hundred times.'

'That the police ought to stand to attention?'

'Yes . . . and that there was a guy with two faces who was after him.'

She drinks more Pepsi and shakes the cup, making the ice-cubes rattle.

'In what way was the guy after him?'

'I didn't ask.'

Tamara dips two fries in ketchup and puts them in her mouth.

'What did he mean, two faces?'

'I don't know. He was drunk. Maybe he meant that the guy had two sides,' Tamara suggests.

'What else did he say about this man?'

'Nothing. It wasn't important. It was just talk.'

'Was he going to meet him?'

'I don't know. He didn't say anything about that . . . I just wanted him to be happy, so I got him talking about all those paintings on the walls instead.'

'Was he violent with you?'

'He was a gentleman,' she replies tersely.

Tamara picks up the bag of sweets from the table, stands up and weaves over towards the door. Saga has just gone after her when her phone rings. She looks at the screen and sees that it's Janus.

'Bauer.'

'We've been through all the security footage from the Foreign Minister's hard-drive . . . thirteen cameras, two months, almost twenty thousand hours of footage,' Janus says.

'Is there any sign of the killer? Doing reconnaissance or something?'

'No, but someone else is very visible in one of the recordings – you need to see this. Call me when you reach the building and I'll come down and let you in.'

Saga knows that Janus is bipolar, and she's worried he's having a manic episode, he must have stopped taking his medication for some reason.

'Do you know what time it is?' Saga asks.

'Who cares?' he replies quickly.

'I need to get some sleep. I'll see you tomorrow,' she says gently.

'Sleep,' Janus repeats, then laughs loudly. 'I'm fine, Saga, I'm just eager to make progress, same as you.'

She walks towards the car park, looking at the traffic below, and calls Jeanette.

Sofia appears to have been working as a prostitute, just as she said. She's probably been telling the truth all along – and is in no way connected to the murder.

So why was she allowed to live? Saga asks herself as she stops in front of the car, all too aware that they still have no idea of what the murderer wants.

27

There is a large white house with a pale thatched roof on Ceder Street outside Helsingborg. This early in the morning the surrounding parkland is draped in grey mist, but yellow light is shining from the ground-floor windows.

Nils Gilbert wakes with a start. He must have dozed off in his wheelchair. His face feels hot and his heart is pounding. The sun hasn't risen above the treetops, and the house and park are heavily shaded.

The gloomy garden resembles the realm of the dead.

He tries to see if Ali has arrived, if he's taken the wheelbarrow and shovel from the shed.

Just as Nils rolls over to the kitchen door to let in some fresh air, he hears an odd scraping noise. It sounds like it's coming from the large living room. It must be the cat trying to get out.

'Lizzy?'

The sound stops abruptly. He listens for a while, then leans back.

His hands start to shake on the armrests of the wheelchair. His legs twitch and bounce in a meaningless dance.

He hid the signs of Parkinson's for as long as he could: the stiffness in one arm, the foot that dragged ever so slightly, the way his handwriting changed until it was so small that even he couldn't read the microscopic scrawl.

He didn't want Eva to notice anything.

And then she died, three years ago.

Eva had complained about being tired for several weeks.

It was a Saturday, and she had just come home from Väla with lots of heavy grocery bags. She was having trouble breathing and her chest felt tight. She said that she was probably coming down with a real stinker of a cold.

By the time she sat down on the sofa, sweat was dripping down her cheeks.

She lay down, and was already dead by the time he asked if she wanted him to turn the television on.

So now it's just him and fat Lizzy.

He can go weeks without talking to anyone. Sometimes he worries that his voice has disappeared.

One of the few people he sees at all is the girl who looks after the pool. She walks around in jeans and a gold-coloured bikini top, and seems very uncomfortable when he tries to talk to her.

The first time he attempted to say anything to her she looked at him like he was ninety years old or had a serious mental illness.

The people who bring his food are always in a rush. They barely get his signature before hurrying away. And the physiotherapist, an angry, large-breasted woman, just does her job. She gives him curt commands and pretends not to hear his attempts to make conversation.

Only the Iranian man from the garden-maintenance company has any time for him. Ali sometimes comes in for a cup of coffee.

It's really for his sake that Nils keeps the pool open, but he still hasn't plucked up the courage to ask if he'd like a swim.

Ali works hard, and often gets sweaty.

Nils knows that he books him far too often, which is why the garden looks the way it does, with precisely clipped shrubs and hedges, leafy archways and perfectly swept paths.

It's quiet. It's always so quiet here.

Nils shivers and pushes himself over to the jukebox.

He bought it when he was twenty years old: a genuine Seeburg, made by the Swedish Sjöberg company.

He used to change the singles from time to time. He would make new labels on his typewriter and slip them in under the glass top.

He inserts the coin into the slot, hears it rattle down and activate the mechanism before rolling out into the tray again.

He's used the same coin all these years.

He taps the buttons for C7 with his shaking hand. The machine whirrs as the record is placed on the turntable.

Nils rolls away as the fast drum intro to 'Stargazer' starts to play. He is thrown back in time to when he saw Rainbow live at the Concert Hall in Stockholm in the late 1970s.

The band were over an hour late starting, but when Dio walked on and started to sing 'Kill the King', the audience moved as one towards the stage.

Nils goes over to the big windows. Every afternoon he lowers the shades on the west-facing windows to protect his paintings from the strong light.

Through the nylon gauze the window looks even darker and greyer.

To Ali, this whole place must look like a tragic manifestation of the absence of children and grandchildren.

Nils knows that the house is ridiculously showy, that the park is overblown, and that no one ever uses the pool.

His company produces advanced electronics for radar and electronic guidance systems. He's had good government contacts and has been able to export dual-use products for almost twenty years now.

His arms suddenly shiver.

Over the loud music he thinks he can hear a small child chanting a nursery rhyme.

He turns the wheelchair and makes his way out into the hall.

The voice is coming from the abandoned upper floor. He rolls over to the staircase that he hasn't climbed in many years, and sees that the door to the bedroom at the top is standing ajar.

The music from the jukebox stops. There's a clicking sound as the single is slotted back into place among the others, and then silence descends.

Nils started to be afraid of the dark six months ago, after having a nightmare about his wife. She came back from the dead, but could only stand upright because she was impaled on a rough wooden post that ran between her legs, right through her body and neck, and out through her head.

She was angry that he hadn't done anything to help her, that he hadn't called for an ambulance.

The bloody pole reached all the way to the floor, and Eva was forced to walk with a strange, bow-legged gait as she came after him.

Nils puts his hands on his lap. They're twitching and shaking, darting about in exaggerated gestures.

When they are still again he tightens the strap around his waist that prevents him from sliding out of the chair.

He rolls into the living room and looks around. Everything looks the way it always does. The chandelier, the Persian rugs, the marble table and the empire-style sofa and armchairs that Eva brought from her childhood home.

The phone is no longer on the table.

Sometimes Eva's presence in the house is so real that he thinks her older sister has a spare key and is creeping around like in some *Scooby-Doo* cartoon in order to scare him.

He sets off towards the kitchen again, then thinks he sees something out of the corner of his eye. He quickly turns his head and imagines he sees a face in the antique mirror, before realising that it's just a blemish in the glass.

'Lizzy?' he calls out weakly.

One of the kitchen drawers clatters, and then he hears footsteps on the floor. He stops, his heart pounding, turns the chair and imagines the blood running down the pole between Eva's legs.

He presses on silently, rolling towards the big double doors, the wheels making a faint sticky sound on the hardwood floor.

Now Eva is walking bowlegged through the kitchen. The pole is scraping across the slate floor, leaving a trail of blood before catching on the threshold to the dining room.

The stupid nursery rhyme starts up again.

The radio in the kitchen must be switched on.

The footrest of the wheelchair hits the back door with a gentle clunk.

He looks towards the closed door to the dining room.

His hands are shaking, and the stiffness in his neck makes it hard for him to lean forward and press the button controlling the shades.

With a whirr, the grey nylon fabric glides up like a theatre curtain, and the garden gradually brightens.

The garden furniture is set out. There are pine needles gathering in the folds of the cushions. The lights around the pool aren't switched on, but mist is rising gently from the water.

As soon as the shade has risen enough, he'll be able to open the door and go outside.

He's decided to wait outside for Ali, ask him to look through the house. He'll admit that he's scared of the dark, that he leaves the lights on all night, and maybe pay him extra to stay longer.

He turns the key in the lock with shaking hands. The lock clicks and he tugs the handle and nudges the door open.

He reverses, looks over towards the dining room and sees the door slowly open.

He rolls into the patio door as hard as he can. It swings open and he catches a glimpse of a figure approaching him from behind.

Nils hears heavy footsteps as he rolls out onto the deck and feels the cool air on his face.

'Ali, is that you?' he calls in a frightened voice as he rolls forward. 'Ali!'

The garden is quiet. The tool-shed is locked. The morning mist is drifting above the ground.

He tries to turn the wheelchair, but one of the tyres is caught in the crack between two slabs. Nils can hardly breathe. He tries to stop himself from shaking by pressing his hands into his armpits.

Someone is approaching him from the house and he looks back over his shoulder.

A masked man, carrying a black bag in his hand. He's walking straight towards him, disguised as an executioner.

Nils tugs at the wheels to pull himself free.

He's about to shout for Ali again when cold liquid drenches his head, running through his hair, down his neck, over his face and chest.

It takes just a couple of seconds for him to realise that it's petrol.

What he thought was a black bag is actually the lawnmower's petrol tank.

'Please, wait, I've got lots of money . . . I promise, I can transfer all of it,' he gasps, coughing from the fumes.

The masked man walks around and tips the last of the petrol over Nils's chest, then drops the empty container on the ground in front of the wheelchair.

'God, please . . . I'll do anything . . .'

The man takes out a box of matches and says some incomprehensible words. Nils is hysterical, and he can't make sense of what the man is saying.

'Don't do it, don't do it, don't do it . . .'

He tries to loosen the strap over his thighs, but it's tangled and is now too tight to take off. His hands jerk as he tugs at it. The man calmly lights a match and tosses it onto his lap.

There's a rush of air, and a sucking sound, like a parachute opening.

His pyjamas and hair burst into flames.

And through the blue glare he sees the masked man back away from the heat.

The childish nursery rhyme rolls through his head as the storm rages around him. He can't get any air into his lungs. It's as if he's drowning, and then he feels absolute, all-encompassing pain.

He could never have imagined anything so excruciating.

He leans forwards in the foetal position and hears a metallic crackling sound, as if from a great distance, as the wheelchair starts to buckle in the heat.

Nils has time to think that it sounds like the jukebox is searching for a new disc before he loses consciousness.

28

The inmate from Hall is on his way towards D-block, where the atmosphere is tense.

Through the reinforced glass, the guards can see that for once Joona is eating breakfast at the same table as the leader of the Brotherhood, Reiner Kronlid. The two of them talk for a while, then Joona stands up, takes his coffee and sandwich, and goes to sit at another table.

'What the hell's he playing at?' one of the guards asks.

'Maybe he's heard something about the new guy.'

'Unless it's about being granted leave?'

'His application was approved yesterday,' the third guard nods. 'First time for him.'

Joona looks over at the three guards who are watching him through the glass, then turns towards Sumo and asks the same question he just asked Reiner.

'What can I do for you tomorrow?' he asks.

Sumo has already served eight years for a double murder, and now knows that he killed people over a misunderstanding. His face is a picture of grief these days. He always looks like he's been crying but is trying to hold it together.

'Buy a red rose . . . the best one you can find. Give it to Outi and tell her she's my rose, and . . . And say sorry for ruining her life.'

'Do you want her to come out here?' Joona asks, looking him in the eye.

Sumo shakes his head, and his gaze slides towards the window. He stares at the grey fence topped with barbed wire, and the monotonous, dirty yellow wall beyond it.

Joona turns to the next man at the table, Luka Bogdani, a short man whose face is locked in a permanent state of derision.

'How about you?'

Luka leans forward and whispers:

'I want you to check if my brother's started to get rid of my money.'

'What do you want me to ask?'

'No, fuck it, no questions. Just look at the money, count it. There should be exactly six hundred thousand.'

'I can't do that,' Joona replies. 'I want to get out of here, and that money's from a robbery, and if I—'

'Fucking cop,' Luka hisses, and sends his coffee cup flying.

Joona walks on around the tables in the dining room. He asks them all what he can do for them when he's outside. He memorises greetings and errands as he waits for Salim Ratjen to arrive.

Joona told the Prime Minister that he needs thirty-six hours' leave, starting on Monday, in order to infiltrate Ratjen's organisation.

'That won't leave you long in here to find out what he knows,' the Prime Minister had warned.

Joona didn't tell him that the limited amount of time was an advantage.

Before leaving the visitors' room, Joona had asked how far he was allowed to go in extreme circumstances. The corners of the Prime Minister's mouth had twitched slightly when he replied:

'If you can stop the terrorists, you can do pretty much whatever you need to.'

Reiner Kronlid gets up from his table, wipes his mouth nervously, then stares at the hallway and airlock. He stands there stiffly, his neck tense, before licking his lips and sitting back down again. The others at the Brotherhood's table lean forward as he talks.

Joona sees the light in the hallway behind the reinforced glass dim as a grey shadow appears.

The lock whirrs and two guards hand over Salim Ratjen.

Salim Ratjen's face is round and intelligent. His thinning hair is combed across his head, and his moustache is streaked with grey.

He is carrying his belongings in a grey, prison-service duffle, and is careful not to look anyone in the eye.

One of the guards takes him first to his cell, then the dining room.

Salim sits down on the empty chair next to Magnus Duva with a bowl and mug.

Joona stands up and goes over to them. Looking at Magnus, he sits down by their table and asks what he can do for him while he's outside.

'Go and see my sister and cut her nose off,' Magnus says.

'She sends you money every month,' Joona says.

'Don't forget to film it,' Magnus says.

Salim listens, eyes lowered, as he eats his muesli.

Reiner and two of his men stand talking in front of the window to the control room, blocking the view for the few moments required.

The other two members of the Brotherhood walk across the dining room, their muscled arms hanging stiffly by their sides. One of them has a tattoo of a wolf encircled by barbed wire. The other has a dirty bandage around his hand.

This is the wrong time for a murder, Joona thinks, and turns towards Salim Ratjen.

'Do you speak Swedish?' Joona asks.

'Yes,' Salim replies without looking up.

The men head off towards the bathrooms.

'You might have figured out that I have some leave soon, and I'm asking everyone in the block if there's anything they want me to do for them outside . . . We don't know each other, but you're probably going to be here for a while, so I'll ask you too.'

'Thanks, but I'm OK,' Ratjen says in a low voice.

'Because I'm an infidel?'

'Yes.'

The plastic spoon trembles in Salim Ratjen's freckled hand.

Chairs scrape the floor and the two Malmö guys get up on the other side of the room. Imre with the gold teeth is almost six foot six, and Darko looks like a sixty-year-old miner.

Reiner's group start complaining noisily that the coffee is weak. They turn towards the window.

'You can't fucking fool us!' one of them yells. 'Before the Albanians got here there was always enough coffee!'

Behind the glass the two prison guards get ready to go in and calm things down.

The men from the Brotherhood start to head towards Salim. They pull up their hoods and keep their backs to the security cameras.

They're not armed, they just want to intimidate him.

Joona stays where he is, realising that they're about to strike. Salim controlled a lot of the drug trade at Hall, and Reiner Kronlid needs to scare or kill him straight away in order to show him who's in control.

'You'll be put in the laundry room to start, but you can choose to study instead,' Joona says calmly. 'We've got a study group if you're interested. This year three of the guys got their GCSEs, and—'

The first of the two men shoves Salim, and his chair topples over, taking him with it. His bowl hits the floor, sending its contents flying.

Salim tries to get up, but the second man kicks him in the chest and he stumbles back into the chairs behind him.

His right leg flies out and the sole of his shoe slips on the spilled food.

Joona sits where he is, drinking his coffee.

The guys from Malmö appear and force their way into the scrap. They're a head taller than everyone else. They push the men from the Brotherhood away, talking in Albanian with smiles on their lips.

The prison guards rush into the dining room to separate the men.

Salim gets to his feet. He tries to look unconcerned, tries to hide his fear as he rubs his bruised elbow and sits back down again.

Joona hands him a paper napkin.

'Thanks.'

'You got some milk on your shirt.'

Salim wipes the smear and folds the napkin. Joona feels like the attack was feigned, some sort of diversionary manoeuvre.

He glances over at Reiner, trying to read his reaction, and concludes that a second wave is on its way.

The guards are talking to the two attackers, who are swearing blind that Salim Ratjen provoked them.

The situation has already been defused by the time the rapid response team comes rushing in, batons and pepper spray at the ready.

Joona knows that his only chance of getting close to Salim and his organisation before Wednesday is to exploit the fact that Salim was moved from Hall without warning.

There he had presumably built up a network to protect himself and communicate with the outside world.

He probably knew his plot might be discovered, but he wouldn't have thought he'd be transferred.

If he has actually been directing the terrorist group from inside the prison, he is now completely cut off.

As an operational leader, he would have to find a new messenger at once, set up a new network of contacts if he is to be in a position to give the go-ahead for the murder on Wednesday.

If the Security Police are right, Salim Ratjen is in a desperate situation.

Joona looks at Salim, who is sitting with his hand around his cup. A pale film has settled on the dark-brown surface of the coffee.

'I wouldn't drink that,' he says.

'No, you're right,' Salim says.

He quickly thanks God for the food and stands up.

Joona tells Salim to give the study group some serious thought.

They all have ten minutes to get ready before they have to go off to the laundry room and the workshops, or to their studies.

When Joona gets back his cell has been ransacked: the bed has been pulled apart, his clothes are all over the floor, and his letters, books and photographs have been stepped on.

He goes in and hangs the photograph of his daughter Lumi back up, pats her cheek and then gets to work cleaning up the mess.

He picks up the letters he's saved and smooths them out, but stops, Valeria's first letter in his hand, remembering that he received it at Christmas. They had eaten their Christmas dinner, no alcohol of course, and then Santa Claus showed up.

'Ho, ho, ho, are there any naughty children here?' he had asked.

When he sat in his cell that evening and read Valeria's first letter, it felt like the most wonderful Christmas present:

Dear Joona,

You're probably wondering why I'm writing to you after all these years. The answer's simple. I just haven't dared to get in touch before. I've only plucked up the courage now because you're in prison.

We both know that we chose very different paths in life. Maybe it wasn't all that much of a surprise that you joined the police, but I never had any idea that I'd end up going in the opposite direction – you know that. I didn't think I had it in me, but things happen, you pick a path that winds off in front of you, and leads you to a place you never wanted to be.

I'm a different person today, I live a normal life. I'm divorced, with two grown-up sons, and I've been working as a gardener for many years now. But I will never forget what it's like to serve time.

Maybe you're married. Maybe you have lots of kids who come and visit you all the time, but if you're feeling lonely I'd like to come and see you.

I know we were very young when we met, and we really only had that last year in high school, but I've never stopped thinking about you.

Very best wishes,
Valeria

Joona folds the letter and puts it with the others. He picks the bedsheets up from the floor and shakes them. He doesn't dare think about the fact that the Prime Minister's mission could lead to a pardon.

Being locked up and the feeling of impotence that goes with it would quickly become overwhelming if he started to fantasise about freedom. He'd start dreaming of going to Paris to see Lumi, of seeing Valeria, of visiting Disa's grave in Hammarby Cemetery, of going up north to where Summa is buried.

He stifles his longing as he makes the bed, stretching the sheets over the mattress, plumping the pillow and putting it back in place.

29

After studying for three hours, Joona and Marko are let out of the library and start to walk back through the tunnel for lunch.

The security system at Kumla is based on limiting both the range of the inmates' movement and the opportunities for contact between individuals.

The prisoners are responsible for getting themselves from one place to another, section by section, in order to prevent any trouble spreading between the different wings. Violence still flares up, but tends to die down in the same place it started before it can spread.

They reach the T-junction, where Salim and the guys from Malmö are already waiting for the door to be opened. Imre presses the button again.

Salim looks at the old mural from the 1980s: a pale beach with a young woman in a bikini.

'While you were busy washing twenty tons of underwear, I got my high-school diploma,' Marko says with a smile.

Instead of answering, Salim writes 'Fuck you' on the woman's back with a stub of pencil.

After lunch the inmates are allowed an hour's exercise in the yard. That's their only time outside, when they can feel the wind on their faces, watch a butterfly float past in the summer, crunch the ice on a puddle in the winter.

When Joona gets out he sees that Salim is alone. He's standing with his back against the fence.

The yard isn't particularly large. It's framed by buildings on two sides, and fences on the others. Further back is the tall wall, and beyond that the electric fence.

You can't even see the treetops over the top of the wall, just the grey sky.

Two prison guards are watching the inmates.

Most of them are smoking; some of them talk in groups. Joona usually spends his time running, but today he walks with Marko, taking care to stay close to Salim, but not too close.

Joona and Marko pass the battered greenhouse. Reiner is standing by the volleyball net facing one of the security cameras. The rest of the Brotherhood are huddled together talking.

Joona knows that there's a serious risk of trouble, and has already told Marko to get the guards if anything happens.

They pass the thin strip of sunlight reaching over the wall, and their long shadows stretch all the way to Salim Ratjen, who's still standing with his back to the fence.

Marko stops to light a cigarette. Joona keeps walking, and as he passes Salim he takes a step towards him.

'Why would you want to do me a favour?' he asks, looking at Joona with sombre, golden-brown eyes.

'Because then you'll owe me when I get back,' Joona replies matter-of-factly.

'Why should I trust you?'

'You don't have to,' Joona says, and keeps walking.

Rolf from the Brotherhood is walking straight towards them. Reiner is bouncing the ball on the ground, and shouts something to the two men who attacked Ratjen at breakfast.

'I know who you are, Joona Linna,' Salim Ratjen says.

'Good,' Joona replies.

'The court was pretty tough on you.'

'I have to ask you to keep your distance,' Joona says. 'I don't belong to any groups. Not yours, and not anyone else's either.'

'Sorry,' Salim says, but doesn't move.

Joona can see that the two men from the Brotherhood are dragging their feet in the dirt, kicking up a cloud of dust.

Marko glances anxiously to his right and comes closer to Joona.

Reiner passes the volleyball to Rolf, who throws it straight back.

The dust from the path slowly drifts through the sunlight. Reiner holds the ball with both hands as he approaches Salim.

'Reiner's going to make his move any second now,' Joona says.

He turns around and sees that the other two men are approaching from the opposite direction. They're both carrying concealed weapons close to their bodies.

They kick up more dust, joking and jostling each other as they get closer.

Some other members of the Brotherhood have stopped Marko. They're holding him by his shoulders, keeping him out of the way, making out like it's all just for fun.

The Albanian guys from Malmö are smoking with the prison guards.

The dust in the yard grows thicker and the guards start to realise that something's going on.

Joona takes a few steps closer towards Rolf with his hands outstretched, attempting to calm the situation.

'Put the weapon down,' he says.

Rolf is clutching a sharpened screwdriver, a simple weapon which limits the variety of possible attacks. Joona assumes that he's likely to aim straight for his throat, or swing in from the right, beneath Joona's left arm.

Reiner is still holding the ball in one hand as he approaches Salim from behind. He's trying to hide a knife in his other hand.

Joona backs away, drawing Rolf after him.

Marko pulls free and manages to call the guards before he gets punched hard in the stomach.

Salim hears the cry and turns around. The ball hits him in the face and makes him take a step back, but he still manages to grab hold of the arm clutching the knife as Reiner lunges at him. He holds the blade away from him, but stumbles and falls backwards against the fence.

It's a much more aggressive and dangerous attack than Joona was expecting.

Rolf mutters something and jabs with the screwdriver. Joona twists his body away, reaches past the arm with the weapon and grabs Rolf's sleeve from behind. With full force he drives his left elbow up under the man's shoulder. The blow is so hard that Rolf's arm breaks. The end of the bone juts uselessly from his shoulder socket.

Rolf groans as he stumbles forward from the force of Joona's blow. The screwdriver falls to the ground and his arm swings loose, held together by muscles and ligaments.

One of the men on the path runs over, clutching a homemade baton made of heavy nuts screwed to a large bolt.

Joona tries to parry the blow but he's too late. The baton hits him in the back, and pain flares between his shoulder-blades. He falls forward onto his knees but manages to get to his feet again, coughing hard. He sees the next blow coming, jerks his head out of the way and feels the baton whistle past his head.

Joona grabs the arm clutching the weapon. He uses the momentum to pull the man towards him, flips him over his hip and sends him crashing to the ground. Joona lands heavily on top of him with one knee on the man's chest.

Rolf is still staggering around, clutching his shoulder and bellowing in agony.

Salim is on the ground, but uses his bleeding hand to push himself to his feet.

Marko comes running over, panting for breath. He stops in front of Joona and wipes the blood from his mouth.

'I'll say it was me,' he says.

'You don't have to do that,' Joona replies quickly.

'It's OK,' Marko gasps. 'You've got to get out, to see Valeria.'

The dust is settling as Joona walks up to Salim Ratjen.

Reiner drops the knife on the ground and backs away.

The guys from Malmö are approaching from the other direction. The guards are talking anxiously into their radios.

Joona leads Salim straight past the Malmö guys. They make way to let them through, then close ranks again.

Marko goes over to the man Joona sent flying, shoves him

in the back again, and hits him in the face just as the guards start hitting him with their telescopic batons.

Marko falls to the ground and curls up. They keep beating him. He tries to protect his face and neck, but they continue until his body goes limp.

'I'm sorry about this,' Salim says to Joona.

'Tell that to Marko.'

'I will.'

Salim's arm and hand are bleeding, but he doesn't bother to look at his injuries.

'Reiner is unpredictable,' Joona says. 'I don't know what he wants with you, but it would be best to stay out of his way.'

They watch as more guards come into the yard carrying stretchers.

'What are you planning to do outside?' Salim asks.

'I'm going to apply for a job.'

'Where?'

'The National Crime Unit,' Joona replies.

Salim laughs, then grows serious as he eyes Reiner, who is standing over by the volleyball net.

'You seem to think you'll still be going,' Salim suddenly says.

'Marko's taking the blame.'

'Can I ask you to do me a favour?'

'If I have time.'

Salim rubs his nose, then takes a step closer to Joona.

'I really need to get a message to my wife,' he says quietly.

'What message?'

'She needs to call a number and ask for Amira.'

'That's all?'

'She's changed her number, so you'll have to go to her flat. She lives outside Stockholm, in Bandhagen: 10 Gnestavägen.'

'And why would she open the door for me?'

'Tell her you've got a message from *da gawand halak*, that's me. It means the neighbour's boy,' he replies with a brief smile. 'Parisa's very shy, but if you say you've got a message from *da gawand halak*, she'll let you in. Once you're in she'll offer you tea. Accept the offer . . . but wait until she's taken out the olives and bread before passing on the message.'

30

David Jordan kicks his shoes off. He's on the phone with the director of programming for news and social affairs at TV4.

The director is explaining that he's putting together a long item about the Foreign Minister for the ten p.m. news.

DJ heads into the house and walks to the dining room. Light reflecting off the choppy sea floods in through the windows.

'Did you know that Rex Müller and the Foreign Minister were old friends?' DJ asks.

'Really?'

'And I think . . . well, I know that Rex would be happy to contribute if you wanted a personal angle,' he says, his eyes wandering over the rocks down towards the jetty.

'That would be great.'

'I'll tell him to give you a call.'

'Yes, as soon as possible, please,' the director says.

Waves are breaking over the jetty. The boat is straining at its ropes, its fenders bouncing against the water.

When they hang up DJ sends Rex a text telling him that the director of programming took the bait, but that he should wait forty minutes before calling so as not to appear too eager.

DJ has already composed a number of posts for Rex to use on social media. He's fairly confident that those posts, combined with the television interview, will be enough to prevent a scandal.

If people do find out that Rex pissed into the Foreign Minister's swimming pool, they'll interpret his action as a final prank between old friends. Rex will say that he's sure the Foreign Minister must have burst out laughing when he looked at the security-camera footage before his morning swim.

DJ stays by the window. Thoughts are running through his mind. He's taken care of Rex's problem, and now it's time to get to grips with his own. A lot of things have happened in his life recently that he can't talk to anyone about.

Rex would listen, of course, but DJ's job is to help Rex, not burden him with his own worries.

DJ goes into the kitchen and stops in front of the black leather folder on the marble counter, thinking that he should at least look at its contents before making a decision.

The waves below are lit up like molten glass.

David Jordan reaches out and tries to open the catch of the folder with his right hand, but can't do it. It's too stiff. His fingers don't seem to have any strength. An immense tiredness settles over him. His neck can barely manage to hold his head up.

He fumbles weakly in his pockets, finds the little tub of Modiodal, and tips the pills onto the counter. He lets go of the empty container, which rolls onto the floor as he puts one pill on his tongue and swallows.

He can no longer close his mouth, but feels the tablet slip down his throat. Very gently he tries to lie down, and ends up on his side. He closes his eyes, but can still see the light through his eyelids.

He wakes up on the floor half an hour later.

David Jordan has suffered from narcolepsy and cataplexy for seven years. Whenever he gets upset or scared, he loses control of certain muscles and falls asleep.

According to his doctor, the disorder – which is inherited – was probably triggered by strep throat, even if he prefers to say that it's because he was part of some secret experiment when he was in the military.

He sits up. His mouth feels completely dry. He leans on the floor with both hands, gets to his feet, head throbbing, and gazes out at the sea.

He tries to gather his thoughts before looking at the leather folder again.

His hands are shaking as he opens it and pulls out the contents.

He leafs through the information about Carl-Erik Ritter. His heart is beating so hard that his ears roar as he stares at the photograph.

He tries to find some sort of inner calm, and concentrates on reading.

After a while he has to put the documents down, go over to the cupboard and pour himself a glass of Macallan.

DJ drinks it, then refills the glass.

He's thinking about his mother, and closes his eyes tightly to hold back the tears.

He isn't a good son. He works too hard and doesn't visit her nearly enough.

She's ill, he knows that, but he still has difficulty accepting her dark moods.

He feels ashamed that his visits always make him feel so awful.

Most of the time she doesn't say a word to him, doesn't even look at him, just lies there in bed staring out of the window.

Throughout David Jordan's childhood his mother received treatment for depression, delusions and self-destructive behaviour. A year ago he had her moved to an exclusive clinic that specialises in long-term psychiatric care.

There her depression is being treated as a side-effect of chronic PTSD. Her medication and therapy have been drastically adjusted.

The last time he visited she was no longer lying passively in bed. She took the flowers he had brought and put them in a vase with shaking hands. The illness and various medications have made his mother look very old.

They sat at a small table in her room drinking tea from cups with deep saucers, and eating ginger biscuits.

She kept repeating that she should have cooked him a proper meal, and each time he replied that he'd already eaten.

A film of raindrops covered the little window.

Her eyes were timid and embarrassed, and her hand fluttered

anxiously over the buttons of her cardigan when he asked how she was, if the new medication was better.

'I know I haven't been a good mother,' she said.

'Yes, you have.'

He knew it was because of the altered medication, but this was the first time in many years that his mother had spoken directly to him.

She looked at him and explained in an almost scripted way that her suicide attempts when he was young were a reaction to trauma.

'Have you started to talk to your therapist about the accident?' he asked.

'Accident?' she repeated with a smile.

'Mum, you know you're not well, and sometimes you weren't able to take care of me, so I went to live with Grandma.'

Slowly she put her cup down on the saucer, then told him about the horrific rape.

She described the whole sequence of events in a subdued voice.

The fragments of memory were sometimes chillingly precise, and sometimes she sounded almost delusional.

But suddenly everything made sense to David Jordan.

His mother never let him see her naked when he was little, but he still managed to catch glimpses of the scars on her thighs and her damaged breasts.

'I never reported it,' she whispered.

'But . . .'

He remembers how she sat there with her thin hand over her mouth, sobbing, then whispered the name Carl-Erik Ritter.

His cheeks flushed. He tried to say something, but suffered his worst ever attack of narcolepsy.

DJ woke up on the floor to find his mother patting his cheek. He almost couldn't believe it.

He had spent his entire adult life being disappointed in his mother for not fighting harder against her depression.

A car crash can be a terrible thing, but she had survived, after all. She got out OK.

Now he could see how fragile she was. Her aged body was

still frightened, still flinched instinctively, always expecting violence and pain.

Some times were better than others, and sometimes they lived almost normally, but then she would fall into a deep hole, and it had been impossible for her to take care of him.

He feels so incredibly sorry for his mother.

Even though he knows there's no point, he has tracked down Carl-Erik Ritter in order to be able to look into his eyes. Maybe that's enough. Maybe DJ doesn't even need to ask Ritter if he ever thinks about what he did, if he has any idea of the suffering he caused.

While Carl-Erik Ritter's life went on, the rape condemned his mother to a life of recurrent depression and multiple suicide attempts.

Ritter might deny everything. The event is buried deep in the past, and the statute of limitations on the crime has long since passed. But DJ can still tell him that he knows what happened.

Since Ritter has nothing to fear legally he may even be prepared to talk.

He turns over the picture and looks at the face again.

David Jordan knows that the meeting probably won't grant him any relief, but he can't stop thinking about it. He needs to face his mother's attacker.

31

It's almost eleven o'clock at night, and a cold wind is blowing around the flat buildings near Axelsberg metro station. David Jordan crosses the square, heading for a neighbourhood bar, El Bocado, where Carl-Erik Ritter goes most evenings.

DJ tries to breathe calmly. He knows that emotional turbulence can trigger a narcoleptic attack, but the pills he took back at home ought to keep him awake for several more hours.

On the other side of the square a drunk man is shouting at his dog.

The urban landscape is dominated by hulking tower blocks and a red-brick shopping centre.

He glances at the newsstand, the hair salon and the dry-cleaner's next to the bar.

Black mesh is visible behind the newsstand's window, along with a faded poster advertising a big lottery jackpot.

Two women in their forties finish smoking outside the hair-dresser's and go back inside the bar.

Heavy traffic thunders past on the overpass above the square, and old McDonald's wrappers swirls around an overflowing dustbin.

David Jordan takes a deep breath, opens the door to the bar and walks into the gloom and hubbub. The air smells like fried food and damp clothes. The whitewashed walls above the booths and tables are cluttered with old garden tools and paraffin lamps. An illuminated green emergency exit sign hangs from the low ceiling, and cables running from the dusty stereo are taped to the beams.

Two couples are sitting at a table by the door having a loud argument.

Under a little tiled roof a group of middle-aged customers is lined up along the tatty bar, drinking and talking. A yellowing sign advertises the full menu, as well as a special offer on meals for pensioners.

David Jordan asks for a bottle of Grolsch and pays cash. He takes a first, soothing swig and watches as a man with a ponytail tries to show an older woman something on his phone.

A man wipes beer from his lips and laughs at another man trying on a pair of sunglasses.

DJ turns and looks the other way, and finds himself staring at the man he has come here to see.

He recognises him immediately from the photograph.

Carl-Erik Ritter is sitting at the back of the room with one hand around a beer glass. He's wearing a pair of worn jeans and a knitted sweater with holes at the elbows.

DJ picks up his beer and pushes his way through the crowd, apologising as he goes. He stops at the last table.

'OK if I sit down?' he asks, sliding into a chair across from Carl-Erik Ritter.

The man looks up slowly and peers at him with watery eyes, but doesn't answer. DJ's heart is beating way too fast. A dangerous tiredness sweeps over him and the bottle comes close to slipping from his hand.

DJ closes his eyes for a moment, then puts the bottle down on the table.

'Are you Carl-Erik Ritter?' he asks.

'I was the last time someone tried to borrow money for a drink,' the man replies gruffly.

'I'd like to talk to you.'

'Good luck,' the man says. He drinks some beer and puts the glass down, but doesn't remove his hand.

Carl-Erik has eaten steak: the plate it was served on is next to his glass, bearing traces of mashed potato and half a grilled tomato. An empty shot-glass with a dark residue is standing by the napkin-holder.

DJ takes out a photograph of his mother and puts it down on the table in front of him. It's an old picture. In it she's eighteen years old, wearing a pale tunic-dress, smiling brightly at the camera.

'Do you remember her?' DJ asks when he's sure his voice isn't going to break.

'Listen,' Carl-Erik Ritter says, raising his chin. 'I just want to sit here and drink myself into oblivion in peace. Is that too much to ask?'

Carl-Erik tips the last drops from the shot-glass into his beer.

'Look at the picture,' DJ asks.

'Leave me alone. You hear?' the man says slowly.

'Do you remember what you did?' DJ asks. His voice is getting shrill. 'Admit that you—'

'What the hell are you saying?' Carl-Erik Ritter exclaims, and slams his fist down on the table. 'You can't just show up here and throw accusations at me!'

The barman glances at them over the top of the stereo.

DJ knows he has to calm down. He can't get into a fight, that could rebound on Rex, and they can't afford any bad publicity right now.

Carl-Erik's hand is trembling as he holds the empty shot-glass over his beer again. His fingernails are filthy, and he's missed a patch on the side of one cheek when he was shaving.

'I'm not here to cause trouble,' DJ says quietly, moving his bottle aside. 'I'd just like to ask—'

'Leave me the hell alone, I said!'

A man at the next table looks at them as he unwraps two sugar cubes and puts them in his mouth.

'I just want to know if it's ever occurred to you that you ruined her life,' DJ says, doing his best to fight back tears.

Carl-Erik leans back. The neck of his shirt is dirty, his face is wrinkled and ruddy, and his eyes are little more than slits.

'You've got no damn right to come in here and throw accusations at me,' he repeats in a rasping voice.

'OK. I know who you are. I've seen you, and you got what you deserved,' DJ says, and stands up.

'What the hell are you talking about?' Carl-Erik slurs.

David Jordan turns his back on him and pushes his way towards the door. He hears the man calling gruffly to him to come back.

DJ's whole body is shaking by the time he emerges into the square again. It's dark, and the air is cool on his face.

There are a few people standing outside the ICA supermarket on the other side of the square.

DJ starts to cough, and stops outside the hairdresser's, resting his forehead against the glass. He tries to breathe calmly. He knows he should go home, but he can't help thinking that he'd just like to lie down for a while.

'Come back here!' Carl-Erik Ritter shouts as he comes stumbling out after him.

Without bothering to reply DJ starts walking again, but stops outside the dry-cleaner's and reaches out for the wall with one hand. He stares at a mannequin wearing a white dress in the window. He hears footsteps behind him.

'I want you to apologise,' Carl-Erik Ritter shouts.

David Jordan suddenly loses all strength. He leans his forehead against the cool window and struggles to stay on his feet. Sweat is dripping down his back, and his neck feels too weak to bear the weight of his head.

A bus passes on the overpass.

Carl-Erik is drunk, and staggers as he grabs the lapels of David's coat and pulls him towards him.

'Don't do that,' DJ says, trying to pry his fingers off.

'Kiss my hand and apologise,' Ritter snarls.

DJ tries to bring the argument to an end, but a train thunders past, drowning him out, so he has to repeat himself.

'I'm sick. I need to go home and . . .'

Carl-Erik grabs him by the head and tries to force it down to kiss his hand. They stumble backwards together, and DJ can smell the sweat of the other man's body.

'I want a fucking apology!' he yells, yanking at DJ's hair.

David pushes him off and tries to walk away, but Carl-Erik grabs his coat again and hits him from behind.

'That's enough!' DJ shouts as he spins around and pushes the man in the chest.

Carl-Erik takes two steps backwards, loses his balance and crashes into the shop window. The glass breaks behind him and he tumbles into the dry-cleaner's.

Large shards crash out into the square, shattering on the pavement.

David Jordan hurries over and tries to help him to his feet. Carl-Erik lurches forward and clutches at the glass with one hand. One side gives out beneath him and he falls to his knees. His neck slides across a protruding piece of glass.

Blood sprays up onto the mannequin's white dress and the yellowing poster advertising a special offer on shirts.

His jugular vein has been severed.

Carl-Erik pushes himself up with a groan and falls back onto his hip. The glass breaks beneath him. Dark blood is pulsing out from the wound in his neck, pouring down his body. He's bellowing and coughing and tossing his head around, trying to get away from the pain and panic.

David Jordan tries to stem the flow of blood, and shouts across the square for someone to call an ambulance.

Carl-Erik collapses onto his back and tries to push David's hands away.

Blood spreads out across the pavement in front of the building.

Ritter's body shakes as he throws his head back and forth.

He stares at DJ, opens his mouth and a quivering bubble of blood appears between his lips.

His legs twitch as the pool of blood spreads out beneath him and seeps towards a rusty manhole cover.

32

Rex is listening to Wilhelm Stenhammar's three fantasies for piano as he empties the dishwasher. Earlier that evening he was at TV4, recording a conversation about his friendship with the Foreign Minister.

He has never felt like such a fraud in his life, but after the piece aired he received a torrent of positive responses on social media.

Sammy is at a concert at Debaser, but has promised to be home by two o'clock at the latest. Rex is afraid to go to bed before his son is back. Wearily he fills a pot to boil water for tea and tries to suppress his anxiety. His phone rings. He sees that it's DJ and answers at once.

'What did you think of the interview?' Rex asks. 'I felt like—'

'Is Sammy home?' DJ interrupts.

'No, he's—'

'Can I come up?'

'Are you nearby?'

'I'm sitting in the car outside.'

Only now does Rex notice the odd tone in his friend's voice, and starts to worry that he's brought bad news.

'What happened?'

'Can I come up for a little bit?'

'Of course,' Rex says.

He goes downstairs and unlocks the front door, then opens it as soon as he hears the lift stop on the landing outside.

Rex gasps and takes a step back when he sees DJ standing in the bright light.

David Jordan's arms, chest, face and beard are covered in blood.

'Christ!' Rex exclaims. 'What happened?'

DJ comes in and closes the door behind him. His eyes are glassy and blank.

'It's not my blood,' he says tersely. 'It was an accident . . . I'll tell you, I just need . . .'

'You scared the shit out of me.'

'Sorry, I shouldn't have come . . . I think I'm probably in shock.'

DJ leans against the door as he takes his shoes off, leaving a bloody handprint on the wood.

'What on earth happened?'

'I don't know how it ended up . . . or rather, it's complicated, but I ended up getting into an argument with a drunk. He came outside after me, then fell and cut himself.'

He looks up at Rex sheepishly.

'I think he was hurt badly.'

'How badly?'

DJ closes his eyes and Rex sees that he even has blood on his eyelids and lashes.

'Sorry to drag you into this,' DJ whispers. 'I'm supposed to keep you out of anything like . . . Shit . . .'

'Just tell me what happened.'

DJ doesn't answer. He walks past Rex into the guest bathroom and starts to wash his hands. The red water fades to pink as hundreds of droplets hit the white tiles behind the tap.

DJ uses a wad of toilet paper to wipe his face. He flushes it, looks at himself in the mirror, sighs heavily and turns to Rex.

'I panicked. I don't know, it made sense at the time. I just walked away and got in the car when I heard the ambulance.'

'That's not great,' Rex says quietly.

'I just didn't want . . . I didn't want it to affect you,' he tries to explain. 'It can't, not when we're getting new backers, not now that everything's really moving along.'

'I know, but . . .'

'Lyra's at home,' he goes on. 'I didn't know where I could go, so I came here.'

'We'll figure out what to do,' Rex says, rubbing his face.

'I might as well call the police and explain I didn't do anything. It wasn't my fault,' he says, and starts to search for his phone in his pockets.

'Hang on,' Rex says. 'Tell me all about it. Let's go upstairs.'

'Why does everything have to be so complicated? I just went to a bar in Axelsberg and . . .'

'What on earth were you doing out there?'

DJ slumps into one of the chairs at the kitchen table. The pot boiled dry a while ago, and the kitchen smells like hot metal.

'Sometimes I just need to go somewhere where I don't know anyone,' DJ explains.

'I can understand that,' Rex says, putting fresh water in the pot.

'But there was a silly argument and I walked out,' DJ says, sliding his elbows across the table. 'The drunk followed me and wanted to fight, and in the end he fell into a shop window and cut himself.'

DJ sits back again and tries to breathe more slowly. There are streaks of blood on the table from the sleeves of his jacket.

'And now there's blood here,' DJ says. 'We need to wipe it off before Sammy gets home.'

'He'll probably be out half the night.'

'I think there's a lot of blood in the car as well,' DJ whispers.

'I'll go down and take a look while you take a shower,' Rex says.

'No, what if someone sees you? You need to stay out of this. I'll take care of the car tomorrow when Lyra's at art college.'

Rex sits down across from DJ.

'I still don't get it,' he says. 'You were fighting? A proper fight?'

DJ's eyes are shiny and bloodshot.

'Look, he was drunk, staggering around. He kept telling me

to go back in . . . and I was trying to fend him off when he stumbled into the window.'

'How bad was it?'

'He cut his neck. I'm not sure he's going to make it. There was . . .'

'But if the ambulance got there quickly?'

'There was an awful lot of blood,' DJ concludes.

'So what are we going to do?' Rex asks. 'Do we just hope no one saw you?'

'No one in the bar knew me, and the square was pretty dark.'

Rex nods and tries to think clearly.

'You need to take a shower,' he says. 'I'll get you some clothes . . . put everything in the washing machine and get yourself cleaned up, and I'll see if there's anything about it online yet.'

'OK, thanks,' DJ whispers.

Rex gets the bleach out and sprays the table and chair where DJ was sitting. He uses paper towels to wipe it off, then goes downstairs and cleans the bloodstained doorpost, the door-handle of the guest bathroom, the tap, the sink and the tiles behind it. He goes back upstairs, wiping the banister as he goes, then leaves the bleach and paper towels in the middle of the table so he doesn't forget to clean the shower and washing machine once DJ has finished.

He takes out a bottle of Highland Park and a tumbler for DJ, then checks the news on his phone. There's nothing about any fight or accident matching what DJ said.

Maybe it's not as bad as he thought.

If the man had died, the news would be out there by now.

33

The prison warden has granted Joona's application for a thirty-six-hour leave.

Joona reaches the end of the underground tunnel. The prison guard in front of him hesitates for a few seconds, then raises his hand and opens the door. They walk through, wait until the lock clicks, then walk to another door and wait for central command to authorise their progress into the next section.

Just as Joona had predicted, Salim Ratjen concluded that Joona was his only chance to get a message out before Wednesday. Ratjen's message seems to consist of little more than a telephone number and a name, but it could still be coded authorisation for a murder.

After retrieving his belongings, Joona is led to Central Command by another guard.

His suit fitted him perfectly at his trial two years ago, but since then Joona has spent four hours a day exercising and now it's too tight across the shoulders.

The lock whirrs and he opens the door and leaves the huge wall behind him.

A familiar pain behind his left eye flares up as he starts to walk across the asphalt. The electric fence with its coil of barbed wire is the last obstacle before freedom. Tall floodlights rise up ahead of him, their white pylons standing out against the steely grey sky.

He resists the temptation to walk faster, and finds himself thinking back to when he was a child, following his dad through the forest to fish for char.

Whenever he spotted the sparkle of the lake through the trees he became so excited that he wanted to run the last stretch, but he always forced himself to hold back. His dad had explained that you had to approach the water carefully.

The huge gate slides back with a heavy metallic whirr.

The sun emerges from behind a cloud, prompting him to look up. For the first time in two years he can see the horizon. He's looking out across fields and roads and forests.

Joona leaves the prison grounds and reaches the car park. The gate slides shut behind him. It's like breathing fresh air into his lungs, having a drink of water, catching his dad's eye in unspoken agreement.

The memory of those fishing trips comes back again, the way they would walk slowly towards the shore and see that the water was full of fish. The bright surface was broken by little rings, as if it was raining.

The feeling of freedom is overwhelming. Emotions are churning in his chest. He could easily stop and weep, but he keeps walking without looking back. As he walks to the bus-stop, his muscles start to relax.

He feels like he's slowly getting back to his normal self.

In the distance he can see the bus approaching through a cloud of dust. According to Joona's pass, he has to get on and travel to Örebro, and then catch the train to Stockholm from there.

He climbs onto the bus, but knows he won't be catching the train. Instead he's going to meet a handler from the Security Police. The meeting is due to take place in the car park beneath the Vågen shopping centre in forty-five minutes.

He checks his watch, then leans back in his seat with a smile.

He has the plain Omega watch that he inherited from his dad back again. His mum never sold it, even though they could have used the money.

The sun has disappeared and the wind has picked up by the

144

time Joona steps off the bus and makes his way to the shopping centre. Even though he only has five minutes, he stops at a fast-food stand and orders a 'Pepper Cheese Bacon Meal with Future Fries'.

'Drink?' the owner of the restaurant asks as he prepares the food.

'Fanta Exotic,' Joona replies.

He puts the drinks can in his pocket, then stands next to the little red flag advertising ice-cream and eats his hamburger.

Down in the car park, a man dressed in jeans and a down jacket is standing beside a black BMW, staring at his phone.

'You should have been here twenty minutes ago,' he says sullenly when Joona appears and shakes his hand.

'I wanted to get you a drink,' Joona replies, and hands him the can.

Taken aback, the handler thanks him and takes it before opening the car door for Joona.

On the back seat are a basic mobile phone, a debit card and three bulky envelopes from Saga Bauer containing the forensics report from the Foreign Minister's murder. Everything Joona has requested is in the envelopes: the preliminary investigation report, the initial findings from the post-mortem, the lab results and printouts of all the witness interviews.

They drive past the railway station and out onto the highway towards Stockholm.

Joona reads up on Salim Ratjen's background, how he escaped from Afghanistan and sought asylum in Sweden, then got dragged into the drug trade. Apart from his wife, his only other family member in the country is his brother, Absalon Ratjen. The Security Police have conducted a thorough investigation, and are confident that the brothers haven't been in contact in eight years. According to correspondence they have uncovered, Absalon severed all ties with Salim when Salim asked him to hide a large block of hash for a dealer.

Joona has just picked up the folder of photographs from the Foreign Minister's home when his phone rings.

'Were you able to establish contact with Ratjen?' Saga Bauer asks.

'Yes. He's given me a task, but it's impossible to know where that might lead,' Joona says. 'He asked me to see his wife and tell her to make a phone call and ask for Amira.'

'OK. Good work. Really good work,' Saga says.

'It'll be a big operation tonight, won't it?' Joona asks, looking down at the glossy photographs: blood, splattered kitchen cabinets, an overturned potted plant, the Foreign Minister's body from various angles, his blood-soaked torso, hands, and crooked, yellowish toes.

'Do you really think you can pull this off?' she asks seriously.

'Pull it off? This is what I do,' he replies.

He hears her laugh to herself.

'You're aware that you've been away for two years, and that this killer is particularly efficient?'

'Yes.'

'Have you read the forensic timeline?'

'He knows what he's doing, but there's something else, I can feel it. There's something disturbed about it.'

'What do you mean?'

34

Just before they reach Norrtull the handler is given a new destination. He pulls into the car park in front of the Stallmästaregården restaurant and stops.

'The team leading the operation are waiting for you in the pavilion,' he says.

Joona gets out of the car and sets off towards the yellow summerhouse that looks out onto the waters of Brunnsviken. Not long ago, this area was incredibly beautiful, but these days the restaurant is ensnared in a tangle of highways, bridges and viaducts.

When he opens the thin wooden door one of the two men at the table stands up. He has strawberry-blond hair and almost white eyebrows.

'My name is Janus Mickelsen. I'm in charge of the Rapid Response Unit of the Security Police,' he says as they shake hands.

Janus has an oddly jerky way of moving.

Beside him sits a young man with a lopsided smile. He's looking up at Joona with an earnest expression.

'Gustav will be in the first group, leading the National Response Unit's ground operation in the field,' Janus says.

Joona shakes Gustav's hand, and holds it a moment too long as he looks into the man's eyes.

'I see you've grown out of your Batman costume,' Joona says with a smile.

'You remember me?' the young man asks sceptically.

'You two know each other?' Janus asks, and smiles, revealing a network of laughter lines around his eyes.

'I used to work with Gustav's aunt at National Crime,' Joona explains.

Joona thinks back to the party at Anja's summer cottage on the shores of Lake Mälaren. Gustav was only seven years old. He was dressed in a Batman costume, and spent the entire time racing around on the grass. They sat on blankets eating cold-smoked salmon and potato salad and drinking beer. Later, Gustav sat with Joona and kept asking what it was like to be a policeman.

Joona removed the magazine from his pistol and let the boy hold it. Afterwards Anja tried to persuade Gustav that it wasn't a real pistol but a practice one.

'Anja's always been like a second mother to me,' Gustav smiles. 'She thinks being in the police is too dangerous.'

'Things could get very dangerous tonight,' Joona nods.

'And no one will thank you if you get yourself killed,' Janus says with an unexpectedly bitter tone in his voice.

Joona recalls that Janus Mickelsen had been some sort of whistle-blower many years ago. It was a big deal at the time, at least for a few weeks. He had made his career in the military, and was part of a pan-European operation against piracy in the shipping lanes off the coast of Somalia. When his superiors refused to listen to him, he spoke to the media about how the semiautomatic rifles they had been issued became overheated very quickly. Janus claimed the weapons were so inaccurate that they were a security risk. The semiautomatics stayed, and Janus lost his job.

'We'll start the operation at Salim Ratjen's wife's home. We begin at seven o'clock this evening,' Janus explains as he unfolds a map.

He points at a building in a patch of woodland where the Response Unit will lie in wait, just opposite Parisa's house.

'Have you managed to find out anything about who this Amira

is, and where the phone with that number might be?' Joona asks.

'We don't have any matches on the name. The phone with that number is somewhere in the Malmö area, but we don't have any way of tracing it at the moment.'

'For the time being we're concentrating on the operation ahead of us,' Gustav says. 'Ratjen's wife works as a nurse at a dental clinic in Bandhagen. She finishes work at six, and will be home around six forty-five if she stops to go grocery shopping at the supermarket like she usually does.'

'Ratjen has planned the second attack for Wednesday,' Janus says. 'This is our chance to stop it.'

'But you still don't know what his wife's role is?' Joona says.

'We're working on that,' Janus replies, wiping the sweat from his freckled forehead.

'Maybe she's just a middle-man.'

'We don't really know anything,' Gustav says. 'This is a gamble, sure, but at the same time . . . We don't need much to fit these pieces together, one tiny detail could do it. If you can find out anything about how the plan works, who the target of Wednesday's attack is going to be, or where it's going to take place, then we might be able to stop this whole thing right now.'

'I want to talk to the witness before the operation,' Joona says.

'Why?'

'I want to know what the killer did between the first shot and the one that killed him.'

'He said that stuff about Ratjen and hell. It's in the report, I must have read it a hundred times,' Janus says.

'But that doesn't account for the remaining time,' Joona persists.

'He picked up the spent shells.'

The internal forensic analysis isn't complete, but Joona has studied the splatter patterns, the blood on the floor and the convergence points, and he's sure that the post-mortem is going to show that more than fifteen minutes elapsed between the first two shots to the victim's torso, and the fatal shot to his eye.

For now, the forensics experts estimate that the sequence of events took no longer than five minutes in total.

Picking up the shells, moving around and uttering those few sentences could account for those five minutes.

If Joona's right, though, there are still more than ten minutes that can't be explained.

What happened during that time?

The killer is a highly skilled professional. There has to be a reason why he didn't carry out the execution as quickly as possible.

Joona has no idea what that reason might be, but he has a feeling that there's a vital piece missing from the picture, something much darker than what they've seen so far.

'I'd still like to see her, if possible,' he says.

'We'll arrange it,' Janus nods, and tears open the seal on a large padded envelope. 'There's time, since the operation won't be starting until seven o'clock. We're meeting for a final briefing at five.'

He hands Joona a well-worn service pistol with an extra magazine, two boxes of ammunition, 9x19 parabellum bullets, and a set of Volvo keys.

Joona draws the pistol from its holster and looks at it. It's a matte black Sig Sauer P226 Tactical.

'Good enough?' Janus says, and smiles as if he's just said something very funny.

'You don't have any other shoulder holsters?' Joona asks.

'This one's standard issue,' Gustav replies, slightly bemused.

'I know. It doesn't really matter, it just moves around a little too much,' Joona says.

35

Joona follows his handler's black BMW down into the depths of the garage beneath Katarinaberget and parks in front of a rough concrete wall.

They're far below the shelter's immense, sliding doors.

He's heard rumours that the Security Police had a secret prison, but didn't know it was here.

His handler is waiting for him. He runs his ID through a card-reader and taps in a long code.

Joona follows the man into the airlock. Once the door to the garage has locked behind them, the man runs his card through another reader and taps in another code. They are let into the security control room. Joona slides his ID through a hatch and the guard behind the reinforced glass checks it.

Joona signs himself in and his irises and fingerprints are scanned.

He puts his jacket, pistol and shoes on a conveyor-belt, walks through the body-scanner and is allowed past the next airlock, where he introduces himself to a female agent whose dark-brown hair is in a thick plait over one shoulder.

'I know who you are,' she says, blushing slightly.

She returns his pistol, watches as he puts the holster back on, then hands him his jacket.

'Thanks.'

'You're a lot younger than I expected,' she adds, and her blush spreads to her neck.

'So are you,' he smiles, and puts his shoes back on.

They start walking, and the agent explains that they've moved Sofia Stefansson from the old ice-store to an isolation room in the machine house.

Joona has read and compared all the interviews that have been conducted with Sofia.

Her testimony is fairly consistent.

The few discrepancies can be ascribed to her fear: she wanted to be helpful and said what she thought her interrogator wanted to hear.

Saga's interview with Sofia is the most useful: it's fairly exceptional given the circumstances. She managed to help the witness remember the short conversation in which Ratjen's name was mentioned by highlighting specific details.

Without that interview, they wouldn't even have a case.

But if Joona is right about the timing, the witness has been keeping quiet about a large chunk of what happened.

The killer fired two shots, then moved quickly and purposefully, running over to grab the Foreign Minister by the hair, force him down on his knees, and then press the pistol to one of his eyes.

The killer treated his victim like an enemy, Joona thinks.

If you ignore the missing minutes, the attack looks more like something that happened in the heat of battle than an execution.

Sofia slipped and hit the back of her head on the floor, then lay there listening to the brief conversation about Ratjen before the Foreign Minister was killed by a shot to the eye.

'I'm thinking,' Joona explains, without the agent having asked.

'You don't have to explain,' she says, stopping in front of a metal door.

The agent knocks on the metal door, tells Sofia she has a visitor, and lets Joona in, locking the door behind him.

Sofia is sitting on a dove-blue sofa in front of a television, watching an episode of the BBC's adaptation of *Sherlock Holmes*. The television is connected only to a DVD-player. There are piles of discs in front of her, alongside a large plastic bottle of Coke.

Her face is pale and she's not wearing any make-up. She looks like a child with her fragile body and light-brown hair pulled up into a ponytail. She has on grey tracksuit bottoms and a white T-shirt with a sparkly kitten on the front. One of her hands is bandaged, and she has grey bruises around her wrists.

Joona can see that, although she hasn't accepted her new life yet and she's terrified that they're going to start torturing her again, she has started to understand that they aren't going to kill her, but they aren't going to let her go any time soon either.

'My name is Joona Linna,' he says. 'I used to be a detective . . . I've read all the interviews with you. Everything tells me that you're entirely innocent, and I understand why you're frightened given the way you've been treated here.'

'Yes,' she whispers, switching the television off.

He waits a moment before sitting down beside her. He is aware that sudden movements or sharp noises can trigger post-traumatic stress which would make her clam up. He saw her tremble when the agent locked the door: perhaps the metallic sound reminded her of the noise of a spent bullet.

'I don't have the authority to get you released,' he explains frankly. 'But I'd still like you to help me. I need you to make more of an effort than ever to remember the things I ask you about.'

He can feel her trying to read him, her survival instinct attempting to break through the shock.

Very slowly he pulls out the two composite sketches that have been produced using her description.

In one of them the balaclava covers the murderer's head so that only his eyes and mouth are visible.

In the other they've attempted to imagine his face without the mask – but the lack of detail makes it look like the face is still covered.

There's nothing particularly distinctive about the killer's features. His eyes are maybe strangely calm, his nose more prominent than usual. His mouth is almost white, and his jaw is fairly broad, but he has an unremarkable chin.

He has no beard or moustache in the sketch, but from the colour of his eyebrows they have chosen to give him mousy-blond hair, in a nondescript cut.

'They tried a longer nose and I said "I don't know",' she explains. 'They made it shorter and I said "Maybe, I don't know", they made it thinner and I said "I don't know", they made it wider and I said "Maybe" . . . In the end they got annoyed and decided it was good enough.'

'It looks good,' Joona said.

'Maybe I just feel unsure about everything because they kept questioning my memory the whole time. He was black for a while, but I hadn't said anything like that. Maybe they were trying to get me to remember other things, like the colour of his eyes and eyebrows.'

'They understand how people remember faces,' Joona nods.

'He had long hair for a while, with straggly bits around his cheeks,' she says with a frown. 'It suddenly popped into my head that I'd seen that, but I knew he'd kept the balaclava on the whole time, so it couldn't be true, I couldn't have seen his hair.'

'What do you think you saw?' he asks gently.

'What?'

'If it wasn't hair?'

'I don't know. I mean, I was lying on the floor at the time . . . but there was something hanging down his cheeks, like strips of fabric.'

'You don't think it could still have been hair?'

'No, it was thicker, more like leather, maybe.'

'How long were the strips?'

'This long,' she says, putting one hand to her shoulder.

'Can you draw them on this picture?'

She takes the sketch of the masked face and she adds what she saw hanging down beside his face with a trembling hand.

At first it looks like big feathers or quills, but then it starts to resemble matted hair. The point of her pen makes holes in the paper.

'Oh, I don't know,' she says, pushing the picture away.

'Did the Foreign Minister say anything about a man with two faces?'

'What?'

'It could have been a metaphor,' Joona says, looking at the picture.

'Doesn't everyone have two faces, then?'

36

Sofia sits still with her eyes downcast, eyelashes quivering. Joona is struck by the fact that she seems to remember everything as if she's watching herself from outside of her body.

'Do you think the killer was a terrorist?' he asks after a pause.

'Why are you asking me? I don't know.'

'What do you think?'

'It felt personal . . . but maybe it is to terrorists.'

First she witnesses the two shots from a distance, then the killer starts to move. She tries to escape and slips on the blood.

'You fall, and end up lying on the floor,' Joona says, showing her a photograph of the bloodstained kitchen that was taken from her perspective.

'Yes,' she says quietly and looks away.

'The Foreign Minister is on his knees, bleeding from the two shots to his torso. The killer is holding him by his hair, and presses the barrel of the pistol to his eye.'

'His right eye,' she whispers, her face impassive.

'You mentioned the conversation between them – but what happened after that?'

'I don't know. Nothing. He shot him.'

'But that didn't happen right away, did it?'

'Didn't it?' she asks meekly.

'No,' Joona replies, and sees the little hairs on her arms stand up.

'I hit my head on the floor. Everything seemed to be happening very slowly,' she says, getting up from the sofa.

'What happened?'

'It was like time stopped, and just . . . No, I don't know.'

'What were you going to say?'

'Nothing,' she replies.

'Nothing? We're talking about a ten-minute span,' he says.

'Ten minutes.'

'What happened?' Joona persists.

'I don't know,' she says, scratching one arm.

'Did he film the Foreign Minister?'

'No, he didn't – what are you talking about?' Sofia groans, then walks over to the door and knocks on it.

'Did he communicate with anyone?'

'I can't do any more of this,' she whispers.

'Yes, you can, Sofia.'

She turns back towards him, and her face is distraught, desperate.

'Can I?' she asks.

'Did he communicate with anyone?'

'No.'

'Did it look like he was praying?' Joona asks.

'No,' she says, wiping tears from her cheeks.

'Could he have forced the Foreign Minister to say something?'

'They were both silent,' she replies.

'The whole time?'

'Yes.'

'You lay there looking at them, Sofia. Did the killer really not do anything?' Joona asks. 'I mean, did he seem frightened, was he trembling?'

'He seemed calm,' she replies, wiping her eyes again.

'Could he have been fighting an internal battle . . . Maybe he wasn't sure if he should kill him or not?'

'He didn't hesitate, it wasn't that . . . I think he just liked standing there. The minister was breathing really fast the whole time. He was on the verge of losing consciousness, but

157

the murderer never let go of his hair. He just kept looking at him.'

'What made him shoot?'

'I don't know . . . after a while he just let go of his hair but kept the pistol pressed against his eye . . . then suddenly there was a bang, but not from the pistol, that just made a rattling sound . . . The noise came from the back of his head, I think? When his skull exploded?'

'Sofia,' Joona says gently. 'I'm going to take my pistol out in a moment. It isn't loaded. It isn't dangerous at all, but we need to look at it to figure out the last details.'

'OK,' she says, her lips turning white.

'Don't be scared.'

Slowly he loosens his Sig Sauer from its holster, takes it out and puts it down on the table.

He notices that she has trouble even looking at the pistol, the veins in her neck are throbbing.

'I know it's hard,' Joona says quietly. 'But I'd like us to talk about how he was holding the gun. I know you can remember because you said the killer was holding the pistol with both hands.'

'Yes.'

'Which hand did he use for support?'

'How do you mean?'

'One hand holds the pistol, finger on the trigger, and the other hand is used to support it,' he explains.

'He used . . . his left hand for support,' she replies, and tries to smile at him before lowering her gaze again.

'So he was aiming with his right eye?'

'Yes.'

'And he had his left eye closed?'

'He was looking with both.'

'I see,' Joona says, thinking about how unusual the technique is.

Joona also fires with both eyes open. It gives him better peripheral vision in delicate situations, but you have to practise diligently to be able to do it correctly.

He continues asking questions about the way the killer moved.

He runs her through the way the killer's shoulders were angled when he shot from a distance, how he moved the pistol to his other hand so he wouldn't lose his line of fire when he picked the shells up from the floor.

She tells him again how slow everything seemed, the shot to the eye, how the body fell backwards at an angle, with one leg stretched out and the other bent underneath, then how the killer stood over the body and shot him in the other eye.

Leaving his pistol on the table, Joona stands up and gets two glasses from the little kitchen area. He's thinking about how the Foreign Minister's killer didn't have to switch magazines.

But if I was in his shoes I would have done that right after the fourth shot, so I had a full magazine in the pistol when I left, he thinks to himself as he pours the Coke.

They drink, then both put their glasses down carefully on the table. Joona picks up the pistol and waits while Sofia wipes her mouth with the back of her hand.

'After that last shot . . . did he replace the magazine in the pistol?'

'I don't know,' she says tiredly.

'You have to loosen the catch and slide the magazine into your hand, like this,' Joona says, demonstrating. 'And then you insert a fresh one.'

The sound makes her shake. She swallows and nods.

'Yes, that's what he did,' she says.

37

Joona is driving slowly down the bumpy gravel track to Valeria's nursery, thinking about Sofia's description of the killer: he shoots with both eyes open, takes his bullets and shells away with him, and inserts a full magazine in his pistol before he leaves the house.

In order to fire a single-action firearm, the hammer has to be cocked manually to feed the bullet into the chamber.

There are a number of different ways of doing that. Swedish police officers place their left hand over the hammer, aim at the floor and pull back, upwards.

But the killer put his thumb and forefinger over the pistol, and instead of pulling back he thrust the pistol forward in order to be able to fire immediately. That isn't a technique that comes naturally, but once you've learned it, it can save you valuable seconds.

Joona remembers once examining some old footage from Interpol, a security camera recording of the murder of Fathi Shaqaqi outside the Diplomat Hotel in Malta.

The attack was carried out by two Mossad agents from a spearhead unit known as Kidon.

The grainy black and white footage shows a man with his face concealed feeding bullets into the chamber in precisely that way. He shoots the victim three times, then gets on a motorcycle driven by another man and rides away.

Everything Sofia described reinforces the idea that the killer received first-class military training.

Throughout the course of the attack the pistol never wavered from head-height, and its barrel was always aimed in front of him.

Joona can see the man in his mind's eye, how he fires, runs and changes magazine, all without losing his line of fire.

He is reminded of the Polish special forces unit, GROM, or the US Navy Seals. Yet the killer still chose to remain at the scene far longer than necessary.

He isn't frightened or anxious, he just lets time pass as he observes his victim's death-throes.

Joona looks at his watch. In three hours he will be conveying Salim Ratjen's message to his wife.

He parks outside Valeria's little cottage with its leafy garden and picks up one of the two bouquets from the passenger seat. The branches of large weeping willows touch the ground. The late summer air is warm and humid. There's no answer when he knocks at the door, but the lights are on, so he goes around the back to look for Valeria.

He finds her in one of the greenhouses. The glass is misted with condensation, but Joona can see her clearly. Her hair is pulled up in a loose knot, and she's wearing a pair of faded jeans, boots, and a tight red fleece jacket with mud-stains on it. She's moving several heavy pots containing orange trees. She turns around and sees him.

Those dark eyes, that curly, unruly hair, that slender body.

It's as if he's gone back in time.

Valeria was in the same class as him in high school, and he couldn't take his eyes off her. She was one of the first people he ever told about his dad's death.

They met at a party, and he walked her to the door. He kissed her with his eyes wide open, and can still remember what he thought: no matter what happened to him in the future, at least he had kissed the most beautiful girl in school.

'Valeria,' he says, opening the door to the greenhouse.

She keeps her mouth closed to stop herself from grinning, but her eyes are smiling. He hands her the bouquet of lily-of-the-valley. She wipes her hands on her jeans before taking it.

'So you got leave to come and apply for an apprenticeship?' she asks, looking him up and down playfully.

'Yes, I . . .'

'Do you think you'd be able to handle normal life when you get out? Working as a gardener can be pretty tough at times.'

'I'm strong,' he replies.

'Yes, I believe that,' she smiles.

'I promise you won't regret it.'

'Good,' she whispers.

They just stand there looking at each other for a while, until Valeria lowers her gaze.

'Sorry I look like this,' she says. 'But I have to load fifteen walnut trees . . . Micke and Jack are picking the trailer up in an hour.'

'You look more beautiful than ever,' Joona says, following her into the greenhouse.

The trees are in big, black plastic pots.

'Is it OK to lift them by their trunks?'

'Better to use this,' she replies, pulling out a yellow trailer.

Joona lifts the first walnut tree onto the trailer and Valeria pulls it backwards through the door and up the path. The bright green foliage trembles as Joona lifts the trees onto the trailer.

'Nice of the boys to help out,' Joona says after he's put the pot down with a heavy thud.

They get more trees and put them on the trailer. The leaves rustle and soil spills onto the grass path.

Valeria clambers up into the trailer and shoves the trees further in so there'll be room for all of them.

She gets down, blows the hair from her face, brushes her hands, and sits down on the towbar of the trailer.

'It's hard to believe they're grown-ups,' she says, looking at Joona. 'I made my mistakes, and the kids grew up without me.'

Valeria's amber eyes darken and turn serious.

'What matters is that they're back now,' Joona says.

'But I can't take that for granted . . . considering what I put them through while I was locked up in Hinseberg. I let them down so badly.'

'They should be proud of the person you've become,' Joona says.

'They'll never be able to forgive me completely. I mean, you lost your dad at a young age, but he was a hero. That must have meant a lot, maybe not at the time, but later.'

'Yes, but you came back. You could explain what had happened, the mistakes.'

'They don't want to talk about it.'

She lowers her gaze and a line appears between her eyebrows.

'At least you're not dead,' he says.

'Even though that's what they told their friends because they were so ashamed.'

'I was ashamed that Mum and I had such a hard time financially . . . That's why you and I never went back to my place.'

Valeria turns her head and looks into Joona's eyes.

'I always thought your mum wanted you to date Finnish girls,' she says.

'No,' Joona laughs. 'She would have loved you. She had a thing for curly hair.'

'So what were you ashamed of?' she asks.

'Mum and I lived in a one-room flat in Tensta. I slept in the kitchen on a mattress that I had to roll up every morning and tuck out of the way in the wardrobe . . . We didn't have a television or a stereo, and the furniture was all old . . .'

'And you had a part-time job in a warehouse – didn't you?'

'A lumber-yard in Bromma . . . we couldn't have paid the rent otherwise.'

'You must have thought I was very spoiled,' Valeria mumbles, looking down at her hands.

'You soon learn that life isn't fair.'

38

Valeria sets off towards the greenhouse again, taking the barrow with her. They keep loading the walnut trees onto the trailer in silence. The past is drifting around them, dragging up old memories.

When Joona was eleven years old his father, Yrjö, a policeman, was shot and killed while on duty during a domestic dispute in an flat in Upplands Väsby. His mum, Ritva, was a housewife, and had no income of her own. The money ran out and she and Joona had to move out of their house in Märsta.

Joona soon learned to say he didn't want to go to the cinema with his friends, and he learned to say he wasn't hungry whenever they went to a café.

He lifts the last tree onto the trailer, tucks one of the branches in, then closes the trailer door carefully.

'You were talking about your mum,' Valeria says.

'She knew that I felt ashamed of our circumstances,' Joona says, brushing his hands. 'That must have been hard for her, because we really weren't that badly off. She worked as much as she could as a cleaner, and we borrowed books from the library. We would read together and talk about what we'd read in the evenings.'

After putting the trailer away in the shed they walk up to her little house. Valeria opens a door that leads directly into the utility room.

'You can wash your hands here,' she says, turning on the tap of a large metal sink.

Standing beside her, he rinses his filthy hands in the warm water. She lathers a bar of soap and starts to wash his hands.

The only sound is the water running into the sloping sink.

The smile fades from her face as they wash each other's hands.

They keep their hands in the warm water, suddenly conscious of their touch. She gently squeezes two of his fingers in one of her hands, and looks up at him.

He's much taller than she is, and even though he leans down to kiss her she has to stand on tiptoe.

They haven't kissed since they were in high school, and afterwards they glance at each other almost shyly. She takes a clean towel from the shelf and dries his hands and arms.

'So, here you are, Joona Linna,' she says tenderly, and strokes his cheek, tracing his cheekbone up towards his ear and messy blond hair.

She pulls off her shirt and washes under her arms without taking off her discoloured bra. Her skin is the same colour as olive oil in a porcelain bowl. She has tattoos on both shoulders, and her upper arms are muscular.

'Stop looking,' she smiles.

'It's hard not to,' he says, but turns away.

Valeria changes into a yellow vest top and black tracksuit bottoms with white stripes.

'Shall we go upstairs?'

Her house is small, and furnished simply. The ceilings, walls and floors are all painted white. Joona hits his head on the lamp when he enters the kitchen.

'Watch your head,' Valeria says, and puts the flowers he brought her in a glass of water.

There are no chairs around the kitchen table, and the counter is covered with three trays of bread rising under tea-towels.

Valeria puts some more wood in the old stove, blows on the embers, then gets out a pan.

'Are you hungry?' she asks, taking bread and cheese out of the pantry.

'I'm always hungry,' Joona replies.

'Good.'

'Are there any chairs?'

'Only one . . . so you'll have to sit on my lap. No, I usually move the chairs out when I'm baking so I have more space,' she says, gesturing towards the living room.

He walks into the next room, which contains a television, sofa and an old hand-painted dresser. Six kitchen chairs are lined up along the wall, so he picks up two of them and carries them back to the kitchen. He hits his head on the lamp again, stops it swinging with one hand, then sits down.

The lamp keeps swaying for a while, its light sliding over the walls.

'Valeria . . . I'm not really here on leave,' Joona says.

'Did you escape?' she asks with a smile.

'Not this time,' he replies.

She lowers her bright, brown eyes, and her face turns almost grey, as if she were trapped behind a wall of ice.

'I knew it would happen. I knew you'd go back to being a police officer,' she says, swallowing hard.

'I'm not a police officer, but I've been forced to do one last job. There was no other option.'

She leans gently against the wall. She's still not looking at him. The veins in her neck are throbbing hard, and her lips are pale.

'Were you ever in prison for real?'

'I accepted the job the day before yesterday,' he replies.

'I see.'

'I'm done with the police.'

'No,' she smiles. 'Well, you may believe that, but I could always tell you wanted to get back in.'

'That's not true,' he says, even though he realises that it is.

'I've never been as in love with anyone as I was with you,' she says slowly, switching the stove off. 'I know I've failed at most things in my life, and I know being a gardener isn't much to brag about . . . But when I found out that you were in Kumla . . . I don't know, I felt like I didn't have to feel ashamed in front of you, that you'd understand. But now . . . You don't want to work here. Why on earth would you? You'll always be a police officer. That's just who you are, and I know that.'

'I'd be happy here,' Joona says.

'It wouldn't work,' she replies, her voice catching.

'It would.'

'Don't worry, Joona, it's fine,' she says.

'I'm a police officer. It's part of who I am. My dad died when he was on duty . . . He wouldn't have wanted to see me in uniform, but he'd rather that than prison clothes.'

She looks down and folds her arms over her chest.

'I'm probably overreacting, but I'd like you to leave,' she says quietly.

Joona nods slowly, runs his hand along the table, then stands up.

'OK, how about this,' he says, trying to catch her eye. 'I'll book a room in a little hotel in Vasastan, the Hotel Hansson. I have to be back at Kumla again tomorrow, but I hope you'll visit me before I go, regardless of whether or not I'm a police officer.'

When he leaves the kitchen she looks away quickly so he won't see that she's on the verge of bursting into tears. She hears his heavy footsteps in the hall, then hears the door open and close.

Valeria goes over to the window and watches him get in his car and drive away. When he's gone she sinks to the floor with her back against the radiator and lets the tears come, all the tears that have been dammed up inside her since high school, when a chasm opened up between them.

39

Saga locks her motorcycle and starts walking down Luntmakar Street while she thinks about how quickly Joona infiltrated Salim Ratjen's organisation. The operation is supposed to start in two hours.

She passes a vegetarian Asian restaurant and sees a couple in their fifties having a meal. They're holding each other's hands over the table between the dishes and glasses.

Saga realises that she's forgotten to eat anything since the Foreign Minister was murdered.

Everyone has been affected by the threat facing the country.

Jeanette went home sick after their trip to see Tamara at Nyköpingsbro. Saga had to drive back to Stockholm while Jeanette lay curled up on the back seat with her eyes closed.

Janus's eyes were bloodshot and he was chugging water when she met him in the office that morning.

He hadn't shaved, and admitted that he hadn't been home to his family, he'd slept in his car. It occurs to her that she needs to talk to him about the importance of taking his medication. She knows he spent several weeks in hospital after he was dismissed from the military, but that he has managed his illness very well since then.

Janus's colleagues have looked through the security-camera footage from the Foreign Minister's hard-drive. There's no sign of the killer, even though he must have been there at least once before to do reconnaissance.

But three weeks ago the cameras caught another intruder on film.

In the middle of the night Rex Müller, the celebrity chef, was filmed climbing over the fence, crossing the lawn and weaving his way up onto the deck.

The recording shows him urinating straight into the illuminated swimming pool. Then he goes around collecting garden gnomes and throwing them into the pool, one after the other.

It's hard to see any connection to the murder, but it's undoubtedly an aggressive and unbalanced act.

Wiping the sweat from his upper lip, Janus stressed several times that no expression of hatred could be disregarded. A few hostile words in the comments section or on a Facebook or Instagram post could be the prelude to a horrifying hate-crime.

Rex fetches the ashtray Sammy has left on the balcony, rinses it, and is putting it in the dishwasher when the doorbell rings. Leaving the tap running, he hurries downstairs.

The most beautiful woman he has ever seen is standing outside his door.

'My name is Saga Bauer. I work for the Security Police,' she says, looking directly at him.

'The Security Police?' he says.

She shows him her ID.

'OK,' he replies, without looking at it.

'Can I come in?' she asks.

Rex backs away, hears the water running in the kitchen and remembers that he was busy washing dishes.

The police officer kicks off her worn trainers and nudges them aside.

'Can we go to the kitchen?' he says weakly. 'I was just filling the dishwasher and . . .'

She nods and follows him up the stairs to the kitchen. He turns the water off and looks at her.

'Do you . . . would you like a cup of coffee?'

'No, thanks,' she says, looking out at the view of the city. 'You knew the Foreign Minister, didn't you?'

She turns to look at him, and Rex notices that one of her big toes is sticking out of a hole in her sock.

'I can't believe he's gone,' he replies, shaking his head. 'I didn't know it was so serious, he hardly ever mentioned his illness . . . Typical of men of a certain age, I suppose, always thinking they have to keep things to themselves . . .'

His voice fades away.

She goes over to the kitchen table, stares at the bowl of limes for a while before looking up at him again.

'But you were fond of him?'

Rex shrugs his shoulders.

'We hadn't seen a lot of each other in recent years. We've both been so busy . . . That's always the way if you want a successful career. Everything has its price.'

'You'd known him a long time,' she says, putting her hand on the back of one of the chairs.

'Since high school. We were at the same boarding school, Ludviksberg. We were in the same gang . . . spoiled kids, really, no joke was too coarse for us, no prank too extreme,' he lies.

'Sounds fun,' she says drily.

'Best time of my life,' he smiles, then turns towards the dishwasher because he can't bear the insincerity on his own face.

When he looks over at her again he feels a sudden cramp in his chest. Some of the blood from the night DJ came to his flat is clearly visible on one of the kitchen chairs. How could he have missed it when he was cleaning? Somehow the blood has run under the armrest and frozen into dark, congealed drops.

'Why do I get the impression you're not telling the truth?'

'My face, probably,' Rex suggests. 'It just looks like this, there's no point trying to change it.'

She doesn't smile, just lowers her gaze for a moment, then looks up at him again.

'When did you last see the Foreign Minister?'

'I don't remember. We met for coffee a few weeks ago,' he lies, running his hand nervously through his hair.

The look in her pale eyes is serious, thoughtful.

'Have you spoken to his wife?'

'No. I don't really know her, we've only met a couple of times.'

He can't think about anything but the blood. It feels like everything he says is empty and false.

She takes her hands off the chair and walks around the table without taking her eyes off him.

'What are you hiding from me?'

'I need to keep a few secrets so you have to come back.'

'You don't want me to come back, believe me.'

'Yes, I do.'

'I'll shoot you in the kneecap,' she says, but can't help smiling at his stupid grin.

'Shall we go and sit in the orangery?' he suggests with a vague gesture. 'It's a bit cooler there . . .'

She follows him to the covered part of the roof terrace and sits down on one of the fluffy sheepskin armchairs around the old marble table.

Rex tries to think of a reason to go back inside, so he can wipe the chair with bleach and get rid of the evidence before she has time to react.

'Can I get you a glass of water?' he suggests.

'I won't be long,' she says, stroking the leaves of a large pot of lemon balm with one hand.

'Champagne?'

She smiles wearily and he notices the scar running across her eyebrow. Somehow it only makes her seem more alive.

'Did the Foreign Minister ever mention feeling threatened?' she asks.

'Threatened? No . . . I don't think so,' he replies, and feels his skin crawl as it dawns on him that the Foreign Minister was murdered.

Why else would the Security Police be involved?

The Foreign Minister wasn't sick, that's just what the public is being told.

Rex feels sweat break out on his top lip when he thinks back to what he said just now about the Foreign Minister not wanting to talk about his illness. He implied that he knew about it but didn't understand how serious it was.

'Well, I must be going,' she says, and gets to her feet.

He goes back into the kitchen with her. She stops by the table and turns to look at him.

'Is there anything you want to tell me?' she asks seriously.

'No, just what I already said, really . . . that sometimes we went a bit too far with our jokes.'

Instead of leaving, the agent pulls the chair away from the table, sits down and looks up at him with an expression that tells him she's expecting to hear the truth now.

'But you did occasionally go and see him out in Djursholm?'

'No,' he whispers, looking at the kitchen cupboard where the bleach is kept.

If the Foreign Minister really was murdered, then his little prank won't just be seen as a scandalous act, it will make him a suspect.

Rex can feel himself starting to panic, and wonders if he ought to admit what he really thought about the Foreign Minister, then swear that he could never hurt anyone.

He's never done anything violent, but realises that his attempt to help DJ the previous evening could also have serious consequences.

There hasn't been anything about an assault or murder in the local news, but there was a lot of blood, and DJ was convinced that the man was seriously hurt.

Maybe he's still on the operating table? If he dies, Rex could be charged as an accessory to murder, or at least go down for harbouring a felon.

If the police officer moves her hand just a fraction further forward, she'll feel the congealed blood.

'When was the last time you were in Djursholm?'

Rex stares at her hand.

'I'd love to talk about old memories, but I need to get going . . . I'm changing the menu at the restaurant, and . . .'

She drums her fingers on both armrests, then leans back and looks at him intently. Her fingers are right next to the blood.

'Did he ever mention a man with a double face?'

'No,' he replies quickly.

'Shouldn't you be wondering what I mean?' she asks. 'If you didn't know what I was referring to?'

'I suppose so, but . . .'

Her index finger idly nudges one of the sticky drops of blood. 'But what?'

Rex comes close to running his hand through his hair again, but manages to stop himself.

'I really am in a bit of a hurry and . . . well, to be honest, I don't really see how I can help you.'

'Don't be surprised if I come back,' she says, and stands up.

She walks around the chair, slowly tucks it back under the table and looks him in the eye for a few moments before heading towards the stairs.

40

Joona parks beside a battered white trailer at 16 Almnäsvägen out in Bandhagen. He looks at the time and thinks about his interview with Sofia Stefansson again.

They're dealing with a killer who is acting outside the frame of his remit, in spite of his exceptional military training.

He takes meticulous care not to leave any evidence, but he still leaves a witness.

He's incredibly fast and efficient, yet he lets ten minutes pass without doing anything. He's perfectly calm, shows no sign of nerves, he doesn't pray, doesn't ask questions, doesn't make any demands.

That empty period of time must be somehow important to him, it must be a ritual on some level, Joona thinks.

But if that's true, then the motives behind the murder are far more complex than they've assumed. It means that this can't be as simple as a conventional terrorist act.

The door to the trailer opens and a woman in a green raincoat comes out, pulling the hood up over her blonde hair. Joona gets out of the car and goes over to her.

'Joona Linna,' she says.

'That's my name too,' he replies, holding out his hand.

She wipes the smile off her face.

'My name is Ingrid Holm. I'll take you to the boss.'

'Thanks.'

Ingrid leads him through a gate in an unpainted fence between the house and garage, and into a patch of woodland. The air smells like heather and warm moss. As the wind blows through the treetops dry pine needles fall to the ground.

'You need to follow my footsteps exactly so you won't be seen from the road,' she says, stopping him at the brow of the hill.

Ingrid calls someone on her radio, listens, then waits for a few seconds. She tells Joona to crouch down, then leads him past two pine trees and behind a large rock covered in white moss before indicating that it's OK to stand up again. They change direction, and walk along a well-worn path past some tall lilacs and out across a lawn behind a yellow wooden house with white windows and eaves. An old red barbecue and a small trampoline are marooned in the tall weeds next to an old apple tree.

Ingrid leads Joona to the white veranda door. There are police officers in bulletproof vests standing in the hall, kitchen and living room. There's an anxious smell like sweat and gun-grease. Semiautomatic rifles swing from leather straps, black helmets litter the floor. All the downstairs windows have been screened to conceal the activity inside the house.

'The first group are in the kitchen,' she says, gesturing beyond the staircase.

Joona pushes past a group of black-clad men waiting restlessly at the bottom of the stairs.

None of them know that several of them will be dead within a few hours.

The members of Operational Unit 1 are squeezed into the little kitchen. This is Gustav's team, the ones who will be first in behind Joona, forcing their way through the doors and windows if a hostile situation arises.

'Joona?' a man with dark-brown eyes asks.

'Yes.'

'This is Joona Linna, he's going to be the first man in,' the man explains to the others.

'And we're the ones who are going to rescue you,' a man with a shaved head and thick neck says.

'I feel safer already.' Joona smiles, and shakes hands with the four men, who introduce themselves in turn: Adam, August, Jamal, and Sonny.

'This is my day off,' Sonny says. 'But there was no way I wanted to miss this.'

Adam is walking around, making the floor creak. He takes swigs from a small can of Red Bull as he adjusts his vest and clothing.

'Do you want me to call your brother and let him know you have your own wings today?' August asks from where he's sitting on the floor with his back against the wall.

'His big brother's the flight engineer on one of our choppers,' Jamal says.

Sonny looks in the fridge, finds a jar of jam and sniffs at a carton of vanilla yogurt.

'I don't like your chances of finding terrorists in there,' August says, then yawns.

'But if I do, I'll kill them,' Sonny mutters, eating some smoked ham out of a plastic pack.

'Is Gustav upstairs?' Joona asks.

'Yes, he's going through the last details with Janus,' Jamal replies.

One of the men from the Rapid Response Unit is sitting on the bottom step, staring into space. As Joona approaches he jumps up and gets out of the way, his movements jerky with nerves.

Joona goes up the creaking wooden staircase and finds himself in a spacious open landing leading to two bedrooms. Here too the windows have been covered. Everyone is already in position. All conversation is subdued and terse.

Janus is looking at the original plans for the building across the way, discussing something with Gustav.

'Back in black,' Janus says, shaking Joona's hand.

'What are your thoughts about the operation?' Gustav asks.

'Everything will probably go smoothly,' Joona says. 'But if things heat up, I must warn you that the killer is far more dangerous than we initially thought.'

'We've got the situation under control,' Janus says, with a note of impatience in his voice.

'As you know, I spoke to the witness after our meeting . . . and in my considered opinion, our killer has received military training that's at least as good as the training for the US Navy Seals.'

'OK, that's useful,' Gustav says in a serious voice.

'For God's sake, we've got six snipers in position, including me,' Janus says. 'We've got twenty-six men from the Rapid Response Unit armed with automatic machineguns, stun grenades and M46s.'

'I just want you to be prepared for the fact that this guy will be able to see through your tactics without even thinking,' Joona says. 'He'll exploit the things you pride yourself on: he knows how you sweep rooms, how you hold your guns.'

'This is supposed to scare you,' Janus says, patting Gustav on the shoulder.

Beads of sweat are trickling down his freckled brow from his hair.

'We haven't prepared for that,' Gustav says, wiping his mouth.

'If you suffer any losses, you need to abandon standard procedure,' Joona says, wishing that the young man was nowhere near this operation.

'I'll go down and discuss alternative tactics with my team,' Gustav says, blushing slightly. 'I can't have you telling Aunt Anja I made a fool of myself, can I?'

'Just be careful,' Joona says.

'We're all prepared to die in the memory of our esteemed Foreign Minister,' Janus whispers, then grins.

Gustav disappears downstairs with his helmet in his hand.

Joona goes into the bedroom facing the trees and looks at the computer screen that shows what's going on in the street outside. The branches of some bare trees are moving in the wind in front of Parisa's home.

10 Gnestavägen is a yellow terraced house from the 1950s. There's a pile of dry leaves next to the cracked steps, and an old broom leaning against the wall.

Parisa is expected home in twenty-five minutes.

Janus comes in with the plans from the City Council's housing department.'We haven't spotted any sign of activity in the house since Parisa left this morning,' he says, laying the plans on the table. 'But there are a couple of blind spots.'

'The hallway and bathroom,' Joona says, pointing at the paper.

'And upstairs someone could be lying in the bath or on the floor. But the biggest unmonitored spaces are the boiler and utility rooms.'

'The house was built in the fifties, so there could be a pretty big bomb-shelter down there, and—'

'Hang on,' Janus interrupts, and answers a call on his radio. He listens, then turns back towards Joona. 'Parisa's earlier than we expected. She's on her way now, she'll be home in less than five minutes.'

41

Janus changes frequency on his radio and informs all units that Parisa is on her way.

'Joona, you've come up with a lot of warnings, and I just want to say that if things go wrong . . .' Janus says, looking at him intently. 'If we have to break in, make your way upstairs. There's a trapdoor in the wardrobe that leads up into the crawl space and out onto the roof.'

The screen shows Parisa approaching the house carrying bags of groceries. She's wearing a thin black coat, a pink hijab and black leather boots with a slight heel.

She removes some junk-mail from the letterbox, puts her bags down and unlocks the front door.

'We need to get you wired,' Janus says. 'Go into the bedroom on the right and Siv will be with you as soon as I can find her.'

Joona goes back out onto the landing and into the bedroom. A young woman in a black polo-shirt is sitting on the chair by the window facing the street. When she hears him come in she stands up.

'My name's Jennifer,' she says, shaking his hand.

'I don't want to disturb you, but . . .'

'You're not disturbing me,' the woman says quickly, and brushes a lock of hair from her face.

'I just need help with a microphone.'

Jennifer's hair is tied up in a ponytail, and she's wearing black cargo trousers and heavy boots. Her helmet, goggles and bullet-proof vest are on the floor beside the chair.

Joona sees that she's got a sniper rifle, a PSG 90, mounted on a sturdy tripod. She can switch the barrel from one side of the window to the other in one swift movement.

Three extra magazines are lined up on a small table beside a box of ammunition – 7.62mm – and a green bottle of Pellegrino.

A ballistics chart has fallen from the box onto the floor. Joona doesn't think it matters; she won't be needing it anyway. The rifle has an exit velocity of almost 1,300 metres per second, and the distance here is no more than 60 metres.

Joona takes off his jacket and puts it on the bed, loosens his holster and then starts to unbutton his shirt.

'Parisa's up in the bedroom now,' Jennifer says. 'Do you want to see?'

He goes over and looks through the sniper-sight, increases the magnification to eight, and sees Parisa taking off her hijab. Her hair is gathered in a thick, black plait that hangs down her back. In the crosshairs he can see her face clearly: the pores of her nose, the birthmark above one eyebrow, and a thick line down one cheek where she's smudged her eyeliner.

When she goes into the bathroom Joona notes that the door to a large cupboard with gold and brown medallion wallpaper is open.

That must be where the ladder to the crawl space is.

He straightens up and looks at the house. In the gap between the curtains he can see Parisa's shadow moving behind the textured glass in the bathroom window.

The sound engineer from the surveillance group comes in. Siv is a middle-aged woman with dark-blue eyes and shoulder-length blonde hair. She stops, her white blouse straining over her chest as she breathes.

She stares at Joona with a look of concentration on her face. He's standing bare-chested in the middle of the room. All that exercise in prison has given him plenty of muscle. His torso bears the scars from where he's been both shot and stabbed in the past.

She walks slowly around him, feeling below his right shoulder-blade and lifting his arm slightly. Jennifer watches them and can't help smiling.

'I think I'll position the microphone just below your left pectoral muscle,' Siv says eventually, and opens a plastic case with a padded black base.

'OK.'

Siv fixes the microphone in place and tries to smooth the tape.

'Sorry, my hands are cold,' she says hoarsely.

'No problem.'

'I can do it instead,' Jennifer suggests. 'I've got warm hands.'

Siv pretends not to hear her. She adds another strip of tape, then checks that the transmitter works. They hear their voices through the receiver, but the proximity to the microphone creates a powerful echo.

'Can I get dressed?' Joona asks.

Siv doesn't answer, and Jennifer stifles a giggle. Joona thanks her for her help, pulls on his shirt, fastens the holster and then puts his jacket back on.

'This microphone is practically undetectable,' Siv says. 'And the range is more than enough for the house, but won't reach much further, just so you know.'

They're testing the reception once again when Janus comes in holding up his laptop. Joona watches the camera follow Parisa as she goes downstairs in her bra and a pair of soft tracksuit bottoms. She walks into the kitchen and starts eating crisps from a silver bag.

Joona checks his pistol, borrows Siv's tape and straps up the bottom of the butt, the way he always does. He releases the magazine, quickly tests the mechanism, trigger and pin, then puts the safety catch back on, reinserts the magazine and feeds a bullet into the chamber.

'I'll get going,' he says tersely.

As he goes downstairs he sees Gustav standing in the darkened hallway with his hands over his face, his semiautomatic rifle hanging by his hip.

'How are you doing?' Joona asks.

Gustav startles slightly. He lowers his hands and looks embarrassed. His usually happy face is tense and shiny with sweat.

'I've just got this really weird feeling,' he says in a low voice. 'There's something bothering me. Maybe the whole house has been booby-trapped.'

'Just be careful,' Joona says again.

Security Agent Ingrid Holm, who showed him the way through the woods before, is waiting outside to lead him back to his car without being seen from the street.

42

Joona leaves the area and drives around Bandhagen before going back to the quiet residential district again, so the engine isn't cold when he arrives.

He parks a short distance away from Parisa's house.

The leafy tops of some tall birch trees are visible above the tiled roof.

The area is calm. It seems almost asleep.

Joona hasn't seen any sign of the response team, but he knows they're there, waiting for a final command, nervous and impatient, full of the conflicting energy that comes from both longing for the timeless moment when everything happens, and fearing injury or death.

If they were to start firing they could perforate the entire row of houses in less than a minute.

Joona approaches the front door, thinking about the detailed map of the area that was hanging on the wall, which showed the danger zones on both sides of the house. The positions of all operational units and their individual approach trajectories had also been marked.

A tree rustles in the wind. Joona hears a car in the distance.

He reaches out and presses the doorbell.

He knows that snipers are watching the door.

A woman pushing a pushchair emerges from one of the

houses down by the cul-de-sac. Her blonde ponytail bounces as she walks. She comes closer, then stops suddenly and answers her phone.

Joona rings the bell again.

A ventilation fan whirrs into action on a rooftop, then quiets almost immediately. The woman with the pushchair is still standing where she was, talking on her phone.

There's a rumbling sound as a dustbin lorry turns into Gnestavägen and stops with a hiss at the end of the road.

Two men get out to collect the rubbish.

Joona hears footsteps inside the house and moves away from the window. Parisa Ratjen puts the safety-chain on the door before opening. She's fully dressed again, the same pink hijab as before, and a thick sweater that reaches down to her thighs. She's slightly built, not very tall. She's wearing subtle make-up, just lipstick and eyeshadow.

'I've got a message from *da gawand halak*,' Joona says.

Her gaze flutters for half a second. She looks past him, out at the street, then back to him again. She takes a deep breath and closes the door.

The woman with the pushchair ends her call and starts walking again. She approaches Parisa's house just as the rubbish collectors return to their vehicle.

Joona moves aside so the snipers can aim at the crack in the door that will appear if it opens again.

The dustbin lorry rumbles past towards the cul-de-sac.

Parisa removes the safety-chain, opens the door again and asks him to come in. She closes the door behind him, locks it and looks through the spyhole.

The house looks exactly like the plan. On the left is a narrow, curving staircase leading to the bedroom.

Parisa leads him up a couple of steps to the living room, which faces the back of the house.

He follows her, watching the way her clothes hang as she walks.

She's not carrying a gun or wearing a bomb.

The worn floor is partially covered by an attractive rug. The windows and half-glazed terrace door have lace curtains.

'Please, have a seat,' she says quietly. 'Can I offer you some tea?'

'Thank you,' he says, sitting down on the brown leather sofa.

She walks past a brick fireplace with no ash or firewood in it and goes into the kitchen. He sees her glance through the window at the street, then take a pot out of a drawer.

Joona reminds himself of what he knows about the killer, the way the man moved across the floor in the Foreign Minister's home, replacing the magazine in his pistol and feeding a bullet into the chamber without losing his line of fire.

Parisa returns with small glasses of tea on a silver tray, a bowl of sugar and two ornate spoons. She puts the tray on a round brass table, then sits down across from him. Her slender feet are bare and neat, and her toenails are painted dark gold.

'Salim has been moved from Hall Prison to Kumla,' Joona begins.

'To Kumla?' she asks, tugging gently at her sweater. 'Why?'

Her face is lively and intelligent, and her eyes betray a gentle scepticism, as if she can't conceal a weariness at the absurdity of everything that's happened to her.

'I don't know. He didn't explain the reason, but he wanted you to know that he can't make outgoing calls any more, and that no one can contact him for the time being.'

Joona raises the slender glass to his lips as he thinks about what Salim Ratjen said, that he should wait until she served him bread and olives before passing on the real message.

'So you know Salim?' she asks, tilting her head slightly.

'No,' Joona admits frankly. 'But he was put on my block . . . and it's always good to look out for each other.'

'I can understand that.'

'I was granted a day's leave, so you always try to help the others if you can.'

A scraping sound makes Parisa glance quickly towards the garden. The snipers at the back presumably have her in their sights right now.

'So what was the message he wanted you to pass on?' she asks.

'He wanted me to let you know he'd been moved.'

Parisa spills a little tea, and when Joona leans over to pass her a napkin he feels his holster and pistol slip forward slightly.

'Thanks,' she says.

Joona realises that she's seen the gun. Her dark eyes are glassier, and she looks down for a moment, pretends to blow on her tea. He understands that she's trying to control her nerves.

The pistol hasn't necessarily blown his cover. She believes he's a criminal, but the situation has suddenly become more dangerous.

'Let me get us something to eat,' she says, and disappears back into the kitchen.

Joona sees small flakes of ash drifting down from the chimney and hears a dull thud from above.

The operational unit is moving across the roof.

The dustbin lorry stops in front of the house with a heavy wheezing sound.

Parisa comes back and puts a bowl of olives and two small forks on the table.

'I was very young when we got married,' she says quietly, looking Joona in the eye. 'I'd only just arrived from Afghanistan. It was after the 2005 election.'

Joona isn't sure if he should pass on the message. She's offered olives, but no bread. Parisa glances anxiously towards the kitchen. There's a shrieking sound as the dustbin lorry compresses the rubbish. A glass jar shatters with a crack. Parisa startles, then does her best to smile at Joona.

43

Parisa eats some of the olives herself and looks at him. Her pupils are dilated and her hands sink back onto her lap.

'Would you like to send a message back to Salim?' Joona says.

'Yes,' she replies hesitantly. 'Tell him things are fine with me, and that I can't wait for him to be free.'

Joona takes an olive and notices that the shadows of the branches on the wall above the television are suddenly moving to a different rhythm. Something's happening. He imagines he can sense the team approaching from the woods. He doesn't look towards the window overlooking the porch, knows he probably wouldn't be able to see them anyway.

'Afghanistan is so different . . . Yesterday I read an article I'd been saving, from *The Telegraph*, about the "international day of silliness",' Parisa says, smiling gently. 'Suddenly everyone in London decided not to wear trousers on the underground. Does that happen in Stockholm too?'

'I don't know. I don't think so,' he replies, and looks at the big olives.

A startled magpie suddenly lets out a chattering cry. There's a creaking sound from below, as if someone is in the basement.

'I once saw a group of girls get thrown out of the swimming pool because they refused to wear bikini tops,' she says.

'Yes, that's become a bit of a thing,' Joona replies calmly.

A reflected glint of sunlight moves across the wall behind Parisa. She picks up her phone, taps a message and sends it.

'I understand that it's about equality,' she says, putting her phone down again. 'But even so . . . why do they want to show their breasts to everyone?'

'Swedes have a fairly relaxed attitude towards nakedness,' he says, moving forward so that his pistol will be easier to reach.

'Even if you don't ride on the underground without trousers here,' she smiles, and rubs her legs nervously.

'That'll probably come,' Joona replies.

'No,' she laughs, and a tiny bead of sweat trickles down her cheek from her hair.

'Swedes are very fond of swimming naked when they get out in the countryside.'

'Maybe I'll learn to do that too,' she says, and looks out through the window at the forest.

She stares dreamily for a few seconds, then turns back towards the room. There's a strange stiffness in her neck.

It looks almost intentional when she drops her teaspoon. It tinkles against the hardwood floor.

She picks it up carefully and puts it on the tray. When she looks up at him again, her eyes are frightened and her lips are pale.

Janus told Joona to make his way up to the crawl space via the cupboard and run across the rooftops towards the cul-de-sac, where a helicopter would get him.

'Salim was a different man when we got married,' she says, standing up. 'I've got our wedding photograph in the hall.'

Joona stands up and follows her to the hall, which is one of the few places in the house where none of the snipers can see them.

The photograph is hanging on the wall by the stairs. Salim looks happy, in a white suit with a red rose in his buttonhole. Parisa is very young, in a white wedding dress and hijab. They're surrounded by relatives and friends in long dresses and suits.

'He doesn't have as much hair now,' Joona says.

'No, he looks older,' she sighs.

'Unlike you.'

'Do you think?'

'Who's that?' Joona asks, pointing at the other man in a white suit.

'That's Absalon, Salim's brother. He cut off all contact with Salim after Salim got caught up in drugs . . .'

They fall silent.

'This is Salim's team, FOC Farsta,' she says after a pause, pointing at a picture of a football team, young men lined up in dark-red tracksuits.

'Were they any good?'

'No,' she laughs.

A shadow flits past the window in the front door.

'I've got more photographs in the basement,' she says, and takes a deep, nervous breath. 'You wait on the sofa, I'll be right back.'

She turns away, leaning against the wall with one hand, then opens a narrow door and starts to go down a steep flight of steps.

'Why don't I come with you instead,' he says, and follows her.

Joona finds himself in a cramped utility room, with a washing machine and a pile of laundry on the tiled floor. There's an old-fashioned hand-wringer in one corner.

'The storeroom's through there,' Parisa says in a tense voice, pulling on a pair of shoes. 'You can wait here.'

She walks down a narrow passageway, past shelves of winter shoes and boxes, to a metal door.

If Parisa is hiding anyone in the house, it will be in the basement, Joona thinks as he follows her.

As she unlocks the door he slips his hand under his jacket, loosens the strap and takes hold of the pistol. The hairs at the back of his neck stand up as she pulls the heavy steel door open and turns the lights on.

A tunnel several hundred metres long flickers in the light before the fluorescent tubes settle down.

'Do all the houses share this storage space?' Joona asks, even though he doubts that any signal from his microphone can still be picked up.

He follows her along the cool passage, passing a couple of

dozen closed metal doors before they turn left and find themselves in an even longer tunnel.

Parisa is walking as fast as she can, holding her hijab in place with her right hand.

They pass the closed armour-plated doors of an underground bomb-shelter, and ventilation drums clad in silvery foil.

Eventually Parisa opens another sturdy cellar door and together they climb up some stairs, go through a communal bin room and emerge into an entrance hall.

They walk out through the door.

The long tunnel has led them under the main road to an area full of blocks of flats.

Over by the edge of the forest are a small slide and some swings with broken chains. Wild roses shake in the gusty breeze and rubbish blows around.

Parisa goes over to a dirty Opel parked among a number of other cars. She unlocks it and Joona gets into the passenger seat beside her.

'You know . . . I was only being polite when I said I wanted to see more photographs,' Joona jokes, but doesn't get even the slightest hint of a smile in response.

44

Parisa Ratjen slows down before pulling out onto highway 229. Without speaking, they drive past low industrial units and scrappy patches of woodland.

Her face is pale, her mouth tense. She's sitting bolt upright, clutching the wheel with both hands.

Joona has given up asking where they're going. They're way beyond the range of his microphone now.

All he can do is try to keep his cover for as long as he possibly can. Maybe Parisa's role is to take him to the terrorists' hiding place.

She brakes behind a truck with a yellow tarp over its trailer. There's a sharp crack as a stone hits the windshield.

'I don't know what side you're on, but Salim wouldn't ask you to give me a message if it wasn't important,' she suddenly says, changing lane. 'Can you tell me why you haven't passed on the real message?'

'You didn't offer me any bread.'

'Good,' she whispers.

They're alongside the truck now, the steel railings on their left flicker past, as the trailer sways in a gust of wind.

'Salim gave me a phone number,' Joona says. 'You need to phone 010 6893040 and ask for Amira.'

The car swerves as Parisa's grip slips at the sound of the name.

The front wheel of the truck looms large in Joona's passenger window and the roar of its engine fills the car.

'That was all,' Joona says quietly.

She grips the wheel tightly, accelerates and pushes past the huge vehicle.

'Say the number again,' she says, swallowing hard.

'040 6893040.'

Parisa pulls into the right-hand lane again and turns off the main road so sharply that a road atlas on the back seat falls to the floor.

They drive past a large, pale yellow industrial building and onto a large tarmacked area between a petrol station and a McDonald's. She turns the car around, reverses back against the grass and stops.

The headlights shine dully over the asphalt towards the petrol pumps.

Off to the left a family emerges from the fast-food restaurant.

Parisa leaves the car in neutral and winds down the windows on both sides. Without saying a word she opens her door and gets out. She feels under the seat, pulls out a Glock, and points it at him through the open window.

'Get out of the car very slowly,' she says.

'I'm not involved, I'm just passing on—'

'Put your hands up,' she snaps. 'I know you're armed.'

'It's just for protection.'

The pistol is shaking in her hands, but her finger is on the trigger and she would probably still hit him if she were to fire now.

'I have no idea what this is all about,' she says. 'But I grew up in Afghanistan. I saw the sniper in the window on the other side of the street.'

'I don't know what you think you saw, but—'

'Out of the car, or I'll shoot,' she says, raising her voice. 'I don't want to, but I'll shoot you if I have to.'

'OK, I'm coming,' Joona says, and slowly opens the car door.

'Keep your hands where I can see them,' she says, licking her lips.

'Who's Amira?' he asks as he puts his right foot on the ground.

'Walk away from the car without turning around.'

Joona straightens up with his back to her. He notes that there are three cars parked outside the McDonald's. The wind is tugging at the flags flying outside.

'Further away,' she says as she steps closer to the car, keeping the gun trained on him.

Joona starts to walk towards the parked cars.

Parisa gets back in the driver's seat, still pointing the pistol at him.

'I might be able to help you,' he says, and stops walking.

'Keep walking,' she calls out behind him.

He takes another couple of steps, and sees a large man come out from McDonald's carrying a bag of food. He gets into the front seat of his car, puts the key in the ignition and starts to eat his hamburger.

'Just so you know,' she says, with a trace of hysteria in her voice: 'If you try to use me to put pressure on Salim, it won't work, because I've already filed for divorce. He won't care what happens to me.'

'I'm not involved,' Joona repeats, and hears her put the pistol down on the passenger seat.

'Keep walking. I swear, I'll shoot if you stop again.'

The moment he hears her put the car in gear and accelerate he starts to run. He vaults the low hedge surrounding the car park, opens the door of the car in which the large man is eating a hamburger. He yanks him out onto the ground. His big cup of Coke falls to the ground, scattering its ice-cubes.

Joona sees Parisa almost lose control of her car as she drives past the yellow industrial building.

He quickly puts the car in gear, slams his foot down and drives straight through the neatly trimmed hedge.

The golf clubs on the back seat rattle when the rear wheels hit the road on the other side.

The heavyset man gets to his feet and stands there surrounded by the remains of his hamburger as his car heads straight up the steep grass bank beside the road.

Joona drives across the grass divider, makes a sharp right and thuds down onto the main road. The Volvo lurches across the three lanes. The back end of the car is still sliding sideways as he slams his foot down on the accelerator pedal.

The left rear wheel hits the central guard rail with a thump.

The hubcap flashes in the rear-view mirror as it bounces onto the other side of the highway.

Joona sees Parisa turn onto Huddingevägen. A warning light appears on the dashboard.

He passes a white van, hitting one hundred and forty kilometres an hour, then brakes when he sees her dirty Opel a couple of hundred metres ahead.

Joona pulls into the right-hand lane, leaving two cars between them, then draws out his phone and calls Janus Mickelsen, and gives him all the information about Parisa's car and their current position and direction.

'OK, I've got it,' Janus says. 'Keep us informed. I'll get the go-ahead to redirect our operation.'

'I don't know what this is about or where we're going,' Joona says. 'But I've only got enough petrol for another fifty kilometres, so I'll need backup before then.'

When the warning light first comes on, there are eight litres of fuel left. That would give fifty-four kilometres of normal driving, but because he's driving unusually fast it could be considerably less.

He has no idea where Parisa is going, and he can't see any other option but to follow her for as long as he can.

They're heading north, just west of Stockholm. He thinks about her peculiar nervousness, and her efforts to make conversation before she spotted one of the snipers and decided to make a run for it.

Thirty minutes later Joona is driving down a long hill beside a golf course. The wind is blowing hard, tugging sideways at the car.

He sees a petrol station and a row of rental cars. But if he stops he might lose sight of Parisa.

And then she'd be gone.

He has to gamble and keep driving, even though the petrol is going to run out in about four kilometres.

Joona calls Janus and gives him a concise update, telling him that they've passed Åkersberga and are heading out along Roslagsvägen. As he drives, the forests and meadows are swallowed up by dusk.

Parisa's red rear lights are visible far ahead of him. Sometimes they vanish briefly, only to reappear when he emerges from a bend in the road.

The road leads through a dark patch of forest. The tree-trunks look like a stage-set in the glow of the headlights.

Joona thinks about the look on Parisa's face when he passed on Salim's message. The emotions he saw were fear and surprise.

He's just passed an isolated side-road blocked by a rusty barrier when there's a whirring sound.

The engine sounds like it's racing, then it goes completely quiet. Joona pulls over to the hard shoulder, stops and switches on the hazard lights.

Far in the distance he sees the lights of Parisa's car flicker and then disappear.

Grabbing his phone, Joona gets out of the car and starts running along the road after her.

The sound of her engine has already vanished.

Even on a winding road like this one Parisa can drive something like three times as fast as he can run. With every minute the distance between them is growing exponentially.

There's dense forest on either side of the road.

He passes a deserted bus-stop and runs down a slope. The forest opens up, revealing misty meadows in the darkness.

He's running fast, and he knows he can keep this pace up for more than ten kilometres.

Far off in one of the fields, two deer raise their heads as he runs past.

45

Even though there's still some light left in the sky, the surrounding forest is completely dark. Parisa brakes as she heads down a long hill. She slowly steers right, then starts to drive down a gravel track beside an overgrown patch of land with a wrecked car at the far end.

She thinks about the tall man who came to her home with a message from *da gawand halak*. He said Salim had just been transferred to his unit at Kumla, but that he didn't really know him. Presumably Salim had felt obliged to send a message with the first person granted leave.

Salim gave him a code which meant that he was someone whose loyalty couldn't be guaranteed, but that she should still listen to what he had to say.

She had seen that the blond messenger was armed, but didn't actually start to panic until she saw the sniper from the kitchen.

On the upper floor of the house across the street.

A window ajar, a black ring and a glowing circle: barrel and sights.

It was impossible to tell if he knew the sniper, if they were working together.

Maybe the messenger was the sniper's target?

Thoughts are buzzing through her head. She can't figure out

how everything fits together, but right now her sister is the only thing that matters.

Once she'd forced the man out of the car she called the number he'd given her, and the call was forwarded automatically. There was a second ringtone, then after a long wait a man answered in a Slavic language. She asked if he spoke English, and he said of course he did.

The gravel crunches beneath the tyres, and the trees around the car quiver in the darkness. The headlights illuminate a small stream through the trees on the left.

Parisa had asked the man where her little sister Amira was. She explained that Amira was among the group from Sheberghan that was expected to arrive in Sweden on Wednesday.

The man spoke to someone else nearby, then replied that the journey had been quicker than normal, and that they had arrived at the rendezvous five days early. Her little sister was already in Sweden. Amira had been waiting three days for her, and she hadn't known.

The forest opens up to reveal a brighter night sky and, a short distance away, the sea. Parisa crosses a junction and heads down towards a marina.

A large corrugated-metal workshop rises up above more than a hundred beached boats: big yachts with huge keels and long, narrow motorboats that look like sleek arrowheads.

There's light coming from a low barrack-like building. It illuminates a sign on the wooden wall: 'Nyboda Boatyard'.

Parisa turns the car around, and reverses towards the wall.

When she gets out the sea breeze cuts right through her knitted sweater. She's only wearing that and her comfy tracksuit bottoms, and just has trainers on her feet.

Tarps knock against hulls, plastic rustles and the line on the flagpole slaps rhythmically.

She can see movement behind the dirty curtain of the barrack.

A narrow path between the tall metal workshop and the densely packed rows of boats leads down to the water.

Parisa hangs the bag with the pistol in it over her shoulder and goes up the steep flight of steps to the barracks. She knocks, waits a few seconds, then goes inside, into an office with a shabby desk and nautical charts stapled to the walls. A man who looks to be over seventy is sitting at the desk going through some receipts. In a wicker chair in the corner sits a woman of the same age, knitting.

The man is dressed in a short-sleeved shirt, and his hairy lower arms are resting on the desk. He's wearing a scratched gold watch around his wrist. The woman lowers her knitting to her lap and looks up quizzically at Parisa.

'I'm here to pick up my sister,' Parisa says calmly. 'Her name is Amira.'

The man runs one hand over his bald head and invites her to sit down in the visitor's chair.

Parisa sits down and hears a gentle clicking sound behind her back as the woman in the wicker chair resumes knitting.

'We were starting to think no one was going to come and get the last one,' the man says as he reaches for a folder.

'She wasn't supposed to get here until Wednesday,' Parisa explains coolly.

'Really? Well, this is going to cost quite a bit,' the man goes on disinterestedly, then licks a finger and leafs through the shipping dockets in the file.

'Everything's already been paid for,' Parisa says.

'If you'd picked her up when she arrived,' the man replies, giving her a quick glance.

'Doesn't she want to pay?' the woman asks anxiously.

'Oh, she'll pay,' the man says, pointing at a pink sheet of paper in the folder. 'Three days' room and board, cleaning charge, and administrative costs.'

The woman starts knitting again behind Parisa as the man taps some numbers into a pocket calculator next to a dusty telephone.

Parisa hears a sander in the workshop.

The man licks his wrinkled lips and leans back in his chair.

'Thirty-two thousand and three hundred kronor,' he says, turning the calculator towards her.

'Thirty-two thousand?'

'We can't afford charity. Sadly there's no leeway,' he explains.

'Do you accept cards?' Parisa asks, even though she knows she doesn't have that much money in her account.

'No,' he smiles.

'I don't have that much cash.'

'Then you'll have to go to Åkersberga and take the money out, but do bear in mind that the debt will keep rising the longer she stays here.'

'I need to speak to her first,' Parisa says, standing up.

'If we start making exceptions, then—'

'She's my sister,' she explains, raising her voice. 'Don't you understand? She's come all this way. She can't speak a word of Swedish. I have to talk to her.'

'We understand that you're upset, but it isn't our fault that you didn't come and get her, and—'

'Tell me where she is!' Parisa interrupts, waits a few seconds, then walks past the woman and out through the door.

'Just wait here. I'm sure we can sort this out,' the man calls after her.

Parisa goes down the steps and hurries along the narrow track between the boats and the large workshop. Further down she sees a crane shaking in the wind, etched against the approaching clouds. The waves are breaking over the rocks and the boat ramp.

Parisa realises that there are lights shining through the plastic covering several of the boats.

The smell of warm oil dredges up memories from Afghanistan, and she finds herself back in the engineering workshop where her father and grandfather worked, by the Safid River on the outskirts of Sheberghan.

'Amira?' she calls across the marina. 'Amira?'

46

Parisa calls her sister's name again. She thinks she sees shadows moving behind the illuminated plastic covering a large motorboat down by the water.

She starts to walk towards the boat, but trips over a rusty outboard motor. There are engine parts and other junk everywhere: windows, buoys, damp boxes full of rolls of tape, anchors, and a clutch of neon tubes leaning against a big forklift-truck.

'Miss!' the man calls after her. 'You can't just . . .'

'Amira?' Parisa shouts as loudly as she can.

The elderly couple have emerged from the office now, and over her shoulder she sees the man help the old woman down the steep steps, slowly and unsteadily.

The sound of the sander in the workshop stops abruptly.

Parisa detects movement from some distance away. Someone is climbing down an aluminium ladder from one of the boats closest to the water.

It's Amira.

She's sure it is.

Her little sister is wearing a blue down jacket, with a shawl covering her head and mouth.

'Amira!' she cries out, and starts running down the narrow path.

The old man calls out again. Parisa waves at her sister. She stumbles over a sawhorse but manages to get past it.

Her sister is squinting, trying to see her through the growing darkness in the sprawling boatyard.

Suddenly a large man in overalls comes around the corner of the workshop. He's limping, leaning on a crutch as he walks towards Parisa. He's clutching a heavy sander in one hand. The cable snakes off behind him, and white dust is swirling from the dislodged filter.

'Amira!' Parisa calls again, just as three spotlights on the front of the building are switched on.

The man with the sander is heading right for her, followed by her sister, who has a look of fear in her eyes.

'Stop shouting,' the man mutters, walking into the furthest light beam.

'Anders, go home,' the older man calls out behind her.

'I want my wife,' he mutters, and stops.

He stares at Parisa through smeared protective goggles. Amira is standing behind him, as if paralysed, unable to get past.

'Hello,' Parisa says.

'Hello,' he replies quietly.

'I didn't mean to disturb you,' she says. 'But I was trying to make sure my sister could hear me.'

'Parisa, they're crazy, you need to get help!' her sister calls out in Pashto.

When the man hears Amira's voice he turns towards her, steps further into the harsh light from the building and hits her hard across the cheek with the crutch. The blow knocks her sideways and she falls to the ground. He moves after her, bellowing, and tries to hit her in the face with the heavy sander. He misses and loses his grip. The machine flies off, dislodges the frame of an old window, and thuds to the ground.

'Stop!' Parisa shouts, trying to open the bag where her gun is hidden.

Amira is lying on her side, trying to crawl away. The man is kicking out at her, and waving his crutch.

'My wife!' he yells.

'Stop it!' Parisa cries, pulling the pistol from her bag with shaking hands.

He turns towards her and she pulls the catch back and takes aim at him.

'Dad said she was my wife now,' he says in a thick voice.

Parisa sees him looking towards the office building, and turns to see that the old man is still supporting the woman as they slowly approach along the gravel path.

'She was given to me,' the thickset man says, wiping snot from his nose with his sleeve.

'Get out of the way,' Parisa says sharply.

'No,' he says, shaking his head obstinately.

Parisa marches over and hits him in the face with the pistol, right in the goggles. He stumbles back and lands in the weeds in front of the building.

Holding the pistol with both hands and keeping it trained on him, she calls to her sister. Amira starts crawling towards her, but lets out a frightened shriek when the man rolls over and grabs one of her ankles.

'Let go of her, or I'll shoot!' Parisa roars.

She raises the gun and fires into the air, then quickly aims at his chest as the shot echoes between the buildings.

'Let go of her!' she shouts again, her voice cracking.

'Anders doesn't understand. He's only a child,' the older man calls out behind them.

With a gasp, Parisa spins around and aims the pistol at the old man as he comes closer. The old woman is sitting on a stack of starter-motors further up the path.

'Dad, you said I was going to have a wife,' the large man wails from the ground.

'Anders,' his father pants. 'I said . . . that if no one wanted her, you could have her.'

Parisa can feel hysteria flaring in her chest. The elderly man holds his hands up and takes a step towards her.

'Stop or I'll shoot,' Parisa yells at him. 'Amira's coming with me. I'll pay you later. You'll get your money, but—'

Her head flashes and her vision fades as something strikes the back of her neck hard from behind. She lurches forward, then her knees buckle and she hits her forehead against a post, drops the gun and falls sideways. She feels blood start to run down her face.

With a groan she struggles to get up, but it feels like someone's pressing a scorching hot sponge against her neck.

The ground sways beneath her. As she fumbles for something to grab hold of she hears Amira screaming with fear. She tries to pull herself up against the cold metal wall, spitting blood. She sees that other migrants have clambered down from different boats and are cautiously coming closer.

'You don't exist!' roars a bearded man in his fifties. He clutches a shotgun.

He lashes out a second time with the barrel of the gun and she collapses, spilling an old pushchair full of used oil filters, and scraping her shoulder on the gravel.

She raises her head and tries to see where her gun is, but the blow to the back of her head has affected her vision. The world is flickering and shaking. She can only just make out the heavyset man with the goggles as he moves towards Amira.

Gasping for breath, Parisa tries to stand up again. She spits blood, and hears the bearded man say he's going to wipe them out.

He kicks her in her ribs and she rolls over. She tries to catch her breath but he looms over her and yanks off her veil so hard that the friction against her neck stings.

'You've got faces – fucking hell, you've got faces!' the bearded man yells.

'Linus, that's enough,' the elderly father says.

Wiping her mouth, Parisa tries to locate her pistol. Above the man with the shotgun she sees the flagpole shake in the wind, its blue and yellow pennant twitching and fluttering.

The bearded man, Linus, walks over to Parisa, presses the end of the shotgun hard between her breasts, then lowers the barrel, sliding it over her stomach and in between her thighs. Then he stops, and stands there breathing hard.

'Please,' she begs quietly.

'Linus, calm down,' the father says.

The bearded man trembles, then quickly jerks the gun towards Parisa's face and puts his finger on the trigger.

203

'Or would you rather not have a face? You don't really want one, do you?' he asks.

'Stop it now,' the father cries with fear in his voice.

'She doesn't want a face,' he replies.

Parisa tries to move her head, but he follows her movements with the gun.

Anders is crying, covering Amira's mouth and nose with his hand. Her legs are kicking weakly, and her eyes have rolled back.

'Please, Linus, don't go too far, we don't want the cops here,' the father pleads.

Sweat runs from the man's beard down his neck. He mutters something and presses the cold barrel of the shotgun to Parisa's forehead.

47

Joona is running along Roslagsvägen through the darkness. Almost twenty minutes have passed since he left the car by the side of the road. He hasn't seen anyone else in all that time. The only things he has heard have been sudden gusts of wind in the treetops and his own breathing.

He's running down a long slope, so he lengthens his stride and speeds up even more. He can just make out the glow of a building in the distance, through the trees.

His pistol bounces against his ribs.

He runs across a small viaduct with dusty railings, but stops when he hears a sharp bang behind him.

A pistol shot.

He turns and listens.

The sound is carried off across the water and bounces back between the islands.

Joona starts running back as fast as he can, towards an unpaved side-road he passed a short while ago. A car is heading towards him at high speed. Dazzled by the headlights, he climbs into the ditch and pushes his way through the tall grass. The ground shakes as the car passes, then everything is dark again. Joona clambers up onto the road and runs a bit further, until he finds the dirt road leading towards the building and turns into it.

The road leads him past a rusty car, and into a tunnel of black trees.

When he emerges from the patch of woodland he sees Parisa's car. It's parked outside the office of a small boatyard. As he moves towards the rows of boats he reports back to Janus, giving his coordinates using GPS and asking for backup from the Rapid Response Unit.

'But hold back,' he repeats. 'Hold back until I've evaluated the situation. I'll get back to you as soon as I can.'

He hears agitated voices and creeps closer, switching his phone to silent as he takes cover under a large motorboat.

Crouching down, he moves nearer through the narrow space between the boats.

He sees an old woman sitting on a stack of starter-motors before he catches sight of the others.

An elderly man is standing on the gravel path with a Stanley knife hidden in his hand, and another man is sitting on the ground holding a girl in his arms.

Joona quickly moves closer. Dry grass rustles beneath his feet.

The tarpaulin covering one boat lifts like a sail, giving him a glimpse of what's going on. A bearded man hits Parisa in the back of the neck with the butt of a shotgun, then aims the barrel at her.

Water trickles to the ground as the tarp falls back down.

The bearded man is standing still with the barrel of the shotgun pointed between Parisa's legs. It's a double-barrelled shotgun that can fire two rounds without needing to be reloaded.

Joona creeps under a sail boat. The sound in his left ear gets distorted as he passes close to the rusting keel.

The bearded man yells something, and aims the barrel at Parisa's face.

Joona steps quickly from his hiding place, straightens up, approaches the bearded man from the side and twists the barrel of the shotgun upward, away from Parisa's head.

He follows through, yanking the butt of the shotgun down with his other hand, out of the man's grasp, then spins it around and puts his finger on the trigger.

Joona jabs the barrel into the man's face. He staggers backwards, clutching his hands to his mouth. Maintaining his line of sight, Joona takes a step forward, turns sideways and strikes him hard across the cheek with the butt of the gun. A cascade of blood squirts from his mouth.

Joona quickly turns the weapon on the old man.

The bearded man hits the ground, crashes over a box of aerosol cans and comes to rest face-down.

The old man stands still and drops the knife on the ground.

'Kick the knife away and get down on your knees,' Joona says.

The old man does as he's told, leaning against the side of the building as he kneels down.

It's almost silent, the wind and the rustle of plastic are the only sounds. Parisa looks up and sees that the blond man has followed her. Pointing the gun at Anders's chest, he pulls Amira from his grasp.

'Don't play with guns, boys,' he says in his Finnish accent.

Anders just looks at him in astonishment, licking snot from his top lip.

When Parisa rolls onto her side it feels like her head is going to explode. She gasps for breath, but forces her eyes open and sees Amira stumble towards her and sink to her knees.

'Amira,' she whispers.

'We have to get away from here. You need to get up!'

Parisa can't move. She leans her cheek on the rough ground and sees three more migrants approaching along the path. First a small boy with serious eyes, followed by an older woman in traditional costume.

Behind them is a man in a shiny black tracksuit.

Parisa knows she's seen him before, but it takes her a few moments before she realises he's a famous football player. Salim used to point him out in matches because he came from the same town as them.

48

Joona tries to make a quick assessment of the situation, and turns the gun on the bearded man when he starts to move again.

Some sort of conflict has clearly arisen between the human-traffickers, migrants and Parisa.

The old woman is still sitting on the stack of starter-motors with her knitting, and the old man is on his knees with his hands on his head.

'We need to get out of here,' Joona says.

Three refugees are walking towards them along the narrow path between the workshop and the boats.

Joona hears a rhythmic sound and glances towards the water before turning back to Parisa.

'Is this everyone?' he asks, noting that the lights in the house further away have gone out.

'There's just my sister and the three others left,' she replies.

'Tell them to come with us.'

Parisa gasps something, and her sister calls to the other three. They look confused as they come closer. The older woman is reluctant, but the boy pats her hand and tries to calm her.

'Come on,' Joona says, turning the gun on the old man.

The boy points, says something, then crawls in under a white yacht. He emerges a few moments later clutching Parisa's pistol.

He looks pleased with himself as he brushes his knees and holds the gun out towards her.

One arm around her sister's shoulders, Parisa reaches out with her other hand.

The boy steps into the white glare of the spotlight, then his head whips sideways and the right side of his face disappears.

The others see blood, brain tissue and fragments of skull splatter the sleek hull of the yacht before the sound of the rifle shot reaches them.

'Follow me, come on!' Joona calls, trying to pull Parisa and her sister towards the large forklift.

The rhythmic sound gets louder and louder, then the sharp clatter of a helicopter rotor envelops them from all sides, hitting their chests and necks.

'Down on the ground!' Joona yells above the noise.

The Rapid Response Unit helicopter sweeps around, a dark shape against the black sky. A sniper is hanging out of the cabin with his feet on the landing strut.

The older Afghan woman crawls in under the boats, and the football player runs at a crouch along the side of the building. The man Joona hit rolls towards the tall weeds near the building and disappears from view.

Joona manages to get Parisa and her sister behind the forklift, lays the shotgun on the grass by the wall of the workshop, and tries to call the Security Police.

All he can hear is a vibrating sound, but he repeats several times that they have to break off the operation, that there are no terrorists in the boatyard.

Anders stands up, using his crutch, then points at the helicopter with a smile and starts walking towards the water. The treetops rustle and the noise of the helicopter changes as it performs an abrupt swerve behind them.

The four searchlights on the underside of the helicopter shine like white beacons.

Joona can see five members of the Response Unit hanging from a SPIE rope beneath the helicopter. They're all wearing helmets and bulletproof vests and carrying semiautomatic rifles.

They are oddly inert as they approach the ground, like puppets on a string. The jetty's wet wood shimmers in the beam of the searchlights as they fly across the water.

Anders is standing by the edge of the water, laughing at the helicopter.

The sky is dark, but the three spotlights on the front of the workshop illuminate part of the gravel path.

The clattering sound gets even louder. Joona tries calling again, sees from the screen that someone has answered, and shouts at them to break off the operation, that there aren't any terrorists in the boatyard.

'Break off the operation at once!' he repeats.

Everyone has taken cover except Anders and the old woman, who is still sitting on the stack of motors.

Joona watches as the helicopter gets closer to the shore and hovers above the narrow strip of beach.

The water is pushed back in a frothing circle. Waves break over the swaying pontoon jetties. The searchlights cast trembling shadows across the path and wall of the workshop.

A sudden crosswind makes the helicopter lurch, and the mechanic tries to hold the cable away from the cabin with his foot.

The sound of the rotors gets deeper as the helicopter hovers in the air. The five response team officers are still swaying on the SPIE rope. The plastic covering one of the boats comes loose and blows away.

The men reach the ground and quickly free themselves from the cable, then run for cover. The helicopter rises again and turns to move slowly away.

A gun goes off nearby and the echo rebounds from the island opposite the marina.

The rifle shot came from behind Joona, and he has time to think that the Security Police must have brought in more snipers before he sees the helicopter losing height and realises what's happened.

There's another human-trafficker in the boatyard: one who turned out the lights in the house, fired a hunting rifle at the helicopter, and managed to hit the pilot.

Joona sees the main rotor hit the mast crane. There's a loud bang, followed by a shower of sparks. The helicopter is knocked sideways like a moth that's burned itself on a lamp.

The helicopter careens towards the ground and slams into the row of covered motorboats. The sound of the stuttering engine and the plastic being torn to ribbons cuts through the air.

There are three more bangs, and half of one of the rotor-blades just misses Anders's head.

The blade slams into the tin wall of the workshop and shatters.

A yellow fireball fills the sky for a few seconds. The heat of the explosion ignites the grass and the edge of the forest, as well as the cabins of the surrounding boats.

49

Gustav is leading the first unit, and has taken cover with his two fire-and-manoeuvre teams behind the concrete foundations of a fuelling station. He hears a hacking sound and sees the helicopter losing height. Adam yells something and stands up.

'Lie down!' Gustav shouts.

Adam manages to take half a step towards the water before he gets knocked off his feet by the pressure wave from the explosion.

He falls backwards and his helmet hits the ground hard.

The heat sets fire to the surrounding trees.

Pieces of metal rain down on the boatyard, but at first Gustav can't hear anything but a rushing sound, like wind passing through leaves.

And when he calls out to the others to stay down, his voice only seems to exist inside his own head.

The panel of the fuelling station is burning.

He looks at the flames, hears a faint crackle, then suddenly his hearing comes back, and with it the chaos. Adam is screaming desperately next to him.

'Markus! Markus!'

Adam has lost his brother. His voice cracks as he stands up again. Before Gustav has time to react, Adam fires his semi-automatic. He empties the entire magazine into the rows of luxury motor cruisers, then just lets go of the weapon and lets it dangle from its strap.

'Get down, they've got a sniper,' Gustav calls.

Adam tears off his protective goggles and stares at the fire. Boats are burning and toppling over, and smaller explosions are still going off. Jamal leaves his cover, drags Adam to the ground and holds him there.

With his hands shaking, Gustav radios Janus.

Glass splinters and pieces of wood are flying through the air.

They've lost the helicopter and its four-man crew.

Gustav can still see the sparks in the darkness from the rotor-blade hitting the crane.

Like the crackling blow of an immense magic wand.

He fights back the tears as he recites the names of the colleagues he believes are dead.

'Groups three and four are on their way, but you need to go in immediately and capture or neutralise the terrorists,' Janus says.

'And Joona?' Gustav asks. 'What's happened to Joona Linna?'

'We haven't heard from him since he arrived at the scene,' Janus replies. 'We have to assume he's dead.'

'We have no way of knowing if they're holding hostages or—'

'Civilian losses are acceptable,' Janus interrupts. 'Backup's on its way, but you need to do everything in your power to stop the terrorists immediately. That's an order.'

Gustav ends the transmission and tries to calm his breathing as he looks at the men around him. Jamal is biting his bottom lip, August's mouth is hanging open, and Sonny's eyes are blank.

Adam is on his knees, crying as he inserts a fresh magazine into his rifle. His older brother Markus was the mechanic in charge of the rope, the guy who made sure they got to the ground safely just before the helicopter crashed.

'OK, listen,' Gustav says, clicking the butt of his semiauto-matic into position: 'Our orders are to capture or neutralise all the terrorists.'

'When are we getting backup?' Jamal asks.

'They're on their way, but we're going in right now,' Gustav replies. 'Adam, you stay here.'

Adam runs his hand over his face, looks at him and shakes his head.

'I'm coming,' he says hoarsely. 'I'm fine.'

'I still think it would be best if you stay here.'

'You need me,' Adam insists.

'Then you're number four, and I'm last,' Gustav says, feeling another flash of the bad feeling he had earlier. 'Jamal, you take point.'

'OK,' Jamal replies.

'Don't take any risks. Think three-sixty degrees. You can do this. Now let's go!'

Jamal points, gets up into a crouch, and runs over towards the boats through the burning grass. He waves at them to follow him, then starts to make his way through the narrow gap between two rows of luxury yachts.

They move forward like a single unit, trying to secure every angle as they go. The marina is hard to get an overview of, and there hadn't been time to study a map of the terrain. The flames from the helicopter and burning boats rise up behind them. The fires give them extra light, but they also give the illusion that everything is in motion. The flames reflect off pieces of metal, and large shadows quiver and dart across the hulls of the boats.

Somewhere up ahead of them is a sniper, but it's practically impossible to know how visible they are to the shooter. They could be standing out clearly against the fire, or they could be merging into the darkness of the boats and surrounding ground.

Gustav forces himself not to think about the officers who have just died. He needs to be focused.

The group moves at a crouch through the narrow passage. They cover all the angles and secure each line of fire instinctively.

Gustav looks back and quickly scans the area behind them. The ground is dry under the boats, and rubbish has blown in and caught on the cables and supports.

The smell of smoke is getting stronger.

The tall flames reflect off the men's helmets.

Suddenly Jamal signals to them to stop, then squats and puts

214

his left hand on his lower right arm: a signal that indicates the presence of hostiles.

Jamal is no longer certain, but he thought he saw a face out of the corner of his eye.

His heart is beating so hard that his chest hurts.

He gets down on one knee and looks under the hull. Maybe he just saw the fire reflected off a white rudder.

Jamal keeps his finger on the trigger, and moves forward cautiously. He tries to peer around the front of the keel.

Through the clutter he can see the wall of a hangar-like tin building, and a yellow forklift.

Someone is moving very close to them, under the next boat.

A black cat slinks away as Jamal's finger quivers on the trigger.

Glowing embers are raining down between the rows of boats.

Gustav maintains his position as last man, and watches Jamal move on, straight ahead. He wishes he could call out to him to secure the area to their right instead.

Jamal looks left. A sheet of blue plastic moves in the wind, and drops of water fall to the ground.

Suddenly a pair of eyes flashes over by the building. Jamal spins his weapon around in an instant and looks at the face through the sights.

Someone groans behind him: Adam, tripping over a protruding beam. The barrel of his gun strikes one of the posts with a metallic clang.

Jamal doesn't know how his finger didn't succumb to the instinct to squeeze the trigger. Adrenalin turns his blood cold when he realises how close he came to killing the old woman with her knitting.

He puts one hand against a white hull and breathes out.

Gustav turns to check the area behind them. The fire is still spreading, and sheets of burning plastic are drifting across the water. The wind carries the flames, which sets more boats on fire.

Jamal waves them on, and Gustav looks forward, past his men and up towards the parking area. To the left a wrecked car stands among the weeds. Thistles and grass are sticking out from the open bonnet.

Adam is whispering to himself as he pulls out his magazine, looks at it, then clicks it back into place again.

A man in a black tracksuit rushes out from his hiding place behind the wrecked car.

Sonny reacts instantly and fires six shots.

The man's torso is shattered. Blood explodes into the air, and his left arm is torn off. It's held on only by the tracksuit sleeve, which wraps around his neck like a scarf as he twists and falls.

At the same time Jamal sinks to the ground. He lies down on his side, as if he needs to rest.

Gustav can't see what's going on. Crouching, Sonny runs up to him, then the end of a barrel in front of them flares up.

The sound of the shot is brief but deafening.

The bullet goes straight into Sonny's face and out through the back of his head. Gustav sees the blood spray onto Adam. Sonny's helmet flies off and the shot is still echoing as he falls backwards.

Gustav throws himself down and rolls under a huge yacht. The smell of dusty soil and dried grass fills his nostrils. He crawls over to a concrete plinth at the bow and steadies his gun on it.

Sonny's body is making a wheezing, almost bubbling sound.

Gustav scans the area where he thought he saw the gun's flare through his rifle-sights. He can see grey earth, smaller boats, a skip. Everything looks like it's made of lead, dusted with soot. He keeps searching and sees the low bushes, a sealed bin-bag, an empty paint-tin.

Adam is cradling Sonny in his arms. His chest is smeared with blood.

'Dear God in heaven . . . Sonny,' he whimpers.

Gustav is breathing jaggedly as he keeps looking through the rifle-sights. Grass sways in the breeze as sooty embers fall around him. The smoke catches in his throat. Burning boats crash to the ground behind him. Their hulls knock together, and the weights holding down the tarp above him start to sway.

He sees the barrel of a rifle behind a rusty pallet, and his heart starts to beat hard. A bush jerks in the wind just behind the sniper.

Gustav wipes the sweat from his eyebrows in order to see

216

better, and adjusts his goggles. He's usually a very good shot, but right now he can feel his hands shaking.

He carefully adjusts his sights to the position where he thinks the sniper's head will appear when he looks up to shoot again.

'They're all dead,' Adam says to no one in particular. 'I think they're all dead.'

Gustav's sights tremble and slip down the tiles. He can't reply. He needs to stay focused.

Only he and Adam are visible.

Gustav knows he won't get many seconds before the sniper fires.

One of the weights sways on its rope in front of the sights.

Gustav sees the sniper's rifle move slightly to the left, then a head appears for a few seconds before disappearing again. The barrel slides down and stops. Then the head is there again, its eye to the rifle, looking for a new target.

Very gently, Gustav moves his rifle until the face appears in the crosshairs, then he squeezes the trigger.

The G36 jerks back against his shoulder. The sniper is gone. Gustav blinks several times, and tries to slow his breathing. The gun is gone. He starts to think he must have missed when he sees something dark dripping off the branches of the bush behind the sniper's hiding place.

50

Joona is standing by the forklift, watching the flames and oil-black smoke twist up furiously towards the sky.

Parisa is hugging her sister, who is curled up in fear. She is covering her ears and sobbing hopelessly like a child.

'Ask your sister if she can run. We should try to get to the edge of the forest,' Joona says quickly.

'We have to find Fatima, the woman who was here a moment ago,' Parisa says. 'We can't leave her. She saved my sister, told everyone she was her daughter so she'd be left alone.'

'Where is she? Do you know?'

'She was going to get her things – you see that big boat without any plastic?' she points.

'It's too dangerous . . .'

Suddenly they hear automatic gunfire, a whole magazine being emptied down by the water. Bullets slam into wood and ricochet off the steel cradles holding the boats.

Joona tries to see where the Rapid Response Unit is.

They hear smaller explosions as glass shatters and boats topple.

He pulls out his phone and calls Janus again, then suddenly sees that Parisa has left her sobbing sister and crept away with the shotgun. She's running bent over, along the side of the workshop towards the boat she indicated.

Joona draws his pistol and pulls back the hammer.

The fire from the burning helicopter is stretching off to one side, and seems to fade into the dark sky.

Joona sees Parisa slow down when she reaches the end of the workshop. Her shadow ripples across the corrugated metal wall.

Her sister is sitting in silence, her hands over her ears.

Parisa glances towards the water, then steadies herself against the wall and gets ready to run across the open patch of gravel to the boat.

Joona sees her take a step forward and look around the corner, then her whole body trembles, she collapses onto her backside and sits there, a blank expression on her face.

Suddenly she falls backward and hits her head on the ground. Then she's dragged away by her feet.

It looks like some predator has brought her down and dragged her into the undergrowth.

Holding his pistol close to his chest, Joona runs down the path beside the wall, then stops and raises the weapon as he approaches the corner where she disappeared.

He listens, feeling the billowing heat from the fire on his face.

Glowing fragments of burning plastic are drifting through the air.

He quickly glances around the corner and scans the scene: the concrete ramp, the five-metre-tall doors to the workshop.

The trunks of the pine trees at the edge of the forest are lit up by the yellow glow of the fire.

There's a white trailer parked a little further into the forest, behind a chicken-wire fence.

Joona runs over to a smaller doorway, pushes the handle, opens it and looks inside the workshop.

Machinery shimmers dully in the darkness, and further away there's a dark-blue motorboat with damaged bows.

Joona darts inside, checks the corners closest to him, then runs at a crouch over to a large lathe.

The smells of metal, oil and solvents mingle in the air.

The door clicks shut behind him.

The fire is still visible through cracks and tiny holes in the metal walls.

He moves towards the boat, making sure to check dangerous angles.

A man roars: 'You're just an animal. You're nothing. You're just a fucking animal!'

Joona runs towards the voice, crouches down and sees them at the far end of the workshop.

Parisa is hanging upside down, raised up by her feet with a pulley and tackle. Her thick sweater has fallen around her head. The white strap of her bra stretches across her naked back.

The bearded man's mouth is still bleeding. Parisa is trying to hold onto her sweater, and sways as the man yanks it away.

'I'm going to cut your fucking head off!' he cries, raising the axe.

Joona starts to run, but the boat is obstructing his line of fire. He can just see them through the gloom beneath the hull.

Parisa tries to scream even though her mouth has been taped shut. The man mirrors her movements and steps to one side.

'This is Guantánamo!' he yells, and swings the axe with full force.

The heavy blade hits her from behind, in her shoulder, and slices through the muscle. Parisa's body spins around, spraying blood across the floor. Joona rushes past blue barrels of old oil, rolls under the boat and gets a clear view of them again.

'Get back!' Joona shouts.

The man is standing behind Parisa, wiping blood from his beard. One of her trouser legs has slipped up to her knee. She's now spinning back the other way, breathing through her nose and trying to use her hands to defend herself.

'I'll shoot if you don't drop the axe,' Joona calls out, moving sideways to find a better angle.

The man takes a few steps back and stares at Parisa, whose struggling is making the chain creak.

'Look at me, not her. Look at me and back away,' Joona says, moving slowly closer with his finger on the trigger.

'They're only fucking animals,' he mutters.

'Put the axe on the floor.'

The man is about to put the axe down when there's a loud bang as a shotgun hits the metal roof. Small pellets of lead ricochet off the roof and walls, then lose velocity and fall to the floor of the workshop.

'Completely still, now,' the old man's voice says behind Joona.

Joona holds the pistol and his other hand up above his head. After all his years of training he's made the same mistake that killed his father. He got carried away by the situation, by the desire to save someone, and left himself open to attack from behind for a few seconds.

Parisa's stomach is heaving in time with her terrified breathing. Her white bra is soaked with blood and a dark puddle is spreading out beneath her. The bearded man is breathing hard as he puts the axe down.

'Drop the pistol,' the old man says.

'Shall I put it on the floor?'

Joona starts to turn towards him, and sees his shadow on some old tins of paint.

'Toss it away from you,' the old man replies.

Joona turns slowly and sees the man standing four metres away. He's standing next to a diesel engine hanging from a winch. Joona gently lowers the pistol as if he's given up, but he's just waiting for the right moment to fire. He'll aim just below the nose, to knock out his brain stem instantly.

'Don't try anything,' the man calls.

'Which way do you want me to throw the pistol?'

'Easy, now . . . This is a shotgun, I won't miss.'

'I'm doing what you said,' Joona replies.

The old man's face stiffens and the barrel of the gun moves slightly to the right. A dark shadow spreads across the dangling boat engine.

Joona hears the son's footsteps behind him, stands still, then steps quickly forward and sideways when the blow comes. The axe misses, but the edge of the blade cuts into the back of his shoulder.

Joona spins around as he moves and rams his left elbow into the base of the man's neck, breaking his collarbone.

The axe spins through the air, hits a jack and falls to the

cement floor. Joona wraps his arm around the man's neck, tips him over his hip and down onto the floor in front of him to act as a shield as he raises his pistol towards the father.

The old man has already rested the butt of the shotgun on the ground and put the end of the barrel in his mouth.

'Don't do it,' Joona calls.

The old man reaches down and just manages to reach the trigger. His cheeks light up as the blast goes off, simultaneously his head jerks back and fragments of skull and brain tissue spray up at the ceiling and rain down onto the floor behind him.

His body falls forward and the shotgun clatters to the ground beside it.

'What the hell happened?' his son gasps.

Joona quickly ties his arms and legs with thick steel wire, then drags him to his feet and pushes him back towards the dangling engine.

'I'll kill you!' the son screams hysterically.

Joona winds the wire twice around the man's bearded neck and the sturdy axle of the generator, then picks up the control pad from a workbench, and raises the engine just high enough that the man is forced to stand on tiptoe.

Joona hears more rifle shots from outside, then semiautomatic gunfire.

He runs over and lowers Parisa to the ground, telling her repeatedly that she's going to be all right. He rolls her over onto her stomach, quickly wipes the blood away with the palm of his hand and seals the deep wound temporarily with duct-tape.

'You're going to be fine,' he says calmly.

He adds more layers of tape, even though he knows it won't hold for very long. He can see that the wound won't be fatal if she gets to a hospital.

She tries to stand up but he tells her to lie still.

'I just wanted to get Fatima,' she says, trying to control her ragged breathing.

She gets to her knees, then rests for a moment.

She's shaking and wobbling because of the blood she's lost, but he helps her up and supports her through the workshop, though her knees threaten to buckle several times.

They emerge into the cool air. The entire marina is burning, the gusting wind fanning the flames.

Joona leads them up the gravel path along the side of the workshop, clutching his pistol in one hand.

When Amira sees them she gets to her feet beside the fork-lift-truck and walks towards them, her face grey and impassive. Her eyes seem distant, her pupils enlarged. Joona helps Parisa sit down and wraps his jacket around her.

Gustav is standing further up the path. His heavy bulletproof vest and semiautomatic rifle are lying on the ground.

The operation has been brought to a close, and he's reporting back to command in an unsteady voice, saying that they have the situation under control and requesting ambulances and fire engines. He nods, mutters something, then lowers the radio to his side.

'Are there ambulances on the way?' Joona calls.

'The first ones will be here in ten minutes,' Gustav replies, staring at Joona with wet eyes.

'Good.'

'God . . . I'm sorry. I'm so sorry, Joona. I did everything wrong.'

'It'll be OK.'

'No, it won't. Nothing's going to be OK.'

A few metres behind him the old woman is sitting on the stack of motors, still knitting with a sad expression on her face. Her youngest son is lying on the ground, his arms fastened with zip ties.

'We were given orders to go in immediately,' Gustav says, wiping tears from his cheeks.

'Orders from whom?'

There's a loud crack and Gustav takes a small step forward.

The bang echoes between the buildings as the smell of powder dissipates.

The old woman is holding Parisa's pistol in both hands. Her knitting is on the ground by her feet.

She fires again and Gustav fumbles for the wall with one hand. Blood is running from his stomach and a wound in his upper arm. Adam, who is standing next to the woman, grabs the gun and wrestles her to the ground, breaking her arm at the shoulder and holding her down with his boot.

Joona catches Gustav when he collapses and lowers him gently to the ground. Gustav looks confused and his mouth is moving as if he wants to say something.

51

Joona spent two hours waiting in the hallway outside the operating theatre where Gustav was being treated. Eventually he had to leave, but there was still no word about whether Gustav was going to survive.

He parks the car next to the top of Tule Street and feels the cool air from the park. He remembers that part of one of Sjöwall and Wahlöö's books took place here, in an flat overlooking Vanadislunden.

As he walks down the hill towards the hotel, the local anaesthetic he was given for the axe-wound starts to fade. He had to get eleven stiches, and now the pain is starting to flare up again.

The shoulder of his jacket has been taped together, but it's still crumpled and spattered with blood. He smells like smoke, has a cut across his nose, and his knuckles are raw.

The woman in reception stares at him open-mouthed. Joona realises that his appearance has changed quite a bit since he checked in.

'Rough day,' he says.

'So I can see,' she replies with a warm smile.

He can't help asking if there are any messages, even though he doesn't really expect Valeria to have called.

The receptionist checks her computer first, then his cubby hole, but there's nothing there.

'I can ask Sandra,' she suggests.

'There's no need,' Joona says quickly.

He still has to wait while she goes to speak to her colleague. He stares at the empty desk and the pattern of scratches in the varnish as he thinks about the fact that his part of the mission is over.

They all knew that the infiltration and ensuing operation were a gamble, but there was no other option. There wasn't enough time.

Joona has done all he could to help the Security Police, and he wishes he could tell Valeria that now he's just an ordinary inmate out on leave.

'No, sorry,' the woman smiles when she comes back. 'No one's asked for you.'

Joona thanks her and goes to his room. He leaves his muddy shoes on a newspaper, runs a hot bath, then sinks into it with his injured arm hanging over the side.

His mobile phone is on the tiled shelf next to him. He asked the hospital to call as soon as there was any news about Gustav.

The tap drips slowly, rings spread out across the water and disappear. His body relaxes in the warm water and the pain starts to fade.

Salim Ratjen's message had simply meant that Parisa's sister had been smuggled into the country sooner than expected. And before Salim had time to tell his wife, he had been moved from Hall Prison and isolated from the world outside.

The old couple and their three sons had turned their boatyard into a centre for human-trafficking.

Once Joona stopped reporting back, Janus became worried that they were losing contact with the terrorist cell.

And defeating the threat against the state was the absolute top priority.

That was why he made the decision to fly the National Response Unit into the marina.

Janus had seen that Joona was trying to call him, but had heard nothing but static.

From the helicopter, the response team had seen a number

of people next to a large metal building. There were bodies on the ground, and a third person was on their knees. They had to make a split-second decision, and when the sniper saw through his sights that a young man was aiming a pistol at a woman, he had to fire.

The response team couldn't have known that the two men on the ground were human-traffickers, and that the young man with the pistol had fled from the Taliban in Afghanistan.

The family's third son was woken up by the commotion outside the workshop, fetched a hunting rifle from the gun cabinet, crept out of the house and hid behind a pallet of tiles.

When the helicopter had set down the response team, the son fired and managed to hit the pilot in the chest.

The rest of the helicopter crew died in the crash, two of the response team died during the ensuing fire-fight, and two migrants were shot by accident.

There were no terrorists at the boatyard.

The operation was a fiasco.

The father shot himself, the middle son was killed by the response team, and the mother and the two other sons were arrested.

Gustav, the team leader, was shot and seriously injured, his condition still critical. Parisa Ratjen is going to be OK, no lasting injuries. Her sister, Amira, and the older woman are both going to seek asylum in Sweden.

Joona gets out of the bath, dries himself, then calls Valeria. As the phone rings, he looks out at the street. A group of Roma are preparing their beds for the night, on the pavement outside a supermarket.

'I realise you're not coming,' he says when she eventually answers.

'No, it . . .'

She falls silent, breathing heavily.

'I'm done with my job for the police, anyway,' he explains.

'Did it go well?'

'I can't really say that it did.'

'Then you're not done,' she says quietly.

'There's no easy way to answer that, Valeria.'

'I understand, but I feel I need to take a step back,' she says. 'I have a life that works, with the boys, the nursery . . . Look, I don't want to sound boring, but I'm a grown-up, and things are fine as they are. I don't need earth-shattering passion.'

Silence on the line. He realises that she's crying. Someone switches a television on in the next room.

'Sorry, Joona,' she says, and takes a shaky deep breath. 'I've been fooling myself. It could never have worked out for us.'

'Once I get my gardening qualifications, I hope I can still be your apprentice,' he says.

She laughs, but Joona can still hear a sob in her voice, and she blows her nose before answering:

'Send in an application, and we'll see.'

'I will.'

They run out of words again.

'You need to get some sleep,' Joona says quietly.

'Yes.'

They say goodnight, then fall silent, say goodnight again, and then end the call.

Down in the street a group of youngsters emerge from a bar and head off towards Sveavägen.

He can't help thinking how unreal it feels not to be locked up as he gets dressed and goes outside into the cool city air. People are still sitting on the outdoor terraces along Oden Street. Joona walks up to the Brasserie Balzac, and gets a table facing the street. He's just in time to order the pan-fried sole before the kitchen closes.

The police investigation will go on without him.

Nothing is over.

The killer probably isn't connected to a terrorist group.

His motive for killing the Foreign Minister could easily be something completely different.

And something definitely made him behave oddly: he stayed with his bleeding victim for more than fifteen minutes and left a witness alive.

He knew where the cameras were located, and wore a balaclava, but for some reason he wore strips of fabric around his head.

If he hadn't actually killed anyone before, he crossed that line on Friday night. Any fear he felt before the killing would now have been replaced by the sense that he controls the situation. Now there's nothing to stop him from killing again.

52

There's a place in the far corner of Hammarby Cemetery to the north of Stockholm where you can see far across the fields and reed-fringed water.

Even though the city is so close, everything here looks the way it has for a thousand years.

Disa is lying in the innermost row, by a low stone wall, next to a child's grave with a handprint on the headstone. Joona was with her for many years after his separation from Summa, and not a minute goes by without him missing her.

He removes the old flowers, gets fresh water and puts the new bunch in the vase.

'I'm sorry I haven't visited you in a long time,' he says, getting rid of some leaves that have fallen on the grave. 'Do you remember me talking about Valeria, who I used to be in love with back in high school . . .? We've been writing to each other for the past year, and have met up several times, but I don't know what's going to happen to us now.'

A girl comes riding along the bridleway on the other side of the wall. Two birds take off and fly in a wide arc over a large boulder at the edge of the forest.

'Can you believe that Lumi's living in Paris?' he smiles. 'She seems happy, she's working on a film project for college, about the migrants in Calais . . .'

The gravel path crunches as a slender figure with colourful plaits in her blonde hair walks up. She stops next to Joona and stands there in silence for a while before starting to speak.

'I've just spoken to the doctors,' Saga says. 'Gustav's still sedated. He's going to survive, but he'll need more operations. They had to amputate his arm.'

'The most important thing is that he's going to make it.'

'Yes,' Saga sighs, poking at the gravel with her trainer.

'What is it?' Joona asks.

'Verner has already closed this down. Everything's been declared confidential. No one has access. I can't even look at my own damn reports any more . . . If they knew what I've kept on my personal computer I'd lose my job. Verner's pushed for such a high level of secrecy that even he doesn't have access now.'

'In that case, who does?' Joona asks with a smile.

'No one,' she laughs, then turns serious again.

They start to walk back, past the rune-stone with its twined serpents, and the sombre angel by the entrance.

'The only thing we know after the biggest anti-terrorism operation in Swedish history is that absolutely nothing about it points to terrorism,' she says, stopping in the car park.

'What exactly went wrong?' Joona asks.

'The killer said Ratjen's name . . . and we linked that to the conversation the security officers at Hall Prison managed to record . . . I've read the entire translation myself, Salim Ratjen talked about three big celebrations . . . and the date of the first party coincided with the date of the murder of Foreign Minister William Fock.'

'I know that much.'

She swings one leg over her filthy motorcycle.

'But those parties only meant that Ratjen's relatives were coming to Sweden,' she continues. 'There's nothing to suggest that he's been radicalised in prison, and we haven't been able to find any connection to Islamic extremism or organisations that have been linked to terrorism.'

'And Sheikh Ayad al-Jahiz?' Joona asks.

'Yes, well,' Saga laughs bitterly. 'We've got that recording of him saying he's going to find the leaders who supported the bombings in Syria and blow their faces off.'

'And the Foreign Minister was shot in the face twice,' Joona points out.

'Yes,' Saga nods. 'But there's one small problem with that connection . . . The management of the Security Police already knew before the operation that Ayad al-Jahiz has been dead for four years – so he couldn't have been in contact with Ratjen.'

'So . . . why?'

'The Security Police just had its budget increased by forty per cent, so it can maintain the same high level of protection in future.'

'I see.'

'Welcome to my world,' Saga sighs, and kick-starts her motorcycle. 'Come to the boxing club with me.'

53

Narva Boxing Club is almost empty. The chain holding the punchbag clanks rhythmically as a heavyweight metes out hard blows, a distant look on his face. Dust particles dance in the air above the ring. Two younger men are groaning as they do sit-ups on rubber mats beneath the broken speedball.

Saga emerges from the locker room in a burgundy vest top, black leggings and well-used boxing gloves. She stops in front of Joona and asks him to help wrap her hands.

'The security service's main job, in any country, is to frighten its politicians,' she says in a low voice, handing him one of the rolled bandages.

Joona pulls the loop at the end over her thumb, then winds the elasticated fabric across her palm and around her knuckles. She clenches her fist as he does.

'It doesn't really matter to the Security Police that there weren't any terrorists – either way, the threat has been dealt with,' she goes on as he pulls the bandage between her fingers. 'And because politicians can't admit to a waste of taxpayers' money, the operation is being hailed as a triumph.'

The heavyweight boxer is punching faster now, and the two younger men have moved on and are now using skipping ropes.

Joona pulls the gloves over her hands, fastens the laces, then winds sports tape around her wrists.

Saga climbs up into the ring and Joona follows, taking two leather punch pads with him.

'Sweden has been spared,' Saga says, testing the pads. 'But not thanks to us.'

Joona starts circling, changing the height and position of the pads, and Saga follows, striking with a complicated series of hooks and uppercuts.

He counters with one pad, but she slips away and hits out with another sequence of blows that echoes around the gym.

She hunches her shoulders, tilts her head and jabs with her left hand.

'Janus and I are going to keep working on the preliminary investigation to make sure that nothing leads back to the Foreign Minister,' she says, panting for breath.

Joona angles the pads so she can practise straight punches, then swings the right one and hits her on the cheek, before backing away and letting her come at him with two heavy right hooks.

'Lower your chin a little,' he says.

'I'm too proud for that,' she smiles.

'So what happens if you find the murderer?' Joona asks, following her towards the blue corner.

She fires off a sequence of four rapid punches at the two pads.

'My main job is to make sure he doesn't confess to the murder,' she says. 'So he can't be connected to it in any way, can't be prosecuted, or—'

'He's extremely dangerous,' Joona interrupts. 'And we don't know if he's going to kill again. We have no idea what his motives are.'

'That's why I'm talking to you.'

The heavyweight has stopped punching now; he's standing with his arms around the punchbag, staring dreamily at Saga.

'You need to lower your chin.'

'Oh, no,' she laughs.

She slips out of the corner, hits a hard right hook, rolls her shoulders and follows through with a body-blow that makes Joona take a few steps back.

'If I was in the police, I'd try a different approach,' he says.

'What?' Saga asks, wiping the sweat from her face.

'The other Ratjen.'

'Let's take a break,' she says, holding out both her hands.

'Salim Ratjen has a brother in Sweden,' Joona says, removing the tape.

'He's been under heavy surveillance since the Foreign Minister's murder.'

'What have you found out?' Joona asks, untying the laces.

'He lives in Skövde, he's a high-school teacher, and he has no contact with Salim,' she says, climbing out of the ring.

She shakes her gloves onto the floor as she walks towards the locker room. When she comes back she has a towel around her neck and she's taken the tape off her hands.

They go into the little office and Saga puts her military-green laptop on the desk. The walls are lined with glass-fronted cupboards containing medals and trophies, yellowing newspaper clips and framed photographs.

'I don't like to think about what would happen if Verner found out I still have this information,' Saga mutters as she clicks to bring it up. 'Absalon Ratjen lives at 38A Länsmans Street, teaches maths and science at Helena School . . .'

She brushes her hair from her face and reads on:

'He's married to a Kerstin Rönell, who teaches PE at the same school . . . they have two children, both in elementary school.'

She gets up and lowers the blind on the office door.

'Obviously we're monitoring their phones,' she says to Joona. 'We're keeping an eye on their online activities and so on, checking their emails, both private and at the school . . . His wife's the only one who occasionally looks at porn.'

'And he has absolutely no connection to the Foreign Minister?'

'None.'

'So who has he been in contact with in the past few weeks?'

Saga wipes her forehead as she checks the laptop.

'The usual stuff . . . and he mentioned a meeting with a car mechanic that never actually happened . . .'

'Look into that.'

'We also have a strange email from a computer with no IP address.'

'Strange in what way?'

Saga turns the laptop towards Joona and brings up white text on a black background: *I'll eat your dead heart on the razorback battlefield.*

The light of the desk lamp flickers as an underground train passes below them.

'It seems pretty threatening,' she says. 'But we think it's actually jargon related to a competition . . . Absalon Ratjen teaches advanced maths at the school, and his students are taking part in the First Lego League, which is an international contest for programmable robots made out of Lego.'

'Take it seriously anyway,' Joona says.

'Janus is taking it seriously . . . he's working full-time on this email, and a recorded phone call that . . . Well, we don't know if it's a nuisance call or a wrong number. All we can hear is the sound of Ratjen's breathing, and a child reciting a nursery rhyme.'

She clicks on an audio file and a moment later a tentative child's voice echoes from the speaker of the laptop:

> *Ten little rabbits, all dressed in white,*
> *Tried to get to heaven on the end of a kite.*
> *Kite string got broken, down they all fell,*
> *Instead of going to heaven, they all went to . . .*
> *Nine little rabbits, all dressed in white,*
> *Tried to get to heaven on . . .*

The call ends abruptly and is followed by silence. Saga clicks to close the audio file, and mutters that the rhyme could also be connected to the contest as she searches through the report.

'Absalon is the next victim,' Joona says, and gets up from his chair.

'That can't be right,' she objects, smiling despite herself. 'We've examined it from every—'

'Saga, you have to send people down there right away.'

'I'll call Carlos, but can you tell me why you—'

'Make the call first,' Joona interrupts.

Saga takes out her phone and asks to be put through to Carlos Eliasson, head of the National Operations Unit and Joona's former boss.

Ratjen, rabbits and hell, Joona repeats to himself.

He thinks about the high-pitched and slightly bemused child's voice, and the rhyme about the rabbits that end up in hell.

When he was questioning Sofia he'd tried to analyse the composite sketches of the killer.

Sofia told him she had thought the killer had long strands of hair hanging down his cheeks.

Searching her memory, she then described them as strips of thick fabric, possibly leather.

When she tried to draw the strips onto the picture, at first they looked like big feathers, before turning into matted hair.

But they weren't feathers, Joona thinks.

He's almost certain that what she saw hanging over the murderer's cheeks were sliced-off rabbits' ears.

Ratjen, rabbits and hell.

The killer mentioned Ratjen, and said that hell would devour them: he's planning to kill all the rabbits in the rhyme.

Saga is trying to explain to Carlos why they urgently need to send a team to Salim Ratjen's brother in Skövde.

'Look, I need to know why,' Carlos says.

'Because Joona says so,' Saga says.

'Joona Linna?' he asks in surprise.

'Yes.'

'But . . . but he's in prison.'

'Not at the moment,' Saga replies bluntly.

'Not at the moment?' Carlos repeats.

'Just get a team down there at once.'

Joona grabs the phone from Saga's hand and hears his former boss's voice:

'Just because Joona is the most stubborn person in—'

'I'm only stubborn because I'm probably right,' he interrupts. 'And if I am, then there's no time to lose if you want to save his life.'

54

A robot made of red and grey Lego is standing on the kitchen table. It's the size of a wine-box, and resembles an old-fashioned tank with a grab-claw attachment.

'Say hello to our new friend,' Absalon smiles.

'Hello,' Elsa says.

'And he's going to be asleep very soon,' Kerstin says.

She hands out paper towels to use as napkins, looks at her husband's beaming face, and thinks that he must have gained some weight.

The children are already in their pyjamas. Peter's are too short in the leg. Elsa is wearing all her hairbands as bracelets.

Absalon moves the carton of lactose-free milk, a sticky ketchup bottle and the bowl of grated carrot and apple.

The robot starts to roll across the floral-patterned wax table-cloth. Its small rubber front wheels hit the pan of macaroni and trigger the next action. Peter giggles as the moveable upper section of the robot slides forward on two rails. With a plastic rattling sound the wooden ladle sinks into the macaroni, then lifts back up again far too quickly.

The children laugh as macaroni flies across the table.

'Hang on,' Absalon says, leaning forward and adjusting the spring on the grab-arm. He aims the remote at the robot again.

With gentler movements, the robot picks up some more

macaroni, rotates half a turn and then rolls towards Elsa's dish. Her eyes shine as it deposits the food on her plate.

'That's so sweet!' she cries out.

There are sirens in the distance.

'Does it have a name?' Kerstin asks with a wry smile.

'Boris!' Peter declares.

Elsa claps her hands and repeats the name several times.

Absalon steers the robot towards his son's plate, but manages to crash it into the pot of crispy onion pieces, and can't stop it from emptying its spoon into his glass of milk. Peter bursts out laughing and puts his hands over his face.

'Boris, I think you're really smart,' Elsa says consolingly.

'But now he needs to get some sleep,' Kerstin says once more, and tries to catch her husband's eye.

'Can he pick up sausages too?' Peter asks.

'Let's see.'

Absalon runs a hand through his curly hair, then swaps the ladle on the grip-arm for a fork and presses the remote. The robot heads off towards the frying pan too fast, and Absalon doesn't manage to stop it before it collides with the cast-iron rim and topples forward.

'Mum, can we keep him?' the children cry in unison.

'Can we?' Absalon asks with a smile.

'Mum?'

'He can stay as long as we don't have to keep the one in the bathroom,' Kerstin replies.

'Not James,' Elsa says, appalled.

James is a yellow robot who provides toilet paper. Kerstin thinks he's a little creepy, and far too interested in people's bathroom habits.

'We can lend James to Granddad,' she says, taking the fork from Boris and putting sausage on the children's plates.

'Is he coming this weekend?' Absalon asks.

'Can we handle that?'

'I can make a nice—'

Suddenly the kitchen door slams shut in the draught, and the calendar with the children's pictures on it falls to the floor.

'It's the bedroom window,' she says, getting up.

The door feels stuck, as if someone is holding it shut on the other side, and when it opens there's a rushing sound as the air pushes past. She goes out into the hall, closing the kitchen door a little too hard behind her before heading past the stairs and into the bedroom.

The curtains are fluttering.

It's not the window that's open but the patio door. The blinds are rattling in the wind.

The room is cold and her nightgown has blown onto the floor. When Absalon makes the bed, he usually drapes her nightgown across her side of it.

Kerstin crosses the cool floor and closes the patio door, pushing the handle down until she hears the little click.

She picks her nightgown up and puts it on the bed, then turns the bedside light on and notices that the carpet is dirty. Soil and grass have blown in from the garden. She decides to get the vacuum out after they've eaten, and starts to walk back.

Something makes her stop in the darkened hallway.

There's no noise coming from behind the kitchen door.

She looks over at the bundle of coats and bags, all hanging from the same hook.

Very slowly, she moves towards the kitchen, sees the light through the keyhole, and then suddenly hears an unfamiliar child's voice.

'*Seven little rabbits, all dressed in white, tried to get to heaven on the end of a kite. Kite string got broken, down they all fell. Instead of going to heaven, they all went to . . .*'

Thinking that Absalon has decided to demonstrate a new robot while she was gone, she opens the door and walks in, then stops dead.

A masked man is standing by the kitchen table. He's wearing blue jeans and a black raincoat, and is holding a knife with a serrated blade in one hand.

A tremulous child's voice is echoing from a mobile phone on the table.

'*Six little rabbits, all dressed in white, tried to get to heaven . . .*'

Absalon stands up, and macaroni falls from his lap onto the

floor. Elsa and Peter are staring at the man in their kitchen in horror.

'I don't know what you want, but can't you see you're scaring the children?' Absalon says unsteadily.

Five long rabbits' ears are dangling by one of the man's cheeks. They're stained dark red where they were sliced off before being threaded onto wire and wound around the balaclava.

Kerstin's heart is beating so hard that she can barely breathe. With shaking hands she picks up her handbag from the counter and offers it to the stranger.

'There's some money in here,' she says, almost inaudibly.

The man takes the bag and puts it down on the table, then raises the knife and gestures towards Absalon's face with the point.

Kerstin watches her husband weakly try to swat the knife away.

'Stop doing that,' he says.

The hand holding the knife sinks back down, then jabs forward and stops. Absalon draws a ragged breath and looks down. The entire blade of the knife is embedded in his stomach.

A bloodstain spreads out across his shirt.

When the stranger pulls the knife out, a gush of blood follows it and splats onto the floor between Absalon's feet.

'Daddy!' Elsa yelps in a frightened voice, and puts her spoon down on the table.

Absalon stands absolutely still as blood fills the bottom of his tucked-in shirt, then runs down inside his trousers, down his legs and out over his feet.

'Call an ambulance, Kerstin,' he says, dazed, as he takes a step back.

The man watches him, then slowly raises the hand holding the knife.

Elsa runs over to Absalon and wraps her arms around his legs, making him sway.

'Daddy!' she sobs. 'Daddy, please . . .'

She picks up his napkin from the table and holds it to his stomach.

'You're stupid!' she shouts at the masked man. 'This is my daddy!'

As if in a dream, Kerstin goes over and pulls Elsa away from her husband, picks her up in her arms and holds her tight, feeling her small body tremble.

Peter crawls under the table, clutching his head with his hands.

The man looks at Absalon with interest, then brushes the rabbits' ears from his cheek, slowly adjusts the angle of the knife, and thrusts it into the other side of his torso.

The explosion of pain makes Absalon cry out.

The man lets go of the knife, leaving it sticking out, wedged beneath his bottom ribs.

Absalon lurches sideways but his fall is broken by the table. He throws one arm out, and his bloody hand sends a glass of milk flying.

The masked man pulls a machete from a strap inside his raincoat and walks towards Absalon again.

'Stop it!' Kerstin screams.

Absalon slumps onto a chair, holds his hand up in self-defence and shakes his head.

'Please, stop now!' Kerstin sobs.

The ceiling lamp above the table is spinning slowly. The light from the two bulbs wanders across the tablecloth. Milk drips steadily onto the floor.

'What have I done?' Absalon gasps.

He's sweating and breathing fast, on his way to circulatory shock. The masked man stands still and looks at him.

'You must have come to the wrong house,' Kerstin says in a shaky voice.

Elsa is squirming in her arms, trying to escape and see what's going on.

A trickle of blood falls from the chair.

The second hand on the clock ticks slowly on.

There are children playing outside, and Kerstin hears a bicycle bell.

'We're just normal people. We don't have any money,' she goes on weakly.

Peter is sitting under the table staring at his father.

Absalon tries to say something, but a convulsion fills his mouth with blood. He swallows and coughs, then swallows again.

The neighbour's car pulls in and parks next to theirs. Car doors open and close. Bags of groceries are unloaded from the boot.

Absalon's shirt is dark red, almost black. A steady stream of blood is running from the chair, the pool has reached Peter now.

'Daddy, Daddy, Daddy . . .' the boy whimpers in a high voice.

The masked man looks at the time, then grabs hold of Absalon's hair.

'Can I take the children out?' Kerstin asks, wiping the tears from her cheeks.

Elsa is whimpering and Kerstin's field of vision becomes distorted. There's a loud buzzing sound in her head as she sees her husband's lips turn white.

He's in a lot of pain now.

The stranger leans over and whispers something to Absalon. The rabbits' ears sway beside his cheek. He straightens up again and Absalon meets his gaze and nods.

Without any urgency, he lifts Absalon's head and raises the machete.

The lamp above the kitchen table starts spinning the other way.

Peter shakes his head. Kerstin wants to yell at him to close his eyes, but no words will come out.

With great force, the man brings the machete down on the back of Absalon's neck, through his vertebrae.

Blood sprays across the stove.

The dead body collapses onto the floor. Its legs are still twitching, heels hitting the plastic mat.

Peter stares at his father with his mouth gaping open.

Absalon's head is hanging loosely from his body, brightly coloured blood pumps out of his throat in heavy pulses.

Blood is dripping from the handle of the oven.

The man leans over, pulls the knife from Absalon's stomach and shakes the blood from its blade before leaving the kitchen.

55

While Saga is taking a shower at the boxing club, Joona calls Carlos to make sure that the police have gone to Ratjen's home. He tries calling five times before giving up and leaving a voice-mail saying that he's out of prison, and wants to question Absalon Ratjen as soon as possible.

'We might be able to stop the killer before anyone else dies,' he concludes.

Joona and Saga leave the boxing club and walk together towards the car park.

'Verner promised to take care of your release himself,' Saga says.

'If I don't hear anything I have to be back at the prison in three hours.'

They cross the street and walk through the black gates. Suddenly Saga stops.

'My phone just died,' she says, holding it up. 'Look, it's been blocked. I'll have to go to the office and find out what's happened.'

They reach Joona's Volvo, then see two serious-looking men wearing dark suits and earpieces heading in their direction.

'Move away from the car, Bauer,' the younger of the two agents calls out.

Taking her laptop out of her gym bag, Saga does as he says.

'Is this Verner's idea?' she asks.

'Give us the laptop,' the older agent with cropped grey hair says.

'This one?' Saga asks, unable to hold back a grin.

'Yes,' he replies, and holds out his hand.

She tosses the laptop over the roof of the car, and it spins through the air before Joona catches it without changing his expression.

The two agents switch direction and start walking towards him. Melodic folk music is streaming out from an open window at the school. Joona stands still with the computer in his hand. The men walk around the car and approach with don't-mess-with-us expressions.

'That laptop is being sequestered according to paragraph—'

Just before they reach him Joona throws the laptop across the car roof again. Saga catches it with one hand and takes a step back.

'This is just childish,' the older agent says, struggling to suppress an involuntary smile.

They turn around again and start walking towards Saga. The younger one adjusts the cuffs of his sleeves.

'You realise you're going to have to give us the computer,' he says patiently.

'No,' Saga replies.

Before they reach her she drops the thin laptop between the grille of a drain-cover. There's a splash as it hits the water below. The two agents stop and stare at her.

'That was a bit stupid, wasn't it?' the older agent says with a frown.

'You have to come with us, Bauer,' the other one says.

'You should have seen the looks on your faces,' she says, smiling, and heads off along the side of the building with the two agents.

She's much shorter than them, and her leather jacket shimmers damply from her wet hair.

'Do you want me to do anything for you?' Joona calls after her.

'You need to call Verner,' she replies, turning to look at him. 'He promised you wouldn't have to go back to prison.'

Once Saga is in the agents' car and they've driven off, Joona takes out his phone and tries Carlos again, then calls the Security Police Communication Centre.

'Security Police.'

'I want to speak to Verner Sandén,' Joona says.

'He's in a meeting right now.'

'He needs to take this call.'

'Who shall I say is calling?' the woman asks.

'Joona Linna. He knows who I am.'

The line crackles, then Joona hears a recorded voice encouraging him to follow the Security Police on Twitter and Facebook. The voice stops abruptly when the woman comes back.

'He says he doesn't know you,' she says in a reserved voice.

'Tell him—'

'He's in a meeting and can't take any calls right now,' she interrupts, then ends the call before he has time to say anything else.

Even though Joona knows there's no point, he calls the main government building and says that the Prime Minister is expecting a call from him. In a friendly voice, the secretary asks Joona to send an email to the admin department.

'The address is on our website,' he says, then hangs up.

Joona gets in the car and dials Janus Mickelsen's number, but the call doesn't go through and an automated voice informs him that the number is not in use. He tries the other contacts on the borrowed phone, but none of the numbers is in use now.

He looks at his watch.

If he starts driving now, he can be back at Kumla in time. He has no alternative. He can't risk getting an extended prison sentence.

He starts the car and reverses out, then stops to let a woman and guide-dog pass on the pavement before turning right towards Norrtull.

The news on the radio includes a report that says the security services have averted a major attack on Sweden. As usual, no details of the operation are given, including whether the suspected terrorists were arrested. The Security Police's Press Officer has issued a statement praising comprehensive strategic surveillance and a highly successful operation.

56

Joona walks across the wide stretch of tarmac and hears the electronic gates clang shut behind him.

He walks into the shadow of the dirty yellow wall of the prison, stops ten metres from the command centre and makes one last attempt to reach Carlos. A recorded voice informs him that the Chief of Police is busy and will be unavailable all day.

As he is checked back in, it feels like time is slowing down. His hands move sluggishly as they place his watch, wallet, car keys and phone in the blue plastic tray.

A guard with nicotine-stained fingers counts his money, then signs a receipt for the amount.

Joona gets undressed and walks naked through the security scanner. Big bruises have blossomed like thunderclouds across his chest, and the wound from the axe has swollen, making the black stitches stick out.

'I see you had fun out there,' the guard says.

Joona sits down on the worn wooden bench and puts on the colourless prison clothes and trainers.

'It says here that you're going to be put in solitary confinement,' the guard goes on.

'What for? I didn't request isolation,' Joona says, taking the grey sack containing linen and hygiene items.

Another prison guard takes Joona to his new section.

The empty tunnel smells like damp concrete and the only sound is the guard's radio.

Joona tells himself to stop worrying about the killer, he knows he's going to be cut off from the outside world from now on.

He isn't involved in the investigation.

He's no longer a police officer.

They emerge into the isolation unit and he is signed in. He has the rules explained to him, then is led along a silent hallway to his new room, the confined space where he will be spending every hour of the day without any contact with the other inmates.

When the door of the isolation cell slams shut behind him, he goes over to the heavily barred window and stares out at the yellow wall.

'Olen väsynyt tähan hotelliin,' Joona says to himself in Finnish.

He puts the grey sack on the bunk and thinks about the fact that the killer had rabbits' ears tied around his head like trophies, or fetishised symbols.

Perhaps hunting and killing rabbits was a form of ritual preparation before the murder.

He's killed William Fock and is planning to kill Absalon Ratjen, Joona thinks, picking two pieces of grit from the floor and putting them on the narrow windowsill.

Two victims.

He leans over and looks more closely: one piece of grit is yellowish quartz, with a pointed end, and the other has a shiny surface, like a fish-scale.

Joona thinks about the recording of the child's voice, and the rhyme about the rabbits going to hell, one after the other.

Ten little rabbits, he says to himself.

Joona looks under the bed, picks up another eight pieces of grit and lines them up on the windowsill beside the others.

The perpetrator is hunting rabbits. He's going to kill all ten of them.

Time doesn't really seem to reach the isolation cell.

People in prison are dying almost imperceptibly.

Joona stands still and watches the light move slowly across

the row of tiny stones. The shadows get longer, turn like the hands of a clock.

Every piece of grit is its own sundial.

The Security Police thought they were hunting terrorists.

A terrorist would have been a hell of a lot easier than an elite soldier who's cracked, he thinks.

A spree killer.

A trained terrorist would never leave a witness alive, but for spree killers it's important not to kill the wrong people.

He could have a religious or political motive, just like a terrorist. The biggest difference is that he doesn't answer to anyone but himself.

And that's what makes him so hard to predict.

Joona runs a hand through his unruly hair.

The chrome around the hatch in the door is full of finger-prints. The light-switch is grimy with dirt, and there are pale lumps of chewing tobacco stuck to the ceiling.

It doesn't really make any difference if the police are hunting a serial killer, a rampage killer or a spree killer. The decisive factor is the way that their motivation and behaviour fit together.

A particular background can nudge someone in a particular direction, which leads to a particular modus operandi.

A 'spree killer' is 'a person who commits two or more murders without any cooling-off period', according to the FBI.

No killer is going to fit any definition perfectly, but some of the pieces of the puzzle can become easier to slot into place with the right knowledge.

A mass murderer commits his killings in one place, whereas a spree killer moves around.

A serial killer often sexualises his murders, whereas a spree killer rationalises his.

The gap between killings is rarely longer than seven days.

Joona looks at the grains of grit on the windowsill.

Ten little rabbits.

The police are dealing with a killer harbouring a sort of rage that in certain circumstances makes him crack and start killing the people he holds responsible.

He's either selecting his victims very precisely, or is targeting a specific group, killing as many members of it as possible.

What initially tends to look coincidental usually turns out to be the exact opposite.

Joona looks at the grains of grit in the window, then walks impatiently across the floor, over to the door, then back to the window, eight paces in total.

If this killer is picking his targets carefully, and if he fits the definition of a spree killer, then there's still something that doesn't make sense, he thinks.

There's a gap in the logic.

Without doubt, they're dealing with an intelligent murderer: he cut a hole in the glass door of the Foreign Minister's home to evade the alarms, he knew where the cameras were, and left no evidence behind.

And the countdown in the rabbit rhyme suggests that he's already decided who's going to die.

He's planned ten murders – and starts with the Foreign Minister.

Why does he do that?

That's where the problem is.

It doesn't make sense.

The killer must have realised that the police would devote a huge amount of resources to their hunt for him. He must have realised that his plan would become a great deal harder to carry out if he started with that murder.

The spree killer starts with the Foreign Minister, Joona thinks. And plans to move on to a high-school teacher in Skövde.

The Foreign Minister and the teacher, he thinks.

Very carefully, Joona touches the first two grains of grit, then puts his finger on the third, and suddenly knows the answer to the riddle.

'The funeral,' he whispers, then walks over to the door and bangs on it.

That's why he killed the Foreign Minister first. His funeral is a trap. One of the people on the killer's list is an even harder target than William Fock.

The murderer knows that it will take a funeral of this calibre to lure his next target into the open.

'Hello! Come here!' Joona calls, knocking on the steel door. 'Hello!'

The spyhole goes dark and Joona moves away. The rectangular hatch opens and he sees the bearded guard's face through the thick glass.

'What's going on?' the guard asks.

'I need to make a phone call,' Joona says.

'This is the isolation unit, and that means—'

'I know,' Joona interrupts. 'But I don't want to be here, I want to get back to D-wing, I haven't asked to be isolated.'

'No, but the management committee thought you needed protection.'

'Protection? What happened?'

'This is none of my business,' the man says, lowering his voice. 'But Marko's dead . . . I'm sorry. I understand that you were friends.'

'How could he . . .?'

Joona falls silent, thinking of how Marko said he'd take the blame for the fight in the yard so that Joona wouldn't lose his leave. The last Joona saw of his Finnish friend was when the guards knocked him out and cuffed his hands.

'The Brotherhood?' Joona asks.

'That's being investigated.'

Joona takes a step closer, but stops and holds up his hands when he sees the fear in the man's face.

'Listen to me, it's extremely important that I make a phone call right now,' Joona says, trying to sound composed.

'Isolated status is reconsidered every ten days.'

'You know I'm entitled to call my lawyer whenever—'

The guard slams the hatch shut and locks it. Joona goes over to the door and slaps his hand over the spyhole just as it turns dark. He hears a thud on the other side of the door, and realises that the bearded man has stumbled back and hit the wall behind him.

'More people are going to die!' Joona shouts, hitting the door. 'You can't do this! I need to make that call!'

Joona takes aim and kicks the door so hard that the walls shake. He kicks again, and sees a thin trickle of cement dust fall to the floor from the side holding the hinges.

He picks up the chair with both hands and smashes it against the window as hard as he can. One leg snaps as it hits the bars and clatters onto the desk. He does it again, then lets the chair fall to the floor and sits down on the bunk with his hands over his face.

57

The evening light slants in through the windows of the orangery, settling in stripes on the kitchen floor.

The strips of potato start to quiver as Rex lowers the cage into the hot olive oil.

DJ is standing by the island prepping the dill.

'I'm a suspect,' Rex says as he watches the fries slowly colour.

'If you were, you'd be lying strapped to a bench with a wet towel over your face,' DJ jokes.

'Really, though,' Rex says. 'Why else would the Security Police come here if they hadn't identified me on the security-camera footage?'

'Because you were the Foreign Minister's friend.'

'I think he was murdered.'

'Then I can give you an alibi,' DJ smiles, and scrapes the dill into the bowl of shrimp.

'But . . . it would be a scandal.'

'It can't be,' DJ says. 'Even if the recordings were made public . . . You have no idea what a response we got to your television interview. Everyone loves the idea of you two playing pranks on each other.'

'I'm so bad at lying,' Rex mutters, lifting the potatoes from the oil.

'We'll go to the funeral tomorrow, and then we're in the clear,' DJ says, rinsing the heavy knife.

'Yes,' Rex sighs, noticing that DJ has somehow ended up with dill in his blond beard.

'We've got the situation under control. It's fine. The only thing that bothers me is that damn fight,' DJ says.

'I know.'

'Rex, I'm so sorry I came here. I panicked.'

'Don't worry about it,' Rex says.

'Surely we'd know if the man had died?'

'Well, you don't know for sure that he . . .'

'I've been through all the news bulletins, everything.'

'What did he want from you?'

'I don't feel like talking about it,' DJ says, shaking his head.

'What is it?'

'No, it's nothing,' DJ whispers, and turns away.

'You need to talk to me,' Rex says to DJ's back.

'I will,' he replies, and takes several deep breaths. Sammy comes into the kitchen without a shirt on.

'DJ?' Rex says.

'Later,' he says quietly.

'What are you two whispering about?' Sammy asks with a smile.

'Lots of secrets,' Rex says with a wink.

Sammy goes over to the French balcony, opens the door slightly and lights a cigarette.

'Are you still thinking of going to that party out in Nykvarn?'

'Yes,' Sammy nods, clicking to make his lighter produce a transparent flame.

'As long as you're home in time for the funeral.'

Sammy takes a deep drag, making the cigarette crackle, then exhales the smoke through the gap in the door before looking at Rex.

'I'd come home tonight but there are no buses after nine o'clock,' he says.

'Get a taxi,' Rex suggests. 'I'll pay.'

Sammy inhales deeply again, then scratches his cheek with his thumb.

'You can't get a taxi out there in the middle of the night . . . it's not exactly Café Opera.'

'Do you want me to pick you up?'

'How?'

'Don't forget you've got the award ceremony tonight,' DJ says, setting the table.

'Aren't you supposed to be staying at Lyra's tonight?'

'Yes,' DJ says.

'Can I borrow your car, then?'

'Of course,' DJ says, setting out cutlery.

'Then I'll pick you up from Nykvarn, Sammy.'

'Sure?' Sammy asks with a smile, stubbing his cigarette out on the balcony railing.

'Give me an address and a time – preferably not too late. I'm an old man these days . . .'

'Is one o'clock too late? Or we can say earlier, something like—'

'One o'clock's fine,' Rex replies. 'That'll give me time to pick up the award and get rid of it.'

'Thanks, Dad.'

'Can I talk to you?' DJ says, leading Rex out into the orangery.

'What is it?'

DJ's face is calm, but his movements are restrained and nervous.

'Borrowing the car might not be such a great idea,' he says. 'I sat in it with blood all over my clothes, and I—'

'But you cleaned it,' Rex interrupts.

'I know . . . it must be the cleanest car in Sweden, but still, you never know . . . We've all seen *CSI*. They could show up with their special lights and find DNA.'

'I don't think the Swedish police would call in CSI,' Rex laughs.

'But what if he died?' DJ whispers. 'I can't stop thinking about it. I don't understand how it could have come to this.'

Sammy appears in the doorway.

'Now you're whispering again,' he says sternly.

58

A red carpet lined with burning torches leads the way to the glazed atrium of Café Opera. Rex is welcomed by a woman with a blonde plait who leads him to a backdrop made up of ads for the biggest sponsors.

The evening's event is to present Rex with an award that he thinks he should have been given a long time ago. So much time has passed that he started to say he didn't want it, that he wouldn't accept the award even if they baked it inside a cake.

When he turned down the invitation to attend this time, he received a phone call from the organiser saying that a little bird had whispered the name of this year's recipient to her.

Among the throng of people between the buffet table and champagne bars, the noise level is deafeningly high.

Rex makes his excuses and pushes his way through to the bar, where he asks for a bottle of mineral water. The music is turned down and the lights change.

A tall woman from the industry magazine *Restaurant World* gets up on the stage and walks into the spotlight.

Even though Rex knows he's going to get the award, his heart starts beating harder and he can't help running his hand through his hair.

When the woman raises the microphone to her mouth, silence spreads around the room.

'For the twenty-fourth year in a row, we've reached the point where we celebrate the achievements of the Chef of Chefs,' she says, breathing so loudly that the speaker system roars. 'One hundred and nineteen of the finest chefs in Sweden have voted, and we have a winner . . .'

While she is talking Rex finds himself thinking of one birthday when Sammy hid under the kitchen table and refused to come out and open his presents. Veronica explained later that he had been so excited that his dad was going to be there that it had all become too much for him.

The audience laughs politely when the woman on stage makes a joke.

Mathias Dahlgren, who has won several times before, is sitting with his eyes closed and a tense expression on his face.

Rex feels his hand shaking as he drinks the last of the mineral water and puts the glass down on the counter.

The woman on stage breaks the seal on the envelope. Crumbs of red wax fall to the floor as she unfolds the paper, holds it up to the light and then looks up at the audience.

'And this year's Chef of Chefs is . . . Rex Müller!'

Applause and cheering break out. People turn to look at Rex. He heads towards the stage, stopping briefly to shake Mathias's hand. He stumbles slightly on the steps, but makes it up onto the stage.

The tall woman from *Restaurant World* hugs him hard and hands him the microphone and a framed diploma.

He tugs at the T-shirt under his jacket to stop his stomach from showing too much. Camera flashes detonate in the darkness.

'Can you hear me OK? Good . . . This is a huge surprise,' Rex says. 'Because I really don't know anything about food, I just like trying things out – at least that's what my professor at catering college in Umeå told me . . .'

'He was right!' his friend from Operakällaren calls out.

'And when I was working at Le Clos des Cimes, head chef Régis Marcon came rushing in,' Rex goes on with a smile, and attempts a French accent: *'Your services might be asked for at McDonald's . . . somewhere outside the borders of France.'*

258

The audience applauds.

'I love him,' Rex laughs. 'But you can understand why this award comes as such a surprise . . . I would like to thank all my very dear colleagues, and promise that next year I'll vote for you, not just myself.'

He holds up the diploma and starts to head towards the steps, but stops and raises the microphone again in the midst of the applause:

'I'd just like to say . . . I wish my son Sammy could have been here this evening, so he could have heard me tell everyone how proud I am of him for being the person he is.'

There's scattered applause as Rex hands the microphone back to the woman and leaves the stage. People make way for him and pat him on the back as he passes.

Rex makes his way to the exit, apologising and thanking people for their congratulations, shaking hands with people he doesn't know and moving on.

It's cool outside, and the gentle rain forms puddles. He looks at the row of limousines, thinks that he ought to go home, but starts walking towards Gamla stan instead.

Halfway across Strömbron he launches the diploma over the railing, watches it sail across the fast-flowing water, and just has time to worry about it striking one of the swans below before it hits the surface and disappears into the swirling darkness.

Rex doesn't know how long he walks through the glistening alleyways before he reaches a bar with a row of coloured lanterns outside. It looks like a small merry-go-round among the dark buildings that surrond it. He stops outside and reaches for the door-handle. He hesitates for a moment, then goes inside.

The bar is warm and softly lit. Rex takes a seat, says hello to the barman and reaches for the wine-list.

'Congratulations, Rex,' he says when he catches sight of himself in the mirror behind the bottles.

'Congratulations,' a woman sitting a short distance away says, raising her beer-glass in a toast.

'Thanks,' he replies, putting on his reading glasses.

'I follow you on Instagram,' she explains, and moves to the stool next to his.

Rex nods and realises that DJ has posted something about the award. He leans towards the barman and hears himself order a bottle of 2013 Clos Saint-Jacques.

'Two glasses, please.'

He tucks his glasses away in his pocket and looks at the woman, who unbuttons her waist-length fake-fur coat. She's a lot younger than him. Her dark hair is curly from the rain, and she has smiling eyes.

Rex tastes the wine, then fills their glasses and pushes one across to her. She puts her phone down beside the glass and looks him in the eye.

'Cheers,' he says to the young woman, and drinks.

He feels the taste in his mouth, then the warmth of the alcohol spreading out from his stomach, and drinks some more. It feels good, not dangerous at all, he thinks as he refills his glass. He got the damn award, and he never really wanted to stop drinking anyway.

'You're too quick for me,' the woman laughs, sipping her wine slowly.

'Life's a party,' Rex mumbles, and takes a large mouthful.

She lowers her eyes and he looks at her pretty face, quivering eyelashes, her mouth and the tip of her chin.

By the time the bottle is finished Rex knows that her name is Edith. She's more than twenty years younger than him, and she works as a freelance journalist for one of the big news agencies.

She laughs when Rex tells her about his enforced AA meetings, the living dead around the table who can only think about one thing as they confess their sins.

'Are you supposed to be sitting here?' she asks seriously.

'I'm a rebel.'

They've finished the second bottle, and Rex has just told her that his grown-up son does all he can to avoid him, and is out every night.

'Maybe he's a rebel too,' she suggests.

'He's just being smart,' Rex replies, picking up her beer-glass.

'What do you mean?'

'I need to go home and sleep,' he mumbles.

'It's only eleven o'clock,' Edith says, licking the tiny red-wine stains from the corners of her mouth.

It's raining hard as he calls for a taxi and stands by the window, looking out into the alleyway.

'Are you going to stay?' Rex asks when the taxi appears outside.

'I'll take the bus,' Edith says.

'Why not come along, if we're going in the same direction?'

'I live in Solna, so . . .'

'Well, then you'll practically be home if you come with me,' he declares.

'OK, thanks,' she says, and follows him out.

Inside the taxi some sort of slow cabaret music is playing. Edith sits with her hands in her lap, a little smile on her lips. She is gazing out through the windshield over the taxi driver's shoulder.

Rex leans back and thinks how pathetic he is, studying his son's face and tone of voice for signs that Sammy has started to like him.

They're never going to be close, it's far too late for that.

The car turns into Luntmakar Street, slows down and comes gently to a halt.

'Thanks for this evening,' Rex says, undoing the safety belt. 'Time for my beauty sleep now.'

'You promise?' Edith asks.

'Absolutely,' he says, pulling his wallet from the inside pocket of his jacket.

'I thought you said you were a rebel,' she smiles.

'An old rebel,' he corrects in a tired voice.

Rex leans forward to use the card reader between the seats. Edith moves slightly to make room for him, but he is still struck by the warm scent of her body.

'Shall I come up with you and make sure you get to bed OK?' she asks.

59

Rex leads Edith through the flat and out to the orangery beside the roof deck. The pale leaves of the olive trees press against the glass roof and the tendrils of the sugar-snap peas have twined around the little marble table.

Edith looks out across the city for a while before sitting down on one of the sheepskin armchairs among all the plants. Rex pours her a glass of red wine, and a large single malt whisky for himself.

He sits down on the other armchair, enjoying the relaxation offered by the alcohol and the knowledge that he can sleep in tomorrow. The Foreign Minister's funeral isn't until later in the day, so he can safely allow himself a little more to drink.

'In this country you end up with a diagnosis the minute you reveal yourself to be the slightest bit human,' he says, then drinks some whisky. 'You know . . . I'm neither anonymous, nor an alcoholic. I only go to those meetings because my boss wants me to.'

'I promise not to say anything,' she smiles.

'What's your boss like?' he asks.

'Åsa Schartau . . . I've worked for her for three years, but she'd fire me in an instant if I ever swore,' Edith admits.

'If you swore? Why?'

'She thinks it sounds coarse. Actually, I don't really know.'

'Well, you can swear now,' he says, refilling his glass.

'No . . .'

'Go on, swear away,' he teases.

'OK, she's a fucking cunt,' Edith says, then blushes hard. 'Sorry, that's unfair.'

'But it felt good, didn't it?' Rex asks.

'It felt unfair.'

'Then it probably was,' he says quietly.

'I like Åsa. She might not have much of a sense of humour, but she's extremely professional.'

Thoughts of Sammy are thundering through Rex's head, and he can no longer hear Edith. He's staring fixedly across at the rooftops.

'I should probably go home now,' Edith says, looking at the time on her phone.

'Do you have time to taste my chocolate mousse before you go?' he asks, filling his glass again.

'That sounds dangerous,' she laughs.

He wobbles slightly when he stands up and leads her into the large kitchen. He takes the mousse out of the fridge, puts the bowl on the white table and hands her a spoon. She leans forward and he finds himself staring at her low-cut top. The lace on her bra has some of her foundation on it, and her breasts push together as she sinks the spoon into the mousse.

Rex puts his reading glasses on, then plays Corelli's *Concerto Grosso* on the speaker system.

He feels giddy as the alcohol courses through his system and the melodic baroque music fills the room. It occurs to him that he'll have to take a taxi to pick Sammy up from his party.

'Since you're a journalist,' he says. 'Have you heard anything about an assault out in Axelsberg?'

'No,' she replies curiously.

'Some drunk who got into a fight,' he says, and realises that he's saying too much.

'Why are you wondering about that?'

'Oh, I don't know . . . a friend of mine saw something, but . . . forget it.'

Rex gets a bottle of Pol Roger from the champagne cooler and sees that it's the exclusive Winston Churchill blend.

'I should go,' Edith mutters.

'Shall I call a taxi?'

He tries to tuck his glasses in his pocket but misses, and he hears them fall to the floor and break.

'I can get the bus from Odenplan. It's not a problem.'

He opens the bottle, tensing as the cork pops, then gets out two glasses for them and starts to pour, waiting for the bubbles to subside before half-filling them. He sees the hesitant look in her eyes.

'I won tonight,' he says.

'Do you want me to stay?'

She strokes his cheek and a tiny frown appears between her pale eyebrows.

'I have a boyfriend,' she whispers, taking the glass.

'I understand.'

They drink and she leans forward to kiss his closed mouth, very softly, then looks at him seriously.

'You don't have to do this,' he says, refilling their glasses.

He tries to see what the time is, but has trouble focusing on his wristwatch.

'I like kissing,' she says quietly.

'Me too.'

He touches her cheek, tucks a strand of hair behind her ear, returns her smile, then leans over and kisses her. She parts her lips and he feels her warm tongue. He caresses her back and buttocks as they kiss. She starts to pull at his belt before they both stop.

'Just so you know, I don't track down celebrities in order to sleep with them.'

'Me neither,' he smiles.

'But I like you.'

'That's where the similarities between us end – I can't pretend to be very fond of myself,' he says, looking away and pouring more champagne.

He drinks as Edith adjusts her clothes, takes her phone out of her bag, dials a number and inserts her earpiece.

'Hi Morris, it's me. I know, sorry, but I haven't been able to call . . . Yes, well, Åsa doesn't seem to think I have a life. That's what I was about to say: I need to be at work early tomorrow, so I'm going to stay over at hers. There's no point getting mad . . . I know, but . . . OK, bye, then. Big kiss.'

They don't look at each other as Edith ends the call. With downcast eyes she slips the phone back into her bag, then raises her glass to her lips with a trembling hand.

Rex picks up the champagne and walks towards the bedroom, swaying and hitting his shoulder on the doorframe. A little cloud of foam spills from the neck of the bottle, dripping down his hand and onto the floor.

Edith has a serious look on her face as she follows him to the bedroom. The dark sky is visible through one of the skylights, and from the foot of the bed you can see the whole of Stockholm, all the way to the white curve of the Globe.

Edith stands beside Rex and strokes his face, tracing the deep scar across the bridge of his nose with one finger.

'Are you drunk?' she asks.

'Not badly,' he says, and hears himself slur his words.

She starts to unbutton her dress and Rex pulls the covers off the bed. The combination of sudden movement and his unexpected intoxication makes him stagger as if he were negotiating the deck of a ship in rough seas.

Edith lays her dress over a chair, turns her back to him and quickly slips her tights off.

With a sigh Rex sits down on the edge of the bed, manages to pull his T-shirt off, and drinks some more champagne straight from the bottle. He knows he's fairly muscular, but far too broad around the waist. A line of hair leads from his chest to his navel.

Edith slips off her pink panties and folds them to hide the pad, then puts them on the chair and lays her bra on top of them. Her bra straps have left red marks across her shoulders, and she's plumper than he had imagined. Her pubic hair is blonde, with an almost tobacco-coloured tint, and her skin is unblemished.

Rex stands up and pushes his trousers and underpants down,

trampling his way out of them, then he turns aside and tugs at his limp penis so it doesn't look so small.

'The men who leave me usually regret it,' she says.

'I believe you.'

'Good,' she mutters, with a stern look on her face.

'My hands are cold,' he whispers as he puts his hands on her hips.

She pushes him back playfully onto the bed, and he lands on his back, shoves an uncomfortable pillow out of the way and closes his weary eyes for a moment. The room spins as if someone were tugging at the sheet beneath him.

Edith's phone starts to ring out in the kitchen, sounding muffled inside her bag. Rex looks at the two champagne glasses on the bedside table, the pink lipstick on one of them, the tiny bubbles clinging to them. He leans his head back and remembers what he said about Sammy at the award ceremony. On the ceiling he discovers two pale circles that must somehow be reflections from the glasses.

He realises he must have nodded off when he feels Edith's unbelievably soft lips close around his penis. She raises her head and looks at him anxiously, then continues.

He sees the bed and his own pale form reflected in the skylight. He can't understand why he ends up in the same situation every time he drinks. It's a script that he sets in motion yet is powerless to prevent.

She crawls up the bed and straddles him, guiding his half-erect cock inside her. She kisses him. He thrusts tentatively so as not to slip out of her. She looks into his eyes and lifts his right hand to one of her breasts. He stiffens inside her and she leans forward and moans into his mouth.

'Your phone rang,' he says groggily.

'I know.'

'Don't you want to know who it was?'

'Don't talk so much,' she smiles.

The gentle waves of her hair are sticking to her forehead. Her lipstick is gone, and her mascara has run beneath her eyes like a black shadow.

She breathes harder and puts her hands on his chest, so that almost her whole weight is resting on him, then leans back and sighs.

Rex caresses her breasts and watches them press together again and again. She's gasping and moving faster. Her thighs start to tremble and she closes her eyes.

'Keep going,' she groans.

He comes without having time to react, ejaculates right inside her. There's no point pulling out now, it's too late, and he just lets it happen, feeling the contractions and the slow comedown.

Edith's cheeks, neck and breasts are flushed. She opens her eyes, flashes him a wide smile, and slowly begins to move her hips again. A shimmering trickle of sweat has run from her armpit down to her hip.

60

Rex wakes up naked in bed, gasping for breath as if he's been underwater. His heart is pounding anxiously. He looks at the time and sees that it's half past two.

Edith is gone.

He must not have noticed her creep out.

With a groan, he sits up and tries to find his phone, but the room is spinning so much that he can't focus. He stands up, head throbbing, and comes very close to falling over. He screws his eyes shut and leans against the wall for a while before he can continue. The phone is under the bed. Odd images swirl around his head as he crouches down and tries to reach it.

His phone says he's missed nine calls from Sammy.

Rex feels a cold shiver of angst.

He tries to call but can't get through. Either his son's phone is switched off, or he's run out of battery.

He sees that Sammy has left three voicemails, and clicks to listen to them. His fingers are shaking.

'Dad, if you feel like coming early that would be great.'

There's a click and the call ends. The next message is from a few hours later, and Sammy sounds considerably more tired this time.

'It's half past one now. Are you on your way?'

After a brief pause his son says in a low voice:

'Nico was mad and ignored me all night, and now he's with some girl and I'm left here with a bunch of idiots.'

Rex hears him sigh to himself.

'I'll be waiting on the side of the road outside the house.'

Rex stands up and listens to the last message. The walls lurch away from him the moment he tries to focus on them.

'I'm going to start walking, Dad. Hope you're OK.'

He pulls on the clothes that are lying on the floor, bangs into a wall and tries to suppress the urge to throw up. He weaves his way out into the hall, finds DJ's car keys on the dresser, pulls on his shoes and jogs downstairs.

When he emerges into the cool air, he walks straight over to some recycling bins and throws up between the green containers.

He shivers as if he has frostbite and throws up again, feeling lumps of the buffet from Café Opera press their way through his throat.

Legs shaking, Rex makes his way to DJ's car. He pulls out Sammy's note and taps the address into the GPS.

Rex drives off towards Nykvarn. His lingering intoxication makes the world spin outside the windshield. His hands shake on the wheel and sweat runs down his back, and he prays silently to himself that nothing bad has happened.

He tries calling Sammy again, but the car lurches and a lorry honks its horn at him.

While he drives, memories from the past evening slowly become clearer: his drinking, Edith's patient coaxing of his faltering erection.

In the early morning light, the city looks like it's rising from the sea: church spires and imposing buildings break the surface, water runs off rooftops, gushes from windows and doors, down streets and squares.

The water runs away, revealing glistening fragments of the night.

Champagne splashing over floors and sheets, her hand on his head as he licked her, her sweating thighs against his cheeks, the floor lamp toppling over and going out.

Somewhere in the middle of it all he started to get dressed

to take a taxi out to Djursholm, before remembering that the Foreign Minister was dead.

He tripped over her bag, picked it back up and saw a knife in there along with her purse and make-up case.

Rex swerves again as an ambulance passes by silently, blue lights flashing.

He shudders and lowers his speed.

After Södertälje the traffic gets thinner and the highway is almost empty.

Rex speeds up again, passes a tranquil lake, and then there's nothing but forest.

He looks at the GPS and sees that the turn-off for Nykvarn is five kilometres away. Then he'll have to make his way to an isolated place called Tubergslund.

He passes a white van with a sheet of cardboard taped across its rear window, turns the indicator on and is about to pull back into the right-hand lane when he sees a thin figure trying to hitchhike on the other side of the highway.

Realising that it's Sammy, Rex reacts instinctively and pulls off onto the gravel at the side of the road, braking so hard that the tyres slide across the uneven surface.

The van driver lets out a long blast of his horn as he drives past.

Rex gets out of the car without closing the door and runs back along the hard shoulder. He waits until a white bus has passed before rushing across the two lanes. He walks down the tall grass divider as a series of cars drive past. He quickly dashes across the other lanes, then starts running after Sammy.

A huge articulated lorry makes the ground shake. The turbulence once it's passed swirls rubbish and dust into the air around him.

He tries to run faster when he sees Sammy up ahead, lit up in the headlights of the lorry as it thunders past. His thin frame turns red for a few seconds in the glow of its rear lights.

'Sammy!' Rex shouts, and stops running, gasping for breath. 'Sammy!'

His son turns around, sees him, but keeps his thumb up as the next car approaches.

Rex hurries on, panting, sweat running down his back.

'Sorry. I'm so sorry, I fell asleep . . .'

'I was relying on you,' his son says, and keeps walking.

'Sammy,' Rex pleads, trying to get him to stop. 'I don't know what to say . . . I don't want to admit it, but the truth is that I'm an alcoholic. It's an illness, and I had a relapse earlier this evening.'

Sammy turns around and looks at him at last. His face is pale and he looks exhausted.

'I'm ashamed,' Rex says. 'I'm so ashamed, but I'm doing my best to deal with it.'

'I know, Dad, and that's really good,' his son replies seriously.

'Did your mum tell you I'm going to AA meetings?'

'Yes.'

'Of course she did,' Rex mutters.

'I assumed you didn't want to talk about it,' Sammy says.

'I just want to say . . . I haven't been taking it seriously, but I will be from now on.'

'Yes.'

'I'm bound to fall off the wagon again, but at least now I'm admitting I've got a problem, and I know it's hurt you . . .'

His voice breaks and hot tears spring to his eyes. Cars rush past, lighting up Sammy's face briefly.

'Can we go home?' he asks, and sees the hesitant look on Sammy's face. 'I don't mean I should drive. We can walk to Södertälje and get a taxi from there.'

They start walking together as a police car passes by on the other side of the highway. Rex turns around and sees it stop right behind DJ's car.

61

Verner Sandén leans back in his chair and looks at Saga, who is standing in front of his large desk.

'I know how the Security Police work,' she says quietly, putting her pistol and ID card on the desk.

'You're not being fired, you're just on leave,' Verner says.

'There's no way—'

'Don't get angry now,' Verner interrupts. 'I can't deal with that.'

'There's no way in hell that I'm going to let a murderer keep killing just because it suits the Security Police,' she concludes.

'That's why we're paying for you to go off to the Canary Islands.'

'I'd rather take a shot in the back of the neck,' she says.

'Now you're just being childish.'

'I can accept the fact that we're saying the Foreign Minister died of natural causes, but I can't let this go. That's out of the question.'

'Janus is in charge of the investigation,' Verner explains.

'He told me he'd been put in charge of the logistics surrounding the funeral.'

'But after that he'll be picking up where you left off,' he says.

'That doesn't exactly scream high priority to me.'

Verner adjusts some papers in front of him, then clasps his hands together.

'There's no need for you to get angry,' he says. 'I think it will do you good to get away for a while, get a bit of distance from—'

'I'm not angry,' she says, taking a step closer to him.

'Saga, I know you're disappointed about the operation at the marina,' he says. 'But the upside is that this has led to us getting an increased budget, and that means we'll be able to fight real terrorists much better.'

'Great.'

'We're already getting requests from other security services to share our experiences.'

'So you're playing with the big boys now,' she says with a smile, as irritable red spots start to appear on her forehead.

'No . . . well, yes, we're at least in the same playing field,' Verner confirms.

'Fine. Then I need to keep working,' she says.

'You had information on your computer that jeopardised the confidentiality of the operation. That's a serious offence against the democratic state.'

'I know what confidentiality is,' Saga snaps. 'But the Foreign Minister is dead – isn't he?'

'He died a natural death,' Verner points out.

'Who's going to find the killer?'

'What killer?' he asks, looking at her without blinking.

'Absalon was sliced open in front of his wife and children by the same—'

'That's very sad news.'

'By the same killer.'

'Janus doesn't think there's any connection between the deaths – which is why we're having to deprioritise the investigation.'

'I have to keep looking,' she says in an agitated voice.

'OK, so keep looking.'

'No damn holiday.'

'Fine . . . but you have to work with Janus.'

'And Joona,' she adds.

'What?'

'You promised Joona an unconditional pardon.'

'No,' he says.

'Don't you dare lie to me,' she says threateningly.

'If you're referring to confidential material, I must remind you that—'

She sweeps her hand across his desk, sending his phone and a stack of reports flying.

'I'll continue the investigation with Joona,' she says.

'Why are we even talking about him?'

'Joona understands killers, I don't know how, but he does. And now you've sent him back to Kumla.'

'You're not to have any contact with Joona Linna, and that's an order—'

Saga knocks a coffee cup and a thick folder to the floor.

'Why are you doing that?' Verner asks.

'You promised Joona, you fucking promised him!' she screams.

'Now you won't get that vacation after all,' he says.

'Fuck the fucking Canaries!' Saga snarls, and marches towards the door.

62

While DJ helps Sammy with his black suit, Rex goes into his bedroom to call Sammy's mother. As the call goes through, he sighs and thinks about everything that happened. The cops towed DJ's car and Sammy and Rex caught a taxi home. Sammy was still asleep when Rex woke up at ten o'clock with a pounding headache. He went up to the kitchen and opened the door of the wine-cooler. He picked the most expensive bottle, a Romanée-Conti from 1996, pulled out the cork, and poured the wine away. He watched the red liquid swirl down the drain before getting the next bottle.

'Hello?'

Veronica sounds stressed. There's a rumbling, rattling sound in the background, and a woman crying wearily.

'It's Rex,' he says, and clears his throat. 'Sorry if this is a bad time . . .'

'What is it?' she asks bluntly. 'What happened?'

'Well, yesterday,' he says, and feels tears prick his eyes. 'I had a drink and . . . I . . .'

'Sammy already called. He said you're getting along fine, that you had a drink yesterday but that it was nothing to worry about, and that everything was good.'

'What?' Rex whispers.

'I'm so happy that Sammy's happy. He hasn't had an easy time of things, you know.'

'Veronica, it's been . . .' he begins, and tries to swallow the lump in his throat. 'It's been good for me to get to know Sammy . . . I hope that's something that we can continue.'

'We can talk later,' she says curtly. 'I've got work to do.'

Rex sits with the phone in his hand. Sammy is much more mature than he thought. He's already called his mother, lying and saying things are fine to make sure she doesn't drop everything and rush home.

Fifteen minutes later Rex is sitting in the back seat with Sammy in a black Uber, listening to DJ tell the driver that they can get out on Regerings Street and walk the last stretch to the church.

The driver tries to turn around, but the side-street is blocked with huge concrete roadblocks and a traffic cop waves them straight on instead.

For security reasons the whole area around St Johannes' Church has been cordoned off.

The guests include members of the Swedish government, the foreign ministers of the Nordic countries, the ambassadors of Germany, France, Spain and Britain. But the main reason for the heavy security is the presence of the acting US Defence Secretary, Teddy Johnson, who was a personal friend of the Foreign Minister's. Because Johnson was involved in the administration's decision to invade Iraq, he's regarded as a high security risk.

'Sammy, I don't know if you noticed, but I got rid of all the wine and spirits in the house.'

'I heard you doing it this morning,' his son says quietly.

'I realise that I can't trust myself,' Rex goes on. 'You know, I despise the alcoholics at those meetings, but I'm no better than any of them. It's hard to admit, but I'm the worst dad in the world, and it serves me right if you hate me.'

The atmosphere is still subdued when they get out of the car and start to walk up David Bagares Street. The three of them are dressed in black suits, white shirts and black ties, but Sammy has tucked a red handkerchief in his breast pocket.

Police officers and security guards have been stationed at strategic positions around the church. Bus routes have been redirected. All the litter bins have been removed, manhole covers welded shut. The airspace above the church has been closed, so that only police and ambulance helicopters are allowed. Neighbouring buildings have been searched, sniffer-dogs have checked the whole of the cordoned-off area.

Blue lights sweep the street as Rex, DJ and Sammy approach the next roadblock. A police van is parked in front of riot barriers, and police officers with automatic pistols hanging by their hips stop them to check their invitations and IDs against the guest list.

'I know not everyone likes me, but this amount of security seems over the top,' Rex jokes.

'We just want to make sure you're safe,' the police officer smiles as he lets them through.

A long line of guests snakes past the graves, up the broad steps leading to the church, to the security check at the church doors.

Rex is following Sammy and DJ through the crowd when a journalist from one of the evening papers stops him and asks for a short interview.

'What did the Foreign Minister mean to you?' the reporter asks, aiming a large microphone at Rex.

'We were old friends,' Rex says, running one hand instinctively through his hair. 'He was a wonderful person . . . a . . .'

The bald-faced lie makes him lose his thread. Suddenly he doesn't know what to say, how to continue the sentence. The journalist looks at him with a neutral expression. The microphone wavers in front of Rex's mouth and he starts to say that he's brought his son to the funeral before stopping himself.

'Sorry,' he says. 'I'm a bit shaken. It's such a loss . . . my thoughts are with his family.'

He excuses himself with a gesture and turns away, then pauses a couple of seconds before moving towards the church to try to find DJ and Sammy in the crowd.

Two bodyguards are following the Prime Minister and his wife up the steps.

A dog starts barking and the security personnel lead one of the guests aside. He's clearly annoyed, speaking strongly accented English as he gesticulates towards his waiting companions.

The noise of a helicopter echoes between the buildings. An elderly man with a walker is being helped into the church.

'Over here!' DJ calls.

Sammy and DJ are waving to him from the line at the foot of the steps. The black eyeliner his son is wearing only accentuates the paleness of his fragile features. Rex pushes his way through to them.

'Where did you go?' DJ asks.

'I was talking to a journalist about my old friend,' Rex replies.

'That's why we're here,' DJ says happily.

'I know, but—'

A woman further up the steps drops her bag. It rolls down and lipstick and other make-up spills out around people's feet. A small mirror shatters as it hits the ground.

Two security guards approach, looking concerned.

On the deck just before the security check Rex is ushered to one side by a reporter from television news. He stands against the red-brick wall with his face suitably composed and talks about his long friendship and all the silly pranks they played on each other.

He walks into the porch, is waved through the security scanner and passes the row of heavily armed guards. By the time he enters the church he can no longer see Sammy and DJ.

Everyone is taking their seats, and sounds echo off the high walls.

Rex walks down the central aisle, but he can't see them anywhere. They must have gone up to the balcony. A man wearing black gloves pushes past him and keeps walking.

The white coffin is lying in the chancel, draped in the Swedish flag.

The bells start to ring and Rex has to quickly squeeze into one of the pews beside an elderly woman. She looks irritated at first, but then she recognises him and hands him an order of service.

A blonde woman with unusually dark eyes meets his gaze, then looks away. She sits with her hands clasped between her thighs for a while before getting up and leaving the church.

The organ starts to play the first hymn and the congregation gets to its feet. Rex turns and tries to find Sammy. The procession slowly moves along the aisle. The children's choir gathers on the steps to the chancel while the priest walks up to the microphone.

More scuffling as everyone sits down again, then the priest starts by saying that they have gathered to say farewell to the Foreign Minister and entrust him into the Lord's hands.

At the front sit the Foreign Minister's family, and one row behind them are the Prime Minister and Teddy Johnson.

Rex sees a sweaty-looking man in front of him tuck his bag under the pew with his feet.

The choir starts to sing and Rex leans back and looks up at the vaulted ceiling, closes his eyes and listens to the high-pitched voices.

He wakes with a start and wipes his mouth when the priest scatters a small amount of dirt on the lid of the coffin and says those unsettling words: 'For you are dust, and to dust you shall return.'

63

The Rabbit Hunter is standing perfectly still, with his eyes downcast, as the lift carries him upward. He is in the northern-most of the two towers that stand on either side of Kungs Street, well outside the area cordoned off by the police.

He wraps the leather strap with the rabbits' ears around his head, ties it at the back, and listens to the whirr of the cables.

He gets off on the fourteenth floor, walks past the milky-white glazed entrance to East Capital and continues up the staircase that winds around the lift-shaft.

The new keys still meet some resistance as he unlocks the door to Scope Capital Advisory Ltd, disables the alarm and walks across the yellow rug covering the granite floor.

There's a vase of tulips on the reception desk, fallen petals curled on its black surface.

The Rabbit Hunter bends down, grabs the corner of the yellow rug and pulls it behind him, past the empty, glass-walled offices.

There are large lunette windows facing all directions – semi-circular frames, like setting suns – and all of Stockholm lies spread out below him.

He doesn't have much time.

He goes into the north-facing conference room, dragging the mat with him over to one of the arched windows.

He smashes the bottom pane of glass with the hilt of his knife, then quickly removes any sharp fragments from the frame using the back of the blade.

Papers blow off a sideboard.

He hurries around the conference table and shoves it across the floor towards the window. It hits the wall, knocking flakes of paint to the floor.

He lifts the rug onto the table, spreads it out and folds it over, then grabs his black duffle bag from the cupboard. He quickly takes out his .300 Win Mag and unfolds it.

He uses an Accuracy International, a repeat-cylinder sniper rifle, the new version with a curved magazine, improved loading chamber and shorter barrel.

It takes him less than twenty seconds to put the weapon together, lie down on his stomach on the folded mat and aim the barrel of the rifle through the window.

Across the rooftops of the buildings along Malmskillnads Street he can see the pale green copper roof of St Johannes' Church, its spire pointing like a dagger towards the sky.

When he was here earlier today, his rangefinder said that the distance to the church door was only three hundred and eighty-nine metres.

He's made a cheek-rest out of hard foam-rubber, which lets his eye rest at exactly the right height in relation to the rifle sight.

The barrel is fitted with a muffler that reduces both the recoil and the flare. No one will be able to hear where the shot has come from. No one will see any flash of light.

The Rabbit Hunter brushes the ears from his face, puts his right eye to the sights, and stares at the gilded letter Omega above the church door, then slowly moves down to the brown-black metal of the door-handle, and thinks back to the dry summer when he was nine years old.

He remembers the excitement he felt as he crept through the abandoned greenhouses. Bleached light poured through the broken, dusty glass. Cautiously he walked out over the yellow grass and raised his little Remington Long Rifle, pressed the butt against his shoulder and rested his forefinger on the mounting.

A dun-coloured rabbit darted and disappeared into the shade of a bush.

He walked across some dirty cardboard lying on the ground, carefully going around a broken wicker chair, and waited thirty seconds. The next time he moved, the rabbit started to run. He followed it with the barrel, moved his finger to the trigger, took aim at the body, just behind the head, and fired. The rabbit jerked and tumbled forward a few times, then lay still.

The door of St Johannes' Church has opened now, and the funeral guests and security personnel are streaming out.

Through the sights he looks at a young girl who has stopped on the second break in the steps. She can't be more than twelve. He slowly moves down her neck. He sees the vein throbbing beneath her thin skin, the friendship necklace that is hanging slightly off-centre.

The priest is standing right outside the door, talking with those who want to exchange a few words. The Prime Minister appears in the doorway with his wife and bodyguards. The Rabbit Hunter moves the sights so that the Prime Minister's right ear is in the middle of the crosshairs.

A flock of pigeons takes off as four black-clad police officers approach the church. The birds' shadows move across the ground towards the steps.

Teddy Johnson emerges between two American bodyguards, then stops to speak to the widow and her children.

In his sights, the Rabbit Hunter can see the peeling skin of Johnson's suntanned scalp through his thinning hair, and the drop of sweat trickling down his cheek. The politician nudges his glasses further up his nose, utters some consoling words, and moves down the steps.

Without losing his line of fire, the Rabbit Hunter picks up his unregistered mobile phone, sends the text message, then puts his finger back on the mounting again.

He watches as Teddy Johnson, who feels the vibration, pulls out his iPhone, raises his glasses and looks at the screen.

Ten little rabbits, all dressed in white,
Tried to get to heaven on the end of a kite.
Kite string got broken, down they all fell,
Instead of going to heaven, they all went to . . .

The Rabbit Hunter knows the wind is so weak that it won't have any effect on the bullet. And the distance is far too short for him to have to take account of the Coriolis effect, the rotation of the earth.

64

The Rabbit Hunter has less than one kilo of resistance in the trigger. It's so weak that it almost isn't there.

First you haven't fired the rifle, then you have.

It comes as no surprise, but the action has no defined edges.

Now he can see black-clad, heavily armed police officers talking into their radios. An Alsatian dog is lying down on one of the gravel paths between the graves, panting.

Teddy Johnson looks around, puts the phone back in his inside pocket and fastens the top button of his jacket.

The thin crosshairs rest gently on the back of his suntanned neck, then move slowly down to the small of his back. The Rabbit Hunter's intention is to hit Teddy Johnson's spinal column just above his pelvis.

A branch from a tree moves across his line of fire and he waits three heartbeats before putting his finger on the trigger.

He squeezes it gently, feels the jolt in his shoulder and sees Teddy Johnson collapse to the ground.

Blood pumps out across the steps.

The bodyguards draw their pistols and try to figure out where the shot came from, and if there's anywhere they can take cover, any safe place in the vicinity.

The Rabbit Hunter breathes calmly as he catches a glimpse

of the shot man's face, its look of terror. He can't feel his lower body at all now, and is gasping for breath.

The bodyguards try to protect him, standing in the way of any further bullets, but they don't know where the sniper is.

The crosshairs move down Johnson's right arm. The trigger squeezes and his hand jerks as it is transformed into a ragged, bloody lump.

The bodyguards drag Teddy Johnson to the other end of the steps, leaving a dark-red stain across the stone.

People are panicking, running around and screaming as they try to get away. The stairs are empty now.

The American politician lies there, contorted with pain and mortal dread.

The Rabbit Hunter will let him live for nineteen minutes.

While he waits he strokes one of the rabbits' ears with his fingers, feeling its thin cartilage move beneath his hand as the soft fur brushes his cheek.

Without losing sight of his target the Rabbit Hunter changes magazines, inserting heavier, soft-tipped ammunition, then he watches Teddy Johnson suffer, his drawn-out death-throes.

The first ambulances are already on their way into Döbelns Street.

The police are trying to organise the hunt for the sniper, but they still have no idea where the shots are coming from. Someone stares at the splatter pattern from the first shot and points in his direction, towards the roof of the nearby fire-station.

Three police helicopters hover above the blocks surrounding the church.

The paramedics have reached Teddy Johnson. They're trying to talk to him, then they lift him onto a stretcher.

The Rabbit Hunter looks at the time again. Four minutes left. He needs to delay the rescue operation.

Calmly he turns the gun towards the steps leading down towards the French School, moving the crosshairs from a frightened man with fat cheeks to a middle-aged woman with a depressing hairstyle and a press badge dangling from her neck.

He only shoots her in the ankle, but the ammunition is so powerful that her foot is torn off and bounces down the steps towards the pavement. The blast sends her tumbling over, and she collapses onto her side.

The ambulances back away and panic-stricken people crouch down as they run away from the woman. An old man falls down and hits his face on the dusty path, but no one stops to help him.

The officers from the Security Police are trying to understand what's going on, trying to save the life of the American politician as they beckon paramedics. Another ambulance turns into Johannes Street.

Breathing calmly, the Rabbit Hunter looks at the time.

Forty seconds left.

Teddy Johnson's face is pale and sweaty. He has an oxygen-mask over his nose and mouth, and his eyes are blinking rapidly in panic.

The paramedics wheel the stretcher along the path towards Johannes Street. The crosshairs follow him, quivering over his ear.

They push the stretcher onto the pavement and the Rabbit Hunter fixes the sights on Teddy Johnson's ear again, squeezes the trigger and feels the jolt from the recoil in his shoulder.

The man's head explodes. Bone and tissue spray across the street. The paramedics go on pushing the stretcher for a few seconds before they stop and stare at the American VIP. The oxygen-mask is dangling from its tube by the side of the stretcher, and there is nothing where his face used to be but a small fragment of the back of his skull.

65

It took Rex three hours to get out of the church. The police ushered the funeral guests out one at a time through a gap in the security barrier, down Döbelns Street. They conducted careful identity checks on everyone, took brief witness statements, and offered information about support groups.

He saw Edith among the reporters who had gathered outside the cordon and tried without success to catch her eye.

No one seemed to know what had happened, and the police were refusing to talk.

The Foreign Minister's immediate family and the most important politicians had been allowed to leave the church before everyone else. Rex was still stuck in the crowd in the central aisle when he heard screaming and people started fleeing back into the church.

Forty minutes later the police came in and announced that they had the situation under control.

The fire department started washing the blood from the broad flight of stairs as tearful people milled around trying to find family members.

Rex managed to call Sammy and DJ and they arranged to meet back at the flat, where they would try to figure out what had happened. There were rumours of a terrorist attack, and the media were reporting a serious incident with an unknown number of casualties.

Rex removes the tray of scones and pours the steaming tea while the other two sit at the kitchen table trying to find out more on the Internet.

'It looks like that American politician was killed,' Sammy says.

'What a mess,' DJ says, setting out the butter and jam next to the cups and saucers.

'This is completely fucking insane,' Rex says.

'I tried to get out the same way we got in,' Sammy says. 'David Bagares Street, but it was closed off.'

'I know,' DJ says. 'I tried the steps next to Drottninghuset.'

'Whereabouts were you sitting?' Rex says, carrying over the plate of scones.

'We both ended up on the balcony.'

'I was right by the aisle,' Rex says.

'We saw you, Dad. You were sitting like this the whole time,' his son says, shutting his eyes and opening his mouth.

'I was enjoying the music,' Rex says feebly.

'So obviously you noticed us trying to flick little rolled-up pieces of paper in your mouth?'

'You did?'

'I'm pretty sure I won,' Sammy smiles, running his hand through his hair in exactly the same way Rex always does.

A plaster is hanging off Sammy's lower arm, and Rex catches a glimpse of a row of cigarette burns.

DJ holds his phone up and Rex looks at the picture of Teddy Johnson's suntanned face, plump frame, and the look of arrogance in his bright blue eyes.

'They're saying that there are no links to any known terrorist organisations,' Sammy says.

'So did they catch the guy?' DJ asks.

'I don't know. It doesn't say . . .'

'What is it with this summer?' Rex says heavily. 'It feels like the whole world is falling apart. Orlando, Munich, Nice . . .'

He falls silent when the doorbell rings, then mutters that he

288

really doesn't want to deal with any reporters right now, and leaves the kitchen. As he goes down the stairs the bell rings again. He reaches the door and opens it.

Outside stands a man with shoulder-length red hair and a sweaty face. He's wearing a tight leather jacket with shoulder pads and a wide belt.

'Hi,' he says, smiling so broadly that the lines around his mouth and eyes scrunch together.

'Hi,' Rex says uncertainly.

'Janus Mickelsen, Security Police,' the man says, holding up his ID. 'Do you have a minute?'

'What's this about?'

'Good question,' he smiles, looking over Rex's shoulder.

'You've already been here.'

'Yes, exactly, that's right, Officer Bauer . . . I'm working with her,' he replies, tossing his hair back from his face.

'OK.'

'So you really liked the Foreign Minister,' the man says with a familiarity in his voice that sends shivers down Rex's spine.

'You mean politically?'

'No.'

'We were old friends,' Rex says guardedly.

'His wife says she's never met you.'

'I clearly didn't make much of an impression,' Rex says, forcing a smile.

Without returning the smile, Janus walks into the hall and shuts the door behind him. He glances around, then looks at Rex intently again.

'Do you know anyone who was . . . less fond of the Foreign Minister than you were?'

'If he had any enemies, you mean?'

Janus nods.

'We talked about old times when we met,' Rex says.

'Happy memories,' Janus mutters, fastening one of the buttons on his fly.

'Yes.'

'We can offer witness protection. I can personally guarantee the very highest level.'

'Why would I need protection?' Rex asks.

'I just mean, if you have information that you don't want to talk about because you're worried something might happen to you,' he explains in a low voice.

'Is there some kind of threat against me?' Rex asks.

'I hope not; I love your stuff on TV,' Janus replies. 'All I'm saying is that I help people who help me.'

'I'm afraid I don't have anything to tell you.'

Janus pretends to be taken aback by this, as if he doubts Rex's words or is at least very surprised by them.

'I'm picking up energies from you. I like them, but they feel a bit hemmed in,' he says, squinting at Rex.

'I'm sorry?'

'I'm joking. I can't help it. Everyone seems to think I look like a hippie.'

'Peace,' Rex says with a wry smile.

'Is that a Chagall?' Janus asks, pointing at a print on the wall. 'Wonderful . . . the falling angel.'

'Yes.'

'You told my colleague you had coffee with the Foreign Minister a couple of weeks ago.'

'Yes.'

'What day was that, exactly?'

'I don't remember,' Rex says.

'But you do remember which café you went to?'

'Vetekatten.'

'Coffee and cake?'

'Yes.'

'That's great. I mean, they ought to remember you: Rex the celebrity chef and Sweden's Foreign Minister sitting there eating cake,' Janus smiles.

'Sorry, but can we do this later . . . we just got back from the funeral, and . . .'

'I was just about to ask about that.'

'OK, but I need to take care of my son. We're pretty shaken . . .'

'Of course, I understand,' Janus says, raising a trembling hand to his mouth. 'Actually, I'd like to talk to him too, when it's convenient.'

'Give me a call and we can arrange a time,' Rex says, opening the door.

'Do you have a car?'

'No.'

'No car,' Janus repeats thoughtfully before disappearing down the stairs.

66

Joona spends the evening exercising in his tiny cell while repeating his Dutch lieutenant's words about courage and fear: 'It's all about the strategic distribution of energy and the importance of concealing your best weapons for as long as you can.'

Joona sleeps fitfully that night and wakes early. He washes his face and starts to work through the case in his head. He examines every detail he can remember, looks at everything from all three hundred and sixty degrees, piece by piece, like the tiny cogs in a clock, and becomes increasingly confident about his theory.

Rain is falling against the window from a solid grey sky. Time passes.

It's already afternoon when two prison guards knock on Joona's door, unlock it and ask him to go with them.

'I need to make a phone call, even though it's probably already too late,' he says.

They lead him through the tunnel without replying. As if repeating the events from a few days earlier, he is led to a meeting he hasn't requested. This time he is shown into one of the smaller rooms beyond the usual visiting-rooms, where inmates usually see their legal representatives.

The guards let him in, then lock the door behind him.

A man is sitting with his head in his hands. The desk divided across the middle by a screen thirty centimetres high. One wall of the room is adorned with a black and white photograph of Paris. The Eiffel Tower has been tinted a golden yellow colour.

'Is Absalon Ratjen dead?' Joona asks.

Carlos Eliasson leans back in his chair and takes a deep breath. His face is in shadow, and there's an anxious darkness in his otherwise friendly eyes.

'I just want you to know that I took you seriously. I sent two response teams.'

'Was he shot?' Joona asks, sitting down across from his former boss.

'Stabbed,' Carlos says in a subdued voice.

'First in the gut. He bled profusely but retained consciousness despite the extreme pain. Then about fifteen minutes later he was dispatched by . . .'

'A machete to the back of his neck,' Carlos whispers in astonishment.

'By a machete to the back of his neck,' Joona nods.

'I don't understand how you could have heard about that. You've been kept in isolation, but . . .'

'And because you hadn't figured out the killer's plan,' Joona goes on, 'you couldn't see that the Foreign Minister was the first victim because the murderer needed a big funeral to lure his next victim into the open.'

Carlos's face turns red, and he stands up and loosens his bowtie.

'The acting US Defence Secretary,' he mumbles.

'Who was right?' Joona asks.

Carlos pulls a handkerchief from his pocket and wipes his head.

'You were right,' he says helplessly.

'And who was wrong?'

'I was. I did what you said, but I still doubted you,' Carlos admits, and sits back down.

'We're facing an intelligent spree killer with top-class military training . . . and he has another seven victims on his list.'

'Seven,' Carlos whispers, staring at Joona.

293

'The killer has a strong personal motive for these murders . . . one that somehow distorts his perception of reality.'

'I've got a proposal,' Carlos says tentatively, and takes out a leather folder.

'I'm listening,' Joona replies gently, just as he did a few days ago when the Prime Minister came to see him.

'This is a signed agreement,' Carlos says, holding up a sheet of paper. 'The remainder of your sentence is being commuted to community service with the police . . . with immediate effect, if you accept the terms.'

Joona merely looks at him.

'And, after the community service, I can guarantee that you'll be reinstated, at your old rank,' Carlos says, tapping the folder.

Joona's expression doesn't change.

'Same pay as before. You can have more if that's important to you.'

'Can I have my old office back?' Joona finally says.

'A lot has changed while you've been in here,' Carlos says, squirming in his seat. 'We're no longer the National Criminal Police, as you know . . . these days we're the NOU, the National Operations Unit. And the National Forensics Centre is the new name for—'

'I want my office back,' Joona interrupts. 'I want my old office, next to Anja.'

'That isn't going to work, not right now, anyway. It's too soon, and it wouldn't work in the building, because after all you *are* a convicted criminal.'

'I see.'

'Don't take it too hard,' Carlos says. 'We've got a great building at Tors Street, number 11 . . . It's not the same, I know, but there's going to be an overnight flat and . . . Well, it's all here in writing. Read it through, then . . .'

'I prefer to trust people,' Joona says without touching the document.

'Is that a yes? You do want to come back, don't you?' Carlos asks.

'This isn't a game for me,' Joona says seriously. 'The risk of another murder increases every day the killer walks free.'

'We can leave right away,' Carlos says, getting up from his chair.

'I need my Colt Combat,' Joona says.

'It's in the car.'

67

Joona has been given access to a four-hundred-square-metre office in a narrow glass and steel building situated on a wedge of land between Tors Street and the shunting yard of the Central Station.

The premises used to belong to Collector Bank, and it looks like they were abandoned in haste. A couple of ergonomic chairs have been left behind, along with a half-dismantled desk, some dusty cables and a scattering of brochures.

The first evening he makes himself a simple pasta dish in the little staff kitchen, pours himself a glass of wine and sits down to eat on one of the office chairs in the unlit conference room. Through the big, dusty windows he has a view of the rusty railway tracks and the trains rolling into the yard.

The news is dominated by the murder of the acting US Secretary of Defence. No arrests have been made. There's talk of it being a disaster for the police, even worse than the murder of Prime Minister Olof Palme back in the eighties. The FBI are sending their own team and exchanges between the two countries have become tense.

The Security Police press officer is sticking to script: all known threats are under continuous strict monitoring, and they are adhering to the very highest international standards.

Joona reads the post-mortem report on Absalon Ratjen, who

was murdered in front of his wife and children. He puts his plate down on a small filing cabinet, and finds himself thinking about the railway tracks, and the merciless junctions.

Once upon a time Joona was married and had a child, and then he became single.

Memories sweep through him: his father, mother, Summa, Lumi, Disa and Valeria.

That night he settles down on a sun-bleached sofa in the reception area. Somewhere in his dreams he hears Summa laughing right next to his ear, and he turns to look at her. She's barefoot, and the sky is burning behind her. She's wearing a plaited crown made of red roots.

At eight o'clock the next morning a delivery from the NOU arrives: computers, printers, photocopiers, and boxes full of the paperwork relating to the investigation.

Now he can get to work.

Joona knows that none of the murders has been carried out by terrorists – it's been a spree killer. He is hunting a killer with a carefully worked-out plan who in all likelihood will kill again soon.

He tapes photographs of the three victims up on a long wall, then draws a complex network of connections to relatives, friends and colleagues. On the opposite wall he draws up a timeline mapping their childhood, education and careers.

In the large conference room he covers the walls with photographs from the murder scenes: overviews, details, sketches, and the in-depth analysis from the post-mortem on Absalon Ratjen's body.

He covers the floor of the hallway leading to the kitchen with the crime scene and medical reports, then lays out the transcripts of interviews with family, friends and workmates.

He spreads printouts of tip-offs from the public across the floor of the office, as well as three emails from a female reporter requesting profiles for both Absalon Ratjen's killer and the sniper in the tower on Kungs Street.

Joona pulls his buzzing phone from his pocket and sees that the call is from the Forensic Department at Karolinska Institute.

'Is this even legal?' Nils 'The Needle' Åhlén's nasal voice asks.

'What?' Joona asks with a smile.

'I mean . . . Are you back in the police again? Are you leading the investigation? Are you authorised to—'

'I think so,' he interrupts.

'You think so?'

'Looks that way right now, anyway,' Joona says.

'Well, I want to remain anonymous when I answer your question,' Nils says, and clears his throat. 'Absalon Ratjen bled for precisely nineteen minutes before he was killed . . . which is exactly the same length of time Teddy Johnson lived between the first and final, fatal shot . . . I'd chalk that up to coincidence if you weren't the one asking.'

'Thanks for your help, Nils.'

'I'm anonymous,' he says pointedly, and ends the call.

Joona turns to the wall with the photographs. From the amount of blood and the splatter pattern in the Foreign Minister's kitchen, he had already estimated that approximately fifteen minutes had passed between the first and last shots.

Now he knows that the precise answer is nineteen minutes.

He's convinced that somewhere there's something that connects the three victims.

That connection is the key that will unlock the case.

There's no way they were picked at random.

There are almost too many links between William Fock and Teddy Johnson, going back to their teenage years at Ludviksberg School, but Ratjen seems utterly divorced from them.

He led an entirely different sort of life.

Nowhere in the wealth of material that's already been gathered is there a single thing linking all three of them.

A newspaper article from the *Orlando Sentinel* includes a picture of the Foreign Minister and Teddy Johnson back when he was Governor of Florida, standing in front of a killer whale as it leaps out of the water.

Ratjen's life was very different.

The lift doors open over in the reception area, then there's a gentle knock on the glass wall of the conference room.

Saga comes in smiling and hands over a salt shaker and a loaf of bread as a housewarming gift.

'You've made it really cosy,' she jokes.

'It's a little bigger than my office at Kumla,' he replies.

Stepping carefully between the sheets of paper on the floor, Saga goes and looks out of the window, then turns back towards Joona again.

'We aren't allowed to have any contact,' she says. 'But at least Verner agreed to let me continue with my investigation . . . I was so delighted, I managed to knock over a stack of papers on his desk . . . and then a report accidentally fell into my bag . . . but I didn't realise that until I got home.'

'What report?'

'The Security Police's file about Salim Ratjen's family,' she says, pulling the report from her bag.

'Wow.'

'You understand that under no circumstances can I forget to take this with me . . . and I certainly can't say that it might be helpful to you if you're still trying to find a link between Absalon Ratjen and the Foreign Minister.'

Joona takes the file and leafs through until he finds the pages about Absalon Ratjen. In the background he hears Saga say she's going to pop down to Lilla Bantorget to get coffee.

'What do you want?' she asks.

He reads about how Absalon Ratjen fled military service, and mutters that he needs to think.

Absalon was seventeen when he came to Sweden, almost three years before Salim did. Joona already knows from the Employment Office's records that Absalon attended language classes and applied for every job that came up, but the Security Police have more information. They found his name in an abandoned investigation into a cleaning company that was suspected of tax offences. He was one of a group of asylum-seekers who were thought to have worked illegally as cleaners, but because they were tricked out of their wages the prosecution had to be abandoned.

Joona goes into a narrow office overlooking Bonniers Konsthall. He's gathered the facts he has about the killer on one side, and the possible parameters on the other. He's also made a list of advanced military training courses around the world that teach the techniques demonstrated by the murderer.

He examines the forensics photographs of the wounds on Absalon Ratjen's body. The knife hasn't yet been identified, but the wide blade had a serrated back, and a very sharp cutting edge.

The fatal blow to the top of his spinal cord was dealt by a machete with a rusty blade.

Joona sits down on the floor to read the rest of the Security Police report.

The threatening email about 'eating your dead heart' was from a colleague in Canada, and concerned an upcoming Lego robot tournament.

The voice message containing the nursery rhyme about rabbits was sent from an unregistered mobile phone that is no longer in use.

Saga returns, and puts a cup of coffee down on the floor next to him.

'Did you find anything?'

Joona leafs past the list of phone numbers, the IP addresses and the timeline. He sips some coffee and reads about Absalon's attempts to get a student loan.

'It looks like one of the children ran a finger through the blood,' Saga says, pointing at the photographs from Absalon's kitchen.

'Yes,' Joona says without looking up.

He scans the list of addresses of the various asylum centres and homes where Absalon lived, comparing them with those of the Foreign Minister and US politician. Both of them were from wealthy families, and when they first left home it was to go to boarding school.

That was roughly the same time Absalon left a communal residence in Huddinge.

A year later his name cropped up in a report to the Environmental Health Board.

Joona feels a shiver run up his spine.

When Absalon was eighteen years old, an advisor at the

Employment Office gave him a chance. The advisor's son worked as a groundskeeper at a boarding school south of Stockholm, but had been having problems with drugs. Absalon was secretly offered half the son's salary if he would take on the grounds-keeper's duties until the advisor's son got back from rehab.

Before the story was uncovered he had been living in the groundskeeper's flat for almost a year, driving without a licence, and handling machinery he wasn't qualified to use.

Joona gets up and goes over to the window, takes his phone out and calls Anja.

He's sure that he's uncovered the link between the three victims.

'I need to know who made a complaint to the Environmental Health Board twenty-two years ago.'

'Do you want to talk about it over dinner?' she says with her mouth too close to the receiver.

'I'd be happy to.'

He hears her humming 'Let's talk about sex' as her fingernails tap on the keyboard of her computer.

'So, what do you want to know?'

'The name of the school and the person who filed the complaint.'

'Simon Lee Olsson . . . headmaster of Ludviksberg School at the time.'

When Joona ends the call Saga drops her cup in the bin and looks him in the eye.

'You found the connection,' she says.

'Absalon did some casual work as a groundskeeper at Ludviksberg School during William and Teddy's senior year.'

'So it's about the school?'

'One way or another.'

Joona goes over to a thirty-year-old school photograph and sees that the two future politicians were not only classmates, but were also on the same rowing team: eight boys dressed in white, with big shoulders and bulging biceps.

'Someone else who went to that school has already cropped up in the investigation,' Saga points out.

'Who?'

'Rex Müller.'

'I recognise the name.'

'Yes, he's a TV chef . . . I know he's hiding something, but he has an alibi for all of the murders,' she replies quickly. 'We spoke to him because he was caught on camera when he was drunk, taking a piss in the Foreign Minister's pool.'

'There's nothing about that in here.'

'Janus has taken over that part.'

'The truth is always etched in the details,' Joona says.

'I know.'

'Why was he pissing in the pool?'

'A stupid provocative prank when he was drunk.'

'First it looks like a stupid prank . . . then another piece of the puzzle falls into place and suddenly Rex Müller ends up the centre of attention,' Joona says.

68

Rex and Sammy are alone in the large kitchen of Smak restaurant. The wide stainless steel counters have been washed and wiped down. Saucepans, sauté pans, ladles, whisks and knives are all hanging on their hooks.

Sammy is wearing a baggy sweater. He's coloured his eyebrows black and is wearing a lot of eyeliner. Rex is wearing a pink rose in his buttonhole, picked from a bouquet that Edith, the pretty journalist, sent him yesterday.

The restaurant will be changing its menu in two weeks, and Rex has been coming in to test each new element of it before the restaurant opens.

Absolute precision under extreme time constraints only works if the prep cooks, line cooks and head chef all do their part perfectly. When the kitchen closes for the night, cooks finally discover the bruises, small burns and cuts that they've suffered during those hours of intense work.

Today Rex is preparing a mushroom consommé with pan-fried rye bread, pickled chanterelles and herb oil; asparagus with béarnaise sauce; and medallion steak from the Säby estate. Just before he left the flat, Sammy asked him out of the blue if he could come along.

While the meat is cooking sous vide, Rex shows Sammy how

to slice the small tarragon leaves and whisk together the egg-yolks, veal stock, mustard and tarragon vinegar.

With a look of concentration, the boy tips an egg-yolk from one half of the shell to the other.

'I didn't know you were interested in cooking,' Rex says weakly. 'I'd have brought you here earlier if I'd known.'

'No worries, Dad.'

Sammy looks up at him shyly through his long, bleached fringe. He's drawn a tear at the corner of his eye with eyeliner.

'Well, you're very good at it,' Rex says. 'I wish . . .'

He trails off, the words catching in his throat, and remembers that it's his own fault he knows next to nothing about his own child.

While Sammy is chopping shallots, Rex makes a consommé of chanterelles, shiitake, celeriac and thyme.

'Some people only filter the stock through layers of cheese-cloth,' he says, looking at his son. 'But I always use egg-white to pick up any impurities.'

'Aren't you supposed to be going away soon?' Sammy asks, putting the knife down.

'I'm meeting a group of investors up in Norrland this weekend . . . just a bit of schmoozing really, to make them feel special.'

'Does that mean you can't let them see that your son is gay?'

'I just assumed . . . if even I'm balking at the idea of a bunch of old men talking shop and hunting reindeer, then I thought that you'd . . .'

Rex mimes throwing up over the stove, sink and his shirt.

'OK, I get the idea,' Sammy smiles.

'But as far as I'm concerned . . .'

He breaks off when he hears the swing-door squeak. He thinks his sous-chef is early, but when the kitchen door opens he sees the beautiful Security Police officer, Saga Bauer, with Janus Mickelsen.

'Hello,' she says, then gestures towards the man by her side. 'This is my colleague, Janus Mickelsen.'

'We've met,' Rex says.

'Old orders from Verner,' Janus explains to Saga.

'This is my son, Sammy,' Rex says.

'Hi,' Sammy says, holding out his hand.

'Are you a chef too?' Saga asks in a friendly voice.

'No, it's . . . I'm nothing,' he says, blushing.

'We'd like to talk to your dad for a few minutes,' Janus says, poking at a lime on the counter.

'Should I go into the restaurant?' Sammy asks.

'You can stay,' Rex says.

'Up to you,' Saga says.

'I'm trying not to have as many secrets,' Rex says.

He gently removes the egg-white from the consommé and lowers the heat.

'I saw you talking about the Foreign Minister on television,' Saga says, leaning against the counter. 'It was good, very touching . . .'

'Thanks, it . . .'

'Even if it was all lies,' she concludes.

'What do you mean?' Rex says.

'You pissed on his deck chairs, and—'

'I know,' he chuckles. 'That was a little over the top, but we—'

'Just be quiet,' she says tiredly.

'That was just our way—'

'Shut up.'

Rex falls silent and looks at her. A tiny muscle below his eye starts to twitch. Sammy can't help smiling as he looks down at the floor.

'You were going to say that it was just part of your friendship,' she says quietly. 'That you shared a wacky sense of humour, played lots of practical jokes . . . but that isn't true. You weren't friends.'

'He was my oldest friend,' Rex tries, even though he realises there's no point.

'I know you haven't seen each other for thirty years.'

'Maybe not regularly,' he replies weakly.

'Not at all. You haven't seen each other at all.'

Rex looks away and sees Janus pick a white cat-hair from the wrist of his leather jacket.

'But you did go to the same boarding school,' Saga says calmly.

'My dad used to run the Handels Bank. We were wealthy, so I should have fitted in very well at Ludviksberg School.'

'But you didn't?'

'I became a cook, not a company director,' Rex replies, lifting the pan from the water-bath.

'What a disappointment,' she smiles.

'I am, actually, in all sorts of ways.'

'Is that what you think?'

'Sometimes . . . sometimes not,' he says honestly, and glances at Sammy. 'I'm a sober alcoholic, but I've had a few relapses. One thing that happens when I'm drunk is that I remember I can't stand our fancy Foreign Minister because . . . well, what the hell, he's dead now. Because he was a bastard when he was alive.'

Janus flicks his hair from his face and smiles, revealing the laughter lines at the corners of his eyes.

69

Rex's relief at finally telling the truth lasts only a matter of seconds before he starts to feel like he's been caught in a trap. He slices the rye bread, but can feel that his hands aren't quite steady, so he carefully puts the knife down on the chopping board. He can't understand what the Security Police want from him.

Maybe they knew about the security-camera footage the whole time?

Did Saga see the blood on the chair when she visited him?

Rex wonders if he should be cautious, whether he should contact a lawyer or just tell them about DJ's fight with the drunk.

'I thought you wanted to talk about Teddy Johnson's murder,' he says after a brief pause.

'Do you know anything about that?' Janus asks.

'No, but I was there when it happened.'

'We already have a lot of witnesses,' Janus says, rubbing one of his ears.

'So what is it you really want to talk about?' Rex asks, clearing his throat.

'I want to know why you called the Foreign Minister a bastard, and why you pissed in his swimming pool,' Saga replies.

'OK,' he whispers.

'Sammy, I want you to know that we don't suspect your dad of any crime,' she says.

'He's only my dad on paper,' Sammy says.

Rex washes his hands and dries them on a napkin.

'When he was younger, our Foreign Minister was – how should I put it? Wille couldn't bear the fact that I always got better grades than him. I mean, obviously he got good grades because his family had helped support the school financially for a hundred years, but that wasn't enough for him . . . When Wille found out I was going out with a girl, he was determined to sleep with her . . . just to wreck our relationship, and to show how powerful he was. So that's what he did.'

'Maybe she wanted to sleep with him?' Saga suggests.

'I'm sure she did, but I was actually in love with her . . . and she didn't mean anything to him.'

'How can you be sure he wasn't madly in love with your girlfriend?' Saga says.

'He said so. He called her horrible things – groupie, fuck-bucket . . .'

'Sounds like a bastard,' she nods.

'I'm very aware that anyone who gets to go to Ludviksberg School is privileged,' Rex goes on. 'But behind the walls, the school was very clearly divided between us nouveau riche kids and the few whose special status had been guaranteed for generations . . . everyone knew there were special rules, scholarships and clubs just for them.'

'Poor Daddy,' Sammy says sarcastically.

'Sammy, I was seventeen years old. It's a sensitive age.'

'I was kidding.'

'I just want to point that out,' he says, then turns back to Saga again. 'Anyway . . . our future Foreign Minister was the chair of a very exclusive club on the school campus. I don't even know what its real name was, but I remember him calling the place where they met "the Rabbit Hole". After Grace got in with the gang that hung out there, I knew I didn't mean anything to her any more. I get that, and of course she didn't know what they were saying behind her back, she saw them as stars, as school celebrities.'

He notices that Saga's face has stiffened slightly, as if something he just said has caught her attention.

'Who else was in this Rabbit Club?' she asks.

'Only they know that. It was all very secret. I really don't care.'

'So you don't know who the other members were?'

'No.'

'This is important,' Saga says, raising her voice.

'Take it easy,' Janus whispers, picking up a wine-glass from the shelf.

'I never got close to them,' Rex replies. 'I have no idea. I'm just trying to explain why I couldn't stand the Foreign Minister.'

'But Grace must know who the members were?' Saga says.

'Of course.'

Janus Mickelsen drops the glass on the floor. It shatters, spraying splinters of glass across the floor.

'Sorry,' Janus says, his pale eyebrows now white with agitation. 'Do you have a dustpan and brush?'

'Don't worry about it,' Rex says.

'Sorry,' Janus repeats, and starts to pick up the biggest pieces of glass.

'Do you know how I can reach Grace?' Saga asks.

'She was from Chicago . . .'

Once Saga and Janus leave, Rex fries some chanterelles and two slices of rye bread in butter, puts them in dishes and pours some of the consommé over them.

He and Sammy stand side by side at the counter and eat.

'It's good,' his son says.

'Take your time, be absolutely honest.'

'I don't know . . . it's just good.'

'I think it might be missing a touch of acidity,' Rex says. 'I might try a squeeze of lime tomorrow.'

'Don't look at me,' Sammy smiles.

Rex can't shake the lingering anxiety from the earlier conversation. Just talking about Grace has made his heart heavy. He remembers that she refused to see him and stopped taking his calls.

'She's amazing,' Sammy says, finishing his food.

'Who?'

'Who,' he laughs.

'Oh, the cop. I know, she's the most beautiful woman I've ever seen . . . with the exception of your mum, obviously.'

'Dad, I can't believe you climbed into the Foreign Minister's yard to piss in his swimming pool,' his son says with a smile.

'I really didn't like him.'

'Obviously.'

Rex puts his dish down on the counter.

'I didn't tell the police everything . . . I just can't get dragged into anything right now.'

'What is it?'

'Oh, nothing . . . I just don't want them to think that I have anything to do with the Foreign Minister's death.'

Sammy raises his eyebrows.

'Why would they think that?'

'Because the truth is that gang at school lured me into the stables one night and beat the shit out of me. I broke several ribs, and they left me with this little reminder,' Rex says, pointing at the deep scar across the bridge of his nose. 'Not that bad, maybe, but you know how it feels when your pride's been hurt . . . I couldn't imagine seeing them every day, pretending nothing had happened . . . so I left the school immediately.'

'It should have been them instead.'

'No chance,' Rex says with a shrug. 'They had all the power, and I had no one on my side . . . The headmaster and the other teachers all protected them.'

'You should tell the police about this,' Sammy says seriously.

'I can't,' Rex replies.

'Come on, Dad, it'll be fine. You're a cook, you're kind. I mean, have you ever done anything, like, really violent in your whole life?'

'It's not that simple,' Rex replies.

Sammy prods the vacuum-packed meat in the water-bath and looks at the temperature and timer.

'The meat's been in for two hours now,' he says.

'OK, get the butter, some sprigs of thyme, one clove of garlic, and . . .'

The sun passes behind a cloud and grey rain falls lazily against the window facing the yard. The electric lighting is bare and uncompromising. Suddenly Rex imagines he can hear something rustling out in the restaurant, like someone walking on plastic wrap.

He walks towards the pass, then stops. He gently nudges the door open and listens.

'What is it?' Sammy asks behind him.

'I don't know.'

Rex goes through the swinging door, into the empty dining room. There's something dreamlike about the restaurant with the rain coursing down the windows, the light rippling on the white linen, cutlery and wine-glasses.

Rex startles when his phone rings in his back pocket. The caller's number is withheld but he still answers. The signal is weak and the line crackles in his ear. Through the big windows he can see cars and people with umbrellas walking in the rain. He is about to end the call when he hears a distant child's voice.

'Ten little rabbits, all dressed in white, tried to get to heaven on the end of a kite . . .'

'I think you've dialled the wrong number,' Rex says, but the child doesn't seem to hear him. He keeps chanting the nursery rhyme.

'Nine little rabbits, all dressed in white, tried to get to heaven on the end of a kite. Kite string got broken, down they all fell. Instead of going to heaven, they all went to . . .'

Rex listens to the rhyme's countdown before the line goes dead.

Through the window he sees a child standing under the bridge fifty metres away. Rex watches him turn his back and walk into the dark car park.

70

The air feels humid and an oily light is hanging over the fields beside Nynäsvägen. Joona passes a lorry carrying a load of dusty rubble.

The acting headmaster at Ludviksberg School refused to hand over any lists of students unless Joona could produce a formal request from either a public prosecutor or the lead detective.

'This is a private boarding school,' the headmaster explained over the phone. 'And we're not covered by the freedom of information legislation.'

The first three victims can be traced back to the school thirty years ago, Joona thinks as he drives towards Ludviksberg School.

It seems highly likely that future victims will share the same connection.

Maybe the killer does too.

The school is the geographic link, Joona thinks.

But somehow everything has to fit together on a deeper level.

He needs to find the algorithm, solve the riddle.

While he drives he listens to a playlist he put together for his daughter, Lumi. Old recordings of Swedish folk music and dance tunes. Fiddles summoning forth the melancholy of summer, the longing of youth and the transformative effect of the bright summer nights.

He thinks about Summa's bridal crown of woven roots, and her smile when she stood on the stool to kiss him.

Joona drives east towards the coast. The narrow road leads him across two bridges and a tunnel.

He's driving across Muskö when Saga calls. The music goes quiet and Joona taps the car's screen and answers.

'I have to talk to you,' she says without any preamble, and Joona hears her kick-start her motorcycle.

'Are you allowed to?'

'No.'

'I'm not allowed to talk to you either.'

Joona considers the irony in the fact that he and Saga are trying to solve a series of murders together even though their official tasks are like night and day: she's supposed to hush everything up; he's supposed to reveal it.

The water is silvery and still, and Joona sees a flock of ducks take flight. Saga is saying that Rex had a girlfriend – Grace Lindstrom – who dumped him for William Fock.

'But here's where it gets interesting,' she says.

'I'm listening,' Joona says as he drives along the edge of a military training area.

'William had some sort of club at the school. It was only for select pupils, I don't know what the point of it was, but the place where they met was called the Rabbit Hole.'

'The Rabbit Hole,' Joona repeats. They're getting close to the answer.

'This is what we're looking for – isn't it?'

'Do you have the names of the members?'

'Only Grace and Wille.'

'No one else?'

'Rex says he doesn't know.'

'But Grace must know,' Joona says.

'Of course, but she seems to live in Chicago . . .'

'I can go,' Joona says.

'No, I've already spoken to Verner, I'm leaving as soon as I get an address.'

'Good.'

Braking gently, he turns into the driveway leading to

Ludviksberg School. The main building looks like an old manor-house, with whitewashed stone walls and a hip roof.

He leaves the car in the visitors' car park and crosses the lawn to the broad flight of stairs. The ground is covered with blue flowers, but deer or rabbits have been eating them. Joona bends over and picks up one of the spoiled flowers.

He passes a group of students wearing navy-blue uniforms and carrying stacks of textbooks in their arms.

In the entrance there's a large colour photograph of the school grounds with arrows and signs. There are four boarding houses for girls and four for boys, as well as a groundskeeper's flat, teachers' homes, stables, sheds, a pump-house, sports facilities and a beach pavilion.

Joona walks through the glass doors to the headmaster's office, shows his ID to the secretary and is shown into a large room with polished oak panels and huge windows overlooking the park. Behind the desk hang framed pictures of members of royalty who have been pupils at the school.

The headmaster is standing in front of a dark leather armchair, a stack of papers in one hand. He's a thin man in his fifties, clean-shaven, with dark-blond hair parted on the side, and a very rigid posture.

Joona goes over and hands him the little blue flower, then pulls out a document in a plastic folder.

'Here's the prosecutor's request.'

'Not necessary,' the headmaster says, without even looking at the document. 'I'm happy to help in any way I can.'

'Where's the student register?'

'Be my guest,' he smiles, making a sweeping gesture towards a built-in bookcase covering one of the walls.

Joona goes over to the library. It contains the bound yearbooks for every year since the school was founded. He traces his way across the spines, back thirty years.

'Can I ask what this is about?' the headmaster says, putting the flower down next to his keyboard before sitting down.

'A preliminary investigation,' Joona says, and pulls out one of the books.

'I appreciate that, but . . . I'd just like to know if it's anything that might reflect badly on the school.'

'I'm trying to stop a spree killer.'

'I don't know what one of those is,' the headmaster says.

Joona pulls out another four yearbooks and puts them on the table.

He starts to leaf through the thirty-year-old photographs, looking at pictures from a lecture by the author William Golding, as well as St Lucia celebrations, tennis tournaments, cricket, dressage, show-jumping.

He looks at graduation pictures of students wearing white caps, school balls with big band music, Sunday dinners with white tablecloths, crystal chandeliers and serving staff.

According to the yearbooks, the boarding school is home to about five hundred and thirty students at any one time. Taking teachers, administrative staff, boarding house staff and other employees into account, there are some six hundred and fifty names in each book.

One picture shows a very young William Fock, the man who would later become Sweden's Foreign Minister, receiving a prize from the headmaster at the time.

Joona slowly packs the five yearbooks into his bag.

'This is a reference library,' the headmaster protests. 'You can't take our yearbooks . . .'

'Tell me about the Rabbit Hole,' Joona says, zipping his bag.

The headmaster's gaze wavers in momentary surprise, and he sets his chin.

'I have to agree with the international media. The Swedish police might want to try a little harder to find Teddy Johnson's murderer. Just a little tip, seeing as you and your colleagues seem to be having trouble finding things to occupy your time.'

'There's a club here at this school,' Joona says.

'I'm not aware of it.'

'Maybe it's secret?'

'Sadly I don't believe that we have any dead poets' societies,' the headmaster says coolly.

'So you don't have any old-fashioned clubs or associations?'

'I've allowed you to get insight into our activities, even if I

315

find it hard to believe that you'll find your killer here, but I won't answer any questions about the private affairs of our students, or any groups they might or might not belong to.'

'Have any members of staff worked here for more than thirty years?'

When the headmaster doesn't answer, Joona walks around the desk and begins to search the computer himself. He opens a set of accounts and finds the employee payroll.

'The stable master,' the headmaster says weakly.

'What's his name?'

'Emil . . . something.'

71

A group of students are smoking down by the stables. One girl is riding in a paddock, and several horses are grazing in a field behind the building. Students can board their horses at the school, fully serviced, while school is in session.

Just as Joona is walking into the stable his phone buzzes with a text message from Saga. She's taking the next direct flight to Chicago to talk to the only known habitué of the Rabbit Hole.

Grace Lindstrom.

Now that Joona is near the stalls, the air is heavy with horse, leather and hay. The stable consists of twenty-six stalls and a heated saddle room.

A thin man in his sixties, wearing a green quilted jacket and wellington boots, is grooming a coffee-brown gelding.

'Emil?' Joona says.

The man stops and the horse snorts. Its ears twitch nervously at the unfamiliar voice.

'He looks very good across the withers and loins,' Joona says.

'That he does,' the man says without turning around.

With shaky hands, he puts the brush down.

Joona walks over to the gelding and pats him on the shoulder. The horse is sensitive and his skin reacts instantly, contracting beneath his hand.

'Bit too twitchy, that's all,' Emil says, turning towards Joona.

'Too eager, maybe.'

'You should see him gallop, he runs like the wind.'

'I was just talking to the headmaster, and he said you might be able to help me,' Joona says, showing his police ID.

'What's happened?'

'I'm in the middle of piecing together a complicated puzzle, and I could use some help with one of the pieces from someone who's worked at the school for a long time.'

'I started as a stable-boy thirty-five years ago,' Emil replies warily.

'Then you'd know about the Rabbit Hole,' Joona says.

'No,' the man says abruptly, then looks towards the low window.

'It's where some sort of club meets,' Joona says.

'I need to get back to work,' Emil says, grabbing a shovel.

'I can see you know what I'm talking about.'

'No.'

'Who used to meet at the Rabbit Hole?'

'How should I know? I was a stable-boy. I'm still only the stable master.'

'But I'm sure you see things, have seen things. Haven't you?'

'I mind my own business,' Emil replies, but he lets go of the shovel as if all the energy has gone out of him.

'Tell me about the Rabbit Hole.'

'I heard it mentioned in the first few years, but . . .'

'Who met there?'

'I have no idea,' he whispers.

'What did they do there?' Joona persists.

'Partied, smoked, drank . . . the usual.'

'How do you know that?'

'Because that's how it looked.'

'Did you attend the parties?'

'Me?' Emil asks with his chin wobbling. 'You can just go to hell.'

The horse picks up on his nervousness and gets anxious, stamping and knocking the sides of the stall, making the bridle swing against the wall.

'You looked up towards the pump-house the first time I mentioned the Rabbit Hole – is that where it is?'

'It's no longer there,' Emil says, breathing out hard.

'But that's where it was?'

'Yes.'

'Show me.'

They go out together, up the gravel track, past the grounds-keeper's flat and over to the pump-house, where they leave the road and head off towards the edge of the forest.

Emil leads Joona to the foundations of an abandoned building covered by weeds and birch saplings. He stops hesitantly in front of a small hole in the ground, picks some strands of long grass and starts pulling them apart.

'Is this the Rabbit Hole?'

'Yes,' Emil replies, blinking away tears.

Huge roots have disturbed some of the foundation, and Joona can see a narrow flight of stairs blocked by earth and stones between some thorny bushes.

'What did this place used to be?'

'I don't know. I'm not welcome up here,' Emil whispers.

'Why did you stay at the school all these years?'

'Where else would I get to be with such fine horses?' the man says, then turns to walk back to the stables.

The overgrown foundation lies fifty metres behind the main residential block of the Haga boarding house.

Joona puts his bag down on the grass, takes out the oldest yearbook and leafs through the pictures again, looking more closely each time the Haga boarding house appears.

He stops at a winter picture of blond children with rosy cheeks having a snowball fight.

Behind them is a beautiful blue pavilion.

Standing precisely here.

The Rabbit Hole wasn't an underground passageway. It wasn't the cellar beneath an old, abandoned building.

Thirty years ago there was a beautiful building right here.

In the photograph the pavilion's shutters are closed. Gold lettering above the doors spells out 'Bellando vincere' as a sort of motto.

Joona kicks the ground hard at the edge of the overgrown foundation, walks around, pulls up some of the weeds with their roots, leans over and picks up a piece of charred wood. He turns it over, and sees that it's part of an arched window.

He returns to the main school building and marches straight in to see the headmaster again, closely followed by the secretary.

'Ann-Marie,' the headmaster says tiredly. 'Can you explain visiting hours to the detective, and—'

'If you lie to me again, I'll arrest you, and drag you to Kronoberg Prison,' Joona says to the headmaster.

'I'm calling our lawyers,' the man gasps, reaching for his phone.

Joona puts the blackened piece of wood on the desk. Soil and tiny crumbs of charcoal scatter across the polished desktop.

'Tell me about the blue building that burned down.'

'The Crusebjörn Pavilion,' the headmaster says quietly.

'What did the students call it?'

The headmaster lets go of the phone, runs his hand across his forehead and whispers something to himself.

'What did you say?' Joona asks sharply.

'The Rabbit Hole.'

'Presumably the school's management committee was in charge of the maintenance of the pavilion?' Joona says.

'Yes,' the headmaster admits.

Large sweat-stains are spreading out under the arms of his white shirt.

'But the committee allowed the pavilion to be used by some sort of club?'

'Power isn't always visible,' the headmaster says dully. 'The headmaster and school board don't always make the decisions.'

'Who belonged to the club?'

'I don't know. That's way above my level. I'd never be granted access.'

'Why did it burn down?'

'It was arson . . . the police weren't involved, but one student was expelled.'

'Give me a name,' Joona says, looking at him with cold grey eyes.

'I can't,' the headmaster says. 'You don't understand. I'll lose my job.'

'It'll be worth it,' Joona says.

The headmaster looks down for a few seconds, his hands trembling on the desk. Eventually he says quietly:

'Oscar von Creutz . . . He was the one who burned down the pavilion.'

72

Joona runs through the main entrance to Danderyd Hospital. The Rabbit Hole is a black hole, pulling everything else towards it.

Right now there are two threads to follow.

Two names.

One is a member, the other is the man who burned the place down.

Saga has managed to track Grace down, and Joona has asked Anja to help him find Oscar.

Ludviksberg School had no records of who had access to the Rabbit Hole.

School management was used to handling certain families' privileges with discretion.

The members themselves were the only people who knew who belonged to the club.

William Fock had flaunted his membership to prove how powerful he was to Rex.

Anja is a short distance away, waiting by the lifts. She's wearing a bright yellow dress that clings to her full figure.

Her strong shoulders betray the fact that she was once an Olympic medallist in swimming. Now she works for the NOU, and before Joona was sent to prison, she was his closest colleague.

The lift dings just as Joona reaches Anja. They walk in at the same time, look at each other and smile.

'Fifth floor?' Joona asks, and presses the button.

'You're supposed to spend a few more years in Kumla,' Anja mumbles, squinting at him.

'Maybe.'

'Seems to have done you good though. You look more handsome than ever,' she says, hugging him tight.

'I've missed you,' he whispers to her head.

'Liar,' she smiles.

They stand there embracing until the doors open on the fifth floor. Anja reluctantly lets go of him and dabs at the corners of her eyes as they head down the hallway.

'How's Gustav doing?'

'He's going to be OK,' she says, trying to make her voice sound bright.

They pass a glass wall leading to an unmanned reception desk and a waiting room.

Gustav's room is further away, but before they reach it Anja stops.

'I'll go and get some coffee, I think he'd like to speak to you alone,' she says in a subdued voice.

'OK,' Joona replies.

'Be nice to him,' she says, then disappears.

Joona knocks on the door and goes in. The room is small, with cream walls and a narrow pale wooden wardrobe.

There's a large bouquet of flowers in front of the window.

Gustav is lying in a hospital bed with a blanket over his legs. He's hooked up to an IV. The bandage from the amputation covers his whole chest.

'How are you doing?' Joona asks, sitting down on the chair beside the bed.

'I'm fine,' Gustav says, looking at Joona.

He gestures towards the stump at his shoulder.

'I'm a little high all the time, because they're pumping me full of drugs, and it seems like all I do is sleep,' he says, almost managing to squeeze out a smile.

'Did Anja bring the flowers?'

'They're actually from Janus. I hope he's not in trouble, because he's OK. He's a good leader, a good marksman, and, like you said, he can't let anything go.'

His usually amiable face is clenched and pale, his lips almost white.

'Joona, I've thought a lot about what I'd say to you when I got the chance . . . and the only thing I keep coming back to is that I'm ashamed . . . and I'm so incredibly sorry. I know I'm not supposed to talk about this, but I have to tell you that the operation was a disaster. I still can't understand it. I lost Sonny and Jamal. I lost the helicopter. I lost Markus, and . . .'

His eyes glaze over and he shakes his head and whispers: 'Sorry.'

'You can't predict how anything will unfold, no one can,' Joona says quietly. 'You do your best, but sometimes things still go wrong. You paid a high price.'

'I was lucky,' Gustav says. 'But the others . . .'

His words fade away and he closes his eyes, seeming to disappear into thought. Slowly his head slips towards his chest, and Joona realises that he's asleep.

When Joona comes out into the hallway, Anja is standing outside the door eating cinnamon buns. He hands her the bag containing the yearbooks from Ludviksberg School and asks her to check all the names against the databases to see if any of them have a criminal record, are missing, or have died.

'I'm just going to say hi to Gustav,' she says.

'Did you find out anything about Oscar von Creutz?'

'I should get a response any minute now,' she says, offering him the bag of buns.

When he puts his hand in she grabs it, and laughs a bit too loudly when he tries to pull free. Then her phone buzzes.

'OK,' she says. 'Oscar von Creutz's registered address is on Österlång Street . . . and he also has a house on the French Riviera. He's single, but he's seeing someone, a Caroline Hamilton, who in my opinion is far too young for him. Neither of them are answering their phones.'

The beautiful nineteenth-century building reaches high above the buildings around it.

Oscar von Creutz hasn't been at work all day, and his girlfriend Caroline hasn't showed up for any of her classes at school.

Joona rings the doorbell for the penthouse flat, waits a few seconds, then looks through the letterbox and sees post on the hall floor.

He tugs the handle and can feel that the door hasn't been double-locked.

The sun is shining through the stained glass window in the stairwell.

Joona inserts his lock-pick, nudges it carefully, unlocking cylinder after cylinder, then twists it and hears the mechanism click.

The door to Oscar von Creutz's flat swings open and letters and advertisements spill out onto the landing.

'Police!' Joona shouts. 'I'm coming in!'

Drawing his pistol, he moves inside the large hallway, which is lined with built-in cupboards. Heaps of clothes have fallen off hangers and are lying strewn across shoes and boots.

A plastic bag with shampoo, conditioner and soap has fallen over, and a pool of pink liquid has spread out across the textured limestone floor.

Joona walks cautiously into a living room. The still air is heavy and stagnant, and yellow light is falling onto the shimmering floor through the windows.

The top of the coffee table has been smashed, and tiny shards of glass litter the floor.

The lights are on upstairs. Their glow illuminates the curtain behind the glass wall.

Joona stands still for a few seconds, then slips into the hallway leading to a kitchen lined with family portraits.

There's white powder on the floor, and footprints leading to a closed door.

'Police!' Joona shouts once more.

He gently reaches out his hand and pushes the door open. Silence. He can see part of a bathroom.

He quickly goes inside, aiming his pistol into the gloom, sweeping the barrel across the walls and into the corners.

Lipstick, face cream, and eyeshadow are all scattered across the bathroom floor and sink.

He goes over to the bath and sees that it was full of water. The level has sunk, leaving a dirty ring.

Beneath a bathroom cabinet with an open mirrored door lie some pill bottles and plasters. He can see the hallway behind him in the mirror, and when he moves to one side he sees that someone has dragged their hand across the wall in the direction of the kitchen.

He thinks about the rabbits trying to get to heaven on a kite.

The floor creaks under his weight.

Joona reaches the kitchen, steps over a torn packet of flour, and edges along the wall to the right, aiming his pistol at the dining room.

A tub of Kalix whitefish roe, some free-range bacon and a bag of stir-fry vegetables stand in the middle of the island, lit up by sunlight.

The kitchen counter is lined with jars and cereal packets. Most of the wall-mounted cabinets are open.

Joona walks over to the heavy dining room furniture – a dark-wood table and eighteen chairs – and stops at one end.

Beside a half-full coffee cup and a plate with an untouched slice of toast lies the morning paper. The news of Teddy Johnson's murder outside St Johannes' Church is all over the front page.

Joona goes upstairs and searches the second bathroom and both bedrooms. In one he finds a half-full suitcase on the unmade double bed. In the other room someone has left underwear and sock drawers open.

Oscar didn't find out about Teddy Johnson's death until he sat down to breakfast with the morning paper.

The murder sent him into a blind panic. He started to pack, throwing clothes around, and ended up arguing with his girl-friend.

Oscar was scared.

And he didn't think there was any time to lose.

Maybe he and his girlfriend left everything behind, maybe they managed to take a few things with them.

The food laid out in the kitchen suggests they were planning to take supplies with them, so they weren't on their way to the house in France. They were going to a hiding place.

73

When Saga wakes up, the plane is over Lake Michigan. From three thousand metres up the water looks perfectly smooth and shimmers metallically.

She wipes her mouth and thinks about the short text message she received from Joona, telling her that the Rabbit Hole was a building that burned down during Rex's senior year.

The fire wasn't reported to the police, but did have one very unusual repercussion: Oscar von Creutz, a student from a prominent family, was expelled.

Joona went to Oscar's home, but says Oscar appears to have fled in panic.

The cabin crew repeat their request for passengers to prepare for landing.

Saga pulls her paperback from the seat pocket, tucks it in her bag, then leans back and waits for the plane to land.

Her trip is covered by an agreement between the Security Police and the FBI after the murder of the acting US Defence Secretary in Sweden, and falls within the remit of the Counter Terrorism Group and international legal cooperation.

Even if Saga doesn't think the murder was committed by a terrorist, she caught the first flight to Chicago.

Now that Joona has convinced her that they're trying to find a spree killer, there's no time to lose. The killer's clearly entered a very active phase, where there are no quiet periods, no rest. And the tempo is only going to get faster and faster.

He's murdered three people, and is planning to murder another seven.

Ten little rabbits.

Saga thinks about the rhyme, the cut-off rabbits' ears, and the Rabbit Hole.

Right now the Rabbit Hole is the only lead they have.

Young William, who would go on to become Sweden's Foreign Minister, was the club's chair, and Rex lost his girlfriend to him when she became a member.

Maybe Oscar von Creutz was in the club – unless he set fire to the pavilion because he wasn't allowed to join?

But Grace is the only living member they are certain about.

She was there, and she met the others.

Grace is the key to this, Saga thinks as the wheels touch down.

She unbuckles her seat belt, stands up and walks past the passengers in business class. One of the stewards is about to tell her to sit down, but ends up letting her leave the plane ahead of everyone else.

After passport control Saga jogs past baggage claim, through customs and emerges in the arrivals hall. She pretends not to see the FBI driver waiting for her.

She doesn't have time to make small talk with the FBI and pretend to be investigating an act of terrorism.

Saga stops at duty-free to buy a small tin of Swedish Dream Cookies, then hurries to the exit.

Grace attended Ludviksberg School when her father, Gus Lindstrom, was posted to the US Embassy in Stockholm as Defence Attaché.

She later moved back to Chicago for her final year of high school, at the school her dad used to attend.

Grace is now a little over fifty years old, has never married, has no registered phone and isn't active on social media. For the past year she has been living in the exclusive Timberline Knolls Residential Treatment Centre. Saga called and spoke to a receptionist and one of the managers, and asked them to pass on a message to Grace, but she hasn't heard anything back.

Joona sent a photograph of Grace, a blonde girl with perfect teeth, holding a tiny prize trophy. She has a double string of pearls around her neck, and the clasp sparkles in the flash of the camera.

Saga runs past the row of airport taxis. The warm air is full of the smell of fried food and exhaust fumes.

Saga crosses the road to the car-hire centre. She enters an ice-cold office and rents a yellow Ford Mustang.

Is Grace just a privileged girl who left Rex for the snobs in the exclusive club, the spoiled daughter of an American diplomat who was never happy in Sweden, and who just wanted to get back to her friends in Chicago?

During her last term at Ludviksberg School she was evidently deemed worthy to enter the Rabbit Hole, despite her lack of aristocratic connections.

Saga drives through the Waterfall Glen Forest Preserve, then slows down and turns onto tree-lined Timberline Drive, where she parks in front of the main building.

The air smells like damp forest and freshly mown grass.

Less than half an hour has passed since she left the airport.

In the reception area a woman smiles at her from behind a tall cherry-wood desk with a rack of glossy brochures on it.

In English, Saga explains why she's there, saying she's an old friend of the Lindstrom family who's come all the way from Sweden to visit Grace.

'I'll just check her schedule,' the woman smiles. 'She's got art therapy in an hour . . . and after that there's yoga.'

'I won't be long,' Saga assures her as she signs herself in.

'Take a seat, and someone will show you through,' the woman nods.

Saga sits down and leafs through the brochures, where she reads that Timberline Knolls is a holistic and spiritual rehabilitation centre for women and girls aged twelve and up.

'Miss?' a gruff voice says.

A heavyset man in a tight guard's uniform is staring at her. He's breathing through his nose and has beads of sweat on his forehead. A club, Taser and a large-calibre revolver hang from the belt beneath his bulging stomach.

'My name is Mark, and I have the honour of escorting you to the school ball,' he says.

'Great,' she says, without smiling back.

Relatives are walking with residents or sitting on benches in the lush grass.

'Are any of your patients violent?' she asks.

'You can feel perfectly safe with me, miss,' he says.

'I couldn't help noticing your revolver.'

'Some of our guests are famous, and extremely rich . . . so I'd ask you not to stare,' he says, breathing hard.

'I'm not staring.'

'And if you run over and try to get a selfie with Kesha, I'll put six million volts through your sweet ass.'

The guard rocks as he walks, and wipes sweat from his face with an unbleached paper towel.

'Tough talk,' Saga mutters.

'Yes, but if you're nice to me, I'll be nice to you.'

They pass a large structure with white pillars and a sign saying 'Timberline Academy', then a stone building being used as a painting studio.

Mark is out of breath by the time he ushers her into a modern building. He leads her past a dayroom with leaded windows looking out on the park, into a hallway with pale blue walls.

'Call reception when you want to be picked up,' he says, then knocks gently on a door and nods at Saga to go inside.

74

Saga walks into the small room, which contains a bed, a chest of drawers and an armchair. A few beads of clay are lying on the floor next to a potted palm. A thin woman is sitting by the window looking out onto the path, picking at the grey rubber seal between the glass and the frame.

'Grace?' Saga says gently, and waits for her to turn around. 'My name is Saga Bauer, and I'm from Sweden.'

'I'm not well,' the woman says in a weak voice.

'Do you like cookies? I bought some at the airport.'

Grace turns towards Saga and brushes one cheek nervously. The years have left their mark on Grace, rubbing away all trace of the young girl and leaving a prematurely aged woman.

Her grey hair is gathered in a limp plait over her thin shoulder, her face is sunken and wrinkled, and she has a lifeless prosthetic eye in one eye-socket.

'We have a coffee machine in the cafeteria,' she says weakly.

They set out small plates and cups on the little round table by the sofas and sit down across from each other. Saga offers her the plate of cookies, and she says thank you as she puts one on her plate.

'There are lots of people of Swedish descent in Chicago,' Grace says, plucking her grey cardigan. 'Most of them ended up in Andersonville. I read that for a while there were more

332

Swedes here than in Gothenburg. My dad's grandmother Selma came from Halland . . . she arrived in May 1912, and became a housemaid.'

'And you've managed to hold onto the language,' Saga says, to keep her talking.

'Dad travelled to Sweden a lot . . . eventually he ended up as Defence Attaché in Stockholm,' Grace says with a hint of pride.

'Defence Attaché,' Saga repeats.

'There's a lot of history and tradition . . . Did you know that the first diplomatic relations between the US and Sweden were established by Benjamin Franklin?'

'I didn't know that.'

'Dad was very loyal to the ambassador,' Grace says, putting her cup down.

'You lived in Sweden?'

'I loved those light nights . . .'

The sleeve of her cardigan slips down as she gestures towards the ceiling, and Saga sees that her arm is lined with scars.

'You attended school outside Stockholm.'

'The best there was.'

She falls silent and lets her thin hands drop to her lap. Saga remembers that Grace's father stayed in Sweden, even after his daughter moved back to Chicago.

'But you moved back here after just two years?' she says curiously.

Grace, startled, glances up at her.

'Did I? Maybe I was homesick . . .'

'Even though your parents stayed in Sweden?'

'Dad had just started his post.'

'But before you moved home again, you belonged to a club at Ludviksberg School,' Saga says calmly. 'You used to meet in a pavilion known at the Rabbit Hole.'

Grace's face trembles.

'That was just a silly name,' she mutters.

'But it was a fancy club . . . for students from the very best families,' Saga says tentatively.

'Now I know what you're getting at . . . I had a boyfriend

who took me to the Order of the Crusebjörn Knights . . . that was its real name. I was only eighteen, a real idiot . . . a good girl from Chicago who used to go to the Swedish Lutheran Church every Sunday. I never dreamed I would ever date anyone before I got to Sweden . . .'

Her breathing has become oddly shallow, and she fumbles in her pocket for her medication. She ends up scattering the pills on the floor.

'So you know who the members were?'

'They were like film stars . . . Just being there and having them notice me made me feel like Cinderella.'

Grace takes the pills that Saga has picked up, thanks her and swallows one of them dry.

'What was your boyfriend's name?'

'Boyfriend isn't really the right word . . . but it was all so long ago,' she concludes.

'You don't look happy.'

'No,' Grace whispers, then sits silently again.

'Not all boyfriends are nice,' Saga says, trying to catch her eye.

'By the time I realised he'd put something in my drink, it was already too late, I felt sick, tried to get to the door . . . I remember them staring at me . . . the room was spinning . . . I tried to say I wanted to go home . . .'

Grace puts her hand over her mouth.

'They hurt you,' Saga says quietly, trying to sound calm.

Grace lowers her shaking hand.

'I don't know, I was lying on the floor,' she says in a monotone. 'I couldn't move. They held my arms and legs while Wille raped me . . . I kept thinking about Mum and Dad, and what on earth I was going to say to them.'

'I'm so sorry,' Saga says, and squeezes her hand.

'But I never said anything, I couldn't tell anyone that they did that to me . . . The whole club was lined up, pushing and shoving. I couldn't understand why they were so angry at me, they kept shouting and slapping my face.'

She picks at the biscuit crumbs on the table.

'Tell me what you remember,' Saga says.

'I remember . . . I remember it started to hurt really badly. It was wrong. I was seriously hurt . . . but they just kept going, grunting and groaning, kissing me on the neck, groping me . . .'

Her voice fades away, and she's breathing hard.

'They changed places and I saw blood on their hands . . . I begged and pleaded with them to call an ambulance . . . When I wouldn't stop crying they hit me in the face with an ashtray, then they broke a bottle . . .'

She hunches over, panting for breath.

'The last thing I remember is Wille pushing his thumb into my eye . . . I thought I was going to die. I should have died, but I only passed out . . .'

She's sobbing hard now, her shoulders shaking. Saga says nothing, just holds her tight and lets her finish her story.

'I woke up on the manure pile behind the stables, that was where they dumped me. The man who looked after the horses found me. He was the one who took me to the hospital.'

Saga holds her until she's calmed down.

'Do you remember their names?'

Grace wipes the tears from her face and looks down at her hands.

'Teddy Johnson, and . . . what was his name? Kent . . . and Lawrence. Hold on,' she whispers, and shakes her head. 'I know all their names.'

'You said Wille before,' Saga prompts. 'He went on to become Sweden's Foreign Minister.'

'Yes . . .'

'He was your boyfriend, wasn't he?' Saga asks.

'What? No, my boyfriend's name was Rex . . . I was so in love with him.'

'Rex Müller?' Saga asks. She feels sweat break out on her back.

'He was the one who arranged it all,' Grace says. 'He was the worst one. It was all his fault . . . oh, God . . . he tricked me into going into the Rabbit Hole, and . . .'

She stops speaking abruptly, as if she's run out of voice. Saga looks at the fragile woman. She needs to call Joona as soon as possible.

'Did Rex take part in the rape?' she asks.

'Of course,' Grace says, closing her eyes.

'Do you remember any other names?'

'Soon,' she whispers.

'You mentioned Wille . . . so, William Fock, Teddy Johnson and Kent . . .'

The door of the room is suddenly thrown open and two men in dark-grey suits walk in.

'Special Agent Bauer?' one of them asks, holding up an FBI badge.

75

The dark-blue hull bounces through the waves and foaming water hits the cabin's windshield. One of the fenders breaks free of its rope and rolls across the wet deck.

'Hold the wheel,' the captain tells Joona, leaving the cabin.

As its speed increases even further, coastguard vessel 311 starts to plane.

Through the streaked windshield Joona watches as the captain grabs the loose fender and ties it down. He lurches as the bow hits a large wave and water sprays over the railing, but manages to keep his balance, and makes his way back into the cabin, where he takes the wheel again.

The captain wears his long hair in a plait. He has tattoos all the way to his fingertips, and black eyeliner around his eyes. The rest of the crew seem delighted by his Captain Sparrow act, and call him Jack.

'Can you get her up to thirty-five knots?' Joona asks.

'If I dig my spurs into her flanks,' Jack replies, smiling to reveal his crooked teeth.

He speeds up. One of the crew claps his hands and lets out a whistle.

'Jack,' a muscular man calls out. 'At this speed you'd better watch out for the coastguard.'

'I've heard they can be pretty tough,' the captain replies.

'Not as tough as us!' the others call back in chorus.

Joona smiles and looks out over the rough water.

Neither Oscar's nor his girlfriend Caroline's phone is in use, but Anja found Caroline's last Instagram post. She'd taken a picture of herself looking sulky, with the caption 'Quality time'.

In the picture she's leaning against a stack of grey pallets, and behind her is a red Department of Transport sign with information about Stavsnäs jetty.

Anja quickly discovered that Oscar's half-brother owns a small house in the outer archipelago, not far from Stavsnäs.

'I understand that it's something of an honour to be giving you a lift,' the captain says, glancing at Joona.

The engines make the deck vibrate. They swerve around a cluster of rocky outcrops and find themselves rolling as the waves hit the side of the boat. Water breaks over the deck.

The captain points towards a greyish-black island, barely visible in the darkness.

'Bullerön isn't just another island . . . it used to be owned by Bruno Liljefors, the painter, but he sold it to newspaper magnate Torsten Kreuger, and during his time guests like Zarah Leander, Errol Flynn and Charlie Chaplin all came out here, to this little island, which is pretty much nothing but rock. You can walk across it in half an hour – makes you wonder what on earth they did out here, doesn't it?' Jack says.

As they approach the island the captain slows their speed.

There are no lights on the island. The waves crash on the steep rocks as gnarled trees bow in the wind.

'Are we allowed to know what you're expecting to find out here?' the captain asks.

'I'm looking for someone I need to question,' Joona replies.

They enter the public marina. The captain puts the boat in reverse, but it still hits the pier with a scraping sound before they come to rest.

'This person – is he dangerous?' Jack asks.

'He's probably scared,' Joona replies.

'Should I come with you?'

'Bring your pistol.'

The two men jump ashore and Jack fastens his holster around

338

his hips as they head across the rocks. It's much darker on the island than it was on the open water. The waves crash regularly against the rocks, as the gulls make their plaintive cries.

The house, once a simple fisherman's cottage, lies in a south-facing inlet some distance from the other buildings.

Against the night sky the façade looks black at first, like dried blood, but as they get closer they can see that it's actually a traditional red wooden house extended to link up with a raised boathouse.

The wind tugs at Joona's clothes as he stops to check his weapon.

The house looks boarded up, as if preparing for a hurricane. The doors and windows have been barred from the outside.

Joona and the captain walk down towards the house. There's grass growing from the gutters, and the gooseberry bushes are blowing in the strong wind.

There are some red buoys and floats by the side of the building. At the back of the house is an old frame with rusty hooks that looks like a football goalpost.

'No one here,' Jack says.

'We'll see,' Joona replies in a low voice.

He wonders if Oscar and his girlfriend arrived by private boat, and whether they drove it into the boathouse like a garage.

The boathouse's water entrance could be the only one that isn't barred.

Joona slides down the rocks beside the boathouse, puts his face against the lowest planks in the wall and tries to see between the cracks.

When his eyes get used to the darkness, he sees swaying water.

'There's no boat in there,' Joona declares, and starts to walk back up.

He passes a woodshed containing stacks of birch, sees the axe embedded in the block, and some large splinters of wood on the ground beside it.

He stops next to an ornately carved tool-shed. There's sawdust in the cracks. Joona gestures to Jack to stand still, cautiously approaches the shed and goes inside.

Rows of tools hang neatly from the walls, and in the middle

of the floor, next to a folded sawhorse, is a workbench with a handsaw on it.

'I think they're here,' Joona says, pulling a crowbar from the wall.

'Where?' Jack asks.

'In the house,' Joona replies.

'Doesn't look like it.'

'He nailed the doors and windows shut recently.'

'What makes you think that?'

'Because the wind has been blowing from the west for a couple of days . . . Oscar sawed the timbers in here, then carried them to the house . . . Most of the sawdust has blown away, but not the pieces that were sheltered from the westerly wind, here in these cracks.'

'OK,' Jack says. 'You're right, there wouldn't be any sawdust there if the wind had turned . . . but all the entrances are nailed shut from the outside. No one could be inside unless they'd been helped by someone standing out here.'

They go back to the house for another look. There's some sawdust in a spider's web below one of the barred windows. Joona tugs at the plank, then moves on around the corner. He stops in front of the kitchen door and sees that it opens inwards.

The plank nailed across it is purely for show.

He pushes the handle and tries to open the door.

It's been nailed shut from the inside.

Oscar and Caroline put the plank across the door to make it look like the house was shut up, then went inside and sealed it from within.

Joona returns to the front of the house, picks up a crowbar in the tool-shed and walks down to the main entrance.

76

The four-inch nails shriek as Joona tries to break his way in through the front door. He pushes the end of the crowbar in close to the lock and shoves, and the frame splinters as the door latch comes loose.

Joona pushes the door open and peers into the dark hallway.

'Police!' he shouts loudly. 'We're entering the house!'

His words are soaked up by darkness and silence. Wind blows across the roof, making the weathervane creak.

Jack's breathing speeds up, and he glances around anxiously, whispering to himself. Joona draws his pistol and moves cautiously into the hallway. On the rug there's a small doll whose legs are spread oddly. Someone's scribbled on her face with a pen.

Raincoats hang on hooks above a shoe-rack full of wellington boots and wooden clogs.

Joona opens the fuse-box inside the front door and sees that the main power supply has been switched off.

'There's no one here,' Jack whispers again.

They walk into a small living room with a television and a battered leather sofa. The air is perfectly still, and smells like dry wood and dust.

'Police!' Joona calls again. 'We need to speak to you, Oscar!'

He goes into a bedroom. The top bunk bed is made up. The

wide floorboards creak beneath his weight. A screen is leaning up against the wall, the plug to the standard lamp has been pulled out, and there's a water-damaged child's drawing of a cheerful girl holding a skeleton by the hand on the bottom bunk.

Jack goes into the second bedroom and hears something rustle briefly. There's barely any light in here at all. The curtains are drawn, and the gap between them has been closed with three clothes pegs.

Someone's been lying in the double bed. The covers are pulled back and there are signs of dried blood on one pillow.

When Jack opens the wardrobe, it wobbles because of the uneven floor. All it has in it are a couple of pale T-shirts and a blue bikini.

There's a creaking sound behind him to one side, and he spins around, trying to pull his pistol from its holster.

He takes a step to the side, but can't see anything in the dark corner behind the bed. With his hands trembling he draws the pistol and creeps closer – he can make out a shape, the size of a child's head, beneath the bed.

He hears the noise again, and realises it must be coming from the roof, probably a gull sliding down the tiles.

He keeps walking towards the dark corner, and bends over. His plait falls over his shoulder as he discovers that it's a deflated plastic ball with a yellow Pokémon logo.

Joona peers into the bathroom. On top of the washing machine is a damp packet of laundry detergent and a basket of clothes pegs. Joona marches in and pulls open the limescale-streaked door to the shower. All he finds are a bucket and a red-handled mop.

Leaving the bathroom, Joona meets Jack in the passageway that leads to the kitchen, the last room in the house.

They look at each other and nod.

Jack reaches for the closed door, pushes it open and takes a step back as Joona goes in with his pistol drawn.

There's no one there.

Joona moves quickly around the tall breakfast counter with its four bar-stools, aims the pistol at the fridge, then lowers it.

The window is covered with cardboard on the inside, but in the faint light that manages to get in he can see rows of tins on the worktop.

Joona stops in front of the kitchen door.

It's been nailed shut from the inside.

This was where they got in, just as he thought.

In front of him is a pair of folding wooden doors leading to the boathouse. They look like big window-shutters, and they reach all the way from the floor to the ceiling.

Joona puts his hand on the old wood-burning stove that stands beside the modern electric one.

It's cold.

There's a dustpan and broom in one corner, containing fragments of a bowl and some sweets.

Joona crouches down and inspects bloodstains on one leg of the kitchen table, then sees a trail of blood leading across the floor towards the boathouse.

He raises his pistol, goes over to the folding doors and tries to open one of them, but it catches after opening a crack.

He pulls hard, but the door is stuck.

Suddenly he thinks he can see a white light flash in the boathouse. He leans towards the crack between the door and frame and peers in. From the little he can see through the gap, it looks like this part of the boathouse is used as a dining room. He can make out a long, narrow table, and the backs of the chairs along one side.

Joona tries to pull the door open again, but stops when he hears noises from inside.

Then everything gets quiet again.

He waits a few seconds, then pushes one arm through the gap, right up to his shoulder.

He can no longer see inside the room, but he starts to feel across the back of the door to find out what's blocking it.

Joona hears the banging, thudding sound from the boathouse again.

He presses the barrel of his pistol to the door with his free hand as he feels across the other side.

'What's going on?' Jack whispers.

Joona sinks to one knee and finds a sturdy bolt close to the floor. He carefully pulls it open with his fingertips.

It comes free with a gentle clunk, and the gap opens a little further.

He quickly pulls his arm back in, steps back and aims towards the opening at chest-height.

The banging noise has stopped.

He opens the door and looks into the darkness.

He moves sideways silently, with his gun raised, trying to make sense of the shapes he can see.

Suddenly he realises that there's someone in the middle of the room.

A face, no more than a metre above the floor.

Joona sinks instinctively to one knee, immediately identifies a line of fire and puts his finger on the trigger.

In the faint light from the west-facing window, he can just see that it's a young woman tied to a chair.

Her blonde hair is tangled, and she has tape over her mouth.

She stares at him and starts to rock violently, making the chair legs hit the floor rhythmically.

'Caroline?' Joona says.

77

The bound woman stares at Joona with wide eyes. She has dried blood under her nose, and tape has been wound around her arms and ankles.

'Caroline?' Joona repeats. 'Don't be scared. I'm a police officer, and I'm here to help you.'

Behind her on the dining table there are open tins with spoons in them, crackers and a large container full of water.

'What the hell is this?' Jack whispers.

The boathouse isn't insulated, and a cold draught is blowing through the cracks in the floor. A window covered by a net curtain lets in dim light, and they see a pulley and a lifting hook hanging from the ceiling. On one beam brass lanterns and ropes are hanging. Along one wall is a trunk, and at the far end they can see varnished doors of a large tackle cupboard.

The young woman is shaking her head in terror, and tears start to stream down her cheeks.

'Don't be scared,' Joona says. 'I'm a police officer.'

He puts his pistol back in his holster and walks slowly across the creaking floor. The wind is pushing hard at the single-glazed window. Joona turns and looks back at the door to the kitchen, letting his eyes linger on the motionless shadows before going over to the woman.

Carefully he removes the tape from her face. She coughs

and flexes her mouth several times before raising her head and looking him in the eye.

'I'm going to kill you,' she says quietly.

The sea laps beneath them and the chair legs scuff the floor as she rocks in an effort to get free.

'Oscar thinks you're going to rape me, but I don't.'

'No one's going to rape you – we're police officers.'

'You don't look like police officers.'

'Where is Oscar?'

'I have nothing to do with this,' she whispers with a desperate look in her eyes. 'I don't even know Oscar. I just want to go home. I don't care what you do to him.'

The floor creaks oddly beneath them and the spoon in a tin of ravioli starts to shake with the vibrations.

'Tell me where he is,' Joona repeats calmly.

'There,' she replies, nodding her head over her shoulder at the varnished doors.

There's a weird ticking sound and Joona sees a little white light flicker inside the built-in cupboard, like a mobile phone flashing, only faster.

'Is he armed?' he asks.

'I don't know, but I don't think so,' she replies.

Joona moves towards the closed doors.

The whole room is creaking, like a taut rope.

Joona holds his pistol aimed at the cupboard, glances back towards the kitchen again, then takes a few steps back to get a better view of the entire boathouse.

The floor creaks.

Aiming directly at the doors, he looks quickly at the bound woman, the empty pulley block up in the roof, and Jack, who is approaching along the side of the dining table.

There's a scraping sound beneath the boathouse, like wood being dragged across wood. The draught lifts a tuft of blond hair from the floor.

Jack takes a step forward, holding back the hook on the end of the chain beneath the pulley in order to get past.

'I'm almost there now,' Joona says towards the cupboard. 'Can I ask you, please . . .'

There's a loud crash as two huge trapdoors open up beneath Jack. They drop away abruptly, slam into the wall below and bounce back a short distance.

Jack falls through the hole in the floor, but is still holding onto the chain that runs through the wooden block.

The hook flies up and latches into the pulley.

Jack's fall is abruptly halted and he yells out loud as his shoulder is dislocated.

Tables and chairs splash into the dark water below him.

Jack is swaying precariously, but manages to hold on.

The door to the cupboard opens and Joona sees Oscar rush out with a glass bottle in his hand with a burning rag stuffed in the top of it.

Oscar throws the bottle at Joona, but it hits an old pulley hanging from the roof instead. The glass shatters with a crash, and burning petrol spatters the woman taped to the chair.

She catches fire instantly, and Joona rushes over and pushes her in the chest with his foot. She topples backwards, the chair hits the edge of the large opening in the floor, and she tumbles into the water.

Oscar screams something and tries to light another petrol bomb, but his lighter won't produce a flame.

Joona counts the seconds as he runs across the narrow strip where the hinges of the left-hand trapdoor are attached.

The woman sinks into the black water, her hair billowing around her.

Joona's jacket snags on something and he almost loses his balance as he pulls himself free. He throws one arm out and grabs the curtain.

'Leave me the fuck alone!' Oscar screams.

The lighter sparks again just as Joona reaches the other side and rams his lower arm into the side of Oscar's neck, making his head jerk back and sending his glasses flying.

They both crash into the wall and Joona drives one knee up into Oscar's ribs, yanks him sideways, twists his own body in the other direction and flips him over his hip.

Oscar crashes to the floor with a groan, opens his eyes and stares up at the roof in confusion.

The bottle rolls over the edge and down into the water.

Joona knows that time is running out as he drags the man away from the cupboard.

'No, no, no,' Oscar whimpers, trying to cling onto the floor.

A lamp topples over, scattering broken glass across the floor. Joona drags Oscar behind him, slaps one of his handcuffs around the man's wrist, and the other around a column in the wall.

'Don't kill me,' Oscar gasps. 'Please, listen, I'll pay you . . .'

Joona runs to the hole in the floor and jumps in. He plunges down into the cold water. His ears roar as bubbles surround him like the tail of a comet.

His feet hit one of the chairs and slow his descent.

He spins in the water, kicks his legs and swims down into the darkness.

He can't see anything, but knows he has to get past the floating debris.

With one arm he tries to shove the heavy dining table away, then slides along one side of it and reaches the bottom.

His heavy clothing slows his movements as he searches for the woman among the rough rocks on the seabed.

He moves deeper down the slope, fumbling over the rotting remains of an old rowing boat.

Joona blinks in the dark water and feels the cold hit his eyes.

He swims further down.

His hands slip across colonies of barnacles on one of the boathouse pillars. Suddenly a swaying light spreads down into the water.

Jack is holding a lamp above the surface.

Through the debris and bubbles Joona catches sight of the woman. She's slid down the sloping rock towards deeper water, and is lying on her side, still bound to the chair.

He kicks off and swims down towards her.

She stares into his eyes, her white lips tightly closed as she holds her breath.

He tugs at the chair, trying to push off from the rock with one foot to gain more momentum, but she is caught in the other chairs that have gathered around the base of the pillar.

He draws his knife and quickly cuts through the tape around

her ankles and begins to pull it off. She starts to panic, kicking out with her legs, and can no longer resist the urge to breathe.

The pain as she inhales water into her lungs is instant. Her body jerks backwards as if she's been hit hard, she tries to cough it up, but succeeds only in drawing more water into her lungs, and starts to cramp and convulse.

Joona cuts the tape from her wrists and waist, working fast as she begins to spasm, blood blossoming from her mouth and nose. Joona lets go of the knife, pulls her free from the chair, kicks off with his legs and swims upward.

Fending off the furniture that is drifting in the current, he kicks one last time and manages to get her face above the surface.

She coughs and vomits water, gets some air into her lungs and coughs again.

Jack is holding a burning oil-lamp above the hole in the floor.

'The air ambulance is on its way,' he calls down.

With one arm around the woman's waist Joona climbs up the ladder and lifts her up onto the edge. She crawls forward on her knees, coughing and gasping for air, sobs and then coughs again, spitting blood as they hear the sound of the helicopter approaching.

'Take her, you can have her,' Oscar whimpers to himself. 'We're through. I'll stay here. I won't say anything, I promise. I haven't seen either of you.'

Joona helps guide the young woman through the dark house and out onto the rocky hillside behind the house as the helicopter starts to descend. Jack follows them, holding his wounded arm with the other hand as his clothes flap around his body. His eyeliner is streaked across his face.

78

As soon as the helicopter has disappeared across the water, taking Jack and Caroline with it, Joona goes back into the house, grabs a towel from the bathroom and returns to the boathouse.

Oscar von Creutz is sitting with his back to the wall. When he sees Joona come back he stops biting his thumbnail and tries to shuffle away.

Joona walks over and looks at the trapdoors and the empty pulleys in the roof.

The ropes run through the pulleys, so you can gently remove the crossbar beneath the floor and lower the two trapdoors, allowing you to get to your boat.

'Please, don't do it, you don't have to do it,' the man pleads, trying in vain to pull his hand through the cuff.

'My name is Joona Linna. I'm a detective with the Swedish National Operational Unit.'

'Really?' he mutters confusedly.

'Yes.'

'I don't get it,' he says, and bites his nail again. 'This is sick. What the fuck do you want? What are you doing here?'

Joona walks around the edge of the hole, past the drop to the water, stops in front of the trembling man, and waits until their eyes meet.

'You're suspected of kidnapping, attempted murder and grievous bodily harm,' he says calmly.

'That's all bullshit. I have the right to defend myself,' Oscar hisses, and looks down at the floor again. 'What the fuck do you want with me? I don't get it . . .'

He stops speaking and sits for a while with his free hand over his face, breathing hard.

'Tell me about the Rabbit Hole,' Joona says.

'I want to talk to a lawyer first.'

'Anything that happened back then has passed the statute of limitations.'

'Really? Doesn't feel like it,' Oscar says.

'Maybe not,' Joona says darkly.

'I need protection.'

'Why?' Joona asks, picking up Oscar's glasses from the floor.

'Someone's hunting us, killing us, one by one, like rabbits.'

'You've heard the nursery rhyme?'

'Have I already said all this?'

'No.'

'I'm not paranoid. I can tell you everything. I know who it is . . . I swear, it's a student from Ludviksberg. He hates us. He's like a demon, he's waited thirty years before making his move.'

'Who?'

'If you really are a police officer, you have to stop him.'

'Give me a name,' Joona says, handing him his glasses.

'You don't believe me, do you?'

'No.'

'I can prove it all,' Oscar says, putting his glasses back on. 'It makes sense if you realise who we were . . . a small gang who ruled that school. We were like gods. You asked about the Rabbit Hole . . . it was a pavilion that belonged to the Order of the Crusebjörn Knights, dating back to the court of Fredrik I, blah, blah, blah. We knew all that, but we really didn't give a shit, it was just one of a thousand little privileges that went with our status. We'd go to the Rabbit Hole to get drunk and sleep with the best-looking girls in school.'

Oscar smiles sardonically to himself and wipes his upper lip before he goes on.

'It was a different world in there. We used to watch porn and we swapped the portrait of Prince Eugen for a poster of NATO's Evolution Squadron because they had a Playboy bunny as their logo.'

'But you burned the pavilion down,' Joona says gently.

Oscar bites his thumbnail and stares into space.

'You say someone's hunting and killing you,' Joona goes on. 'Does that have anything to do with the fire?'

'The fire?' Oscar says, as if he's just woken up.

'Yes.'

'This is totally fucking real,' he says, rubbing his face with his free hand. 'People are dying, I'm not just imagining it . . .'

'I'm leaving now,' Joona says.

'Please, wait . . . I'm just trying to explain everything so you believe me when I give you the name,' he says anxiously. 'There was this guy in class, his name was Rex. We thought he was a total loser, but he was always hanging around, wanting to be part of the gang, getting beer for us, doing our homework . . . I have a very clear memory of a rainy summer's day when we were smoking behind the main building – there were some bricked-up cellar steps where we used to go – and Rex was hanging around, and said he was going out with a girl named Grace. Wille knew who she was and looked interested, he wanted to know more, and got Rex to boast about having sex with her in the meadow behind the school. It was all a bit pathetic, but Wille enjoyed teasing him. Then just a few hours later he was talking to Grace and telling her that Rex had joined the club and that she could become a member too seeing as they were together. I don't really know what he said, but the idea was that Rex had organised a secret party for her that night. Most of the students weren't allowed out after eight o'clock, but the grounds-keeper used to help us, and he unlocked the boarding house and brought her over to the Rabbit Hole.'

A cold night wind blows through the hole in the floor. The doors bang against the edge of the drop.

'I think about it every day,' Oscar whispers. 'The fact that . . . that she'd made such an effort to look nice, and was so ridiculously happy about everything, blushing and talking about

Rex, thinking he was about to show up, but he was locked up in the stables.'

Oscar's thin mouth stretches into something that's supposed to be a smile, but his eyes are dark.

'Wille locked Rex in and told him that Grace was his now, that it was just the way things went.'

He shakes his head slowly. The wind sweeps across the roof of the building, making the windows rattle.

'Go on.'

'I don't think I want to say any more,' he whispers.

'How old were you when this happened?'

'Nineteen,' he replies.

'So you can't blame anyone else,' Joona says.

'I'm not, but Wille liked humiliating people,' Oscar goes on quietly. 'He liked to make them squirm, make them feel ashamed, but this, what happened when Grace realised she'd been drugged, it was so . . . the hell he kicked off, the things he got us to do . . . we were drunk, I don't even want to think about who did what. Some of us were shouting, others were like animals. I refused, but everyone had to do it, they wanted everyone to do it, so they put a sort of crown of rabbits' ears on me and I did it. I don't know how, but I did it, it was there inside me after all. I was so fucking scared, but I did it . . . they even got the fucking groundskeeper to do it with her before he carried her out.'

'Absalon Ratjen?'

He nods, then sits there motionless, staring into space for a while before he goes on.

'Afterwards, when we let Rex out of the stables, Wille told him he'd had sex with Grace. He made up lots of crap about what the two of them had done, and how much she'd liked it. I just felt numb. I was empty, my soul had been sucked out and all I could think about was getting away from the school, and I started to walk. But when I reached the outdoor swimming pool, just before the bridge, I made up my mind to go back and set fire to the pavilion.'

'You got expelled.'

'I'm not telling you this to get some sort of forgiveness. What

I did was wrong, I know that, but I don't want to die,' Oscar says. 'Christ, all I want is for you to believe me when I say Rex Müller is the one hunting us down.'

'You seem very sure.'

'I am.'

'But you thought I was the murderer just now?' Joona says.

'Rex has money. He doesn't need to get his hands dirty unless he wants to.'

'You're sure Rex was locked up while the rape was taking place?'

'I helped do it . . . and I helped let him out afterwards,' he replies heavily.

Joona pulls his damp phone from his inside pocket, looks at the blank screen and realises that it's ruined.

The victims' nineteen minutes of suffering must correspond with how long the rape took.

Rex was locked inside the stables. All the other boys took part, but someone other than Grace was inside the Rabbit Hole.

'You said everyone joined in,' Joona says.

'Yes.'

'But that isn't entirely true, is it?'

'Isn't it?' Oscar mumbles.

'Was there a witness?'

'No.'

'Who saw you?'

'No one.'

'I need the names of everyone who was in the Rabbit Hole,' Joona says.

'Not from me,' Oscar says.

'I need to make sure they get protection.'

'But I don't want them to get protection,' Oscar replies, looking at Joona with empty eyes.

79

Valeria is walking down towards the greenhouses. It's cool, and she wraps her worn cardigan more tightly around her. She's thinking about asking Micke to help her with the frame of the new polytunnel. She loves her nursery: the fresh air, the racks of seedlings, the rows of plants and trees.

But today her chest feels empty.

She knows she should transplant her cuttings into pots, but can't summon up the enthusiasm.

She closes the glass door behind her, moves some buckets out of the way and sits down on the metal stool and stares out into space. When Micke opens the door she jumps and gets up.

'Hi, Mum,' he says, holding up a bottle of champagne in a gift-bag.

'It didn't work,' she says bitterly.

'What didn't work?'

She turns away and starts to remove dead leaves from a sugar plum just to give her hands something to do.

'He leads a different kind of life,' she says.

'But I thought . . .'

He trails off, and she turns to look at him again with a sigh. It still surprises her that he's an adult. Time froze when she was locked up in prison, and her sons somehow remained five and seven years old in her head. They will forever be two little boys in their pyjamas who love it when she chases and tickles them.

'Mum . . . he seems to make you happy.'

'He'll never stop being a policeman.'

'That doesn't matter, does it?' Micke says. 'I mean, you're not really in a position to dictate how people should live their lives . . .'

'You don't understand . . . while he was in prison I didn't have to feel ashamed of the way I turned out.'

'Has he made you feel ashamed?'

She nods, but suddenly isn't sure if it's true. An unpleasant chill blossoms in her chest.

'What exactly happened, Mum?' Micke asks, carefully putting the bottle of champagne down on the floor.

Valeria whispers that maybe she should call and talk to him. She leaves the greenhouse, wiping tears from her cheeks, and tries to stay calm, but still finds herself walking faster. She pulls her boots off in the hallway and hurries into her bedroom, picks up her phone and calls him.

She gets put through to Joona's voicemail. She hears the short bleep and takes a deep breath.

'I need a police officer to come and arrest me for being so stupid,' she says, then ends the call.

A sob rises in her throat and her eyes fill with tears. She sits down on the bed and covers her face with both hands.

80

The Rabbit Hunter leaves the car on a forest track, slings his bag over his shoulder and walks to the guest marina at Malma Kvarn, where he selects an older model Silver Fox with a powerful engine. He climbs on board, breaks open the ignition cover, connects the cable from the starter engine to the one from the battery, and immediately hears a dull rumble.

Thirty metres away, a family are unloading a sailing boat. The youngest children are standing on the pier looking very tired in their red life jackets.

Clouds sail across the sky.

The Rabbit Hunter unties the boat and steers out through the sound.

The wind is strong out on the open water and he has to take care to steer into the largest of the waves. The radio crackles as he tries to find the right frequency, and he hears fragments of a coastguard conversation about a rescue operation.

The Rabbit Hunter steers towards Munkön, in order to make his way through the outer archipelago to reach Bullerön.

A wave hits the windshield and the water runs down the glass just as he manages to pick up the coastguard's message over the radio.

There seems to have been some sort of accident.

The air ambulance has reached Södermalm Hospital.

The aluminium hull shudders as the bow hits the waves, then he hears that the police have arrested a man on Bullerön and have him on board coastguard vessel 311.

In order to hear better the Rabbit Hunter pulls the cables apart, stopping the engine.

The man has been arrested for attempted murder and kidnapping, and is being taken to Kronoberg Prison in Stockholm.

It's Oscar, they've taken him.

The Rabbit Hunter thinks of a grey rabbit changing direction as it runs, its paws kicking up a cloud of dust.

He sinks onto the deck and covers his ears with his hands.

Oscar got rich from hedge-fund money and other people's retirement accounts – and, many years ago, he raped a girl with his friends. He kicked her, put on a pair of white rabbit's ears and a bowtie, then raped her a second time with a bottle.

The boat is rolling hard on the waves, and he has to cling on to stop himself from pitching over.

He can't understand how the police managed to trace Oscar so quickly. It's simply not possible.

Oscar is getting away, like a rabbit darting into its hole.

He had been so sure he would succeed.

It was like following a rabbit with myxomatosis, the disease that covers them in sores around their nose and eyes, blinds them, and makes them so weak that in the end you can just walk up and kill them by standing on them.

He doesn't want to think about it, but his brain conjures up images of him as a boy rinsing the slaughterhouse bench and tiled floor with a hose – the blood and viscera swirling down into the drain.

There's a sudden bang and he falls sideways, gets up and realises that he's drifted onto some rocks. A large wave foams over the railing, and he hits his head on the steel frame of the windshield before regaining his balance.

He fumbles with the cables again and there's a spark. He does it once more, and the engine comes to life.

The boat lurches sideways. Water splashes in around his legs, and the hull buckles against the rocks, shedding dark-blue flakes of paint.

He puts the boat in reverse and it floats reluctantly backward. The rocks scrape a silver groove along the painted side before the boat comes to a halt again.

He screams so loud that his voice breaks.

The next wave rolls in and pushes the boat forward with a shriek of metal, and white spray fills the air. He powers up the engine as the water turns and lifts the boat from the rocks. Moving backwards, he turns and steers back towards Värmdö again.

Tomorrow he will be waiting outside Police Headquarters until the custody hearing is complete. If Oscar is released on bail, he'll try to flee the country, either by car or boat. But everything will be far more complicated if he's remanded in custody until his court date.

81

The Chicago FBI is headquartered in a shimmering glass complex in a drab part of the city.

Saga is sitting with a Commissioner Lowe, in a conference room with a wall to wall blue and yellow carpet.

Saga has apologised and explained that she didn't see anyone waiting for her at the airport, and that she assumed they would be meeting up after her visit to the treatment centre.

Since her visit to the rehab centre Saga has called Joona more than ten times, but his phone has been switched off.

It's evening now, and the office is almost empty. A detective from Washington comes into the conference room and puts her bag down on the table. The short woman with black eyes and plaited hair has a deep furrow across her brow.

'Special Agent López,' she says in English, without a trace of a smile.

'Saga Bauer.'

They shake hands and López unbuttons her jacket.

'Our acting Defence Secretary was murdered in Sweden because you and your colleagues did such a terrible job.'

'I'm sorry about that,' Saga says.

'What can you tell me about the terrorists?' López asks, leaning back in her chair.

'Speaking personally, I don't think we're dealing with

360

terrorists. But obviously we're following all possible lines of inquiry.'

López raises her eyebrows sceptically.

'Such as coming here?'

'Yes.'

'What did you find?'

'It's way above my pay-grade to determine the extent to which I can share information—'

'I don't give a damn about that,' López interrupts.

'I need to speak to my boss,' Saga says.

'Go ahead.'

Saga gets out her phone and tries Joona again, and this time the call goes through.

'Joona.'

'At last,' she says in Swedish.

'Have you been trying to call?' he asks.

'I've left messages.'

'My phone got wet,' Joona explains.

Saga looks at the whiteboard containing the erased remnants of red, green and blue writing as she explains that she, as a Security Police agent, absolutely can't tell him that Grace was subjected to a brutal gang rape in the Rabbit Hole.

'She remembers the names of the perpetrators . . . William, Teddy Johnson, Kent, Lawrence and Rex Müller.'

'Rex Müller?' Joona says. 'She named him?'

'Yes,' Saga replies, and smiles at López, who stares back at her blankly.

'Which means that Rex has been identified both as a rapist and the man who's avenging the rape.'

'What? What are you talking about?' Saga asks.

'I've arrested Oscar von Creutz . . . I want to question him again, but he told me what happened and it's pretty clear that Rex wasn't part of it,' Joona says. 'They locked him in the stable while they raped his girlfriend. Oscar's convinced that Rex is the person who's started taking revenge on them.'

'So Rex didn't participate in the rape?' Saga says.

'No.'

López digs around in her bag and takes out dark lipstick.

'And you don't think he's the murderer?' Saga says.

'He's got enough money to pay someone to do it for him, but . . .'

'None of this feels right,' Saga concludes.

'The murders have to be about what happened in the Rabbit Hole,' Joona says. 'We've got a spree killer who's murdering the rapists one by one.'

'But why?'

'He must have been there.'

'A witness?'

'Something else,' he says. 'Something else must have happened, something we don't know about, some unknown factor, a third element.'

'Who could it be?' she asks.

'We've got a victim and the perpetrators . . . but something's missing.'

'What?'

'That's what we need to find out.'

'I'll talk to Grace, and you talk to Rex and Oscar,' Saga says.

'There's no time to lose.'

Saga ends the call, puts her phone in her pocket and turns back towards López with a smile.

'My boss says he'll contact you tomorrow,' she explains.

'I understand Swedish,' López says coolly in English.

'Then you already know that,' Saga replies, and gets up from her chair.

The corner of López's mouth twitches at her own bluff, then she nods.

'Your boss is going to say that you should tell us everything you know.'

'I hope so,' Saga says.

'I'll pick you up from your hotel after breakfast.'

'Thanks,' Saga says, and walks out of the conference room.

On the ground floor she hands her visitor's badge back in at reception, then gets into her yellow car and starts to drive back to the exclusive rehab centre.

The traffic in the suburbs has died down and the rainy

Chicago sky looks like dark-grey clay by the time Saga parks the car on Timberline Drive.

Five hundred metres away she can see the lights in the security lodge and the closed gates glinting in the floodlights' sharp glare.

Visiting hours are long over, and the patients are probably all in bed.

She walks quickly along the road, but before she reaches the lights she jumps over the ditch and heads through the trees.

The only sounds are the rain dripping through the leaves, and her own footsteps on the grass and dead leaves.

She heads away from the security lodge, towards the fence, and holds the branches back as she tries to see through the trees.

There isn't time to wait until morning, she needs to get in and talk to Grace immediately. Because regardless of whether the killer has been hired or is acting on his own behalf, he clearly intends to kill everyone on the list as efficiently as possible. Both his motives and modus operandi are emotionally charged, and all the evidence suggests that he has a warped and chaotic personality.

She wades through a grove of wet ferns, hears a shuffling sound behind her back, and looks up into the dark treetops to see a large bird moving through the upper branches.

Saga hurries on into the dense darkness before she sees light up ahead.

There's no time to lose because this perpetrator has all the hallmarks of a spree killer.

Each murder is merely a step along the way, a small part of a final solution.

Saga emerges into an area where the trees have been cleared, and stops in front of the tall, black steel fence.

Every few metres signs warn that trespassing is forbidden, and list the name of the security company patrolling the area.

Saga runs over and grabs one of the thinner poles that make up the fence, puts her foot on a yellow sign that says 'Security cameras in operation', and heaves herself up, then jumps down on the other side.

A network of illuminated paths criss-crosses the park.

Saga runs between the trees and follows one of them beyond the reach of the lights.

If Grace hasn't taken her medication, it might be possible to talk to her about what happened in the Rabbit Hole.

Saga approaches the buildings and slows down.

The lampposts cast a desolate glow over damp paths and wet park benches. The buildings are dark, their windows blind reflections.

Leaves drip and rustle behind her.

Someone is approaching. Saga steps back and sinks down behind the bushes.

It's a man from the security firm, checking that the doors of one of the buildings are locked. Saga hears him report back over his radio before he moves on, out of sight.

82

The park is silent, and everything is glowing gently in the muted light from the lampposts. Saga approaches one of the buildings, and stops to listen.

Just as she starts walking again a light goes on in one of the windows, falling across the freshly mown grass.

Saga moves cautiously into the cover of a large tree. There's a snap as she stands on a dry branch.

A naked woman appears in the window.

She can't be more than twenty years old.

Saga watches her pale face as she stares out into the night before turning and tottering away from the window.

Saga waits a little while, then hurries across the grass to the path that leads to Grace's building.

Only now does she notice that her jeans are soaked through to her knees.

She's close to the art studio now, and hears her own footsteps echo softly off its stone façade.

Saga is planning to tell Grace that Rex didn't participate in the rape, that he was locked up all night.

Maybe that will prompt Grace to tell her exactly what happened.

Maybe Grace will be able to identify the unknown factor that they need.

Saga has just started to walk cautiously towards the corner of the building when she hears giggling behind her.

She turns around.

A woman in a thin nightie is standing behind her with a blonde wig in her hand.

'My little doll!' she says, sounding astonished.

The woman's face is oddly unguarded, almost boundless in its expressiveness. Saga moves slowly away but the woman follows her.

'I had to do it, Megan,' she says, making a sad face. 'Grandpa said I couldn't have you.'

'You think—'

'I swear,' she interrupts sternly. 'Ask him yourself. He's standing over there, under that tree.'

The woman points nervously towards the shadows of the park.

'OK,' Saga says, and turns to look.

'He just hid!' she gasps.

'I have to go,' Saga says softly.

'Come on,' the woman hisses, and starts walking towards the park. 'We'll run away together . . . heedless of all danger, rushing through the forest . . .'

Saga hurries off in the other direction, along the side of the building, and glances back to see that the woman has stopped on the path.

Saga runs across an open space, away from the studio and towards the building where she met Grace earlier.

The entrance is lit up but all the windows are dark. Saga walks up to the door and tries it, but it's locked. She looks in through the glass, sees the dark cafeteria and the glow of the snack-vending machine.

She startles when she hears an unsettling noise behind her – like bare feet running across a wet floor – and quickly looks around.

There's no one there. Everything is peaceful: the stillness of the pond, the park with its dripping leaves.

Saga hurries around the building and walks across the grass towards a park bench next to a large rhododendron, then stops to figure out which window is Grace's.

She hears manic laughter and darts into the shadows, then sees the woman with the wig hiding behind a tree, waving in her direction.

Saga stands motionless and watches as the woman smiles and turns away, rubs her nose hard, then wanders off into the park.

Saga quickly drags the bench under the window, then climbs up and tries to see into Grace's room.

Between the curtains she can just make out a bedside table with a porcelain musical box on it.

Saga barely has time to register the figure rushing towards her before she feels a jolt of pain in her back, like the bite of a raging dog. Her legs buckle and she tumbles sideways, hitting her chest on the arm of the bench and letting out a groan.

Her back is throbbing painfully, her body is jerking spasmodically, and she doesn't know how she ended up on the ground.

She opens her eyes and stares up at the dark, rain-filled sky, assuming she's lost consciousness.

There's another burst of pain, like someone kicking her repeatedly in the side, and her vision fades, but she can feel herself being dragged by the legs across the path and out onto the wet grass.

Saga gasps for air, opens her eyes and sees Mark, the guard from earlier, leaning over her with his Taser in his hand.

He's breathing hard and has a fevered look in his eyes as he stares at her.

She tries to raise one hand to push him off, but has no strength in her muscles.

'I'm a big boy, a nice boy too, but the rules say I have to check if you're armed.'

Saga's heart starts to beat faster as he unzips her jacket. He finds her phone and throws it hard against the nearest tree. It shatters, and the pieces fly out across the grass.

He leans over her again and shoves his cold hand under her shirt, beneath her bra and pinches one of her nipples hard.

'Nothing here,' he mumbles, and pulls his hand out again.

He's breathing hard through his half-open mouth as he holds the Taser to her neck and unbuttons her jeans. She manages to raise her right hand and grab the sleeve of his uniform, and tugs at it feebly.

'Stop,' she snarls.

'I need to look for concealed weapons,' he says.

Mark starts to pull down her jeans and underwear, but then his radio crackles. He rests one hand on her chest and presses, forcing the air out of her lungs as he stands up.

'We've got an intruder – get the police out here,' he says, walking into the light beneath one of the lamps.

Saga tries to pull her trousers back up as she sees two guards running towards them from between the buildings, and two nurses approaching anxiously from the other direction.

83

The day after Joona arrested Oscar von Creutz a short custody hearing is held in Police Headquarters.

Oscar sits in silence between his defence lawyers, looking up at the high windows. The sun emerges from behind the clouds and makes the dust particles in the air sparkle.

As if from a great distance he hears the prosecutor request that he be remanded in custody on suspicion of kidnapping, attempted murder and aggravated assault.

They're serious charges, but he knows he can be held only if there's a risk he might reoffend, destroy evidence or attempt to evade justice.

When the court decides that Oscar should be granted bail he hides his smile behind his hand. It occurs to him that he ought to say thank you, but he doesn't. He just walks towards the exit with his lawyers.

'Now you don't have to worry about this any more,' one of them smiles when they stop in the doorway.

'Thanks, Jacob,' Oscar replies quietly, shaking their hands.

His legal team have already put together a defence plan if the prosecutor can't be persuaded to drop the preliminary investigation.

During Oscar's first meeting with his lawyer, a doctor was present, and took eight blood samples from him. They weren't going to be sent to a laboratory, but could later be used during any ensuing trial.

Seeing as they know precisely which substances the prosecutor's office tests for, they'll base their defence on the substances the prosecution is guaranteed to have missed.

The fact that those substances were never in Oscar's blood is irrelevant.

The plan is to fabricate a convincing picture of illness, where different doctors have prescribed different medications without checking the side-effects and their interaction. The lawyers will be able to prove that Oscar's temporarily confused and erratic behaviour was the result of that interaction.

Oscar doesn't care about the trial. He's paid to be freed because he can't just sit in a cage waiting to be shot.

Prison can't offer him any protection.

That's why he's thinking of leaving the country and staying away as long as it takes for the police to catch the murderer.

But Oscar doesn't know that the Rabbit Hunter is waiting for him outside Police Headquarters, watching as he walks away from his lawyers.

He doesn't notice someone follow him, walk past him through the park, and overhear him call a taxi to the Silja Line terminal in Värtahamnen.

During the drive to the harbour Oscar books a cruise on the M/S *Silja Symphony*, pays for the taxi in cash, then checks in and goes on board.

He finds his cabin in the back, a suite with sloping glass windows between sea and sky. He locks the door carefully and gives the handle an extra tug just to make sure. As soon as he gets to Helsinki he's planning to catch the ferry to Tallinn, then hire a car and drive south through eastern Europe, all the way down to southern Turkey.

Oscar gets up and opens the minibar door, which rattles with bottles. He takes out two small brown bottles of whisky, fills a glass and then sits by the window and looks down at the long line of vehicles slowly rolling onto the ferry.

*

Rabbits are nervous creatures. They huddle up; sitting motionless they'll remain unseen, but they can't handle it if the hunter stops to wait them out.

The silence makes them panic and start running, because they think they've been spotted.

The Rabbit Hunter goes down into the garage beneath Rådhusparken, opens the boot of the car, and makes sure he can't be seen on any security cameras as he packs a black overnight bag with weapons, a change of clothes, vinyl gloves, wet-wipes, bin bags, tape, box cutters and a special crowbar for opening security doors.

Taking the bag with him, he leaves the garage and walks down to Fleming Street, where he catches a taxi for the ferry terminal and buys a cheap ticket under a false name.

He's been given another chance to stop Oscar, but knows there's still a lot that could go wrong. There are always unforeseeable factors. The plan is to get off the ferry before it leaves, but Oscar may be sitting in a crowd of people in one of the restaurants when the boat leaves. In that case he'd have to go with him to Finland in order to get the job done.

The Rabbit Hunter is planning to slice open Oscar's stomach and pull his intestines out.

He wants each of them to have to confront his own death.

The purpose of the rhyme is to prepare them.

At the beginning, he wants them to hope that they might survive, despite all the pain and fear, so that they struggle desperately even as it slowly dawns on them that any future life will be very different from the one they've known.

They need to realise that they will be blind, or missing a limb, or paralysed.

They should go on fighting for their lives until the second stage, when they realise that there is no mercy, that this pain and fear are the last things they will ever experience.

The Rabbit Hunter takes no pleasure in their suffering, but he is filled with an elevated sense of justice – and then when they finally die, the world becomes completely still, like a winter landscape.

In the terminal he checks in using one of the automated

machines, prints his boarding card, then follows the stream of people on board. The M/S *Silja Symphony* is more than two hundred metres long, with thirteen decks, and with its almost one thousand cabins, it carries more passengers than the *Titanic* did.

The Rabbit Hunter holds up his fake ID. He's given the made-up last name 'von Creutschen' so that he ends up next to Oscar on the passenger list. He makes a note of Oscar's cabin number from the screen, goes over to the map by the lifts, then goes downstairs to the staff quarters.

The Rabbit Hunter waits outside the staffroom. After a minute or so, a woman comes out. He catches the door, holds it open for her, and asks after Maria, to demonstrate that he has a valid reason for being there as he goes inside. He passes two men changing out of their street clothes, and says hello to a woman who is typing a message on her phone.

'Do you have a master key-card?' he asks.

'I need mine,' she replies without looking up.

'I'll get it back to you in no time,' he says with a smile.

'Ask Ramona,' the woman replies, nodding towards the bath-room.

There's a grey and pink imitation-leather gym bag on the bench outside the bathroom. He unzips it and searches through the clothes, running his hands over the bottom of the bag as the toilet flushes.

He quickly searches the two inside pockets as he hears her wash her hands and pull out some paper towels. He opens the two side pockets and finds Ramona's ID and master key-card just as the lock on the door clicks.

As the door swings open he walks away calmly, card in his hand.

He'd allowed himself fifteen minutes to find a key-card, but it's only taken five.

Not needing to use his crowbar will give him more time with Oscar in his cabin.

He carries his bag up the carpeted stairs, past decks housing the bars and restaurants, the avenue of tax-free shops, the hall-ways of meeting rooms, one-armed bandits and the casino.

The top deck, named after Mozart, is where the most exclusive suites are.

A drunk woman emerges from a cabin and stumbles towards him. She blocks the hallway with her arms, as if they are playing a game.

'You look nice,' she says with a giggle. 'Do you want to come to my cabin and help me with . . .'

It's as if something snaps in his head, he hears a crackling sound in one ear and reaches out for the wall for support as he remembers how he wept when he nailed up the remains of his latest kills around the door next to the rotting rabbits.

Now they'll stay away, now they'll stay away, he whispered.

The Rabbit Hunter merely smiles at the woman as he passes her. Sweat is running down his back and he finds himself thinking about the heat from the burning wheelchair.

He found the petrol in the tool-shed, and the matches in the kitchen, then he updated Nils Gilbert's Facebook status with a suicide note.

He went out and poured petrol all over him, told him why he was going to die, and then tossed the lit match on his lap.

The heat made him back away as he listened to Gilbert's growling roar and watched the contorting body through the flames for nineteen minutes.

The body shrank in on itself and turned black.

Everyone knew that Gilbert was lonely and depressed, and the police would never think of linking his suicide with the other deaths.

Now the Rabbit Hunter stops at the back of the ship, in front of the door leading to a suite bearing the peculiar name 'Nannerl'. He hears voices behind him as he slips on a pair of vinyl gloves, goes into the suite using the master key-card, and closes the door silently behind him.

He puts his bag down on the floor and takes out a blood-smeared plastic bag from which he pulls out the leather strap with the ten rabbits' ears fastened to it.

84

The Rabbit Hunter turns towards the mirror in the hall, puts the strap around his head and ties it at the back of his neck. With a familiar gesture he flicks some of the ears away from his face, then looks at his reflection, which fills him with cold power.

Now he's a hunter again.

He pulls out one of his pay-as-you-go phones and sends the audio file to Oscar. He hears a smartphone beep in the bedroom, then the sound of the rhyme playing.

Oscar is probably alone, but the Rabbit Hunter still checks the bathroom just to be sure, then quickly makes sure the living room is empty.

He can see the oil-black water of the harbour through the streaked windows.

He pushes the bedroom door open and marches in.

A football match is muted on the television. A bluish-grey glow reflects off the walls of the room.

He realises at once that Oscar is hiding in the wardrobe, behind the white glass sliding door, and that he's probably trying to call the police right now.

Everything is so mundane, yet simultaneously so strange when death comes calling.

There's a glass of whisky on the bedside table.

He sees the dented table legs, the frayed bedspread, the dark marks on the carpet, and the smears on the mirror.

The Rabbit Hunter hears Oscar drop his phone. Oscar knows that the noise has given him away, but keeps hiding regardless because his brain is trying to tell him that the murderer might not have heard anything, that the murderer might not actually find him.

Some hangers clatter against each other inside the wardrobe.

The floor starts to vibrate as the ferry's engines warm up.

The Rabbit Hunter waits a few seconds, then walks over and kicks the sliding glass door to pieces. He backs away instinctively as the fragments fall to the floor around Oscar von Creutz's legs.

The middle-aged man slides to the floor in fear, and ends up crouching in the wardrobe staring up at him.

A flash of memory comes back to him, and he thinks about the rabbits' terror when he checked the traps, turned the cages upside down, and grabbed them by their back legs.

'Please, I can pay, I've got money, I swear, I—'

The Rabbit Hunter strides over and grabs one of Oscar's legs, but he squirms and tries to get away, and the Rabbit Hunter loses his grip. He hits Oscar twice in the face, holds his arms back with one hand and grabs his leg again.

Oscar screams as the Rabbit Hunter pulls him out onto the floor and fastens his ankle to one leg of the bed with a zip tie.

'I don't want to!' he roars.

Oscar lands a kick on the Rabbit Hunter's upper arm, but he flips Oscar over, pushes him down on his side and locks his arms behind his back.

'Listen, you don't have to kill us,' Oscar pants. 'We were young, we didn't understand, we—'

The Rabbit Hunter tapes his mouth shut and then takes a couple of steps back and stares at him for a while, watching him struggle to break free, watching him try to move his body even though the zip ties are cutting into his skin.

He did two tours of Iraq, so he knows how state-sanctioned killing feels. He's aware of the force of will required, and the exhaustion that follows.

He used to think they were all fairly ordinary guys when they were doing their basic training together.

But the killing in southern Nasiriyah made them overconfident.

The targets weren't people to them, but part of a destructive and dangerous enemy they were risking their lives to fight.

There was a unity, a sense of common purpose.

But killing someone after you've come home and are no longer wearing the uniform is different.

It's lonely, and far more powerful. The decision and responsibility are yours alone.

He looks at the time and pulls out the knife he's planning to use. It's an SOCP knife, shaped like a Chinese ring dagger, with the blade and grip fashioned from the same piece of black steel.

It's a finely honed, well-balanced weapon.

The Rabbit Hunter walks over quickly and blocks Oscar's free leg with one knee, holds his chest down with one hand, and cuts his shirt open across his torso. He looks at the hairy stomach, which is rising and falling rapidly in time with his breathing, and sticks the knife in ten centimetres below the navel. It slides softly through tissue and membranes as he slices Oscar's torso open, almost all the way to his breastbone.

Smiling, he looks into Oscar's bulging eyes as he sticks one hand into the opening in his gut and feels the heat of his body through the plastic of the glove. Oscar's body is shaking. Blood is streaming down his sides. The Rabbit Hunter grabs his intestines and pulls them out, leaving them hanging between Oscar's legs. Then suddenly there's a knock on the door to the suite.

A loud knock.

He stands up, turns up the volume on the television, goes over to the small hallway, closing the bedroom door behind him, and looks through the peephole.

An elderly man dressed in white is waiting outside with a room service cart. Oscar has evidently already ordered food, and now he's going to have to accept the delivery.

The man knocks again as the Rabbit Hunter pulls his gloves off and closes his bag. He quickly removes his trophies, hangs them on a hanger, looks in the mirror, wipes the blood from his face, turns the light out and opens the door.

'That was quick,' he says, blocking the door.

Loud bangs are coming from the bedroom as Oscar tries to attract attention by kicking something.

'Would you like me to serve in the sitting room, sir?' the older man asks.

'Thanks, but I'll do it myself,' he replies.

'I'm happy to do it,' the man says, glancing into the suite.

'It's just that I'm not quite ready to eat,' he says as the whisky glass crashes on the bedroom floor.

'Then I'm happy with a signature,' the man smiles.

The Rabbit Hunter remains in shadow as he takes the receipt and pen. As he signs for the food he realises that the bottom of his right arm is covered in blood, all the way to the elbow.

'Is everything all right, sir?' the waiter asks.

He nods, looks the man in the eye and tries to work out if he is going to have to drag him into the bathroom and slit his throat over the Jacuzzi.

'Why shouldn't it be?'

'I didn't mean to be impertinent, sir,' the man says apologetically, and turns towards the cart.

The banging from the bedroom starts again as the waiter hands him the tray. The Rabbit Hunter thanks him, backs into the hall and pushes the door shut.

He puts the tray on the floor and looks through the peephole, ready to rush out and grab the waiter. Through the wide-angle lens he sees the old man release the brakes on the small wheels of the trolley, then walk slowly off along the corridor.

He quickly pulls on a fresh pair of gloves, wraps the rabbits' ears around his head and returns to the bedroom.

It smells like blood, whisky and vomit.

Oscar is about to lose consciousness and is kicking only weakly now, letting his heel fall to the floor. His face is white and sweaty, and his eyes are darting about.

The Rabbit Hunter turns the television off and walks straight over to Oscar, grabs hold of his intestines and pulls them out a whole metre, jerks hard and then lets them fall to the floor.

The pain brings Oscar back to almost full consciousness again. He's breathing quickly through his nose and trying instinctively to push himself backward.

Oscar is going to die in three minutes, and the noise inside the Rabbit Hunter's head gets louder as he stares into his terrified eyes. The room is silent, but inside the Rabbit Hunter's mind it's like someone is drumming on saucepans and throwing plates into a bath. Oscar raped a young woman, left her unconscious and bleeding on a manure pile, and thought he could get away with it.

The floor lurches beneath the Rabbit Hunter's feet.

He leans against the wall, trying to focus and breathe calmly, then he sees the bloody handprint on the wall and makes a mental note to wipe it off before he leaves, even though there's no way it could be traced back to him.

'I can tell you know why this is happening,' he says, taking the knife out again. 'That's good. That's the point.'

Oscar whimpers and writhes, fighting to pull free. Blood from his torso is pouring onto the floor and soaking into the carpet, which is now shiny and black.

The loudspeakers announce that the ferry will be departing in thirty minutes. The Rabbit Hunter is confident that he'll have time to get back to shore before then.

Oscar won't be found until the next morning, in Helsinki, the Rabbit Hunter thinks to himself, looking at the knife in his hand.

It's like the black tongue of a demon, pointed and jagged.

Soon he will slide the blade into Oscar's heart, right through the breastbone.

The whole world clatters and rings like a casino.

Then a wind sweeps through him, leaving silence in its wake.

It's like when a rabbit is lying on the ground kicking one leg. When the animal finally stops moving, a calm seems to settle on the entire world.

Time comes to a stop.

He has always been on his way towards this point.

Ever since those Sundays after mass, back when he lived with Grandma and Grandpa.

85

Rex gets off the underground at Mariatorget, and is walking along Sankt Pauls Street when his phone buzzes to let him know he's received a new voicemail. It's from Janus Mickelsen, telling him he's organised a secure safe-house for Rex and Sammy, with reinforced glass, a steel door, alarm and a direct line to the emergency control room.

'I understand that you can't speak freely if you feel threatened. I get it, I really do. This is a good solution, short-term. My boss has given the go-ahead and I'd like you to meet me tonight at 19.00 just outside Knivsta, at a safe-house belonging to the Security Police, so we can talk through the situation,' Janus says, then repeats the full address twice before the message ends.

Rex decides to go and find out more about this threat the Security Police seem to be taking so seriously.

He walks through the glass door of 34 Krukmakar Street, where the Pool Hall has its rundown basement premises, thinking that there appears to be a tug-of-war between the Security Police and the National Operative Unit.

He passes the bar and goes downstairs, making his way between the tables.

The only sound is clicking as balls knock together and roll silently across the felt table.

At the end of the room is one pool table that's bigger than

the others. Beside it stands a tall man with unruly blond hair and eyes as grey as driftwood.

'The yellow ball is called the Kaisa,' Joona says.

The Finnish pool game, Kaisa, is like Russian Pyramid. It requires a larger table, bigger balls and longer cues. You can play Kaisa in teams, but usually it's a duel between two players.

Rex listens as the taller man runs through the rules and hands him a long cue.

'Sounds a bit like snooker,' Rex says.

'First to sixty wins.'

'Is this why I'm here?'

Joona doesn't answer, just sets the balls out in their positions. If Rex isn't involved in the murders, then he's probably one of the intended victims. The murders appear to revolve around the rape, but there's something more to it than that, maybe further parties, an unknown participant, Joona thinks.

'If you beat me you can leave, but if you lose I'll arrest you,' he says, shooting a sharp glance at Rex.

'Sure,' Rex smiles, running his hands through his unkempt hair.

'I mean it,' Joona says seriously. 'You had a strong motive for the Foreign Minister's murder.'

'Did I?'

Joona hits his white cue-ball, and there's a loud click as it strikes the yellow ball and sends it rolling across the table, where it hits the cushion, rebounds and disappears into one of the pockets.

'Six points to me,' Joona explains.

Rex looks at him uncomprehendingly.

'I had a motive because I pissed in the Foreign Minister's swimming pool?'

'You said he was a bastard and that he stole your girlfriend in high school.'

'Yes,' Rex concedes.

'But you didn't mention you were locked up all night.'

'There were three of them,' he says reluctantly. 'They gave me a beating and then locked me up – not great, but no reason to—'

'Why did they do it?' Joona interrupts.

'What?'

'Lock you up.'

'So that Wille could see Grace without being disturbed, I assume.'

'And did he?'

'He always got what he wanted,' Rex mutters, chalking his cue.

'Aim for the Kaisa,' Joona says, pointing at the yellow ball. 'She needs to go into this pocket.'

Rex leans forward and takes the shot, but ends up hitting one of the reds, which rolls into the other red.

'And that's a kiss,' Joona says. 'No points for that.'

Rex shakes his head with a smile as Joona steps up and hits the Kaisa straight into the corner pocket.

'What does Grace say?' Joona says as he continues with his turn.

'About what?'

'About the evening you were locked up,' he replies, taking another shot and potting Rex's white cue-ball in the same pocket.

'I don't know. I never saw her again,' Rex says. 'I left the school and she never answered my letters or phone calls.'

'I'm talking about now, though,' Joona says.

'I heard she moved back to Chicago, but I haven't seen her for thirty years.'

'You've been accused of murdering the Foreign Minister,' Joona says.

'Who'd accuse me of that?' Rex manages to say.

'You're in serious trouble here,' Joona says, backing away from the table.

'I've done lots of stupid things,' Rex tries to explain as he adjusts the position of his cue. 'But I haven't killed anyone.'

His shot misses. The white cue-ball rolls past the Kaisa, hits the cushion and bounces off.

'If you're not involved in the murders, then you could be on the list of future victims.'

'Am I going to get protection?'

'If you can explain why,' Joona says.

'I have no idea,' Rex says, wiping his forehead.

'Revenge?' the detective suggests, taking his shot.

'That's not very likely.'

Joona gives him a sideways glance, then takes another shot.

'It depends on what you've done,' he says.

'Nothing,' Rex protests. 'What the hell, I get under people's skin, maybe I sleep with women I shouldn't, say stupid stuff, and no doubt there are plenty of people who'd like to take a swing at me, but—'

'Forty-one,' Joona says, then straightens up and looks at him seriously.

'I don't know what to say,' Rex says.

'So you've done lots of stupid things,' Joona reminds him.

'I pissed in the Foreign Minister's pool, but I—'

'You already said that,' Joona interrupts.

'I've done it more than once,' Rex confesses, suddenly blushing.

'I don't care where you've pissed.'

'A hundred times, maybe,' he says, with a peculiar intensity in his voice.

'Get a different hobby.'

'I will, of course I will. What I'm trying to say is that I saw something once when I was there.'

Joona leans over and takes another shot, to prevent Rex from seeing the satisfied smile on his face. The balls click together, and one of them hits the cushion and rebounds into a pocket.

'Forty-nine,' Joona says, slowly chalking the end of his cue.

'Listen,' Rex goes on. 'I'm a sober alcoholic these days, but before things changed, before I started to take it seriously, I used to go there a lot . . . Sometimes I threw those hideous garden gnomes of his in the water, sometimes terracotta pots and garden furniture. I mean, he must have known about it, and just didn't care, unless he thought it was fair payback.'

'You thought you saw something?' Joona prompts, as he moves around the table checking the angles.

'I know I saw something, even if I was drunk . . . I don't remember when, but I still know what I saw . . .'

He falls silent and shakes his head sadly.

'You can think what you like,' he says in a low voice, 'but I saw someone in a mask with a weird, bulging face . . . inside the Foreign Minister's house.'

'How long ago?'

'Four months, maybe? I'm not really sure.'

'What were you doing earlier that day?'

'No idea.'

'Where did you get drunk?'

'Just like Jack Kerouac, I try to do my drinking at home, to limit the damage, but it doesn't always work out.'

Joona takes another shot, the balls click and the Kaisa disappears into the corner pocket.

'Which month was it?'

He knocks Rex's cue-ball into the same pocket, simultaneously hitting a red ball, which rolls diagonally across the table and down into the opposite pocket.

'Don't know,' Rex says.

'Fifty-nine points,' Joona says. 'What did you do afterwards?'

'Afterwards?' Rex says, trying to remember. 'Oh, yeah . . . I went to Sylvia's, she never sleeps, and tried to tell her what I'd seen. It seemed like a really smart idea at the time, but . . .'

'And what did she think?' Joona asks, holding back on his final shot.

'I didn't say anything,' he says, sounding frustrated.

'You went to see Sylvia . . . and said nothing?'

'We had sex,' he mutters.

'Do you usually see Sylvia when you're drunk?' Joona asks.

'I hope not,' Rex says, leaning his cue against the wall.

'We can stop playing. We can even agree to a tie,' Joona says. 'If you call Sylvia and ask what date it was.'

'No chance.'

'OK.'

Joona leans across the table with his cue.

'Hold on,' Rex says quickly. 'You were joking about arresting me, right?'

Joona straightens up, turns towards him and looks him in the eye with a completely neutral expression.

Rex runs his hand through his hair and takes out his iPhone, puts his glasses on and looks for Sylvia among his contacts. He walks off towards the bar as he makes the call.

'Sylvia Lund,' she says when she answers.

'Hi, it's me, Rex.'

'Hello, Rex,' she says in a measured tone of voice.

He makes an effort to keep his voice friendly and stress-free. 'How are you?'

'Are you drunk?'

Rex looks at the tired-looking man behind the bar.

'No, I'm not drunk, but—'

'You sound strange,' she interrupts.

Rex walks a little way up the ramp towards the street in order to talk in peace.

'I need to ask you something,' he says.

'Can we do this tomorrow? I'm kind of busy,' she says impatiently.

Her voice fades as she turns to say something to someone else.

'But I just need—'

'Rex, my daughter's been invited to—'

'Listen, I just need to know what day I came to see you that night, and—'

The line goes dead as Sylvia hangs up on him.

Rex looks out at the street and sees a balloon floating between the cars. He can feel his hands shaking as he calls her again.

'What the hell do you think you're playing at?' Sylvia asks angrily.

'I just need to know when it was,' he persists.

'It's over,' she says. 'I want you to stop—'

'Shut up.'

'You're drunk, I knew it—'

'Sylvia, if you don't tell me, I'm going to call your husband and ask when was the last time he got home from a trip and you were nicer than usual to him.'

There's complete silence on the line. Sweat trickles down his back.

'The last day of April,' she says, and ends the call.

86

A student with matted hair gets out of the lift at the seventeenth floor, but Joona goes up to the top of the building, cool-box in hand. He feels like he's trying to start a fire by gently blowing on the embers, and he knows that flames are going to leap up any minute now. He's here to see Johan Jönson, a computer expert for the NOU, and one of the best IT analysts in Europe. Johan was known as 'the nerd', until he developed the Transvector decryption program that MI6 have started using.

Johan opens the door with a sandwich in his hand and invites Joona into the large room.

In return for turning down all his lucrative private sector offers, Johan demanded to have the entire top floor of the Nyponet block of student residences at the college put at his disposal.

All the internal walls have been removed and replaced by plain steel pillars. The huge room is stuffed full of electronic equipment.

Johan is a rather short man with a black moustache and a small goatee. His head is shaved, and his dark eyebrows are thick, growing together across the top of his nose. He's wearing a tight shirt that looks like Paris Saint-Germain's uniform, and it's slid up to reveal his bulging stomach.

Joona takes the hard-drive containing the security-camera

footage from the Foreign Minister's home out of the cool-box, removes the bubble-wrap and hands it to Johan Jönson.

'You can find erased material, can't you?' Joona says.

'Erased sometimes means just that,' the analyst replies. 'But usually it just means that you say it's been erased even though it's still there. It's a little like Tetris, the older material just sinks deeper and deeper.'

'This recording is four months old.'

Johan puts the remains of his sandwich down on a dusty monitor and weighs the hard-drive in his hand.

'I think we should try a program called Under Work Schedule, which brings everything up at the same time . . . it's a little like one of those paper garlands you cut and unfold, with lots of angels or gingerbread men all joined together.'

'Quite a long garland,' Joona says.

It's possible to restore deleted digital material, but given the thirteen cameras in the Foreign Minister's home were installed seven years ago, they would effectively have to look through ninety-one years' worth of footage.

Not even Joona could persuade Carlos to provide the resources necessary to look through that amount of material. But now that he has a precise date, nothing can stop him.

'Look for Walpurgis Night,' he says.

Johan sits down on a stained office chair and grabs a handful of sweets from a plastic bowl.

More than forty computers of various types are perched on top of desks, filing cabinets and kitchen tables. Bundles of cables run across the floor between crates full of old hard-drives. In one corner of the huge space is a stack of obsolete equipment: assorted circuit boards, soundcards, graphics cards, screens, keyboards, routers, consoles and processors.

Joona spots an unmade bed with no legs in one corner, behind a bench covered with spare parts and a magnifying lamp. There's a collection of bright yellow earplugs on an upturned plastic bucket, next to an alarm clock. Johan probably has less space to live in now than he did when he was a student.

'Move that printer and sit down,' he says to Joona as he attaches the hard-drive to the main computer in the network.

'We have footage from the last time Rex pissed in the swimming pool in our files already, but we're looking for the thirtieth of April, so it'll be material that's been recorded over several times,' Joona explains, moving the printer and a Thomas Pynchon book from the chair.

'Excuse the mess, but I've just linked up thirty computers with the help of a new version of MPI in order to get the sort of supercomputer I need.'

The date and time are at the bottom of the screen. The image shows the first light of day hitting the front of the house and the closed front door.

'Good cameras, good lenses, ultra-HD,' Johan nods approvingly.

Joona lays out a map showing the location of every camera in the Foreign Minister's property, numbered one to thirteen.

'OK, let's burn some rubber,' Johan mutters as he types commands with a rapid-fire clatter of keys.

The row of computers begins to click, fans whirr into life and diodes start to flash.

'Up comes the underworld . . . slowly but surely,' the analyst says, tugging at his short beard.

A grey image appears on the large screen, like iron filings gathering around shifting magnetic fields.

'It's too old,' Johan whispers.

Several layers of flickering shadows appear, and they can make out parts of the garden. Joona sees two ghostly silhouettes walk down the drive. One is the Foreign Minister, and the other is Janus Mickelsen of the Security Police.

'Janus,' Joona says.

'The Foreign Minister was his first deployment with the Security Police,' Johan murmurs as he types new commands into the main computer.

The image disappears, the house is just about visible through the grey fog, and the snow-covered garden flickers into view.

'The garland's still folded up, but we can start pulling the gingerbread men apart now . . . June fourth, June third, June second . . .'

Pale shapes glide to and fro at a rapid pace, passing straight

387

through each other. It looks like an X-ray, with the outlines of figures moving inside one another, through cars reversing and driving into the garage.

'May fifteenth, fourteenth . . . And here we have thirteen lovely versions of the last day of April,' Johan Jönson says softly.

With the footage running at eight times normal speed, they watch the Foreign Minister and his wife leave the house at 7.30 in separate cars. A landscaping company appears two hours later. One man cuts the hedge and another blows leaves. The postman drives past, and at 2.00 a boy on a bike stops and looks into the garden as he scratches his leg. At 7.40 the first car returns to the double garage and lights go on inside the house. Half an hour later the second car arrives, and the garage door closes. Around 11.00 the lights start to go off, and by midnight everything is dark. Then nothing happens until 3.00 a.m., when Rex Müller climbs over the fence and weaves his way across the lawn.

'Now let's check the cameras in real-time, one by one,' Joona says, moving closer.

'OK,' Johan says, tapping a new command. 'We'll start with number one.'

On the large screen they see a perfectly sharp image of the front door and a view of the illuminated garden down towards the gate. Every so often pink petals from the flowering Japanese cherry trees drift down.

87

After three hours they've looked through that night's footage from all thirteen cameras. Thirteen different angles of a sleeping house on the morning of May 1 between 3.36 and 3.55. Four cameras captured Rex during those nine minutes, from the moment he puts his bottle down in the middle of the road and clambers over the black iron railings, until he leaves the garden and delightedly 'discovers' a bottle of wine in the middle of the road.

'Nothing,' Johan sighs.

Rex is in the grounds for nine minutes, and during that time there is no sign of anyone else in any of the recordings, no vehicles on the road, no movement behind the curtains.

'But he saw the murderer,' Joona says. 'He must have, his description matches what other witnesses have said.'

'Maybe it was a different day,' Johan mutters.

'No, this was the night it happened . . . He saw the murderer, even if we can't,' Joona says.

'We can't see what he saw – all we've got are these cameras.'

'If only we knew exactly when he saw him . . . Start with camera seven, that's the one pointing at the pool.'

Once again they see Rex on the edge of the screen as he stumbles onto the deck at the outer limit of the lens's distorted perspective.

He walks over to the side of the pool, sways for a while, then opens his fly and urinates in the water, before weaving over to the navy-blue garden furniture and letting his urine cascade over the recliners and table.

He buttons his trousers, turns towards the garden and looks at something. He lurches slightly, then walks back towards the house, where he stops in front of the patio door and looks into the living room. He leans against the railing, then disappears out of shot.

'What's he looking at just after he zips his fly? There's something in the garden,' Joona says.

'You want me to enlarge his face?'

On the screen Rex moves backwards towards the pool, circles the furniture and turns his back to the camera.

When he starts to move forward again, Johan zooms in on his face and follows it as he urinates on the table. He rests his chin on his chest, closes his eyes and lets out a sigh before zipping his trousers.

Rex turns towards the garden, sees something and smiles lazily to himself before his face slips offscreen as he loses his footing.

'No, it's not there . . . keep going,' Joona says.

Rex turns to face the house and starts to walk towards it, and Johan zooms in even closer. Rex's drunk face fills the whole screen: bloodshot eyes, bottom lip dark with wine, stubble starting to grow out.

They see him stop in front of the patio doors and look into the living room. He opens his mouth slightly, as if he realises he's been spotted, before the look in his eyes becomes concerned, scared, and he turns away and disappears.

'There! That's when he sees him,' Joona says urgently. 'Run it again. We need to take another look.'

Johan Jönson makes a loop of the twenty seconds in front of the glass door, when Rex sees something and starts to smile before becoming scared.

'What do you see?' Joona whispers.

They zoom out and try to follow his gaze. He seems to be staring directly into the living room.

Without breaking the loop, they switch to camera six and see Rex from behind and slightly off to one side. His face is reflected in the glass, as if he's looking at his own reflection.

'Is he in there?' Joona whispers.

The shift in Rex's face, from bemusement to fear, is visible in the reflected image. Through the glass the living-room furniture looks like indistinct shadows.

'Is there someone standing in there?' Johan says, leaning forward.

'Try camera five.'

The fifth camera is positioned outside the dining room, in the part of the house that's at an angle to the rest of the building. It covers part of the living room from the outside, as well as the entire window, and looks towards the corner where camera six is mounted.

Johan zooms in.

The twenty-second-long clip repeats over and over in its loop, but everything inside the darkened dining room is completely still: the chandelier above the table, its reflection on the tabletop, the chairs neatly tucked underneath, a pair of men's socks on the floor.

'There's no one there – what the hell is he looking at?'

'Zoom in under the sofa,' Joona says.

Johan pulls back, then moves down to the base of the lamp, and follows the cable under the sofa.

There's something lying there. Johan gulps and makes the picture brighter, but loses the contrast. The milky darkness is almost as impenetrable as the black was. The picture slowly pans right, revealing a collection of pale tassels by the leg of the sofa.

'It's just a rolled-up rug,' Joona says.

'I almost got scared there,' Johan smiles.

'There's only one possibility left,' Joona says. 'If the killer isn't inside the room, then Rex is seeing him reflected in the window.'

'He's seriously drunk, though, so it could be nothing,' Johan says tentatively.

'Go back to camera six.'

Once again the screen shows Rex from behind, in front of

the glass door to the living room. Time after time, the expression on his face changes from surprise to fear.

'What's scaring him?'

'He can't see anything but himself.'

'No, that's the Venus effect,' Joona replies, leaning closer to the screen.

'What?'

'If he's being filmed from the side, and we can see his face head on, then he can't be looking at himself.'

'Because he's looking straight at the camera,' Johan says, tugging at his beard again.

'So what he's looking at must be somewhere just below camera six.'

The analyst switches cameras and pans past the large living-room windows to the edge of the image, towards camera six which is mounted on the far corner of the building, with a grove of dark trees behind it.

'Closer, under that weeping willow,' Joona says.

The long branches reach almost to the grass, and are swaying in the gentle breeze.

Joona feels a shiver run down his spine at the first glimpse of the murderer.

The shadows of the leaves move across a masked face, and then it's gone.

88

With his hands trembling, Johan rewinds the footage and halves the speed, and they see the branches of the willow part to reveal the face, then hide it again.

'A little more,' Joona whispers.

The leaves sway slowly and then they see the murderer once more, just as he turns away and vanishes into the shadows.

'Again, from the beginning,' Joona says.

This time he can clearly see the rabbits' ears hanging in front of the masked face.

'Stop . . . go back slightly.'

The screen is almost completely black, but something grey moves across the murderer's head and there's a flicker in the window next to him.

'What the hell's he doing?'

'Zoom in on the darkness,' Joona says.

'What's that?' Johan asks, pointing at the screen.

'Must be the back of his ear.'

'He's taken off the mask?'

'The opposite, I'd say . . . this is where he puts it on, under cover of the shadows.'

The murderer must have figured out that there was a camera shadow in line with the grove of trees, and made his way into the garden using that blind spot before stopping under the willow tree to pull his balaclava over his head.

'Quite the fucking professional,' Johan says breathlessly.

'Try number eight again . . . there was a glimmer of something in the window.'

The picture goes black and the grey movements sweep across the screen as the murderer pulls on his mask with his back to the camera. There's a flicker of something in the window before he turns around, the rabbits' ears swaying in front of his face.

'What's that, glinting off the kitchen window?' Johan asks.

'It's a vase. I saw it before, on camera seven,' Joona says. 'It's on the windowsill, next to a bowl of lemons.'

'A vase.'

'Zoom in on it.'

Johan makes the vase fill the screen, just as Rex's face did a short while before. The curved, shiny metal reflects the window and the garden outside. Along one edge of the vase is a trace of movement, no more than a fleeting shift in the light.

'Back,' Joona says.

'I didn't see anything,' Johan mutters as he rewinds the footage.

The movement along the edge of the vase forms a curved line, the colour of yellowing paper.

'That could be his face before he puts the mask on,' Joona says.

'Shit me sideways,' Johan whispers, taking a high-resolution screenshot of the convex reflection.

They both stare at the curved reflection in the vase, a pale arc running vertically down the screen.

'What do we do? We need to see his face.'

Johan drums his fingers on his thigh and mutters something to himself.

'What did you say?' Joona asks.

'In an almost spherical mirror, the image is so distorted because the rays from the edges and centre of the surface don't meet at the same point.'

'Can that be corrected?'

'I just need to try to find a concave distortion that corresponds

394

exactly with the convex surface, and align that with the main axis . . .'

'Sounds like it would take a long time.'

'Months . . . if Photoshop didn't already exist,' Johan smiles.

He opens the program and starts to flatten the image, little by little.

The only sound is the tapping of keys.

The glare of the reflection is sucked into the white arc, leaving the surrounding space darker. It looks like a peculiar meteorological phenomenon.

'I've got goose-bumps,' Johan whispers.

The pale face slowly widens and finally crystallises in its original form.

Joona takes a deep breath and stands up from his chair. For the first time, he can clearly see the murderer.

89

As Rex puts his suitcase down in the hall he can hear Sammy playing his guitar. He recognises the chord, and tries to remember what song it is as he heads towards the living room.

Rex gave Sammy a steel-stringed Taylor guitar when he got confirmed, but he didn't know that he still played it. As he enters the room he remembers the song: Led Zeppelin's 'Babe, I'm Gonna Leave You'.

Sammy has dirt under his nails and he's written something on his hand. His blond fringe hangs in front of his face as he concentrates.

He plucks nimbly at the strings and sings along quietly, just to hear the tune in his head.

Rex sits down on the amplifier and listens. Sammy keeps playing until he reaches the long instrumental section, then holds his hand over the strings to silence them and looks up.

'You're good!' Rex exclaims.

'No, I'm not,' Sammy says, embarrassed.

Rex picks up his semi-acoustic Gibson and adjusts the amp. There's a buzz as the cables warm up.

'Do you know any Bowie tracks?'

'"Ziggy Stardust" was the first song I taught myself. I felt really cool. Mum must have heard it a million times,' Sammy says, smiling as he starts to play.

Rex sings along, trying to keep pace with his son on his guitar.

Grey clouds are racing across the sky outside the large windows, and it looks like there might be a storm brewing.

As they sing together, Rex looks at Sammy's face and remembers when Veronica told him she was thinking of keeping the baby. He had already said he didn't feel mature enough, and was unable to contain his feelings of powerlessness and frustration. He stood up, tucked his chair in and walked out on her.

'Solo, Dad! Solo!' Sammy cries.

With a look of horror on his face, Rex starts playing the only blues scale he knows, but it sounds all wrong.

'Sorry,' he groans.

'Try E-flat instead,' Sammy says.

Rex changes position and tries again, and this time it does sound a little better, almost like a real guitar solo.

'Bravo!' Sammy says with a smile, looking at him happily.

Rex laughs and they start to play Håkan Hellström's 'It'll Never Be Over For Me', when suddenly the doorbell rings.

'I'll get it,' Rex says, and puts his guitar down on the floor, making the amplifier rumble.

He hurries out to the hall and opens the door.

A young woman with pierced cheeks looks at him groggily. She's wearing black jeans, a Pussy Riot T-shirt, and a black hat, and her skinny left arm is in a cast from the elbow all the way to her fingertips. In her other hand she's carrying a crumpled plastic bag from H&M.

Behind her stands a man in his thirties. His eyes are warm and his face is boyishly attractive, albeit rather haggard, like a rock star. Rex recognises him. It's the man Sammy was at the party with when he took an overdose.

'Come in,' Sammy says behind Rex.

The young woman stumbles over the doormat and hands the bag to Sammy.

'Your stuff,' Nico says, stepping into the hall.

'OK,' Sammy replies.

The woman wraps her arms around Nico and smiles up at his face.

'Is this the gay guy who paid for your car?' she asks.

'He's my Salaì. I love him,' Nico says, stroking her back.

'I thought you loved me,' she complains.

Sammy looks in the bag.

'Where's the camera?'

'Shit, forgot it,' Nico says, and taps his head.

'How are things?' Sammy asks in a subdued voice.

'The court case is in November . . . but I've rented a house in Marseilles, so I'm going to spend the autumn there.'

'He's going to paint a series of pictures of me,' the young woman says, wobbling as she manages to step on Rex's boots.

'Filippa's coming along. There'll be a little gang of us, so it's going to be really cool.'

'I'm sure it will,' Sammy says.

'She doesn't have your eyes,' Nico says quietly.

Sammy looks up at him.

'Damn, you're so handsome,' Nico sighs.

Sammy can't help smiling.

'When can I have my camera?' he asks.

'What are you doing tonight?'

'Why do you want to know?' Filippa whispers into Nico's ear.

'I'm thinking of going to Jonny's party,' Nico says.

'They're so fucking sick, I can't handle that,' she groans, leaning back against the coats hanging in the hall.

'I wasn't asking you,' Nico says, and looks at Sammy. 'Do you want to come? It could be fun, and I'll take the camera.'

'To Jonny's?' Sammy says dubiously.

'He's staying at home,' Rex says sternly.

'OK, Dad,' Nico says, and salutes.

'I'll think about it,' Sammy says.

'Say yes, that would make me—'

'Thanks for coming,' Rex interrupts.

'Stop it, Dad,' Sammy whispers, sounding pained.

Filippa giggles and starts to go through the pockets of the coats behind her. Nico takes her arm and backs out through the door.

'I'll call you,' Sammy says.

Rex closes the door, then stands there holding the handle, staring down at the floor.

'Dad,' Sammy says wearily. 'You can't just do that. That was really shitty.'

'You're right, I'm sorry,' Rex begins. 'But . . . I thought it was over?'

'I don't know what's going to happen.'

'You need to live your own life, but I can't pretend to like him.'

'Nico's an artist. He went to art school in Gothenburg.'

'He's good-looking, and I can see that he's exciting, but he put you in danger, and that—'

'I'm not completely naïve,' Sammy cuts him off irritably.

Rex holds his hands up towards him apologetically.

'Can we just try to get through these weeks together, like we said at the beginning?'

90

The Rabbit Hunter is walking down the narrow pavement on Luntmakar Street, a dark backstreet that runs between the tall buildings in the centre of Stockholm.

Inside his coat the little axe swings on its strap by his waist.

Several pallets laden with shrink-wrapped trays are blocking the pavement in front of one of the restaurants and he's forced to step out into the road.

The Rabbit Hunter feels beneath his nose, as if he has a nosebleed, and looks at his fingers, but it's nothing. He thinks of how he used to tie live rabbits to the dead ones, in long chains, and then set them loose. The living and injured would drag the dead bodies with them, darting in different directions and panicking as they tried to get away.

They would draw strange bloody patterns across the dirty cement floor.

He remembers the twitching back legs, the claws clattering as the creatures tried to escape the weight of the dead. Without hurrying, he walks down the street past a half-open garage. The electronic door seems to be broken, and is being held a metre or so off the ground by a sawhorse. He can hear a woman sobbing angrily inside the garage. She sniffs and says something in an agitated voice.

The Rabbit Hunter passes the opening just as the woman stops speaking.

He stops, turns around and listens.

The woman is crying again, and now a man is shouting at her.

The Rabbit Hunter walks back, crouches down and looks in. He sees a steep ramp with dim lights along the concrete walls. The woman is speaking more calmly now, but stops abruptly as if she's been hit. The Rabbit Hunter ducks under the door and starts to walk down the ramp.

The air inside is stuffy and smells like petrol.

He keeps going until he reaches a small garage. A man in his sixties, wearing a leather jacket and baggy jeans, is shoving a skimpily dressed young woman in between a red van with misted-up windows and a sports car covered in some sort of silvery fabric.

'Are you having fun?' the Rabbit Hunter asks in a low voice.

'Who the fuck are you?' the man exclaims. 'You're not allowed down here!'

The Rabbit Hunter leans against the wall, looks at them and then the van, which is rocking rhythmically, and thinks that he could slice them all open, chop their hands off and watch them run around squirting blood everywhere.

'Get out of here!' the man says.

The woman stares at him blankly.

Pieces of an aluminium ventilation system are laid out on a tarp just behind the man, and further away some rolls of artificial grass are stacked against the wall.

The Rabbit Hunter has never had anything against close combat. When he was going house to house helping to clear the combat area in Ramadi, he was always the first man in.

They would break the door down, then throw in some Polish-manufactured shock grenades. The unit commander would stand aside and give orders to the others.

He always went straight for the target with his M4, a pistol or a knife. He was quick, and could kill four or five men single-handed.

'Get lost,' the man says, coming closer.

The Rabbit Hunter straightens up, wipes his top lip, and looks at the flickering fluorescent light in the ceiling.

'This is a private garage,' the man says threateningly.

'I heard screams when I was walking past, and—'

'It's none of your business,' the man interrupts, puffing his chest out.

The Rabbit Hunter looks over at the young woman again. She has a sullen look on her face, and one of her cheeks is red from where the man slapped her. She's wearing a mid-length raincoat and a white wrap-dress, black tights with skulls on them, and platform shoes.

'Do you want to be here?' the Rabbit Hunter asks her gently.

'No,' she replies quickly, and wipes her nose.

'Look, you've misunderstood the situation,' the man smiles.

The Rabbit Hunter knows he shouldn't be here, but he can't help staying. He doesn't care about the woman. She's not going to escape prostitution, whatever happens here. It's the man who's the attraction.

'Let her go,' he tells him.

'She doesn't want to go,' the man replies, drawing a semi-automatic pistol.

'Ask her,' the Rabbit Hunter suggests, feeling shivers of heat radiate from somewhere deep in his gut.

'What the fuck do you want?' the man asks. 'Do you think you're some kind of hero?'

He points the pistol at the Rabbit Hunter, but is unnerved by his utter lack of fear and takes a few steps back.

'Nothing's going to happen to her,' the man says, a trace of nerves in his voice. 'She's just stuck-up and thinks she's better than the others.'

The Rabbit Hunter follows him, and can't help smiling.

The man has lowered the gun. It's pointing at the floor now, its barrel shaking.

He backs into the large ventilation drum, moving aimlessly, trying to get away like a sick rabbit.

'Leave me the fuck alone.'

The man raises the pistol again, but the Rabbit Hunter gently blocks his hand, turns the gun on him and pushes the barrel into his mouth.

'Bang,' he whispers, then pulls the gun out again, releases the magazine onto the ground and empties the bullet from the chamber. It rolls across the floor to the girl's feet. She's just standing there, her eyes downcast, as if afraid to look.

The Rabbit Hunter goes back up the ramp, wipes his fingerprints off the pistol and drops it in a bucket of sand and cigarette butts. He ducks under the garage door and walks along the shaded pavement.

At Rehns Street he turns right and walks up to the wooden doorway just as a woman with dyed black hair whose arm is in a cast holds the door open for a man with an attractive face.

The Rabbit Hunter catches the door and thanks them, walks straight into the lift and presses the button for the top floor.

He remembers when he and his mother used to help each other with the traps, spraying the cages with apple cider so the rabbits wouldn't pick up the scent of humans.

The lift reaches the top floor just as the lights in the stairwell go out. There's only one door on this floor, a heavy security door.

After Rex dies, he's going to cut his ears off, thread them onto a leather strap and wear them around his neck inside his shirt.

The thought fills his head with a crackling sound, which turns into a deafening rattle, like when you push a shopping cart full of bottles across the car park.

The Rabbit Hunter closes his eyes and tries to compose himself. He needs to bring the silence outside in, and impose it on the chaos.

He rings the doorbell and hears footsteps approaching from inside the flat. He looks down at the marble floor only to see it rotating beneath his feet.

The door opens and Rex is standing in front of him, his shirt hanging outside his trousers. He lets him in, takes a few steps back and almost falls over a suitcase.

'Come in,' he says gruffly.

The Rabbit Hunter goes in and closes the door behind him, hangs his coat up and unties his shoes while Rex goes back upstairs.

He adjusts the axe hanging under his jacket and slowly follows Rex to the brightly lit first floor.

'I'm hungry,' he says when he enters the kitchen.

'Sorry,' Rex smiles, and throws his arms out. 'I was playing guitar instead of preparing the asparagus.'

'I'll do it,' the Rabbit Hunter says, taking out a white plastic chopping board.

'I'll start making the stock, then,' Rex says, grabbing four bunches of green asparagus from the fridge.

The Rabbit Hunter swallows hard. He needs to take his medication as soon as possible. His brain is screaming as if someone were ripping it in half. Rex is one of the men who raped his mother, who left her for dead on a manure heap.

The Rabbit Hunter leans one hand on the counter and pulls a vegetable knife from the block.

Sammy comes into the kitchen holding an apple, glances at the Rabbit Hunter and then turns to his father.

'Can we keep talking?' he asks, then blushes.

The Rabbit Hunter holds the knife-blade against his thumb, presses it gently and closes his eyes for a few moments.

'Sammy,' Rex says. 'I don't have a problem with you living here, that isn't what I said.'

'But it isn't all that fucking great knowing you aren't wanted,' he says.

'Everyone's going to die anyway,' the Rabbit Hunter says.

He looks at the knife in his hand and thinks about his mother again, and the terrible rape that destroyed her.

Now he knows that his mother was suffering from recurrent reactive depressive psychosis during his childhood, and that her dark delusions had a serious impact on both of them.

Their aggressive fear of rabbits, and of those repulsive rabbit holes in the ground.

He used to try to keep his childhood memories at arm's length. The rabbit hunts and his mother's fears were just one part of a secret past.

But more recently those memories have been surfacing more frequently, breaking through all his defences.

They rush in and head straight for him, as if everything is happening at this very moment.

He doesn't think he's psychotic, but the past has proved beyond any doubt that it will never give up.

91

As he chops the shallots, Rex can feel how sore the fingertips of his left hand are from playing the guitar.

'Why would you say you aren't wanted?' he asks tentatively, brushing the chopped onion into a saucepan.

'Because you're always talking about how we have to try to get through three weeks together,' Sammy explains.

Rex scrapes the knife against the edge of the pan, looks at the wide blade, then rinses it in the sink.

'I don't mean that I have to put up with you when I say that,' he says. 'I mean . . . I'm pleading with you to put up with me.'

'Doesn't feel like it,' his son says in a thick voice.

'I've never seen Rex as happy as he is now,' DJ points out as he peels the asparagus.

'Dad, do you remember last time I was supposed to stay with you?' Sammy asks. 'Do you remember that?'

Rex looks at his son, his glistening eyes, sensitive face and thin shoulders. He realises that what he's about to say isn't going to be good, but he still wants him to keep going.

'No, I don't remember,' he replies honestly.

'I was ten years old, and I was so happy. I told all my friends about my dad, and how I was going to live with you in the middle of the city, and how we were going to eat at your restaurant every night.'

Sammy's voice breaks, he lowers his face and tries to calm down. Rex wishes he could go over and hug him, but doesn't dare.

'Sammy . . . I don't know what to say, I don't remember that,' he says quietly.

'No,' Sammy replies. 'Because you changed your mind when you saw I hadn't cut my hair.'

'That's not true,' he says.

'I had long hair, and you kept making a fuss, saying I should get it cut, but I didn't, and . . . when I got to your house . . .'

Sammy's eyes fill with tears, his face turns red and his lips swell. Rex takes the saucepan off the heat and wipes his hands on his apron.

'Sammy,' he says. 'Now I know what you're talking about, and it had nothing to do with your hair. Look, it was like this . . . when your mum brought you, I was so drunk I couldn't stand up. There was no way she could leave you with me.'

'No,' Sammy sniffs, turning his face away.

'That was when I lived on Drottning Street,' Rex says. 'I remember I was lying on the kitchen floor, and I remember you. You were wearing red plimsolls and you had that little cardboard suitcase that . . .'

He trails off as the realisation spreads through his chest.

'But you thought it was your hair,' he says, almost to himself. 'Of course you did.'

He walks around the kitchen counter and tries to hug Sammy, but his son pulls away.

'Forgive me,' Rex says, and gently brushes Sammy's long fringe away from his face. 'Forgive me, Sammy.'

DJ slips a Modiodal pill in his mouth and swallows. He doesn't know how he's going to be affected emotionally by everything that's going on. It wouldn't be good if he suddenly fell asleep on the floor.

He cuts the peeled asparagus stems into slices, saves the tops and then tips the rest into a pan of water.

He's thinking that he can't be a hunter right now, that he's going to have to be DJ the friend for a little while longer.

There's no hurry. Everything is happening at a perfect pace, in the perfect order.

He remembers his mum showing him a school photograph, with all the students gathered in front of the huge main building. The eyes of nine of them had been pricked out, and the tenth wasn't on the picture because he was the groundskeeper. He remembers his mother's trembling hand precisely, and the way the light from the lamp on the table shone through the holes in the paper, like an unfamiliar constellation.

'I can take care of myself,' Sammy says in a subdued voice. 'Don't you get that yet?'

'But I'm responsible for you while you're here . . . and the way things are looking right now, I don't think I should go to Norrland with DJ.'

'We can postpone the meeting,' DJ says, putting the vegetable knife down on the chopping board. 'I can call the investors.'

Rex shoots him a look of gratitude.

DJ smiles and thinks about how he's going to kill him: Rex is going to have to crawl down the hallway in the hotel with his back sliced open until he shoots him in the back of the neck.

Rex squeezes some lime juice into the pan, and Sammy gets the cream from the fridge.

'I don't need babysitting,' Sammy says. 'It may look like I do, but I'm fine.'

'I just don't want you to be on your own,' Rex replies as he starts to peel the shrimp.

'You've been dreaming about going up there and going hunting,' Sammy smiles, pretending to aim a rifle. 'Bang, bang . . . Bambi's dead.'

'It's just business,' Rex replies.

'And I'm ruining it,' Sammy says.

'You could come up to the wilds of Norrland with us,' DJ suggests, imagining a bleeding rabbit crawling across the floor while what's left of its paws lie on the workbench.

'Dad doesn't want that,' Sammy replies quietly.

'Of course I do!' Rex protests, rinsing his hands.

'No, you don't,' Sammy says.

Rex blends the soup together, flash-fries the fat buds of asparagus and grabs the bowl of peeled shrimp.

'It would be great,' he says enthusiastically. 'We could make food for the investors, Sammy, and I promise, you'll love the scenery up there.'

'But I can't kill animals.'

'Neither can I,' Rex says.

'Maybe you'll find out you've got it in you, when it comes down to it,' DJ says, trying to force the sound of his mother's screams from his head.

Only two of the rapists have been hard to kill. One because he knew it would lead to a lot of media attention and a large police operation, and the other because he lives in Washington DC and had been heavily protected by Blackwater for many years.

His plan was so ingenious that no one could have spotted it before it was too late.

He knew that Teddy Johnson would attend the Foreign Minister's funeral.

But he had to entice him at exactly the right time, before he found out that any of his other old friends from the Rabbit Hole had died, otherwise he would suspect a trap.

And then it wouldn't have made any difference what bait the hunter had set at the back of the rabbit cage.

But he had walked into the trap, and DJ had managed to give Rex the slip in the crowded church. He made sure he sat on the balcony, close to the stairs, with Sammy off to his right. During one particularly rousing hymn they threw little balls of paper at Rex.

DJ snuck out of the service, and managed to get up to the top of the tower on Kungs Street ten minutes before the priest's closing words. He knew that the chaos after Teddy Johnson was shot would hide the fact that he had disappeared. People would be running around screaming. It would take hours before the three of them found each other again, back at Rex's flat.

A .300 Win Mag was the obvious weapon of choice. He usually follows his gut feeling when it comes to choosing a weapon.

When he killed the Foreign Minister he had chosen a pistol with a silencer, because he knew all too well that no matter how carefully you prepare and plan and map your victim's routines, there are always things you can't foresee.

He had been there twice before he broke in to identify the locations of the alarms and cameras and to check the security routines. But unlike most people, a man in the Foreign Minister's position could very easily have had armed bodyguards in the house.

The Rabbit Hunter would have preferred to slit his wrists in the bath, but after the prostitute managed to free herself and raise the alarm, he didn't want to take any risks.

There were three reasons to kill the Foreign Minister while he had a prostitute tied to his bed. The first was that he knew his victim only arranged that sort of encounter when the rest of his family were away.

The second was that the Foreign Minister always got rid of his bodyguards before he saw a prostitute.

The third was that the prostitute increased the likelihood that the circumstances surrounding the Foreign Minister's death would be hushed up.

DJ smiles at Rex as they sit down at the table, but inside him his mother screams in terror as the rabbits slip out of the trap. They panic as they try to escape the shovel he's using to hit them with.

92

Joona marches through the hallway on the eighth floor of Police Headquarters. His blond hair is untidy, his grey eyes sharp. He's wearing a new black suit and a pale grey shirt. The jacket is unbuttoned and the butt of his Colt Combat is visible in the worn leather holster beneath his left shoulder.

A young woman with laughter lines on her face smiles at him warmly, and a man with a silvery beard who's standing in the staffroom puts his hand on his heart as Joona walks past.

Outside his boss's office is a map showing Sweden's seven police districts, on which Stockholm is the smallest and the northernmost covers half the entire country.

Carlos is bent over his aquarium and when Joona walks in he jumps as if he's been caught doing something illegal.

'You spoil them,' Joona says, looking at the fish.

'I know, but they love it,' Carlos nods.

He's changed the décor of the aquarium. Instead of the wrecked ship and plastic diver, the fish are now swimming around white spaceships, Stormtroopers, a prone Darth Vader and a Han Solo half hidden by the bubbles from the oxygen pump.

'We've got a picture of the murderer's face now,' Joona explains. 'But the photograph doesn't match anyone with a criminal record or who's ever been a suspect.'

411

Carlos opens the picture on his computer and looks at the face that Johan Jönson was able to extract from the reflection in the silver vase.

The murderer is a white man in his thirties, with blond hair and a neat, full beard, a straight nose and furrowed brow.

The face is turned to the side, his thick neck is twisted, and his neck muscles stand out from the shadows. His mouth is slightly open, and his blue eyes are glistening, and have a distant look in them.

'We need to get this picture out to every unit in the force, and it has to come from you,' Joona says. 'Top priority. We'll give it fifteen minutes, then if there's no response we can get the picture up on the newspapers' websites and ask for information from the general public—'

'Why is it always such a rush when you . . .?'

He cuts himself off when Anja comes into his office without knocking. She walks around the large desk and rolls Carlos and his chair out of the way, as if he's a barbecue that's in the way.

She quickly disseminates the picture across the internal network that covers the entire force, giving it top priority, then opens an attachment to an email she herself has sent, containing a suggested text to newsrooms around the country.

The killer's picture appears on Carlos's own radio display, which is lying next to the keyboard.

'Now we just have to wait,' she says, folding her arms.

'So, what's new around here apart from the name?' Joona asks, looking out at the park through the low window.

'We're working exactly the same way we were before,' Carlos replies. 'Just a little worse.'

'Sounds great,' Joona says, checking his watch and wondering why Saga hasn't been in touch.

A call comes in on another terminal. Carlos realises he's going to have to answer, and fumbles with the buttons until he manages to switch the speaker function on.

'Rikard Sjögren, Stockholm Response Team,' the officer says by way of introduction. 'I don't know if it's any use, but I was part of the operation guarding the Foreign Minister's funeral at St Johannes' Church, and I'm sure I saw this man among the mourners.'

'But you don't know who he is?' Carlos asks, his mouth close to the unit.

'No.'

'Was he with anyone else, or near anyone you recognised?' Joona asks.

'I'm not sure . . . but I saw him talking to that chef who's always on television.'

'Rex Müller?'

'Yes, that's the one, Rex Müller.'

Anja has already started looking through the newspapers' and weekly magazines' archives of photographs from the funeral. Faces sweep past, mostly politicians and businessmen in the bright sunshine outside the church.

'Here he is,' she says. 'That's him, isn't it?'

'Yes,' Joona says.

There's a man standing in a line of people in the background of a photograph of the President of Estonia. He's shading his eyes against the sun, which is shining brightly on his blond beard.

'But no name,' Anja mutters to herself, and goes on looking.

It doesn't take long before she finds another photograph of him, this time standing next to Rex Müller and his son. Rex has his arm around his son's shoulders, and is looking into the camera with a mournful expression on his face, while the murderer is in the process of turning away. His brow is wet with sweat and the look in his eyes seems oddly tense.

'According to the caption, his name is David Jordan Andersen,' Anja says.

We've identified the murderer, Joona thinks. David Jordan Andersen is the spree killer who is murdering the rapists, one by one.

Anja quickly looks up his name and discovers that a David Jordan is the founder of the company that produces Rex's cooking shows, and that he pretty much acts as his manager.

'Where does he live?' Joona asks.

'He lives . . . out on Ingarö, and his company has an office on Observatorie Street.'

'Send one team out to Ingarö, one to the office, and another

413

to Rex Müller's home,' Joona tells Carlos. 'But don't forget that he's extremely dangerous . . . he's very likely to try to kill the first men in.'

'Don't say such things,' Carlos mutters.

Joona and Anja wait while Carlos quickly organises a leadership team and gives the National Operations Unit the order to break into the house on Ingarö, then gives the two other addresses to the local police response teams.

Before he ends his call he stresses the importance of heavy armaments and protective vests.

'He can shoot right through our vests,' Joona says, and leaves the room.

93

The sky is white now that the rain has passed. Faded dog rose petals are stuck to the drain-covers. Water drips from the roof of the Forensic Medicine Department at Karolinska Institute.

Nils 'The Needle' Åhlén drives past the car park in his white Jaguar, pulls up on the pavement and stops right in front of the entrance with one of the back wheels on the flowerbed.

The Needle's thin face is clean-shaven, and he has his white-framed aviator sunglasses perched on his crooked nose. He's regarded as an extremely dedicated and focused pathologist, and today he's in an unusually good mood.

He waves cheerily at the woman at the reception desk, goes into his office, takes his jacket off and pulls his white coat on.

'You know I'm a bad man . . . la, la, la,' he sings as he goes into the lab.

The Needle's assistant, Frippe, has already taken the body out of the store and has laid it, in the sealed bag it was placed in for transportation, on the table ready for the post-mortem.

'I spoke to Carlos, and he says Joona Linna's back,' Nils says. 'Now everything's going to be fine again.'

He stops talking abruptly, clears his throat a couple of times, takes off his glasses and polishes them on the bottom of his coat.

'I'm starting to understand why I had to get Mr Ritter out again,' Frippe says, tucking his hair up in a ponytail.

'Joona thinks he was murdered,' The Needle says, and the corners of his mouth twitch into a smile.

'That's not what I think,' Frippe says.

'Three people who attended Ludviksberg School thirty years ago have been killed this week. But Joona thinks there could be more, so Anja ran all the names from their old yearbooks through the databases. There's one suicide in the south of Sweden that Joona plans to look into . . . and the only other relevant death is this one,' Nils concludes.

'Which was an accident,' Frippe says.

'Joona thinks we've missed a murder.'

'He hasn't even seen the damn body,' Frippe says with barely concealed irritation.

'No,' The Needle says, smiling happily.

'Carl-Erik Ritter was incredibly drunk. He had 0.23 per cent alcohol in his blood. He fell into a plate-glass window on his way home from the El Bocado pub in Axelsberg and cut his carotid artery open,' Frippe goes on, opening the body-bag.

A cloying, swampy smell spreads through the room.

Carl-Erik Ritter's naked body is brown and mottled, and his blackened stomach is distended.

The body has been stored at a temperature of 7°C to slow the decomposition process, but they are losing the fight against decay.

Frippe leans over the grey face, and suddenly notices something red glinting in one of the nostrils.

'What the hell . . .?'

A brownish red liquid starts to trickle from the nose, across the dead man's lips and down his cheek.

'Shit,' Frippe says, jerking his head back.

The Needle hides his smile but says nothing – he reacted that way himself once upon a time. During the process of decomposition blisters often develop beneath the skin and inside the nose; when the blisters suddenly burst and the liquid drains out, it's easy to confuse that with a nosebleed.

Frippe goes over to the computer and stands there for a while, before returning with his iPad and starting to compare pictures from the scene with the dead man's injuries.

'Well, I'm sticking with my evaluation,' he says after a while. 'It's a textbook accident . . . But obviously Joona could be right about other deaths, there are other districts, we could have missed a murder in Gothenburg or Ystad.'

'Maybe,' Nils mutters, pulling on a pair of vinyl gloves.

'The shop window broke and Ritter fell onto the glass. It all makes sense. Take a look at the forensics team's report,' Frippe says, holding out the iPad.

Nils doesn't take it, but instead starts to examine the many superficial cuts on the body, which now look like thin black lines, focused mainly on the hands, knees, torso and face. The only really serious wound is the incision across the throat and up towards one ear.

'One straight, gaping wound,' Frippe reads as Nils picks at the deep gash. 'The internal edges are smooth and not particularly drenched in blood . . . no tissue damage or bruising, and the surrounding skin is intact . . .'

'Fine,' The Needle says, running his finger along the inside of the cut.

'The direct cause of death was a combination of blood loss and blood aspiration,' Frippe goes on.

'Yes, it's a very deep wound,' Nils murmurs.

'He was drunk, lost his balance, smashed onto the plate-glass window with his full bodyweight, and his neck slid down one of the jagged edges . . . like the blade of a guillotine.'

Nils gives him an amused sideways glance.

'But what if those unfortunate circumstances are too perfect?' he says. 'What if he had help from someone applying pressure to his head, someone who made sure his neck slid along the jagged edge so that it cut right through his carotid artery and throat.'

'It was an accident,' Frippe says obstinately.

'He drowned slowly in his own blood,' The Needle declares, pushing his glasses further up his long nose.

'Now it feels like Joona Linna is standing here asking who's right,' Frippe groans.

'But you're convinced you are,' Nils says breezily.

'It was an accident. I removed two hundred and ten glass splinters from the body.'

Nils moves his fingers to the dead man's mouth and opens the congealed wound on the top lip, uncovering his teeth.

'This was done with a knife,' he says curtly.

'A knife,' Frippe repeats, and swallows hard.

'Yes.'

'So it was murder after all,' Frippe says, looking at the body.

'No question,' The Needle whispers, looking him in the eye.

'One single wound . . . One single wound out of two fucking hundred was inflicted with a knife.'

'To give the victim a hare-lip . . .'

94

The National Operations Unit's black minibuses have blocked the narrow road four hundred metres from David Jordan's home on the island of Ingarö. Heavily armed police officers are cordoning off the area, and have laid out spike strips that run all the way across, even down into the ditches.

After consultation with Janus Mickelsen of the Security Police, the ground operation is being led by Magnus Mollander. He's a shy blond man, who split up with his girlfriend just a few days ago. One morning she declared out of the blue that she could no longer live with someone who risked death every time he went to work. There had been no reasoning with her. She just packed her flowery suitcase and left.

While they were driving to the house Magnus checked the satellite images of the property, which consists largely of woodland and steep rocks leading down to the water.

The response team is made up of eight police officers in full gear: helmets, bulletproof vests, stun grenades, pistols and sniper rifles.

Their heavy boots echo as they move down the empty road.

At a signal from Magnus, Janus and two other snipers leave the road and head out into the undergrowth. The rest of the group head towards the fence and move along it in silence.

Birdsong is coming from the treetops high above. A few butter-flies are flitting among the wild flowers.

The response team reaches the neatly maintained driveway to David Jordan's house. Magnus waves his colleagues forward. He's received a report from Janus telling him that the snipers have crossed the fence and are now making their way up the rocks behind the tennis court.

He gestures to the group to spread out in pairs.

Magnus and his partner Rajmo stand still and observe the house.

The snipers report that they're in position.

Magnus is sweating. He can hear his own breathing inside the helmet as he raises his arm and gives his men the signal.

Group one makes its way to the guesthouse and forces the door while group two follow Magnus and Rajmo towards the main building.

Crouching, they run across the open space towards the house. They approach from two directions – Magnus breaks down the front door as other men in group two smash a window and toss in distraction grenades.

Rajmo pulls the door back, knocking the splinters from the frame with the barrel of his gun, then runs over to the first bedroom door, crouches down and opens it. Magnus is right behind him. The burglar alarm shrieks as they check the bedrooms, opening the wardrobe doors and overturning the beds.

As they emerge from the bedrooms they get reports from the rest of the team in the main building. They've searched the other end of the house but found nothing.

Magnus waves Rajmo forward, then runs through the living room, securing the hidden corners before heading into the huge kitchen, full of dazzling light from the sea. Magnus moves forward, and hears the team in the other part of the house shout something. His protective glasses have become dislodged and he pulls them off, but then, from the corner of his eye, he sees someone rush out from a hiding place in the yard. Magnus gasps and points his gun at the window. His finger is resting on the trigger but he can no longer see anyone, just the row of white lounge chairs.

Magnus crouches down to limit the size of target he presents. His heart is pounding in his chest. Outside the leaves on the trees sway in the gentle wind. He wipes the sweat from his eyes and then he sees the figure again.

It's Rajmo, somehow reflected through various windows, making it look as if he's outside on the deck even though he's moving around the dining-room table ten metres away.

Magnus stands up again, looks through the window, takes a step back and sees his partner reflected in the glass once more.

He turns towards Rajmo and says that they need to search the house again.

In the kitchen there's a half-full glass of whisky on the marble counter, next to an open bag of cheese puffs. Magnus removes one of his gloves and touches the glass. It isn't cold. No ice-cubes have melted into it recently.

But someone has been here, and left the house in a hurry.

He goes over to the window. Group one has reached the jetty. Two men have climbed onto the speedboat and are checking the cabin and deck hatches.

Magnus opens the patio door and goes outside. He sees an inflatable fox in a tree. The wind must have carried the toy from the pool area.

The alarm finally turns off and Magnus reports back to NOU command that there's no one home, but that they're going to search the house once more, slowly and systematically.

'Joona Linna will be with you in fifteen minutes,' the chief of staff tells him.

'Good.'

Magnus walks around the house and waves to the snipers, even though they have orders to remain on standby. The red rubber surface of the tennis court is covered with brown pine needles.

Magnus starts to walk along the back of the main building, thinking that they should search the guesthouse once more as well. There must be a shed housing the pump and ventilation for the pool, and someone could be hiding there too.

The lingering summer heat radiates off the dark-brown wood

of the building. There aren't many windows on this side, facing the forest.

The ground crunches beneath Magnus's heavy boots and the air is heavy with childhood smells of sap and warm moss.

He discovers what look like large lobster pots hanging beneath the eaves at the back of the house, and is just about to lift them down when he receives instructions from command to go back into the house, switch on the computer and try to find a calendar or something that details any upcoming trips.

In the distance he can hear a woodpecker. Magnus thinks about how his girlfriend always used to cover her ears when she heard a woodpecker. She couldn't bear it, and was convinced they must get terrible headaches from having to do that.

He starts to retrace his steps, signalling to Rajmo who has followed him around the house, but stops when he sees a hatch in the façade, about a metre and a half high. The catch is hanging loose on the outside.

Some sort of woodshed, maybe, he thinks, drawing his knife. Rajmo moves back as Magnus nudges the door open with the blade.

He doesn't really believe the house could be booby-trapped, despite the warnings he was given.

Nothing happens.

Magnus smiles at Rajmo, puts his knife away, opens the door completely and sees a steep flight of steps leading down into the foundation of the building.

'I'll go down and check,' Magnus says, as he sticks his hand in and presses the light-switch.

There's a click, but the lights don't come on. He attaches the flashlight to his pistol and starts to go down the steps.

'What the hell is that smell?' Rajmo says as he sticks his head through the low opening.

The cloying stench of decay gets stronger the lower they get. The narrow concrete steps seem to lead far beneath the house itself. There are spiderwebs everywhere, with big spiders swaying with their own weight.

At the bottom of the steps is a short passageway containing two metal doors. Magnus signals to Rajmo to be ready, then quickly opens the closest door. He looks into a room containing a radon filter and water purification system. Rajmo opens the other door and shakes his head at Magnus.

'Geothermal heat pump,' he says, pulling the collar of his jacket up over his nose to escape the nauseating smell.

Struggling not to throw up, Magnus sweeps his flashlight across the passageway and sees a narrow wooden door at the end.

They can hear a loud humming noise.

Magnus tries to open the door but it's locked. Rajmo takes a step back and kicks the handle so hard that the entire lock comes loose and the door swings open.

The stench of rotting meat hits them like a noxious wave. The humming becomes a deafening buzz as tens of thousands of flies fill the air.

'Christ,' Magnus groans, clapping one hand over his nose and mouth.

The air is so thick with flies that they can't see the rest of the room.

'What the fuck is this?' Rajmo manages to say.

The flies disperse, followed by a sound like someone dragging a stick across railings, then everything is quiet.

Magnus can feel his legs shaking as he steps inside the stinking room.

The flashlight's beam plays unsteadily across a workbench covered in black blood. It's run down one of the wooden legs and onto the floor. Blood has sprayed across the walls, all the way to the ceiling.

Magnus's flashlight moves across the dissected, splayed cadavers of rabbits, glinting with black flies.

There's a glass jar holding knives with stained wooden handles and blunt blades.

'This is fucking disgusting . . .'

They hear the clattering sound again. Magnus points his gun at the floor and the flashlight lights up a cage. The innards of a large number of animals lie tossed against the wall beside a drain. There's a yellow plastic bucket containing a bloody chopping board and a skin scraper.

The clattering sound is coming from the little cage on the floor. A panic-stricken rabbit is darting around, its claws scraping against the metal mesh.

95

Joona pulls on a breathing mask and vinyl gloves and goes down into the cramped slaughter-room to examine the dead animals. He quickly takes in the stinking innards on the floor, then the dissected animals and hanging body parts, but can't find any remains that are obviously human. What happened here seems to have been a mix of rabbit slaughter and animal torture. He can see attempts to produce rabbit-skins, and the remains of shredded leather on a filthy stretching rack, as well as unsettling evidence of violent dissections, trophy-gathering and mutilation.

On the bloodstained wall behind the workbench is an old newspaper clipping with a picture of Rex holding a silver chef's trophy in his raised hand.

Joona carries the live rabbit in its cage up into the sunlight, then walks a little way into the forest before he lets it go.

Janus has leaned his sniper rifle against the fence surrounding the tennis court and undone his bulletproof vest. He puts a tablet in his mouth, tucks his red hair back and drinks from a bottle of water, leaning his head back and gulping it down.

'I saw you on some of the security-camera footage from the Foreign Minister's home,' Joona says.

'My first job when I started with the Security Police was cleaning up after him . . . A great way to spend taxpayers' money. Some of the girls were so badly hurt that I had to take them to the emergency room . . . and afterwards I was the one who had to get them to keep quiet and disappear.'

'I understand that you were transferred.'

'That was at the Foreign Minister's request. All I'd done was hold him up against the wall, grab him by his tiny cock and tell him that I was obliged to protect him, but that I have two faces, and one of them isn't very nice.'

Magnus Mollander is waiting for Joona when he returns with the empty cage. Magnus's face is grey, as if he has a fever, and he's shivering in spite of the fact that he has beads of sweat on his forehead.

'There's nothing on the computer,' he reports. 'Forensics have done an initial assessment but can't find anything to suggest where David Jordan might have gone.'

He breaks off his report as Rajmo walks over to them to tell them that a woman is heading down the road towards the house.

'Get rid of any obstructions before she sees them,' Joona says. 'Keep out of the way, and we'll see if she's on her way here.'

They all huddle behind the guesthouse where they can't be seen from the road: nine heavily armed police officers, Joona, and the forensics officer.

The gate opens with a gentle creak.

Joona draws his pistol and holds it hidden by his side as he hears the woman's footsteps on the gravel path.

She's getting very close to them now.

Joona takes a step forward.

The woman lets out a yelp of fear.

'Sorry to startle you,' Joona says, with his pistol tucked against his leg.

The woman stares at him, eyes wide open. Her hair is straight and blonde, and she's wearing faded jeans, simple sandals and a washed-out T-shirt with the words 'Feel the Burn' on it.

'I'm with the police, and I need you to answer a couple of questions,' Joona says.

The woman tries to compose herself, takes her phone out of her bag and takes a step towards him.

'I'll just call the police and check that . . .'

She breaks off abruptly when she sees the heavily armed

response unit waiting behind the guesthouse. The colour slowly drains from her face as she takes in their bulletproof vests, helmets, automatic pistols and sniper rifles.

'Where's David Jordan?' Joona asks, putting his pistol back in its holster.

'What?'

The young woman stares up at the house in amazement, and sees the front door lying on the ground.

'David Jordan,' Joona says. 'He isn't at home.'

'No,' she says in a thin voice. 'He's in Norrland.'

'What's he doing there?'

She screws her eyes up as if the sun is dazzling her.

'I don't know,' she says. 'Some work thing, I guess?'

'Whereabouts in Norrland?'

'What's going on?'

'Call him,' Joona says, pointing to the phone that she's still clutching in her hand. 'Ask where he is, but don't say anything about us.'

'I don't understand,' she whispers, and puts her phone to her ear, but lowers it almost immediately. 'It's switched off . . . his phone's switched off.'

'Are you two together?' Joona asks, looking at her with eyes as grey as stone.

'Together? I haven't really thought about it . . . we meet up fairly regularly . . . I like being here, I can paint when I'm here, but it's not like we're that close or anything, I have no idea what he does every day, other than producing Rex's cooking shows.'

She falls silent and drags one foot across the gravel.

'But you knew he was going away.'

'He just said he was going to Norrland, but he knows he doesn't need to tell me his every move.'

'Norrland's the size of Britain,' Joona says.

'He might have mentioned Kiruna,' she says. 'I think it was Kiruna.'

'What do you think he was going to do in Kiruna?'

'I have no idea.'

Without another word Joona starts to walk towards his car.

He calls Anja on his new phone to ask her to book a plane ticket.

'Have you managed to get hold of Rex Müller yet?' he asks, getting in the car.

'Neither he nor his son Sammy are at home, and no one knows where they are. We've spoken to TV4, and the boy's mother, who's out of the country, but . . .'

'Well, it looks like David Jordan travelled up to Kiruna this morning,' Joona says, pulling out onto the road.

'Not according to any passenger lists.'

'Check to see if any private planes have landed at the airport, or any private airstrip.'

'OK.'

'I'm heading to Arlanda now,' he adds.

'Of course you are,' Anja says calmly.

'And I'm counting on you to trace their phones in the meantime.'

'We're trying, but the operators are reluctant to hand over any information, to put it mildly.'

'As long as you get the information before my plane takes off.'

'I can talk to the prosecutor about—'

'Fuck that, roll over them, break the law,' he interrupts. 'Sorry, but if we can't locate Rex and his son they're going to be dead very soon.'

'Fuck that,' she repeats calmly. 'Roll over them and break the law.'

The winding forest road is empty. Joona passes a group of holiday homes around a glittering lake with a diving platform in the middle of it.

Joona speeds up and is just about to pull out onto the main road when Anja calls him back.

'Joona, it can't be done,' she says.

She tells him that the NOU's technicians have tried to locate David Jordan and Rex using GPS tracking. They haven't been able to remotely activate the phones so that they transmit positional data, and because the mobile phone companies are unable to detect any signals from their local masts in Kiruna, the technicians are confident that David Jordan's and Rex's phones aren't just switched off, but smashed.

'What about Sammy's phone?' Joona says.

'We're working on that,' Anja snaps. 'Stop stressing me out. I can't handle this, everyone's miserable all the time, no flirting . . .'

'Sorry,' Joona says, pulling onto the highway.

'But you were right about one thing . . . a Cessna something-or-other from Stockholm landed early this morning at the sea plane harbour in Kurravaara.'

'No passenger list?'

'Wait a second.'

He hears her talking, then thanking someone for their help.

'Joona?'

'Yes?'

'We've traced Sammy's phone. He's somewhere near Hallunda. We've got a precise address, a terraced house on Tomtbergavägen.'

'Good to hear he stayed at home,' Joona says. 'Send a car and get Jeanette Fleming to talk to Sammy . . . I need to know where Rex and David Jordan are.'

96

Rex is standing in his hotel room looking at the hunting gear he's laid out on top of the bed. He opens the wooden box and takes out the broad-bladed hunting knife, then uses it to cut the labels off his new clothes.

That morning they took off from Hägernäsviken in a twin-engined Cessna sea plane. Even though the cabin was pressurised, it was too noisy to speak. The landscape below them changed: cultivated land and built-up areas turned to black-green pine forest, then marshes and tundra.

The plane landed at the harbour in Kurravaara, where a driver was waiting to take them to the hunting lodge.

As they passed the tourism centre at Abisko, they could just make out the half-moon-shaped gap between the twin peaks of Tjuonatjåkka in the distance.

At the resort at Björkliden the car turned off the main road onto a winding gravel road leading to Tornehamn.

The hotel is a relatively modern building on the site of the old base camp for the workers who built the iron-ore railway, Malmbanan, more than a hundred years ago.

They're completely alone up here, two hundred kilometres north of the Arctic Circle.

DJ unlocked the door and switched the alarm off, then showed Rex and Sammy around the deserted hotel.

They walked through the huge dining room and into the large restaurant kitchen, and looked inside the freezers at all the vacuum-packed meat, hundreds of pizzas, thirty boxes of hamburgers, bread and rolls, turbot, Arctic char and vendace roe.

They walked down long hallways lined with thick carpet, then went down the curved staircase to the spa centre, past an empty exercise pool.

The floor was being torn up in the waiting area, and a mountain of furniture blocked the entry and part of the hallway.

Rex is still standing in front of his bed gazing out through the window: beyond the junction in the road and Pakktajåkaluobbalah he can see mountains and valleys, and countless small mountain lakes, like drops of molten lead.

He starts to get dressed for the hunt.

DJ has picked his clothes personally, selecting the right sizes and tracking down exclusive outfits with scent-barriers to stop animals from detecting humans. The material muffles sound and repels water and wind.

Rex turns towards the door. He has the uncomfortable feeling that the room has suddenly got darker.

He puts the rest of his clothes on, tucks the binoculars, water bottle and knife in his bag, then reaches for the door-handle. Once again a sense of unease hits him.

He stops in front of room 23 and knocks. All the electronic locks have been disconnected, but the doors can still be locked from inside.

'It's open,' a subdued voice calls out.

Rex steps into the short hallway, stepping over the shoes towards the spacious bedroom. Sammy has changed clothes, and is sitting on the bed watching television. His all-terrain jacket is open and he's wearing mascara and gold-tinted eyeshadow.

'It's great that you're coming,' Rex says.

'It's not like I can stay here on my own,' his son replies.

'Why not?'

'I already have the urge to ride a tricycle down the hallway and start talking to my finger.'

Rex laughs and explains that DJ thinks it's important that he participate in the hunt.

'I'm just saying it would be nicer to stay here and make food,' Sammy says, switching the television off.

'I agree,' Rex nods.

'Should we go and see what sort of rich old men DJ has managed to lure up here?' Sammy says with a sigh, picking up his bag.

They walk in silence along the cold hallway, and can hear raucous laughter and the clink of glasses. DJ is sitting in front of the roaring fire in the lobby with three men dressed in hunting gear, drinking whisky.

'And here's Rex,' DJ announces loudly.

The men break off their conversation and turn around, smiling. Rex falters. It's like falling into a hole. One of the men is James Gyllenborg. Rex hasn't seen him since the assault thirty years ago. James was in the stable and hit him with a two by four, then kicked him in the crotch when he was on the ground, before spitting on him.

Rex leans on one of the leather armchairs for support and realises that he's dropped his bag on the floor and the hunting knife has slid out onto the carpet.

'Dad, what is it?'

'I dropped . . .'

Rex picks the bag and knife up, forces the nausea down and walks over to the men to say hello. He recognises the other two men from Ludviksberg as well, but can't remember their names.

'This is my son, Sammy,' Rex says, and swallows hard.

'Cheers, Sammy,' James says.

They shake hands with Rex without getting to their feet, and introduce themselves as James, Kent and Lawrence.

They've all aged.

There's something grey about James Gyllenborg's very being, as if the years have washed both the life and colour out of him. Rex remembers him as a vibrant blond youth, with thin lips and nervous blue eyes.

Kent Wrangel is heavily built and has a rather flushed face. He's wearing glasses and a gold necklace. Lawrence von Thurn is also big, with a full grey beard and bloodshot eyes.

'We're delighted that you gentlemen have such faith in this project,' DJ says. 'Because this is going to be so damn good. And of course you already know that Rex has just been presented with the prestigious Chef of Chefs award!'

'Quite undeserved, it has to be said,' Rex smiles.

'Let's drink to that!' James says, and takes a gulp.

The other two clap their hands happily. Rex tries unsuccessfully to catch DJ's eye.

'I want you to know that the reason I've confiscated all our phones, including my own, is that this deal is going to hit this industry like a bomb,' DJ says, topping up the men's glasses with whisky. 'And once it's detonated, everything will get much harder, and much more expensive. So this is something of a game changer . . . regardless of whether you decide to sign up or walk away, the condition is that no information leaks out, so that those of us left are free to negotiate with the most important suppliers before word gets out.'

'This is going to be huge,' Kent says, stretching his legs.

'DJ, can I have a word?' Rex says quietly, and leads him away.

'Exciting, isn't it?' DJ says in a low voice as they walk into the dining room.

'What is this? What the hell are you playing at?' Rex says. 'I'm not going to do business with a bunch of bastards from my old school.'

'I thought . . . well, you all know each other, so it couldn't be any better, could it? And who cares if they were bastards back then, as long as they have money now?'

Rex shakes his head and struggles to appear more composed than he feels.

'You should have let me know.'

'Look, in all seriousness, it's practically impossible to put together any kind of deal in Sweden without running into people who went to Ludviksberg,' DJ says as he sees Kent coming towards them with two glasses of whisky.

DJ goes to meet him, takes one glass and leads him back to the others.

Rex remains standing in the dining room and watches them go. His head is roaring, but he tells himself that he needs to stick it out, if only for one night. He'll put up with it for a few more hours, then come up with an excuse so he and Sammy can go home first thing tomorrow morning.

He tries to convince himself that he's doing this because it's important. It's a way for him to secure his financial future in case Sylvia ever gets so sick of him that she lets him go.

Like everyone at Ludviksberg, he must have treated plenty of people badly in his time. That was part and parcel of being privileged, but Rex could never accept the beating. He walked out of the school before breakfast the next day and he never went back.

'OK, listen,' DJ says, clapping his hands to get everyone's attention. 'The reindeer here are far more elusive than wild ones.'

Rex slowly walks back to join the men in the lounge as DJ goes through the rules.

'I've been reindeer-hunting in Norway,' Lawrence says in his deep voice. 'We sat in a hide for eight hours and didn't get a single clean shot.'

'But here we're stalking our prey,' DJ reminds them. 'You hunt in small teams, creep up on the reindeer, read the terrain, look for tracks. It's fucking exciting . . . to get close enough you have to be absolutely silent, and know which direction the wind is blowing.'

'And we have no backup plan,' Rex jokes with a wide smile. 'If none of us bring down a reindeer, I won't have anything but potatoes to cook for dinner.'

97

Half an hour later DJ is standing on the broad steps of the deck handing out guns and ammunition.

'The rifle I've chosen is a Remington 700 with a synthetic butt,' he says, holding up a blue-green rifle with a black barrel.

'Good weapon,' Lawrence murmurs.

'James, I have a left-handed one for you,' DJ adds.

'Thanks.'

'It weighs 2.9 kilos, so you should all be OK,' DJ smiles, then holds up a brown box. 'We're using .375 Holland & Holland, and you only get twenty rounds.'

He tosses the box to Rex.

'So aim carefully.'

They take their equipment and start to walk around to the other side of the hotel. The sky is grey and unsettled, the air smells like rain, and a gusty wind is blowing through the low bushes.

DJ leads them along a path up the slope, and explains that it's a forty-minute hike to the gates and the feeding grounds.

'The whole enclosure is six hundred and eighty acres, and covers wooded valleys, bare hilltops, and a few small lakes, including Kratersjön, as well as some steep mountain cliffs towards the south, so you need to watch your step.'

The landscape is brown and the air fresh and full of moisture. It smells like forest, heather and wet leaves.

'Having fun?' Sammy asks, with a gentle but unmistakeable note of derision.

'It's just work,' Rex replies. 'But I'm happy you're here.'

His son gives him a sideways glance.

'You don't seem very happy, Dad.'

'I'll tell you later.'

'What?'

Rex is about to admit that he can't handle this, that he wants to get away as soon as possible, when DJ falls in alongside them. He shows them how to load, demonstrates the single-stage trigger and the safety catch on the side.

'How are you doing, Sammy?' he asks with a smile.

'Sorry, but I don't get the point of shooting reindeer in an enclosure . . . I mean, they can't go anywhere. It's like the *Hunger Games*, but without the right to self-defence.'

'I hear what you're saying,' DJ says patiently. 'But at the same time, if you compare this with the meat industry, it couldn't be more free-range. The enclosure covers more than three million square metres.'

Rex looks at James's and Kent's broad backs, the rifles over their shoulders. James turns around and hands him a silver hipflask. Rex takes it and passes it on without drinking.

'How's Anna doing? She was looking better when we saw her at the awards ceremony,' Kent says.

'She has her hair back, but they don't think she'll make it to winter,' James replies. 'My wife has cancer,' he explains to Rex.

'Do you have children?'

'Yes . . . a boy who's twenty, studying law at Harvard . . . and an afterthought, Elsa, she's nine. She just wants to be with her mum all the time, nothing else.'

They climb diagonally up a hillside, and see that the landscape curves down into a deep valley. The view is spectacular.

'So we're all going to put our school uniforms on tomorrow, then?' Lawrence jokes.

'Oh God,' Kent sighs.

'Christ, all that church-going, and those Sunday dinners . . .

we'd never have survived without microwave pizzas and nips of cognac.'

'Or Wille, calling his family's chauffeur and getting him to drive all the way from Stockholm with a case of champagne,' Kent chuckles, then turns suddenly sombre.

'I can't believe he and Teddy are both dead,' James says quietly.

98

Jeanette Fleming is standing next to a lilac bush, staring at rows of brown houses. The silver clip in her short hair glitters in the sunlight. She's wearing a tight skirt and has a Glock 26 in a holster under her jacket.

In the distance she sees her plain-clothes colleagues from Stockholm Police ring the doorbell of the neglected house at the far end of the street.

The NOU have traced Sammy's phone here.

Rex's son could be the only person who knows where his father and the spree killer, David Jordan Andersen, are.

The officers wait a few moments before ringing again.

Some children bike by, and a woman in a burka walks past pulling a wheeled suitcase.

The door opens and Jeanette sees the officers say something to a figure in the hallway before going inside.

Her colleagues' only task is to make sure the house is safe so Jeanette can conduct a brief interview with Sammy there.

Jeanette thinks about how pale her boss had looked when he came into her office after Anja Larsson demanded that he loan Jeanette to them as part of the ongoing collaboration between the two bodies.

She walks around the block of houses and stops at the back. Unlike the other yards, this one is overgrown and wild. She can see an old barbecue through the tall weeds, and there are rusted bicycle parts on the cracked stepping stones.

There's no sign of movement behind the closed blinds.

Jeanette gets her lipstick out of her bag and touches up her make-up. She thinks about the fact that even though she is the best psychological interviewer in the country, she has very little understanding of her own behaviour.

She was on a job with Saga Bauer, at a service station south-west of Nyköping.

Jeanette still can't understand what happened.

She hadn't really believed people actually did that sort of thing.

It could have been tragic, it could have been comical, but her surprise and embarrassment had turned to genuine, unexpected, and inexplicable lust.

The anonymous copulation had taken a couple of minutes at most, and she didn't have time to regret her actions before she felt him come. She was so surprised that she gasped 'Stop!' and pulled away, stumbling and hitting her knee on the floor. She'd rinsed her mouth and crotch, then sat back down on the toilet to let the semen trickle out of her.

For hours afterwards she felt mentally numb, and ever since she has been veering between feeling stupid and feeling oddly liberated.

Sometimes when she sees men out in the street, often older men, ugly and coarse, she is overwhelmed by shame and has to look away, her cheeks burning.

But morally it's really no worse than meeting someone in a bar and ending up in bed with them, no worse than a silly sexual fantasy, a meaningless fuck.

She's asked herself if she subconsciously did it to punish her prudish ex-husband, who was even worried about her masturbating, or her sister, who was so reckless and promiscuous as a teenager but who is now the perfect little wife.

In truth, she thinks she needed to do it for her own sake, to redefine her view of herself. She did it because it was possible, and because the transgressive act just happened to turn her on at the time.

Ever since then she has been expecting to start feeling bad, to be punished somehow, but it wasn't until yesterday that her anxieties caught up with her.

The day before yesterday she had a physical at work, as she does every year. They run blood pressure, blood samples, ECG, TSH – then twenty-four hours later she can log in and check her results.

The doctor would only comment if any of the results was abnormal.

Jeanette hadn't actually thought about it until then, but she suddenly found herself panicking. When she was sitting in front of her computer about to log in, she felt utterly terrified that she might have been infected with HIV.

Her ears were roaring.

The list of results on the screen was incomprehensible.

When she saw that the medical officer had written a comment, her field of vision contracted with fear.

She'd gone to the bathroom to rinse her face with cold water before she could return to the screen.

There was nothing about HIV.

The only comment the doctor had made was that the hCG levels in her blood indicated that she was pregnant.

It still hasn't properly sunk in.

She spent eight years waiting for her husband to get around to thinking about having children, and then he walked out on her. After a long series of failed dates she decided to apply for artificial insemination. Two weeks ago she received a final refusal from the health service, and now she's pregnant.

Jeanette is still smiling when she gets the call from inside the house.

99

Jeanette adjusts the pistol at the small of her back as she walks up to the battered house. The younger of the two police officers opens it before she has time to ring the bell and ushers her into the hall.

'Sammy isn't here. It's just his phone,' he says.

Jeanette steps over a pair of split boots and follows the officer along the hallway. There are framed canvases leaning against the wall, and a roll of blank canvas lying on the floor.

The kitchen smells like cat food and urine. The sink is full of dirty dishes and the linoleum floor is cluttered with bags of wine bottles.

From a hook in the ceiling hangs something that's evidently supposed to be a piece of art: a dozen tiny children's shoes in a red mesh cage.

A young woman wearing nothing but a pair of lilac tracksuit bottoms is sitting on one of the chairs. Both of her nipples are pierced and she has a tattoo of a greyish-black sun over her navel.

She has dark rings under her eyes, a red rash on her forehead, and one of her wrists is in a cast.

On the floor in front of her lies a man on his stomach with his arms cuffed behind his back.

'Can we lose the handcuffs?' Jeanette asks.

One of the officers leans over the prone man:

'Are you going to stay calm now?'

'For fuck's sake, yes,' the man on the floor groans. 'I already said so.'

The officer crouches down, rests one knee on the small of his back and removes the cuffs.

'Sit down,' Jeanette says.

The man gets up from the floor and rubs his wrists. He's bare-chested as well, and skinny. He's dressed in a pair of low-cut jeans, and his dark pubic hair is visible over the top of them. His face is attractive, but prematurely aged. He looks at her blankly, as if he has a bad hangover.

'Sit down,' she repeats.

'What the fuck's your problem?' he asks, but sits down across from her.

There's a black smartphone in the middle of the table.

'Is that Sammy's phone?' Jeanette asks.

The man looks at the phone as if he's just noticed it.

'I don't know,' he says.

'What's it doing here?'

'He must have forgotten it.'

'When?'

The man shrugs and pretends to think.

'Yesterday.'

The man, whose name is Nicolas Barowski, smiles to himself and scratches his stomach.

'What's the code?' Jeanette asks after a pause.

'Don't know,' he says.

Jeanette looks up at the cage of children's shoes hanging from the ceiling.

'You're an artist?'

'Yes,' he replies curtly.

'Is he any good?' she asks the girl as a joke.

'He's the real deal,' she replies, raising her chin.

'Who gives a shit . . . I don't see any difference between my art and Czech porn about group sex,' Nico says seriously.

'I know what you mean,' Jeanette replies.

'I'd rather be in a bunch of porn than paint with oils,' he says, and leans towards her.

'Does that shock you?' the girl says, giggling.

'Should it?' Jeanette says.

'Art isn't nice,' Nico goes on. 'It's dirty, perverse—'

'No, now you're going too far,' Jeanette interrupts with feigned concern.

Nico smiles broadly, nods, and holds her gaze in a flirtatious way.

'Where's Sammy now?' she asks.

'I don't know, and I don't care,' he replies without looking away.

'He's more in love with Sammy than he is with me,' the girl says, brushing something from one of her nipples.

Jeanette walks over to an iPhone plugged in on the floor. She unplugs it, looks at the picture of Andy Warhol on the case, and turns to Nico.

'What's your code?'

'That's private,' he replies, scratching his crotch.

'Then I'll ask Apple for help,' she jokes.

'Ziggy,' he replies, not understanding the joke.

He sits slumped with one hand between his legs and looks at her as she unlocks his phone and checks the log. The most recent text is from Rex's phone.

'Rex Müller sent you fourteen hearts this morning?'

'No,' he grins.

'Did Rex call you yesterday?'

'No,' Nico says, and looks at his nails.

'So Sammy called you from his dad's phone,' Jeanette says. 'What did he say? You talked for six minutes.'

Nico lets out a deep sigh.

'He was upset . . . about lots of things, and he said he had to go on a trip with his dad.'

'Where?'

'I don't know.'

'He must have said,' Jeanette persists, searching the kitchen cabinets for a clean glass.

'No.'

'Was he upset because you stole his phone?'

Nico squirms and scratches his forehead.

'That too . . . but he said his dad was trying to turn him straight by making him shoot reindeer in a cage.'

'They were going hunting together?'

'I don't know,' Nico says wearily.

'Do they do that often? Go hunting together?'

'They don't know each other. His dad's an idiot, he's never given a damn about him.'

Jeanette tips the cigarette butts out of a glass and cleans it.

'What else did he say?' she asks.

Nico leans back in his chair, purses his lips and looks at her.

'Nothing, just the usual,' he replies. 'He said he missed me, that he was thinking about me all the time.'

She puts her finger under the tap, then fills the glass and drinks, fills it again, and turns the tap off.

'You can stay and watch while I have sex with Filippa,' he says softly, touching the girl's left breast.

'I'm afraid I don't have time right now,' Jeanette smiles, then picks Sammy's mobile phone up and walks out.

100

They stop at a stone bench just inside the gates of the enclosure. DJ pours coffee from a flask, hands out the steaming mugs and smiles at the men.

Now he has the last four in a cage, ready for slaughter.

It's going to require a degree of care when he kills the first one, so the others don't try to run.

Towards the end it won't matter if they figure out what's going on and start to panic.

They will all bleed and scream, and feel death creep up and stare at them, until it's finally time.

'We'll split into two teams, in two zones,' he explains. 'Team one will be made up of me, James and Kent . . . and we'll stick to zone one. Lawrence, Rex and Sammy will be team two, in zone two. Everyone OK with that?'

He hands out maps to the two teams, goes through the geographic boundaries, permitted shooting angles and safety regulations.

'We'll break off at five a.m. precisely, and disarm our rifles. No more shots can be fired after that, even if that's the first time you see a reindeer. We'll wait ten minutes, then gather here before going back to the hotel together . . . and don't worry about tonight's meal,' he adds. 'Rex has promised to make the best hamburgers on the planet.'

'We've got plenty of ground fillet steak,' Rex says.

DJ looks at them, takes a sip of coffee and thinks about how he's going to lead Kent and James across the bare stretch of ground and split them up among the rocky crags. His plan is to end up on the same side of the rocks as Kent, then they'll head up the path towards the ravine and rest there before going into the valley.

Kent's in worse shape than the rest of them. He's overweight and suffers from high blood pressure. While they're resting he'll congratulate him on his recent appointment as Chancellor of Justice, draw his hunting knife, slice open the lower part of his fat gut, make him stand at the edge of the cliff and tell him that he's going to push him off in precisely nineteen minutes. He'll still be conscious, so he'll experience the fall.

The men study the maps and point at the landscape and hilltops. Rex puts his rifle down on the bench and walks off, steps over the ditch and stops in the undergrowth facing the fence to pee.

'If you bring down an animal, make sure it's dead, then break off and mark the location on the map,' DJ says. 'The biggest stags in here weigh a hundred and sixty kilos, and have got huge antlers.'

'I am so up for this,' Kent says.

Sammy blows on his coffee, drinks some and wipes the lipstick off his mug with his thumb.

'Didn't you get a rifle?' Lawrence asks, looking over at him.

'I don't want one. I don't understand how anyone can think it's fun to kill an animal,' Sammy replies, looking down at the ground.

'It's called hunting,' Kent says. 'People have been doing for quite a while . . .'

'And real men like it,' Sammy concludes, turning towards DJ. 'They like killing, they like guns and rare meat – what could possibly be wrong with that?'

'Can someone give this little poof a slap?' Kent says with a smile.

DJ looks at Rex, who is walking back through the weeds.

He has no idea that he's one of the prey in the enclosure.

So far Carl-Erik Ritter is the only one who has been at all problematic, like a wounded rabbit retreating into its burrow.

When DJ found out that Ritter was dying from liver cancer, he'd been forced to rethink his plans.

He had to prioritise Ritter to make sure he didn't die of natural causes before he could get to him.

The accelerated plan involved finding him in the bar and luring him outside to the Axelsberg underground. DJ had driven up from Skåne early that morning and maybe he wasn't concentrating enough. He hadn't counted on being attacked in the square. He had to improvise to make it look like an accident. He shoved him into the window, breaking the glass with the back of his head, then turned him around and pushed his neck onto the sharp edge, slicing through his carotid artery.

Even though he tried to hold the wound together, Ritter still bled out quicker than expected. He only took fifteen minutes to die. He was getting away too easy. Maybe that was why DJ cut his lip open with the knife before he lost consciousness.

'OK, let's get going,' DJ says, shaking his mug. 'The sky looks pretty dark off to the east, and there's a chance we might get a bit of bad weather this evening. Kent and James, you come with me, we've got a little further to walk than the others.'

101

Once Rex's group have climbed a little higher they can clearly see the vegetation below them, and how the forest thins out up the slopes and then stops altogether.

The bog arcs between Rákkaslåhku and Lulip Guokkil. The entire valley is like the prow of a huge ship pointing towards Torneträsk.

Sammy pulls out his binoculars and looks around.

Lawrence is holding the map, leading the group down into the valley, towards zone two. The range includes part of the bog and the eastern slopes, and stretches above the treeline to the subalpine heathland and across to the ravine.

Everything is suddenly very quiet.

The only sounds are the clatter of their equipment, their feet hitting the ground, and the wind blowing through the leaves.

The muddy path is covered with the footprints of previous hunters. Clumps of lingon twigs brush against their boots.

'How's it going?' Rex asks, and Sammy shrugs in response.

Between the white stems of the birch trees the light is the colour of porcelain. The valley is like a vast room, a hall of pillars with a canopy of billowing cloth.

'Do you know how deep the snow gets here in the winter?'

'No,' Sammy replies quietly.

'Two and a half metres,' Rex says. 'Look at the trees . . . all the trunks are much whiter up to two and a half metres off the ground . . .'

When he doesn't get any response from Sammy, he goes on in an exaggeratedly pedagogical tone:

'And that's because the black lichen that grows on the bark can't survive underneath the winter snow.'

'Please, can you two try to keep quiet,' Lawrence asks, turning towards them.

'Sorry,' Rex smiles.

'I want to do some hunting, even if you don't. That's why I'm here.'

They walk through a patch of crowberry scrub and emerge into a brighter glade.

'I barely even know how a hunting rifle works,' Rex tells Sammy. 'I got my licence when I was thirty and I still haven't quite figured it out . . . You have to pull the bolt back somehow when you insert more cartridges.'

Lawrence stops and raises his hands.

'Let's split up,' he says, and points at the map. 'I go down into the valley, and you two continue along the path . . . or up that side.'

'OK,' Rex replies, looking along the path towards the side of the mountain.

'You can only fire in that direction . . . and I'll fire that way,' Lawrence says, pointing.

'Of course,' Rex replies.

Lawrence nods to them, steps off the path and heads off down the slope through the trees.

'I've ended up stuck in a cage full of angry apes,' Rex mutters, fastening his knife to his belt.

They walk along the path for a while, and start to head diagonally up the mountainside. After half a kilometre they stop beside a boulder. It's like a tower-block of slate, deposited here when the glaciers retreated.

They stand with their backs to the rock-face, and drink some water.

Rex puts on his reading glasses, unfolds the map and studies it for a while before he gets his bearings.

'We're here,' he says, pointing at the map.

'Great,' Sammy says without looking.

Rex takes out his binoculars and tries to figure out the borders of the zone. He catches sight of Lawrence further down. Rex adjusts the focus and looks at him through the binoculars. His bearded face is wary, his eyes narrow. He's creeping through the undergrowth in the valley, then raises his rifle, stands absolutely still, lowers the gun without firing, and walks on. Rex follows him through the binoculars until he disappears between the trees.

'Let's go higher up,' Rex says.

They head up the side of the fell. The ground is dry, and the low birches are more sparse.

'Will you help me with the burgers later?' Rex asks.

Sammy stares ahead sullenly without answering. They keep walking but stop when they see three reindeer up ahead. The animals are standing between a clump of low trees and some large rocks.

They creep closer, wind in their faces, as they move around an almost black rock-face.

Rex crouches down, raises his rifle and looks at the stag through the sights.

The reindeer lifts his head with its big antlers, looks out across the tundra, sniffs and twitches its ears, and stands absolutely still for a few seconds before it continues eating. It moves forward slowly as it grazes.

Suddenly Rex has the perfect line of fire. It's a magnificent reindeer, a large bull with a pelt like bronze and a milk-white chest.

The crosshairs quiver over its heart, but Rex has no intention of putting his finger anywhere near the trigger.

'Hope you find a hole in the fence,' he whispers, and watches the stag raise its head again.

Its ears twitch nervously.

There's a snap as Sammy steps on a branch behind Rex. The animal reacts instantly and rushes away down towards the edge of the trees.

Rex lowers the rifle and meets Sammy's contrary stare, but instead of being annoyed he smiles.

'I wasn't going to shoot,' he says.

Sammy shrugs and they walk up the slope through the meadow grass. They find steaming reindeer droppings between some alpine flowers and forget-me-nots. The sky is cloudy above the summit of Lulip Guokkil and the wind is noticeably colder.

'Bad weather on the way,' Rex says.

They clamber upward until the ground flattens out and they find themselves on a sort of heath that stretches off towards the dark, steep mountainside.

'Can you carry the rifle for a while? I just . . .'

'I don't want to,' Sammy snaps.

'You don't have to be mad at me.'

'Am I being boring now? Too bitchy for your liking?'

Rex doesn't respond, just points ahead and heads off along a track that leads through thorny bushes and scrub.

He thinks about his alcoholism, all the things he's ruined, and becomes increasingly convinced that he will never win back Sammy's trust. But perhaps they can meet up from time to time in a restaurant somewhere, just so he can hear how Sammy's doing, just so he can ask if there's anything he can do to help.

The wind is getting colder. Dry leaves come loose from the bushes and blow away. 'We'll chargrill the burgers,' he says. 'Cut the crusts off the sourdough, add some slices of Vesterhav cheese, some Stokes ketchup, Dijon mustard . . . tons of rocket, two slices of bacon . . . pickles and dressing on the side . . .'

As he passes the biggest rocky outcrop, Rex feels the first drops of rain. The gusting wind makes the grass tremble, as if an invisible animal were running through it.

'And we'll fry thin strips of potato in olive oil,' he goes on. 'Black pepper, lots of flaked salt . . .'

Rex falls silent when he sees a foaming white stream tumbling down the mountainside up ahead. He can't recall having seen it on the map, and turns to ask Sammy, but his son isn't there.

'Sammy?' he says in a loud voice.

He starts to retrace his steps around the cliff, and sees the empty track running back across the plateau. The low trees and bushes are shaking in the wind.

'Sammy?' he calls. 'Sammy!'

He starts to walk faster, looking out across the landscape. Heavy rain is falling on the southern side of Lulip Guokkil, it looks like a curtain of steel rods. The storm will soon be here. Rex hurries back along the sloping mountainside. Further up small stones come loose and roll towards him.

'Sammy?'

Rex scans the terrain, then steps off the path and starts climbing the steep slope. He goes as fast as he can. He's quickly out of breath and he can feel the lactic acid in his thigh muscles. He's sweating, and wipes his face as he follows a dry stream up the hill, slipping on a rock.

His progress is hindered by the thorny undergrowth. As he moves off to one side, he thinks he sees someone disappear behind a rock up above.

Rex pushes through a gap in the bushes. He's keeping his face down, but still scratches his cheek, and the rifle over his shoulder gets caught on the tangle of branches, so he leaves it behind. It hangs there swaying as he stumbles out and falls forward.

Then he catches sight of James in the distance, up above, between two large rocky crags. Suddenly James turns his rifle towards him and takes aim.

Rex stands up and straightens his back, peering at James, but he's having trouble seeing what he's doing from this distance. Light glints off his binoculars and Rex raises his hand to wave.

The barrel of the rifle flares yellow and then he hears the bang.

Rex lurches as he hears the echo bounce off the mountainside. The bushes behind him rustle and a couple of branches break and fall to the ground with a heavy thud.

Up above he sees James running in a crouch, then kneel and take aim again.

Rex turns and sees the large stag trying to get up. Blood is gushing from its chest and it's rapidly losing strength. It falls sideways into the bushes, kicks its legs and catches its antlers on the thickest branches, making its neck twist in an unnatural way.

The reindeer stag snorts and bellows, tensing its neck as it tries to stand. Another shot rings out and the large head is thrown backwards, and its body slowly slumps to the ground, still twitching.

James runs down the slope towards Rex and the stag, sending loose stones rolling downhill.

'What the hell are you playing at?' Rex shouts. 'Are you out of your fucking mind?'

He can hear the anger in his voice but can't help himself. James stops, panting for breath. His eyes are wide and his top lip is shiny with sweat.

'Are you crazy?' Rex goes on.

'I shot a reindeer,' James says through clenched teeth.

'My son could have been standing there!' Rex shouts, throwing his hand out.

'You're in my zone,' James says, unconcerned.

A strong wind blows in, bringing the heavy rain. It sweeps across the birch trees and the drops start to splatter the slope around them.

Just as the rain starts to pour they hear a whip-crack from the sky.

The two men turn around.

High above the ground a red emergency flare glints through the downpour. It drifts off to one side, then falls slowly, disappearing from view as if sinking into a stormy sea.

102

The storm is right above them, and the wind is gusting hard, driving the rain into their eyes.

When they reach the place the flare went off, Rex finds his son. He's sitting huddled against a tree-trunk with DJ. Their green hunting outfits are drenched and rain is dripping down their faces.

'Sammy?' Rex cries, running over to him. 'What happened? You just disappeared, and I—'

'OK, listen,' DJ says, standing up. Water is dripping from his blond beard onto his jacket, and his pale blue eyes are blood-shot. 'There's been an accident. Kent is dead. He fell into the canyon . . .'

'What the fuck . . .?' James yells through the driving rain.

'He's dead,' DJ shouts. 'There's nothing we can do.'

The rain changes direction on the gusting wind. Their clothes whip and flap around them.

'What happened?' Rex gasps.

'The edge is kind of overgrown,' DJ says. 'He couldn't see the drop. Maybe he didn't know where he was on the map.'

'Sammy?' Rex asks. 'You just vanished . . .'

His son looks at him, then turns his face away.

'He fell,' Sammy says weakly.

'Did you see?'

'He's lying down there,' Sammy says, pointing.

Rex and James walk cautiously towards the edge to look. The rain runs down their necks, over their backs and down into their trousers.

'Be careful!' DJ urges behind them.

It is hard to tell where the ground stops in the heavy rain. They slowly approach the edge and see the deep ravine open up. The wind tugs at James and he stumbles a couple of paces before regaining his balance.

Rex moves forward tentatively, making sure he has firm ground beneath his boots, and holds onto the tangled bushes as he leans out over the edge.

At first he can't see anything. He squints and brushes the rain from his face. His eyes scan the trees, rocks, upturned roots, bushes. And then he sees Kent. His body is lying some forty-five metres below, towards the edge of the drop.

'He's moving,' James exclaims beside him. 'I'll climb down, there must be a way.'

Rex pulls out his binoculars, but has to let go of the bush to be able to see. He moves sideways along the precipice and raises the binoculars to his eyes.

The sheer edge of the cliff is still blocking his view. He moves closer, leans out and manages to see the green-dressed figure. Suddenly the ground moves beneath his feet. Rex grabs hold of some branches and throws himself backward as a clump of moss and compacted earth breaks off from the edge and tumbles into the ravine.

'God,' he mumbles.

A shiver of mortal dread runs through his body, and his heart is pounding as he raises the binoculars again, leans out and adjusts the focus. In spite of the water trickling down the lenses he can see the body clearly now.

The blood from where he must have hit the rocks is being washed away by the rain.

Kent is wedged into a gap in the rocks. His neck must have snapped because he's facing the wrong way, and one leg is sticking up at an impossible angle.

There's no doubt that he's dead.

'We need to get an emergency helicopter here!' James shouts, his narrow eyes dark with panic.

'He's dead,' Rex says, lowering the binoculars.

'I'm climbing down,' James insists.

'It's too dangerous,' DJ calls behind them.

'Shit,' James whimpers, and sinks to the ground close to the cliff-edge.

Lawrence arrives at last, out of breath. His glasses are wet and he must have caught himself on something, because his thigh is bleeding through the fabric of his trousers. His thick grey beard is full of pine needles and twigs.

'What's going on?' he pants, wiping the water from his eyes.

'Kent fell in the ravine,' James replies.

'Is it serious?'

'He's dead,' DJ says.

'We don't know that,' James exclaims angrily.

'There's no way he could have survived the fall,' DJ tells Lawrence, pointing towards the drop.

'He's dead,' Rex confirms.

'Shut up!' James screams hysterically.

'Listen to me,' DJ says, raising his voice. 'Let's go back to the hotel and call the police.'

Lawrence moves away, shaking his head, and sits down on a rock with his rifle on his lap, staring into space. James is standing completely still, his lips white with rage and shock.

'I knew it,' he says quietly to himself.

'There's nothing we can do for him now,' DJ says. 'We need a phone . . .'

Rex goes over and squats down in front of his son, and eventually catches his eye.

'We're going back to the hotel,' he says softly.

'Yes, please,' Sammy replies.

DJ tries to reason with the other two men, but they won't listen to him.

'I know it feels awful leaving him down there,' he says. 'But we need to get the police out here as soon as possible.'

Rex helps Sammy to his feet. DJ indicates a direction away from the cliff-edge and they start walking.

'Come on,' DJ calls. 'We don't want any more accidents.'

The other two men look at him, then slowly start to move. The group walks along the side of the mountain, heading gradually into the valley towards the hotel.

'This is fucking sick,' James says.

The rain is still falling hard, and their clothes hang heavy on their bodies.

'Can't we just go home?' Sammy says.

'I'm so sorry you got dragged into this,' Rex says, then turns towards the others.

He looks at the three men through the rain. Puddles are forming in every depression and hollow, and the ground looks like it's bubbling. The rocks have acquired a ghostly halo from the rain bouncing off them.

'Take care not to slip,' he reminds Sammy.

'I saw him fall,' his son whispers. 'I was heading towards them from the side . . . it was before the rain. It all happened so fucking fast . . . I don't get it . . .'

'We shouldn't have come on the hunt,' Rex says, anxiety and regret gathering in his throat. 'I always think I have to do all these things, but I'm not a hunter, and I could have said that from the beginning.'

'You're too kind to do that,' Sammy says tiredly.

'We could have waited back at the hotel instead,' Rex goes on, holding a branch out of the way. 'Got the food ready, sat and talked, like you wanted.'

'Mum told me I wasn't planned. The opposite, really . . .'

'Listen,' Rex says. 'I was incredibly immature when she and I met. I'd never even thought about having children. It felt like I'd only just started living.'

'Did you want Mum to have an abortion?' his son asks.

'Sammy, everything changed the moment I saw you, when it really sank in that I had a son.'

'Mum's always tried to tell me that you care about me, but it's been hard to find any evidence.'

'I always said I'd be there for you when it really mattered, but I haven't been,' Rex says, swallowing hard. 'I haven't been there for you.'

He trails off when he feels his voice starting to crack. He tries to catch his breath and calm down.

'I want your mum to take that job in Freetown, and I want you to move in with me, properly . . . the way it should be,' he eventually says.

'I can manage on my own,' Sammy retorts.

Rex stops and tries to make eye contact with his son.

'Sammy,' he says. 'You know I really like having you live with me, right? You must have noticed, some of the best moments of my life have been when we've been cooking together, playing the guitar . . .'

'Dad, you don't have to,' Sammy says.

'But I love you,' Rex goes on in a thick voice. 'You're my son. I'm so proud of you, and you're the only thing that really matters to me at all.'

103

The whole valley has vanished in the downpour; it's as if the church and old railway barracks never existed, just a grey world with no real depth.

Rex and Sammy's clothes are soaked through and they're freezing cold when they finally see the outline of the hotel through the driving rain.

DJ, James and Lawrence passed them a while ago, at the gates to the enclosure. The three men hurried ahead and disappeared along the waterlogged track.

When they were halfway back Sammy put his foot down wrong. Now his ankle has started to swell, and he's limping with his arm around Rex's shoulders.

'Dad, wait,' Sammy says, stopping at the bottom of the steps to the deck.

'Is it hurting?'

'It's not that. I just want to say something before we go in. I said I saw Kent fall, but it . . . it actually looked more like he jumped.'

'It could have looked that way,' Rex says.

'And there's something else . . . he only flashed before me for a moment before he was gone . . . but I had time to notice his red scarf trailing behind him.'

'But . . .'

'He wasn't wearing a scarf, was he? It was blood.'

They walk up the steps in silence, then go into the large lobby while they try to figure out how Kent could have been bleeding before he fell.

Maybe he walked up to the cliff-edge and shot himself, Rex thinks.

There are wet footprints on the stone floor of the lobby. Rifles and other equipment are piled on the low coffee table in front of the fireplace.

DJ is standing in the foyer searching the cushions of the sofas and armchairs.

'Did you call the police?' Rex asks.

DJ shoots him a dark look.

'The phones are gone,' he says.

'No, we left them at the reception desk,' Rex says.

'Then they must have somehow slipped off,' DJ says, walking behind the desk.

'Is anyone else here other than us?' Sammy asks.

Rex shakes his head, shivers and looks over at the windows. The rain is still coursing down the glass.

'What are we going to do?' Sammy asks.

'We need to get you into some dry clothes,' Rex says.

'That'll solve everything,' Sammy says, walking off towards his room.

'They're not here,' DJ mutters, searching among the papers.

'Isn't there a landline?' Rex asks.

'No . . . and the computers need a password,' he says in a hollow voice.

'I've got an iPad,' Rex remembers. 'Do you think there's Wi-Fi here?'

'Try it,' DJ says as he searches behind the desk.

'Bloody hell,' Rex sighs, watching Sammy walk off.

DJ stops and looks at him.

'Is it Sammy?'

'I'm trying, I . . . I've got so many emotions right now, but of course I understand that he can't just absorb the fact that I want to be a father to him after all these years . . .'

Rex stops then walks off, unbuttoning his soaking wet jacket as he heads towards his own suite.

When he opens the door it sounds like someone's taken a deep breath.

The wind outside might have caused a difference in air pressure, he reasons as he pulls his boots off in the dark hallway.

He walks out into the main room, and has just pulled his jacket off when he realises that someone is standing in the corner behind the lamp.

The yellow lampshade is hiding his face, but he can see light glinting off the blade of a hunting knife.

'Stay where you are,' a voice says behind him.

Rex turns and sees James aiming his hunting rifle at him.

'No sudden movements now,' he says. 'Put your hands where I can see them, slowly.'

'What are you—'

'I'll shoot, I'll shoot you right in the face,' James yells.

Rex shows his empty hands and tries to figure out what's going on.

'Kill him,' Lawrence whispers from the corner behind the lamp.

'Where's your rifle?' James asks, waving the barrel at him.

'I left it in some trees,' Rex replies, trying to sound as calm as possible.

'And your knife?' Lawrence hisses. 'Where's your knife?'

'In my belt.'

James takes a step closer and stares at him with a fevered look in his eyes.

'Loosen your belt and let the knife drop to the floor.'

'Shoot him instead,' the other man says, shuffling his feet impatiently.

'I'm unbuckling it now,' Rex says gently.

'If you do anything stupid you're dead,' James warns, resting the rifle against his shoulder. 'I promise you. I'd be only too happy to shoot you.'

'He killed Kent,' Lawrence says, in a louder voice.

'Don't do anything stupid,' Rex pleads.

'Shut up,' James shouts.

Rex unbuckles his belt and the weight of the hunting knife pulls it onto the floor beside his leg.

'Kick the knife over here,' James commands.

Rex kicks the knife, but it rolls only a metre across the carpet before coming to a stop.

'Kick it again!' James says impatiently.

Rex moves forward and kicks it harder, sending it over to the armchair.

'Now back away and get down on your knees,' James says.

Rex takes a few steps back and kneels down.

'Shoot him,' Lawrence repeats. 'Right in the forehead.'

'So you seem to think I had something to do with Kent's death?' Rex says tentatively.

James marches over and strikes him in the face with the butt of the rifle.

It hits his right eyebrow, his neck jerks and his vision fades for a few seconds. Rex slumps sideways. The pain throbs and burns.

'You were in our zone!' James shrieks, holding the barrel to his temple. 'I'll shoot. I don't care what happens . . .'

'Shoot him!' Lawrence calls in a gruff voice.

'I was looking for Sammy,' Rex gasps.

'Where the hell are our phones?' James asks, pressing the barrel harder against his head.

'I don't know. I haven't touched them,' Rex replies quickly. 'But I have an iPad in the suitcase on my bed. We can call for help on that.'

'Shut up,' James snorts. 'You know perfectly well that there's no fucking Wi-Fi . . .'

The door opens and someone comes into the room.

'Dad?' Sammy calls into the dimly lit suite.

'Get DJ!' Rex shouts to his son before the next blow hits him.

He falls onto his back, raises his head and sees that Lawrence has already reached the hallway.

'Sammy!' Rex gasps.

Lawrence grabs his son by the hair, drags him across the floor and hits him across the face with the handle of his hunting knife. He forces Sammy down onto his stomach, sits astride him, pulls his head back by the hair and puts the knife to his throat.

James is breathing faster now, and closes his mouth and moistens his lips before standing over Rex, and pressing the rifle to his forehead.

'This ends here,' he says. 'Understand? This ends here. You're done. Getting your revenge doesn't change anything. It doesn't make anything better.'

The barrel is shaking and James steadies it by pushing it harder into Rex's face.

'We didn't know what we were doing,' James goes on. 'It just happened. We knew it was wrong, but we're not bad people, we were just young and stupid.'

'You don't have to apologise,' Lawrence shouts at James.

'What did you do?' Rex gasps.

'I'd never rape anyone. It wasn't me, it was Wille . . . and the whole fucking school looked the other way. We all knew that, because no one cared what we did in the Rabbit Hole.'

'You're talking about Grace?' Rex says.

'Shoot him! Now!' Lawrence pants.

James turns the gun around and hits Rex in the face with the butt several times. The room vanishes with each blow, only to reappear hazily before fading again.

'Dad!'

Rex hears Sammy scream as more blows strike his face. It's like something from a different world. His mouth hurts, and one eye. He's tumbling into darkness. He tries to resist, but loses consciousness.

His head is throbbing when he comes to. His face is sticky with blood, and his wounds are stinging. He can vaguely tell that the men are tearing strips of cloth and tying his arms behind his back. He hears them hunting through his things, and realises that they're looking for the phones.

'I'll go and check the boy's room,' he hears Lawrence say.

Rex tries to turn his head to look at Sammy, but he can't move. He tries to shout, but he can't get any words out. The only sound that emerges is the bubbling of blood in his throat.

104

Four security guards from Timberline Knolls Residential Treatment Centre led Saga to the gates where they waited for the police to arrive. They gave an account of the intrusion and handed her over to the two police officers.

Saga dozed off on a bench in the police station's holding cell. She wasn't allowed to talk to anyone.

The following afternoon she was moved to a windowless interview room. She still wasn't allowed to make any calls, but a female officer took down all the names and contact numbers Saga gave her.

Towards evening, when they began to realise she might actually be telling the truth, the FBI were called in. But because their offices had closed for the day she was taken back to the holding cell, where she slept on a hard rubber bunk.

It's nine o'clock in the morning when Special Agent Jocelyn López arrives at the custody unit. She already seems over-caffeinated, and she somehow looks even more unhappy than last time.

'Did you like the hotel?' she asks once she's signed Saga out.

'Not much.'

They leave the police station in silence and get into López's silver Pontiac.

'I need to borrow a phone,' Saga says.

'To call your boss?' López asks as she starts the car.

'Yes.'

'I've already spoken to him, several times.'

'Then you know that I need to make a call,' Saga says.

'Forget it.'

'It's important.'

'Bauer, you Swedes might be good-looking, but you're not very smart, are you?'

Saga doesn't know exactly how the incident has been resolved between the various authorities, but it seems clear that the Swedish side has guaranteed she'll go back home without causing any more problems.

López leads Saga Bauer into Terminal 1 of O'Hare International Airport, thanks her for her cooperation and pins a large badge of a smiling onion with the words 'My Kind of Town' on her jacket.

A transport officer assumes responsibility for her departure. He seems very good-humoured, and as he takes her to check in he says he's been watching a television show about Vikings.

The lines at security are long. After forty-five minutes they've reached only halfway. The police officer gets a call on his radio, replies, then looks over towards the escalators before turning to Saga.

'I have to go, but you'll be all right, won't you? Your plane leaves in four hours. Grab a hamburger and keep an eye on the boards for your gate number.'

He forces his way back through the crowd and hurries off, talking into his radio.

Saga moves slowly forward in line.

Her phone has been destroyed, so she has no idea what Joona has found out about Rex and Oscar.

It's possible that more people have died because she got stopped before she had time to talk to Grace.

She's not going to cause any more problems. She'll head home, but first she just needs to get out to the rehab centre one last time, and then somehow call Joona.

Something happened during the rape that Grace hasn't told her.

There was someone else in the Rabbit Hole.

Could he be the murderer?

Saga apologises and pushes her way back through the crowd, slings her bag over her shoulder and walks out of the departure hall.

The man behind the counter at the car-rental firm looks oddly hopeful when he sees her come back in.

'Not a chance,' she says before he has a chance to open his mouth.

She rents a Ford Mustang, like last time, and starts to drive back to the treatment centre.

Chicago's suburbs are laid bare in the grey light.

The gates of Timberline Knolls are open and Saga drives straight past the security lodge and pulls up in the visitors' car park.

She bypasses reception and half-runs between the main buildings, cutting across the grass lawn she crept across in the darkness not all that long ago, to get to Grace's building.

She opens the door and walks straight through the cafeteria, where a few patients are having lunch, knocks on Grace's door, and walks in without waiting to be asked.

Grace is sitting with her back to the door, just like last time, staring out at the beautiful rhododendron bush behind the building.

The white pill bottle is on the floor by the woman's feet.

'Grace,' she says gently.

The woman's breath forms a patch of mist on the glass, and she wipes it off with her finger before breathing on the window again.

'Can we talk?' Saga says as she comes closer.

'I'm not feeling very well today,' Grace says, and slowly turns around. 'I think I've taken three, I should probably get some sleep . . .'

'Is three pills too many?' Saga asks.

'Yes,' the slender woman says.

'Then I'll call for a doctor.'

'No, they just make me tired, that's all,' she mumbles.

Grace opens her thin hand to reveal more of the pink capsules,

466

then picks one up and raises it towards her mouth before Saga gently stops her.

'That's probably enough now,' she says.

'Yes.'

'I don't want to upset you,' Saga says. 'But when I was here last time, you told me about the Rabbit Hole, and what the boys did to you.'

'Yes,' Grace says in a low voice.

'Did anything else happen in the Rabbit Hole?'

'They hit me, I fainted several times, and . . .'

Grace falls silent and starts to pick at the buttons of her cardigan with trembling fingers.

'You fainted, but you're still sure that all the boys took part in the rape?'

She nods, then puts her hand to her mouth as if she's about to throw up.

'Shall I call for help?' Saga asks.

'Sometimes I take five pills,' Grace replies.

She looks at the window and runs her finger through the condensation, making a squeaking sound. Saga sees a couple of women in nurses' uniforms approach along the path from the right.

'Grace? You say you're sure they all joined in, but . . .'

'I remember everything,' the woman says with a smile. 'Every little mote of dust in the air . . .'

'Do you remember Rex?'

'He was the worst,' Grace replies, and looks at her through half-closed eyes.

'You're sure? You saw him?'

'He's the reason I ended up there. I trusted him, but he . . .'

Grace rests her cheek against the wall, closes her eyes and lets out a silent burp.

'Did he go with you to the clubhouse?'

'No, they said he would be coming later.'

'And did he?'

'Have you smelled the stench that comes from a rabbit hole?' Grace asks, gets up and walks over to the armchair. 'It's only a tiny opening in the ground, but down below there's a whole labyrinth of dark passageways.'

'But you didn't see Rex, did you?' Saga asks patiently.

'They kept pulling at me, none of them wanted to wait . . . they were growling, all dressed up with big white ears . . .'

She rests her hands on the back of the armchair and rocks forward – it looks like she's nodded off in the middle of a thought.

'You wouldn't rather lie down on the bed?'

'No, it's OK, it's just the pills.'

She slowly tries to settle down on the armchair, but when there's not enough room for her to curl up she gets to her feet again.

Saga can hear knocking and cheery voices, and realises that medical rounds are underway.

'Grace, what I'm trying to say is that memory is a complicated thing. Sometimes we think we remember things because we keep repeating them to ourselves. What would you say if I told you Rex wasn't there, because—'

'He was there,' Grace interrupts, one hand fumbling across her neck. 'I saw . . . I saw at once that they had the same eyes.'

'The same eyes?'

'Yes.'

'You had a child,' Saga whispers, and a shiver runs down her spine when she realises that the child is the unknown factor that Joona had been talking about.

'I had a child,' Grace repeats quietly.

'And you think that Rex is the father?' Saga asks, shaking her head.

'I know he is,' she replies, brushing away a tear. 'But I didn't tell Mum and Dad . . . I spent three weeks in the hospital, and said I'd been hit by a truck, and that all I wanted was to come back to Chicago . . .'

She wobbles again and puts her hand to her mouth.

'I . . . I should probably lie down,' she whispers to herself.

'I'll help you,' Saga says, guiding her slowly across the floor.

'Thanks,' she says, and sinks onto the bed, lies down on her side and closes her eyes.

'Did you give birth alone?'

'When I realised it was time, I went out to the barn so I didn't make a mess,' she says, blinking tiredly. 'They say I became psychotic, but to me it was reality . . . I hid myself away in order to survive.'

'And the child?'

'Mum and Dad used to come some weekends, and when they did he would have to take care of himself, I used to hide him in a cot . . . because I had to be indoors, sit at the table, sleep in my bed.'

Grace reaches to open the drawer in the bedside table. She puts her hand in and closes her eyes for a few moments, gathering her strength before pulling out a framed photograph and handing it to Saga.

In the picture a young man with a shaved head is squinting at the camera. He's wearing sand-coloured combat fatigues, and a bulletproof vest and is holding an MK12 by his side.

He's the unknown factor in the rape.

The man in the picture has burned his cheeks and nose in the sun.

On his shoulder is an oval black and yellow badge, bearing an eagle, an anchor, a trident, a flintlock pistol, and the words 'Seal Team Three'.

The Seals.

'Is this your son?'

'Jordan,' she whispers with her eyes closed.

'Does Rex know about him?'

'What?' Grace gasps, and tries to sit up.

'Does he know you gave birth to a child, and that he's the father?'

'No, he must never know,' she says, and her mouth and chin start to tremble so much that she has trouble speaking. 'He has nothing to do with Jordan. He raped me, that's all. He must never meet Jordan, he must never look at him . . . that would be awful . . .'

She sinks back onto the bed, puts both hands over her face, shakes her head and then lies still.

'But what if he wasn't there?' Saga starts to say, but breaks off when she realises that Grace is asleep.

Saga tries to wake her, but it's impossible. She sits down on the edge of the bed, checks her pulse, and listens to her regular breathing.

105

DJ sits down heavily in one of the armchairs in the foyer and leans back against the headrest. The rain is drumming on the windows and roof. On the table in front of him lie three of the five hunting rifles.

His heart is beating far too fast and his body is twitching spasmodically. His neck tenses, as if someone were holding it tightly. His narcolepsy threatens to overwhelm him.

He's destroyed all the phones, the wireless router and every computer in the hotel.

He's trying to think strategically, keeps asking himself if there are any other preparations he needs to make, but his thoughts devolve into peculiar fantasies each time.

DJ was planning on finishing them all off inside the enclosure, but only managed to get rid of one of them because of the storm.

He had stood in front of the deep ravine, watching the rain sweep in towards the valley.

Over the course of nineteen minutes, Kent Wrangel had begged for his life something like a hundred times, and had sworn he was innocent almost as often.

DJ hadn't wounded him particularly badly, just stuck his hunting knife into his stomach, just above his pubic bone, then held his shaking body upright on the edge of the deep ravine.

He stood there with the knife in Kent's stomach, explaining why this was happening.

Kent gasped for breath as his gut filled up with blood.

DJ had tilted the sharp blade of the knife upward, and whenever Kent got tired or slumped to the ground slightly, the knife cut higher into his guts.

Towards the end Kent had been in agony. One knee almost buckled several times, and the knife had slid up diagonally towards his ribs.

Blood filled his boots and started to overflow.

'And now the kite string breaks,' DJ said, pulling the knife out, looking Kent in the eye and shoving him in the chest with both hands, out over the edge.

DJ wipes his mouth, glances over towards the hallway leading to the hotel rooms, and starts to remove the cartridges from the rifles. He opens the duffle bag on the floor in front of his feet and drops the ammunition into the compartment next to the underwear.

It's time to bring this to a conclusion.

First Lawrence, or possibly James, and then, last of all, Rex.

Maybe he'll have time to kill one of them before all hell breaks loose, before the screaming starts and they start running.

But fear has never saved the rabbits.

He knows that their panic follows simple patterns.

His hands tremble slightly as he fits the silencer to his pistol, inserts a fresh magazine, and puts it back in the bag, next to the short-handled axe.

If they don't come out soon, he'll have to start going from room to room.

He takes out his black SOCP dagger, wipes the grease from the blade, and checks the cutting edge.

His mother was left pregnant after the rape, but it probably wasn't until he was born that her psychosis really hit her.

She was only nineteen years old, and must have been horribly lonely and frightened.

DJ doesn't remember his early years, but now knows that she gave birth to him alone, and kept his existence a secret. She hid him out in the barn. His first memory is of lying under a blanket, freezing, eating beans from a tin.

He has no idea how old he was then.

Throughout his childhood her chaotic psyche became part of his life, part of his perception of reality.

His maternal grandparents didn't move home for good until Lyndon White Holland's long stint as ambassador to Sweden came to an end.

DJ was almost nine when his grandfather found him in the barn.

At the time he spoke a mixture of Swedish and English, and hadn't really understood that he was a human being.

It took time to get used to his new circumstances.

His mother was looked after at home. She was kept heavily medicated and spent most of her time in bed with the curtains drawn.

Sometimes she got frightened and started screaming, and sometimes she hit him for leaving the door open.

Sometimes he told her about the rabbits they had shot that day.

Sometimes they would sit on the floor next to the bed together, singing her nursery rhyme until she fell asleep.

A year or so later he recorded the whole rhyme for her on a cassette tape so she could listen to it if she felt anxious.

His mum never wanted to talk about his dad, but once, when he was thirteen and her medication had just been changed, she told him about Rex.

It was the only time that happened during his childhood, and he can still remember those few sentences by heart. As a child, he clung to every little word, building whole worlds of hope around what she had said.

He had learned that they had been in love, and had to meet in secret, like Romeo and Juliet, before she came back to Chicago.

DJ couldn't understand why he didn't go with her.

She replied that Rex didn't want children, and that she had promised not to get pregnant.

At first DJ believed her, but then he started to think she was hiding from Rex in Chicago because she was ashamed of the way she looked after the truck accident.

He still doesn't know where the idea of the accident came from. He has no memory of her ever having talked about it.

When he was fourteen years old his mum saw a picture of Rex in an article in *Vogue*, about the new generation of chefs in Paris. She went straight out into the barn and tried to hang herself, but Grandpa climbed up to the beam on a ladder and cut her down before she died.

Grandma and Grandpa had her committed to a psychiatric hospital and he was sent to the Missouri Military Academy, which took younger boys.

DJ tucks the dagger under the tablecloth when he hears someone coming down the hallway.

He closes the duffle bag with his foot, leans back again, and wonders which one of the men the fates have chosen to send out first.

His head crackles and he can see his mother huddled on the floor in the stall, covering her ears and whimpering in terror as one of the rabbits they thought was dead suddenly jerks and starts running again.

DJ remembers catching it under a green plastic bucket, sticking his hand inside to grab it, then nailing it to the wall. His mother was shaking uncontrollably, then threw up in terror and screamed at him that he wasn't allowed to bring the rabbits inside.

106

DJ looks up when he hears the footsteps get closer, and Lawrence appears in the light of one of the lamps. DJ raises his hand in greeting, thinking that the man will soon be running from room to room clutching his intestines in his arms.

Lawrence looks like he's been crying. His eyes are swollen and red and he's still wearing his wet clothes.

'Did you find the phones?' he asks, blinking hard.

'Can't find them anywhere,' DJ replies.

'We think Rex took them,' Lawrence says in a tense voice.

'Rex?' DJ says. 'Why would he do that?'

'We just think it's him,' Lawrence snaps.

'You and James? That's what you two think?'

'Yes,' Lawrence says, and his face turns red.

He goes behind the reception desk and switches on one of the computers. The rain is still clattering on the roof. The storm seems to have been catching its breath, then returning with even greater fury.

Just two months after DJ returned from his last tour in Iraq, his grandfather died, leaving a fortune to his only grandchild.

DJ's grandmother had passed away two years earlier. He went to the clinic to visit his mother, but she didn't even recognise him.

He was alone.

That was when he decided to go to Sweden, so at least he could see his father.

Rex was already a successful chef. He'd been a guest on countless television programmes and had published a cookbook.

DJ set up a production company, changed his name to his grandmother's maiden name, and approached Rex without any thought of revealing that he was Rex's son.

Nonetheless, he was incredibly nervous before their first meeting, and suffered an attack of narcolepsy in the dimly lit passageway leading to the Vetekatten café.

He woke up on the floor and arrived at the meeting half an hour late.

They didn't look alike, except maybe around the eyes.

DJ presented Rex with a business proposal. He offered him a ridiculously generous contract, drew up a new strategy, and in less than three years managed to get him a slot on the main Sunday morning breakfast show and turn him into the biggest chef in the country, and a bona fide celebrity.

DJ came to act as a sort of manager, they started to socialise, and gradually became friends.

Even though he was already sure, he couldn't help taking a couple of strands of Rex's hair. He was standing behind Rex's chair, and pulled them out with a pair of tweezers. Rex yelped and put his hand to his head, then spun around. DJ just laughed and said it was a white hair that he hadn't been able to ignore.

Without touching them, he put the hairs in plastic bags and sent them to two different companies that specialised in paternity tests.

There was no doubt about the match. DJ had found his father, but had to bury any happiness he felt.

'There's no Wi-Fi,' Lawrence says from behind the reception desk.

'Maybe try another computer?' DJ suggests.

Lawrence looks at him, wipes the sweat from his hands and nods towards the window.

'Can we walk to Björkliden from here?'

'It's only twenty kilometres,' DJ replies. 'I'll go as soon as the storm has passed.'

476

Throughout David Jordan's childhood his mother was treated for depression and suicidal behaviour. After the most recent visit, when she didn't recognise him, DJ had his mother moved to a more exclusive care home, Timberline Knolls Residential Treatment Centre. The senior doctor there believed her condition was post-traumatic stress disorder, and radically altered her treatment.

Just before Thanksgiving DJ decided to go to Chicago to ask his mother for permission to tell Rex that he was his father.

He didn't even know if she would understand what he was talking about, but the moment he walked into her room he could tell that she was different. She took the flowers and thanked him for them, offered him tea and explained that she had been ill as a result of psychological trauma.

'Have you started to talk to your therapists about the truck accident?' he asked.

'Accident?' she repeated.

'Mum, you know you're sick, and that you weren't able to take care of me, and that I had to live with Grandma.'

DJ saw the odd expression on her face when he told her about the DNA test, that he had got to know his father, and that he now wanted to tell him the truth.

There was a faint tinkle as she put her cup down on the saucer. She stroked the tabletop slowly with one hand, and then she told him what had happened. She became less and less coherent as she went on, but she told him about the rape in gruesome detail, about how the boys had wanted to hurt her, and the pain, the fear, and how she ended up losing herself.

She had shown him a photograph from a boarding school outside Stockholm, then started to stammer as she recited the names of the boys who had taken part in the assault.

He remembers exactly how she was sitting, with her thin hand over her mouth, sobbing as she told him he was the product of rape, and that Rex was the worst of all of them.

After saying those words his mother couldn't look at him.

It was devastating.

'Nothing's working. We're completely isolated,' Lawrence says in an unsteady voice.

'That could be because of the storm,' DJ suggests.

'I think I'm going to head out for Björkliden right away.'

'OK, but make sure you bundle up, and watch out for the cliffs,' DJ reminds him gently.

'Don't worry,' Lawrence mutters.

'Can I show you something before you go?' DJ says.

He folds back the tablecloth and picks up the flat knife, then conceals it by his hip as he walks over to the desk.

107

Lawrence nudges his glasses further up his nose, walks over to the desk with the computer, and looks at DJ.

'Is it difficult getting down to the main road from here?' he asks.

'Not if you know which way to go,' DJ replies in an oddly flat voice. 'I can show you on a map.'

Instead of a map, DJ pulls a photograph from his pocket, puts it on the desk and turns it around so Lawrence can see it.

'My mum,' he says softly.

Lawrence reaches forward to pick up the photograph, then snatches his hand back as if he's been burned when he recognises the young woman in the photograph.

At that moment a black knife slams down into the counter right where his hand had been.

The blade sinks deep into the wood.

Without thinking, Lawrence pushes the computer towards DJ, and the rounded corner of the screen hits one side of his face.

DJ stumbles backwards and almost falls.

The computer's trajectory changes when it reaches the end of the cable. The screen swings back beneath the desk, comes loose and clatters to the floor.

DJ looks surprised as he raises his hand and feels his face.

Lawrence runs along behind the desk and down the steps to the spa as quickly as he can with his bulky frame.

His first thought is to try to get out through the emergency exit he noticed earlier.

For some reason the sign's green glow had stuck in his mind.

Without looking, Lawrence hurries past the photographs of women in Jacuzzis and on white massage tables. He passes a smaller reception desk with towels and a shop selling bathing suits, and makes his way into the locker room. When he closes the door he notices that it has a lock.

He tries to turn it but his hands are shaking so badly that he keeps losing his grip.

The lock's stuck.

Lawrence is gasping for breath and his heart is thudding in his chest as he wipes his hands on his shirt.

Footsteps are approaching.

He pulls at the handle and tries again. It's stiff, but finally there's a scraping sound and he pulls harder, turns it, and slowly the lock slides into place before he loses his grip and scrapes his knuckles.

He sucks the wound, listens and is just about to check that the door is completely locked when someone pushes the handle down on the other side.

Lawrence moves back.

DJ tugs at the handle and shoves the door with his shoulder, making the doorframe creak.

Lawrence stumbles backwards, staring at the door, and feels like shouting at him to kill James instead, that James is in Rex's room.

But instead he retreats further into the dark locker room, thinking in confusion that he needs to find somewhere to hide.

DJ just said that Grace is his mother.

So DJ is the one who's been getting revenge, Lawrence thinks to himself as he walks past the lockers.

He pushes open a frosted glass door and finds himself in an unlit shower room. He takes a few steps and tries to calm his breathing.

His mouth is completely dry and his chest hurts.

He stands with his back to the wall and looks down at the drain. There are some dried hairs stuck to the grille.

Sweat is running down his sides from his armpits.

Lawrence thinks back to the rape in the Rabbit Hole, how they formed a line, and how he was worried they'd be stopped before he got a chance to do it with her.

When he'd seen her lying there on the floor beneath the others he'd felt a surge of adrenalin and fury against her.

He had always known that Grace was too pretty for him, but now she was lying there with her legs open.

He pushed his way forward, leaned over her, hit her in the face with his beer bottle, and held her chin hard to make her look at him.

At first he felt nothing but jubilant triumph inside.

Afterwards he stood up and spat on her, but then two weeks later he had tried to castrate himself in the bathroom of his dorm. He cut deep, but the pain made him stagger sideways, slip and fall. He hit his face on the sink, and when it broke people came running.

After a month in a junior psychiatric ward he was allowed home, and he immediately handed himself in to the police. They wouldn't even listen to him: no one had been raped at the school, and the girl he was talking about had moved back to the US.

He rests his hand against the cool polished granite wall, feels the taste of blood in his mouth, and realises he can't stay in the shower room.

Legs shaking, Lawrence makes his way past the row of showers, the tinted glass door to the sauna, then emerges into the unlit pool area.

All he can hear is the rain against the huge windows.

He knows he has to reach the emergency exit, get out of the hotel and try to find help, or just hide out in the forest.

The pool area is divided by a large, hexagonal bar in the middle.

On one side are the Jacuzzis and the main swimming pool, which still has some water left at the bottom. In the winter you could swim through a plastic curtain right out into the snow, but for now the external part of the pool is covered.

On the other side of the bar, beyond the serving area and relaxation zone, is the emergency exit. The construction workers have dug up the floor and all the furniture has been moved out, and is now blocking the passageway between the bar and the windows. The mountain of wicker chairs and tables is covered with industrial grey tarp.

The only way through to the emergency exit seems to be past the door to the women's locker room.

Lawrence listens for a while, then starts to creep along the pillared walkway. He keeps his eyes glued to the frosted glass of the door to the women's locker room. Every little vibration makes him tense in an effort not to run in panic. He can see through the gap around the door that the changing room is unlit, and he holds his breath and moves past, forcing himself to walk slowly past the window to the solarium.

He glances quickly back at the door, then hurries on.

Through the next window he sees a gym full of exercise machines, treadmills and cross-trainers.

Lawrence is walking towards the other side of the bar when he hears a squeaking, clicking sound.

From this angle the pillars block his view of the entrance to the women's lockers, but a reflected shadow is moving on the wall.

Someone must have come through the door.

Lawrence doesn't know what to do. He doesn't dare run, so he just walks quietly around the end of the bar, where he sinks to the floor and tries to catch his breath.

108

Lawrence is hiding behind the bar, with one hand clamped firmly over his mouth. His racing pulse is thudding in his ears. He knows that DJ is in the spa area, trying to find him.

But everything is silent and still.

Some Coke has dripped down the dark veneer of the bar, and someone has stuck a piece of gum under the edge of the protruding bar-counter.

Lawrence is sweating as he huddles up, making himself as small as he can, trembling.

He's breathing hard through his nose, thinking about how the rape set him on a path away from happiness. He's never had a serious relationship, never been close to anyone sexually, never had a family.

To stop those close to him thinking he's weird, he sometimes pretends to have brief relationships.

To his friends he claims to prefer one night stands. But the truth is that there has never been anyone for him, male or female.

For the past year he has been in touch with a girl he met on a dating site. She's one of the dancers in the musical *Hamilton* on Broadway. Lawrence knows that this may be a lie, that she could be 'catfishing', but they always have interesting and entertaining conversations, and she's never asked him for money. He loves the pictures she sends. She's so astonishingly pretty that it makes his entire body feel happy. Her big, curly hair, and those cheeks, and that smiling mouth. She's too good to be true, but she just sent him a ticket to the show that looks genuine, with a barcode and everything.

He's probably being tricked somehow, but what if it really does mark a turning point in his life?

Lawrence glances over at the emergency exit, then stands up in a crouch and creeps down a broad flight of stairs.

The whole bar area has been cleared and they've started to lay mosaic tiles on the floor. The green exit sign is shining beyond some construction pallets.

Rain is still streaming down the big panes of glass.

Lawrence walks faster, trying to breathe quietly.

If he can get outside, he just has to keep going until he reaches the church, then head along the E10 to Björkliden, and hide somewhere until this is all over.

There's a clatter as his foot hits a black bucket. It slides across the dusty floor, and the trowels inside it rattle when it comes to a halt.

Lawrence starts running, no longer worrying if anyone can hear him, swings around the pallets and reaches the emergency exit. He shoves the handle down and pushes and pulls, but the door won't open.

A heavy padlock is hanging from the handle.

He adjusts his glasses, turns around, and his heart starts to thud in terror when he sees DJ coming down the stairs with an axe in his hand.

Lawrence kicks at the glass but nothing happens.

His eyes sweep quickly across the room and he realises he needs to try to get to the other side of the bar, through the mountain of sofas, cupboards, potted plants, chairs and tables.

Panting, he hurries along the windows towards the stack of furniture. It's tightly packed and reaches his chest. He lifts the plastic cover and squeezes in between a pile of chairs and a round marble table.

The light changes beneath the plastic, becomes hazy and oddly soft.

He holds the cover up with one hand and crawls into a narrow passageway between some cupboards, but stops when he hears a clattering sound behind him. He quickly huddles down and hears the plastic settle on top of the furniture again.

Leaning over and with his knees bent, he forces his bulky frame between two cupboards full of dishes.

He can't help thinking that it's Grace coming after him.

That this is how they've set it up.

In his mind's eye he sees her pink pleated skirt, her blood-smeared thighs and her long hair stuck to her cheeks.

Panting for breath, he pushes past some huge terracotta pots and deck chairs, then suddenly hears footsteps behind him.

On one level he knows it's DJ, but his brain keeps summoning up an image of Grace.

She's here to get her revenge. He can hear her getting closer, dragging a skipping rope behind her, its plastic handle bouncing across the uneven mosaic floor.

Panicking, he shoves one wicker chair out of his way, picks up the next and pushes his way through to a large buffet table, but from there on his path is blocked.

He's reached a wall of heavy cupboards. It's impossible to get through to the pool area this way. He needs to find a different route, possibly under the stack of sun-loungers.

The plastic sheet billows up in a draught, then settles back down with a rustling sigh.

The pain in Lawrence's chest has got worse and his left arm feels oddly numb.

When he bends down to see if it would be possible to crawl under the loungers his glasses fall off.

Shaking badly, he sinks to his knees to look for them, but manages to knock them under a low table instead. He thinks he can see them, and reaches but can't quite grab them.

He lies down on his stomach and starts to slide into the cramped space. Shuffling forward, he blinks and stretches his arm out, touches his glasses with his fingertips and quickly puts them back on.

Still lying on his stomach, he turns his head and looks back towards the mosaic floor when DJ suddenly crouches down and stares straight at him through the table legs and chairs.

He looks like Grace, with his attractive open face and blond hair.

The plastic rustles and Lawrence realises that DJ is squeezing through the stack of furniture.

Lawrence presses on beneath the table, and hears the zip of his jacket scrape across the slate floor.

He's breathing harder now, and with each breath his back presses against the stone slab and it feels like he's about to get stuck.

He thinks about the ticket to the musical again, and how she'll never understand why he didn't show up.

Furniture is crashing behind him and he hears glass breaking as he gets closer to the other side of the table.

He's gasping for breath now as he tries to grab something to help pull himself out.

There's a dull clang as DJ puts the axe on the floor and reaches in after him.

'Leave me the fuck alone!' he screams.

DJ grabs one of his feet and starts pulling him back. Lawrence kicks out and pulls free, slides out from the other side of the table and stands up shakily. It feels like he's about to throw up as he pushes between some heavy sofas. He topples a stack of white cushions and the plastic settles down over him again. He stumbles on, scrambling over the cushions, and just about manages to keep his balance.

He's made it through the barricade, and turns and rushes on, hitting his shoulder on one of the pillars as he hurries around the whirlpool bath, but then he stops.

He's breathing incredibly fast and the fingers of one hand feel completely numb now.

He keeps going, looking back at the bar and seeing DJ's reflection in the glass door.

DJ is running along the walkway with the axe in his hand.

He's heading towards the pool area, past the doors to the locker rooms.

Odd strips of leather are hanging down his cheeks.

Lawrence coughs and walks quickly towards the main pool, thinking he can get outside from here.

His heart is hurting now, and he has to move more slowly as he grabs the handrail beside the tiled steps leading down into the pool. The water at the bottom smells stagnant.

Shaking, he hurries down the shallow steps, wades out and tries to run, but the resistance is too great.

The muck at the bottom swirls up through the thigh-high water.

He pushes laboriously through the water, feeling it splash his stomach and chest.

Plasters, flip-flops and clumps of hair are floating on the surface.

He passes the hanging plastic curtain and heads into the covered outdoor pool. It must be possible to get out from there. The covering is only a tarp, after all, stretched across some low cross-beams.

He wades further out and tries to see if there are any holes in the fabric.

He hears heavy splashing behind him and turns around.

DJ is ploughing towards him through the water.

Lawrence realises it's going to be almost impossible for him to get out of the pool before he's caught.

His fingertips are itching and tingling.

Panting, he turns away and starts to wade towards the closest edge of the pool. He almost falls over, but manages to grab it.

He pushes the tarp up as hard as he can. The coarse nylon fabric is stretched so tightly that he can't open up even the smallest gap.

He tries to pull on the cross-beam in an effort to dislodge it, but it's impossible.

DJ is wading through the water with long strides.

The waves hit the side of the pool and splash up at Lawrence.

He can't get his fingers under the edge of the tarp and tries to push it instead, but he has to give up.

Gasping for breath he starts to wade off into the water again, but his heart is beating too fast. He can't go on. There's nowhere left to run, and he stops and turns around.

109

Lawrence stands still, breathing hard through his mouth. He tries to say something, but is still too out of breath. He's nothing but a rabbit, darting around in its own blood at the bottom of a tub.

The Rabbit Hunter is getting closer now, trailing the axe across the surface of the water.

He had prepared the tape-player and the cassette, and had intended for Lawrence to be pinned to the reception desk by the dagger when the others came out to look for him.

The dirty water has splashed up over Lawrence's checked shirt, and there are big sweat-stains under his arms.

'I know what this is about,' Lawrence says between strained breaths.

He holds both hands up as if to stop him from coming any closer. The Rabbit Hunter takes a short step forward, grabs one of his hands, stretches his arm out and strikes him with full force just above the elbow with the axe. Lawrence stumbles sideways from the force of the blow, and his scream of pain echoes around the walls of the pool.

Dark blood pumps from the deep wound.

He keeps hold of Lawrence's hand, twists it slightly, and strikes again.

The blade slices straight through the bone this time.

He lets go and looks at Lawrence, who staggers backwards with his lower arm hanging from a few last sinews before it falls off and splashes into the murky water.

'Oh God, oh God,' he whimpers, trying to press the stump of his arm back to his body to stem the bleeding. 'I don't know what you want me to do. Please, just tell me. I need help, can't you see?'

'Grace is my mother, and you—'

'They made me do it. I didn't want to. I was only seventeen,' he sobs.

He falls silent, breathing hard. His face is white, as if he were already dead. The Rabbit Hunter looks at him intently: the splashes on his glasses, his snot-streaked beard, the blood smeared across his filthy clothes.

'I understand that you want revenge,' Lawrence says, gasping for breath. 'But I'm innocent.'

'Everyone's innocent,' the Rabbit Hunter says in a low voice.

He thinks about Ratjen, sitting on a chair in his kitchen in front of his children. Ratjen died because he provided the keys, because he opened the door to the boarding house and took Grace to the Rabbit Hole. That's what started it all. If he had said no back then, he could have eaten his macaroni in peace, and then gone to bed with his wife once the children were asleep.

'Wille made all the decisions,' Lawrence gasps.

'Mum identified you. She told me what you did,' he says calmly.

'They forced me,' he sobs. 'I was a victim, I was also a . . .'

Lawrence's voice fades away as the Rabbit Hunter's ears go deaf. He picks at one ear but still can't hear anything. He's lost in the memory of a summer afternoon, the day before his mum's attempted suicide.

He was hunting with his rifle beyond the main road, past the railway line and down towards the silo. He sat down in the grass, leaned back, and when he woke up it was already evening.

It was as if he'd woken up in a dream.

He lay still in the tall grass, thinking that the silo looked like the Mad Hatter's big top hat.

At that moment he was as small as a rabbit.

Lawrence is still hoping he can escape, and stumbles off in the direction of the tiled steps again.

A trail of dark blood billows out across the water around him. The Rabbit Hunter looks at his watch and follows him.

Lawrence passes the plastic curtain, staggers forward, takes one step up and then sits down on one of the bottom steps. He lifts the stump of his arm, whimpering from the pain. Wheezing badly, he tears his shirt apart and winds it around the stump as tightly as he can, pulling at it with his single, trembling hand.

'God, oh God,' he keeps whispering to himself.

Blood seeps through the fabric onto the wet steps.

'You don't need to worry about bleeding to death,' the Rabbit Hunter says, brushing the rabbits' ears from his face. 'Because before you pass out I'm going to hit you in the neck with the axe, so you'll die pretty instantaneously.'

Lawrence looks up at him in despair.

'Did we kill Grace? Why are you killing us, if she's still alive—'

'She's not alive,' he interrupts. 'She never got a chance to live.'

Very soon he's going to go back upstairs and hang James Gyllenborg. He doesn't know why he wants to hang him, in particular. It was just an idea he had when he was watching him when they were out hunting – that he wanted to see him hang.

A flash of memory: the sound when Grandpa cut his mother down from the beam in the barn.

'What are you going to do next?' Lawrence whispers with bloodshot eyes. 'When you've finished getting your revenge? What happens afterwards?'

'Afterwards?' the Rabbit Hunter says, resting the axe on his shoulder.

110

When Rex comes to, his heart starts to race with anxiety. He's lying on his stomach on the floor with his arms tied behind his back. His face feels tight, and is thudding with pain from the repeated blows.

His empty suitcase lies in the middle of the floor, its contents scattered.

He can hear voices and rolls cautiously onto his side. He tries unobtrusively to free his hands, and realises that he can't feel his fingers.

Through half-open eyes he sees Sammy sitting against the wall with his arms wrapped around his knees. Rex makes a slight movement, meets his son's gaze and sees him shake his head almost imperceptibly.

Rex closes his eyes at once and pretends to be unconscious. He listens to his son talk in a subdued voice.

'I have nothing to do with this . . . I'm sure you already realised that. I wouldn't even be here if my dad hadn't been trying to stop me from seeing my boyfriend.'

'You're gay?' James asks curiously.

'Don't tell Dad,' Sammy jokes.

'What's so great about guys, then?'

'I've been out with girls too, but the sex is better with guys.'

'In my day,' James says, 'I could never have said that. So many things have changed, in a good way.'

With ice-cold fingers Rex tries to loosen the tightly knotted strips of cloth.

'I'm not ashamed of who I am,' Sammy replies.

'Do you go out with older men?' James asks in an odd tone of voice.

'What turns me on are individuals, situations. I don't have a big set of rules,' Sammy says calmly.

Rex lies still and hears James walk across the floor. He opens his eyes cautiously and sees James standing in front of Sammy. He's holding the rifle loosely in one hand, its barrel pointing down beside his leg. The overpriced bottles of water and wine that the hotel offers its guests are standing on the coffee table.

James turns around and Rex quickly closes his eyes and tries to make his body limp. James comes over and stops in front of him. The smell of metal tells him that the rifle is pointing at his face.

'Most people I know call themselves pan-sexual,' Sammy goes on.

'What's that?'

'When you think that personality, not gender, is the most important thing.'

'That sounds sensible,' James says, going back over to him. 'I'm sorry Lawrence cut you. Does it hurt?'

'A little . . .'

'You're going to have a scar on that pretty face of yours,' he says with unexpected tenderness in his voice.

'Damn,' Sammy sighs.

'You should probably put something over it to keep the edges closed,' James goes on.

'Dad has some plasters in his toiletry bag,' Sammy suggests.

The room goes silent and Rex keeps his eyes closed. He's almost certain that James is looking at him.

'It's over there, by the armchair,' Sammy says.

Rex feels James take a step away from him and kick the bag across the floor, towards Sammy.

'Thanks.'

Rex hears Sammy unzip the bag, followed by a rustling sound as he finds the plasters.

'You should wash it first,' James points out.

When he hears James pick the water bottle up off the table and unscrew the lid, Rex twists his arms and pulls as hard as he can until he frees one hand from the bindings. His cold fingers tingle and sting as the blood returns to them.

'Sit still,' James murmurs. 'Lift your face up a little . . .'

'Ow,' Sammy whispers.

Rex opens his eyes and sees that James has put the rifle down on the floor and is bending over Sammy holding the water bottle and a bundle of paper napkins.

Very slowly, he gets to his feet. His legs are numb and feel like lumps of wood. One of the strips of cloth is dangling from the cuff of his shirt, but comes loose and falls to the floor, making a soft sound as it lands.

Rex stops and waits.

James hasn't heard anything. He turns the water bottle upside down on the napkins and goes on bathing Sammy's cheek.

Rex moves slowly over to the coffee table and picks up the wine bottle, taking care not to make a sound.

'A bit more water,' Sammy says. 'Ow . . . ouch, that really . . .'

'Almost done,' James says, with an odd intensity in his voice.

Rex walks towards James but manages to step on the shirt that was in his suitcase. It's still in plastic and rustles beneath his foot. He rushes forward, raising the wine bottle, and sees James drop the napkins and turn towards him just as he strikes. James raises his arm to defend himself, but the bottle hits him on his cheek and temple, so hard that the glass breaks. Green splinters and dark-red wine rain down on James and across the wall behind him.

James groans heavily and falls sideways. Sammy moves out of the way and Rex grabs the rifle and backs away. James slumps back against the wall, feels his temple and looks groggily up at Rex just as he steps forward and rams the butt of the rifle against the bridge of James's nose, slamming his head back against the wall.

'Come on,' Rex says to Sammy. 'We have to get out of here.'

They leave the room, close the door and hurry along the cold hallway towards the reception area.

'Nice work, Dad,' Sammy says with a smile.

'You too,' Rex says.

They can hear heavy thudding coming from somewhere, and Rex turns back, but the dimly lit hallway is empty and the door to his room closed. The barrel of the rifle scrapes the wall and Rex raises it slightly. At that precise moment he gets such a splitting headache that he has to stop.

'What is it?' Sammy whispers.

'Nothing, just give me a second,' Rex replies.

'What are we going to do?'

'We're going to get away from here . . . Let me look at you,' he says, and leads his son into the light. 'You might end up with a scar . . .'

'On my pretty face,' Sammy jokes.

'Yes.'

'You should see yourself, Dad.'

Rex looks back at the hallway again, and now he sees that one of the doors they passed is ajar.

111

Rex and Sammy walk towards the lobby in silence. The thick carpet muffles their footsteps.

They emerge into the lobby. There's no one there, but one of the computers is lying on the floor. The rain is still pounding furiously against the black windows. The gutters are overflowing, the water splashing down onto the terrace outside.

'*Ten little rabbits, all dressed in white,*' they suddenly hear a child say. '*Tried to get to heaven on the end of a kite.*'

Rex and Sammy turn around and see an old tape player standing on a table.

'*Kite string got broken,*' the child's voice continues. '*Down they all fell. Instead of going to heaven, they all went to . . .*'

'What's going on?' Sammy whispers.

Rex recognises the rhyme from the phone call he got at the restaurant. He walks over to the table and sees that there's blood on the tape-player buttons.

'*Nine little rabbits, all dressed in white, tried to get to heaven on the end of a kite . . .*'

'Go to the front door,' Rex says nervously.

'Dad . . .' Sammy says.

'Walk down to the main road, then turn right and keep walking,' Rex calls.

'Dad!'

Rex turns and sees James Gyllenborg coming towards them quickly. He's holding a hunting knife in his hand, his clothes are stained with wine, and he's breathing through his mouth as if his nose is broken.

'*Eight little rabbits, all dressed in white,*' the voice on the tape drones on.

James looks at the knife in his hand, then marches towards Rex.

'Just calm down, James!' Rex says, raising the rifle.

James stops and spits some bloody saliva on the floor. Rex backs away and puts his finger on the trigger.

'You're an idiot,' James snarls, holding the knife out in front of him.

There's a crack as one of James's legs snaps at the knee. Blood spurts onto the floor and he collapses. He arches his body back and shrieks with pain.

It takes Rex a few moments to understand what's happening.

DJ is standing in the doorway leading to the spa area, a pistol fitted with a silencer in his hand.

He's wearing a leather strap around his head, strung with rabbits' ears.

Rex notices that his trousers are wet, right up to his thighs. He walks into the lobby, tosses a plastic-covered rope on the floor and tucks the pistol into a shoulder holster.

DJ stops, closes his eyes, then slaps himself on the cheek, across one of the rabbits' ears.

James is screaming and trying to crawl back down the hallway.

DJ looks at him, then walks over to Rex and takes the rifle, removes the cartridges and puts it on the coffee table with the other guns.

'*Six little rabbits, all dressed in white, tried to get to heaven on the end of a kite,*' the child's voice chants on the tape.

James is lying on the floor gasping. A pool of blood is spreading out around his shattered leg.

'We need to bind the wound,' Rex says to DJ. 'He'll bleed to death unless we . . .'

DJ grabs James by his unharmed leg and drags him into

the dining room. Rex and Sammy follow him in. James knocks into one of the tables, sending the candlesticks rolling to the floor.

DJ turns James onto his stomach, puts one knee between his shoulder-blades, fastens his hands behind his back with cable ties, then stuffs a linen napkin into his mouth. Very methodically, he pulls a chair over and feeds the black rope through the chandelier hook in the ceiling.

'What are you doing?' Rex asks.

DJ ignores his questions and ties a noose, then pulls it over James's head, tightens it, winds the rest of the rope around a pillar and then starts to hoist him up by his neck.

The weight of James's body pushes the chandelier to one side, and the prisms tinkle as he twitches and writhes. Panicked quacking sounds can be heard through the linen napkin. Some of the crystals fall to the floor.

'That's enough,' Rex says, and goes over and tries to hold James's weight.

DJ wraps the rope around the pillar several times, then ties a knot and shoves Rex out of the way.

James swings sideways, his legs flailing.

The chandelier tinkles above him.

DJ watches James as he slowly spins, then he pushes the chair over towards him and watches as he stands up on it with his one good leg and tries to keep his balance.

In the lobby, the tape has reached the final verse about the last rabbit who ends up going to hell. DJ looks at his watch, then walks over and loosens the noose slightly. James tries to breathe in through his broken nose. Tears are streaming down his cheeks and his whole body is shaking.

'If you fall or pass out, you'll die,' DJ says calmly.

'Are you crazy? What the hell do you think you're doing?' Rex asks.

'You still don't get it,' DJ says blankly. 'All the others understood, but not you.'

'Dad, let's go,' Sammy says, trying to pull Rex away.

'What is it I don't get?' Rex asks, swallowing hard.

'That I'm going to kill you too,' DJ replies. 'As soon as I'm done with James I will . . . I think I'll slice your back open and pull your shoulder-blades out.'

He holds up an old photograph of Grace from her first year at the school. The photograph has a white fold right across her smiling face.

'She's my mother.'

'Grace?'

'Yes.'

'I just found out she was raped,' Rex says. 'James told me.'

'Dad, let's go,' Sammy says quietly.

'You were there,' DJ says with a smile, swaying slightly.

'No, I wasn't,' Rex says.

'Do you know, everyone says that before I—'

'I've done loads of things I regret,' Rex cuts him off. 'But I haven't raped anyone, I was—'

He's interrupted by a knock coming from the lobby. They stand in silence as another knock echoes through the hotel.

112

The Rabbit Hunter stands absolutely still in the dining room, looking through the door to the lobby and feeling the icy rush of adrenalin through his veins.

But a wave of fatigue comes hot on the heels of his increased pulse, and he realises he's forgotten to take his Modiodal today.

He's not sure he'll need it, but a serious attack of narcolepsy could ruin everything.

He just needs to stay calm.

He hears Rex say that they need to remove the rope from James's neck, but it's as if he's speaking from behind a wall.

The Rabbit Hunter opens his eyes and meets his gaze.

He knew from the beginning who was going to be the last to die. Rex will be left alone, surrounded by the desolation of the battlefield. He will see his avenger come and will fall to his knees in acceptance of his fate.

The dining room is silent.

Rex moves back with Sammy. James is in so much pain that he's on the point of losing consciousness.

When there's a third knock on the door, sparks fly inside the Rabbit Hunter's head as he sees the barn door blow open and snow swirl in across the floor.

His mum is crying like a frightened little girl as she shuffles backwards, holding the butcher's knife to her own throat.

The storm had been raging all night, and his mum had grown more and more scared, not knowing what to do. She sat for hours with her hands over her ears, her eyes screwed shut, and then she got aggressive, picking at the entrails and throwing them at the door, and threatening to smother him when he started to cry.

He knows he has to stop. The razor-sharp memories take up too much space, and he needs to stop himself from turning into his mother, from opening the door to psychosis.

As a child he shared her sickness, but he wasn't sick himself. He just didn't have an alternative – and that isn't a sign of psychosis, he reminds himself.

For her, the rape overwhelmed the reality of the present, her fear of rabbits became a phobia and her terror formed a terrible alliance with her memories.

There's another knock on the door, even harder this time.

The Rabbit Hunter hears himself start to issue orders, but it feels as if it's all happening in another world.

He kicks the chair from under James and watches his body jerk as he pulls off the rabbits' ears, closes the doors to the dining room, then rearranges the rug to cover the bloodstains on the floor.

They go over to the reception area, and DJ takes Sammy behind the desk with him while Rex goes over to open the front door.

The rain is still beating against the black windows, running down the glass, gushing off the roof.

A figure is visible in the storm outside.

DJ puts his rabbits' ears in a drawer containing pens and paperclips. He draws his pistol, takes the safety off and hides the gun behind the desk.

Rex unlocks the door and lets in a tall man holding a petrol can. Rain blows in across the floor before Rex closes the door.

DJ studies the stranger's face and weary movements.

His blond hair is stuck to his wet cheeks. His clothes are soaked through and his shoes and the bottoms of his trousers are caked in mud.

DJ can't hear what he says to Rex, but sees the man put the

empty petrol can down on the mat and walk towards the reception desk.

'The hotel's closed,' DJ says, looking into the stranger's oddly pale grey eyes.

'I realise that, but I ran out of petrol down on the E10 and saw the lights,' the man says in a Finnish accent.

DJ puts his left hand on Sammy's shoulder and holds the hidden pistol with the other. He's an ambidextrous shooter, and doesn't even need to think when he switches hands.

DJ knows that there's a chance that the stranger is a police officer.

He could be, even though it seems unlikely.

Still, he can't allow irrational suspicions to govern what he does in the next few minutes.

No one could have tracked them down in such a short time, and a police officer would never come after him alone.

DJ looks at the way the man's wet clothes cling to his arms and chest, and is sure he isn't wearing a bulletproof vest.

But he could still have a pistol tucked under his left arm or down by his ankle.

The most likely explanation is that the man doesn't have a clue what he's stumbled into; he simply ran out of petrol.

'We'd love to help, but this is a private event,' DJ says, moving the pistol to his other hand under the counter. 'There's no staff here and all the phones have been disconnected.'

113

Joona stands in front of the reception desk as if he's about to check in. He knows Rex recognised him, but treated him like a stranger.

David Jordan has a small streak of blood on his forehead, and is looking at him with curiosity.

Presumably he's trying to figure out if Joona is going to pose a threat to his plan, or if he's just going to leave.

Joona brushes his wet hair from his face and feels the rain trickling down his back as he puts both hands on the counter.

As soon as he landed at Kiruna Airport he spoke to Jeanette Fleming, the psychologist, over the phone. She didn't have an address, but confirmed that both Sammy and Rex had travelled to Kiruna, then repeated what Nico had said about Rex trying to turn his son straight by forcing him to shoot reindeer in a cage.

While Joona hired a car, Anja found the only hunting enclosure with wild reindeer anywhere close to Kiruna. She also discovered that the hotel attached to the enclosure had been rented for a private event this weekend. She begged Joona to wait for reinforcements from the North Lapland Police District.

'I'm sorry we can't help,' David Jordan concludes.

Joona knows that most elite military close-combat training assumes that the opponent will be inferior in terms of both equipment and training.

Because that's usually the case.

Their techniques are extremely effective, but there's also a degree of arrogance built into everything they do.

'You must have a mobile phone, though?' Joona says in a friendly voice.

'You'd think so, wouldn't you, but we've been a bit unlucky with everything technical, so we're on our own until we get picked up tomorrow.'

'I see,' Joona says. 'Where's the nearest place you can think of to get hold of a phone? Would that be Björkliden?'

'Yes,' DJ replies curtly.

Joona had noted the four hunting rifles on the coffee table in front of the fireplace when he came in, which probably means that at least one person is missing.

Both Rex and his son look like they've been beaten, but apart from the injuries to their faces they don't seem too badly hurt.

There's a computer lying on the floor, and the rug in front of the dining-room door is askew.

'Has there been some sort of trouble here?' Joona says, nudging the computer with his foot.

'Go now,' DJ says quietly.

David Jordan had his left hand on Sammy's shoulder when Joona came in, and then he moved the hotel ledger with his right hand.

Both gestures were unnecessary.

It's likely that he wants Joona to think he isn't holding a pistol beneath the desk, to test if he's the first police officer on the scene.

But Joona knows that the murderer is ambidextrous, and he knows that he's in the middle of an unspoken hostage situation.

The murderer would definitely have time to shoot both Rex and Sammy before Joona managed to put his hand under his wet jacket and draw his own pistol from its holster.

He knows he has to wait, even if that might mean incurring losses, and suddenly finds himself thinking of his former lieutenant, Rinus Advocaat, who quoted Wei Liao-Tzu before their first training session in unconventional close combat.

The tactical balance of power is located at the extremities of the Tao, he said in his usual joyless way. If you have something, pretend that you don't have it; if you're missing something, pretend that you have it.

Even a child is familiar with the strategy, but it takes strong will to stick to it in a tense situation where it would normally be natural for a police officer to draw his weapon.

Right now, this extreme game is Joona's only chance of saving the lives of the hostages.

Like all spree killers David Jordan has got a plan, and he'll want to stick to it.

If he thinks Joona is a police officer, he will shoot at once. That's the only rational option, even if it means deviating from the plan. But if Joona is merely a man who's run out of petrol, it makes more sense to wait and let him leave.

The killer has tried several times to show Joona that he's unarmed, to prompt him to act. So by now he's probably started to drop the suspicion that Joona could be an armed police officer.

'What are you guys doing up here?' Joona asks.

'Hunting.'

Every second he lingers takes them closer to a dangerous situation, but as long as Joona pretends not to have a gun, there's a chance he can separate Rex and Sammy from the killer.

'Well, I'd better get going, but . . . I was just thinking,' Joona says with a smile. 'There must be some sort of garage here with snow mobiles, that sort of thing?'

'There should be,' Rex replies, coming closer to the desk.

'It would be great if I could just siphon off a bit of petrol . . . I'll pay, obviously,' Joona says, undoing one of his jacket buttons.

'We only have the keys to the main entrance, and they don't fit the barn or the annexe,' David Jordan says, sounding stressed.

'I see,' Joona nods. 'Well, thanks anyway.'

He turns his back on David Jordan, undoes the last button and starts to walk towards the door.

'Don't you want to wait until the worst of the rain has passed?' Rex says behind him.

'That's kind of you.'

He turns around again and sees that Sammy has started

shaking, and that David Jordan has had his eyes closed for an unusually long time.

Wait, wait, Joona thinks.

David Jordan moves with lightning speed, yet it still feels like he's pushing his arm through gushing water as he raises a pistol and pulls the trigger.

The hammer hits the pin, the percussive gas forces the bullet through the barrel and the bolt clicks.

Blood squirts out behind Rex as the bullet passes through his torso.

David Jordan has already turned the gun on Joona and moves out from behind the desk without losing his line of fire for a second.

He has both eyes open, and is scanning the whole room as he moves. Rex looks bemused as he staggers backwards, clutching his hand to his bleeding stomach.

'Dad!' Sammy cries.

Joona forces himself not to put his hand inside his jacket. David Jordan is aiming at his chest, and his finger is on the trigger.

DJ reaches Rex, grabs him from behind and kicks him in the back of the knee so he slumps to the floor. He never takes his eyes off Joona.

'This is none of your business,' he says to Joona. 'If you stay out of it, you'll get out of here alive.'

Joona nods and holds both hands up in front of him.

'Take my son with you,' Rex gasps to Joona. 'This is between the two of us, we can end it without anyone else here.'

David Jordan pauses for breath, presses the end of the silencer to Rex's temple and closes his eyes again. Joona reaches his hand out and takes Sammy's arm. He pulls him towards the front door, slowly and carefully. They pass the table with the rifles and the dark fireplace. David Jordan looks up at them. It almost looks like he's having trouble staying awake, even though his knuckles on the hand holding the pistol are turning white.

Joona reaches the door and gently pushes the handle down. The killer's eyes start to close again.

'Sammy, I love you,' Rex says to his son.

David Jordan's eyes immediately snap open and he raises the pistol towards Sammy. Joona yanks Sammy backwards just as the bullet slams into the glass behind them.

They stumble out into the rain and biting wind. Sammy collapses onto the stone deck, and the door is thrown back so hard by a gust of wind that the glass shatters.

Joona drags Sammy to his feet and sees through the flying glass that David Jordan is running across the foyer with his pistol raised in front of him.

'We have to take cover,' Joona shouts over the wind, and pulls the boy off to one side.

Water is cascading off the roof, gushing from the overflowing gutters and spraying up from the bottom of the drainpipes.

'Dad!' Sammy cries.

Joona drags him past the rocks on the edge of the deck and straight into the bushes. They tumble over the edge, hit the ground and slide down a drenched slope, dragging stones and soil with them.

Sammy lets out a groan as they come to a stop among a thicket of birch saplings.

Joona is already on his feet, and quickly pulls Sammy further away from the hotel. Torrential rain is pouring down on them, forming new streams and carrying off soil and leaves.

They hide beneath the protruding rock-face and hear David Jordan calling out to them.

'Sammy!' David Jordan shouts from the edge of the terrace. 'Your dad's dying. He needs you.'

The boy is breathing far too quickly, and he tries to sit up. Joona holds him down and sees that his eyes are wide with shock.

'I have to talk to my dad . . .'

'Be quiet,' Joona tells him.

'He doesn't think I care, but I do, and he needs to know that,' he whispers.

'He already does,' Joona says.

The rain is lit up by the light from the windows, and a figure darts across one of the panes. DJ's footsteps send small stones over the edge of the terrace, and Sammy shakes as they hit the ground in front of them.

But suddenly the footsteps stop.

David Jordan has stopped, and is standing absolutely still, listening, waiting for them to start running and give themselves away. Like rabbits.

114

Saga tries her best, but she doesn't manage to wake Grace before the doctor reaches the room on her round. She opens the door, turns away from the staff, walks to the cafeteria and pours herself a mug of coffee.

A middle-aged woman with beautiful green eyes stares at her, then shakes her head.

'It isn't visiting time,' she mutters, then starts to pull a muffin to pieces on her lap.

Saga drinks the weak coffee, puts the mug down and takes another look at David Jordan when he was in the military. His eyes and cheekbones look a little like Rex's, but otherwise they don't look particularly alike.

She picks up the mug again and takes another sip, then walks around the cafeteria and watches as the staff leave Grace's room and knock on the next door.

Saga waits a few more seconds, then hurries back inside, closes the door carefully behind her, goes over to Grace and pats her on the cheek.

'Wake up!' she whispers.

The woman's eyelids tremble slightly but remain closed. Saga can hear that her breathing is shallower now, and pats her cheek again.

'Grace?'

Slowly she opens her heavy eyelids, blinks, and looks up in wonder at Saga.

'I fell asleep,' she whispers.

'You can go back to sleep again soon, but I need to know why you're so sure that Rex is the father of your son, seeing as he didn't—'

'Because I've seen the DNA test,' Grace interrupts, trying to sit up in bed.

'There was no police investigation,' Saga says. 'No samples were taken from you, don't you remember? You said you'd been in a car accident . . . you didn't tell anyone about the rape.'

'I mean the paternity test,' she replies.

Saga looks at Grace in surprise, sits down on the edge of the bed, and then suddenly realises what happened thirty years ago.

'You were seeing Rex before you were raped, weren't you?'

'I was stupid. I was in love . . .'

'Did you have sex?'

'We just kissed,' Grace says, looking at Saga in confusion.

'Is that really all?'

Grace picks at her nightdress and looks down at the floor.

'We did it on the meadow behind the school . . . But, I mean, we stopped before he . . . you know, the way you can stop things . . .'

'That isn't always enough, as you probably know by now?'

'But . . .'

Grace lifts the sleeve of her nightdress to her face and wipes her cheeks and nose.

'Listen,' Saga says, 'Rex was locked up in the stable while you were raped . . . if he's the father of your child, then you must have been pregnant before.'

A trace of recognition flits across Grace's face.

'He was locked in the stable . . . Are you sure?' she asks.

'Yes, I am. The others beat him and then locked him up. He had no idea what was going on.'

'Dear God,' she whispers, and tears start to trickle down her cheeks.

Grace lies back on top of the bed and her mouth opens, but she can't bring herself to say anything.

'Do you have a phone?' Saga asks, patting her hand.

A pane of glass shatters somewhere in the building and an alarm starts to ring in the hall. Saga sees a guard approach along one of the paths.

'Grace,' she repeats. 'I need to know if you have a phone.'

'We're not allowed,' Grace replies.

Something hits the floor hard in a neighbouring room, making the picture on the wall sway.

'It isn't visiting time!' a woman screams through the wall, her voice breaking. 'It isn't visiting time!'

Saga leaves the room and is hurrying towards the exit when the heavyset guard comes running around the corner, his keys jangling. He stops when he sees her, breathing hard, then pulls his Taser from his belt.

Without hesitating she heads towards him, yanks a bright-red fire extinguisher off the wall and marches on with long strides.

The guard stares at her, loosens the safety catch of the Taser and starts to walk towards her.

The heavy fire extinguisher is hanging from her hand, and she swings it up into her arms and rushes at him.

'I need to borrow a phone,' she says, ramming the base of the extinguisher straight into his chest.

He groans as the air goes out of him, staggers backwards and fumbles for support along the wall as she slams the fire extinguisher into his chest again.

He drops the Taser as he falls, reaching out with his hand and pulling down a picture.

Saga moves with him, kicks low and hits him in the calf, knocking his foot out from under him and sending him crashing to the floor. He hits the wall with his shoulder and lands awkwardly on his backside.

'What the hell?' he coughs, staring at her in bewilderment.

Saga drops the fire extinguisher, steps between his legs, grabs his head with both hands, pulls it towards her and hits him in the face with her right knee. His head snaps back, spraying beads of sweat. His heavy body follows and he slumps to the floor, inert. He lies there on his back with his arms out and his mouth bleeding.

'How hard can it be to lend someone your phone?' Saga pants between breaths.

115

DJ comes back in from the rain, walks through the shattered door, yells something, then throws his pistol at the wall. There's a crash, and parts of the gun fly across the floor and under the furniture.

Rex is lying on his side and can hardly breathe. His stomach is burning with pain and every movement hurts so much that he's having to fight not to pass out.

'What were you doing out there?' he asks between shallow breaths.

He tries to get up, but lurches forward as his legs buckle beneath him, and he falls to his knees. He's keeping one hand pressed against the bullet wound. His field of vision contracts for a few moments, then he sees that DJ is putting the leather strap with the rabbits' ears back on again, and coming towards him with a black knife in his hand. The dangling ears sway with each step.

'Sammy's only a child,' Rex pants.

Pain and shock have left him barely able to understand what's going on. DJ pushes him forward and he puts both hands down to brace his fall, then feels himself being cut across the back.

His arms give way and he sinks to the floor.

'You can't,' he whimpers as DJ forces him up onto his feet again.

512

Rex has no idea how deep the cut on his back is – his fear that Sammy might be dead overwhelms everything else. DJ pushes Rex in front of him, through the shattered door and out into the rain.

Rex looks around in horror to see if he can see Sammy's body on the road down towards the church.

The rain is pouring down on him and his clothes quickly become soaked and cold. He's clutching his stomach with both hands and can feel warm blood seeping out between his fingers.

The heavy gusts of rain sweep across the driveway.

DJ shoves him forward again and he takes a couple more steps before feeling a dizzying tiredness. Everything around him seems to be moving jerkily.

'Sammy!' DJ shouts into the rain.

Rex starts crying with relief when he realises that Sammy is OK, that DJ must have lost track of him in the darkness.

'Sammy!' DJ roars, brushing the rabbits' ears from his face. 'Take a look at your dad now!'

Rex stumbles forward and tries to speak, but only coughs up blood.

'Call Sammy,' DJ commands. 'Tell him to come out. Tell him you love him, and that everything will be OK as long as he . . .'

Rex stops at the fork in the driveway. He doesn't want to be part of this any more. DJ walks around and hits him hard in the face with the handle of the dagger. He staggers but manages to keep his balance and raises his chin.

'Call Sammy,' DJ says darkly.

'Never,' Rex gasps.

The rain is lashing the air, and the pools of water look like they're boiling. The old wooden church down in the valley is painted dark red, and looks bloodstained among the white crosses in the churchyard.

'I get it,' Rex snarls. 'I get that you think—'

'Quiet!' DJ roars.

'I didn't rape—'

'I'll cut your throat!' DJ shrieks.

They can see the blue glow of police cars approaching the hotel from the turn-off on the E10 highway.

513

'Sammy!' DJ shouts.

All Rex can think is that Sammy will be OK, as long as he stays hidden.

'Keep walking!' DJ says.

Rex looks him in the eye and then sinks to his knees on the path. He's had enough.

DJ tries to get him to stand up, hits him across the cheek and yells at him to keep walking. Rex doesn't move. It doesn't even hurt as much any more. DJ tugs at him and he sways, but makes no attempt to get to his feet.

He closes his eyes, then opens them, and is just thinking that this is how it ends when he sees a figure through the rain. Someone is walking up the driveway towards them.

Joona has made his way to the driveway and is walking towards the two figures. The ground itself looks like it's shaking. He knew he had precisely nineteen minutes to save Rex from the moment the bullet hit his stomach.

The murderer has followed the same pattern every time.

There are two minutes left.

Joona knew he would have just enough time to get Sammy out, and then return before David Jordan decides it's finally time to execute Rex.

Rain is running through his eyebrows and he's having difficulty seeing. With each step he takes his pistol swings in the holster inside his soaked jacket. He hasn't yet revealed to DJ the fact that he's armed.

The Rabbit Hunter grabs Rex by his hair and pulls his head back, but lets the blade of the knife rest on his shoulder. He stares at the man walking towards them, trying to figure out what he could possibly want. Why is he coming back? He must have realised how serious the situation is, and that he should be doing everything he can to get away from them.

The emergency vehicles will be here in five minutes.

That's fine.

He has time to do what he needs to do. Nothing else matters, he thinks, and looks at his watch.

The symmetry of vengeance is perfect.

Rex spawned his own nemesis during the rape. At the precise moment of the crime, two cells came together to form the life that grew inside Grace's womb, the embryo that went with her to Chicago, the child that was born in secret and grew up to become a rabbit hunter who, thirty years later, has returned to punish the rapist.

The stranger is striding towards them along the drive.

The rain is pouring down on them, lashing the bushes until they're almost flattened.

Without any haste, the Rabbit Hunter moves the blade to Rex's neck and watches as the tall man seems to slow down mid-stride. He unbuttons the last button on his jacket, puts his hand in and pulls out a pistol, then raises it, all in the same fluid, concentrated movement.

The Rabbit Hunter doesn't have time to react. It's as if he can't comprehend, can't accept that this is happening.

Joona strides through the rain as he shoots David Jordan three times straight in the chest.

The recoil kicks back, and the final white flare of the barrel shimmers in the grey light like a small explosion.

David Jordan is thrown backwards and lands heavily on his back. The sound of the gunshots echoes off the mountains.

Joona walks the last few steps towards the killer with his pistol aimed at him, and kicks the knife away. The rain is still pouring down on them, rebounding off the ground. David Jordan lies on his back, staring up at him.

'You had a gun the whole time,' he says in amazement.

Joona sees that the three entry wounds are all in the centre of his chest and knows that David Jordan has no more than a couple of minutes to live.

There's no hope of saving him.

Water is gushing down the driveway, carrying the blood away with it.

Joona holds the pistol against David Jordan's forehead as he quickly searches his clothes, then he stands up and puts his pistol back in its holster.

David Jordan coughs up blood and stares up at the black sky. The falling rain gives him a dizzying sense of being carried upward at great speed.

Rex hasn't moved. He's still kneeling on the drive. At first he doesn't want to lie down when Joona tries to help him.

'Sammy,' he gasps.

'Don't worry, he's fine,' Joona says, gently laying Rex down on his side.

Rex's lips are white and his body is shaking, as if he has a fever. Joona rips Rex's shirt open and sees blood seeping from the bullet-hole in his abdomen. One of his kidneys has probably been hit. He's in serious pain, and will soon go into shock.

Joona's phone rings. He sees that it's an American number and guesses it's Saga. He answers, and says he can't talk right now.

'This is important,' Saga says. 'I've talked to Grace again, and Rex is David Jordan's father.'

'But he didn't take part in the rape,' Joona says.

David Jordan is lying on his back with his mouth open, but his eyes are still blinking when the raindrops hit them.

The first of the emergency vehicles are driving past the little church, their blue lights sweeping across its dark-red wood.

Joona switches his phone to speaker and puts it down.

'Did you hear what I said?' Saga says.

'Yes,' Joona replies as he helps Rex to raise his knees slightly to ease the pressure in his blood-filled abdomen.

'It might not matter any more,' she says. 'But David Jordan wasn't the result of the rape, like he thought – he was actually the fruit of true love.'

Saga goes on talking, but the phone starts to crackle and fade, then her voice vanishes altogether when the screen goes dead.

Rex tries to turn his head to look at DJ, but he doesn't have the strength. Blood is seeping out between Joona's fingers and onto the driveway.

Police and paramedics are running towards them now.

DJ has stopped breathing. His face is perfectly calm. Maybe he heard Saga's words before he died and understood what she was saying.

Joona stands up slowly and starts to walk down the slope. He sees Sammy walk towards the ambulance beside his father. The stone-coloured rain is still battering the valley and lake, and the entire landscape is etched in silver.

epilogue

Rex walks over to the edge of the swimming pool and looks at the smoke drifting over the teal water. He raises his head and watches the moths flying around the lanterns in the leafy garden.

The fat sizzles as it drips onto the coals, and tiny flames flare up around the thick steaks.

Sammy has set the long table on the deck, and is now blowing up a big, pink inflatable rabbit. Veronica is sitting a short distance away on the hammock, drinking red wine with Umaru, a man she met in Sierra Leone. His nine-year-old daughter comes out through the doors with a bowl of salad.

Rex flew to Chicago with David Jordan's body, and sat next to Grace at the funeral, holding her hand. She'd taken so many tranquillisers that he had to help support her at the church. As they walked past the pews after the brief service he heard her whisper 'Sorry', over and over again.

Rex goes over to the grill and turns the steaks, sees that they look perfect, and drinks some mineral water before putting Sammy's soya steaks on the grill. He's just about to get the potato and artichoke gratin from the kitchen when his phone rings.

'Rex,' he says as he answers, poking the steaks with the tongs.

'Hello Rex, this is Edith,' a high voice says.

'Hello,' he says uncertainly.

'We met just after you won the Chef of Chefs award.'

'I know – I've been thinking about calling, but—'

'I'm pregnant,' she says.

'Congratulations,' he says without thinking.

'And you're the father.'

It's already evening when Valeria picks up the apples and carries the baskets into the store. She goes up to the house and runs a bath, adding some oil and a few drops of perfume.

With a sigh she sinks into the hot water and feels her muscles relax as she thinks about the fact that Joona never called back after she left that voicemail.

She understands why, though. She pushed him away for no reason, simply because he was who he was.

He's always going to be a police officer.

Valeria let two months pass but couldn't stop thinking about him, so last week she picked up the phone and tried to contact him again. It turned out that he'd never received her message.

She smiles to herself, closes her eyes and listens to the sound of her own breathing, the drips falling into the bath, and the soft lapping of the water.

For some reason she can't remember if she locked the basement door earlier this evening.

Not that it really matters, but she usually does.

She's almost asleep, so she puts one foot on the edge of the bath, then stands up slowly to stop herself from getting dizzy. She steps carefully out of the bath and starts to dry herself. Her skin is steaming hot, and the mirror above the sink is foggy with condensation.

She squeezes the water from her hair, then pushes the bathroom door open and waits a few moments, looking along the hallway at the shadows on the wallpaper.

Over the past few days she's been getting an odd feeling in the house. She's not usually scared of the dark, but she's been more wary since her time in prison.

Valeria leaves the bathroom and walks naked along the hallway, pulling the wet plasters from her hands and wrists. She was clearing a patch of brambles in a large garden in Saltsjöbaden the day before yesterday, and the thorns went right through her gloves.

She walks into the bedroom and sees through the window that the treetops beyond the greenhouses are still darker than the sky. She goes over to the chest and opens the top drawer, takes out a clean pair of knickers and puts them on, then gets out her yellow dress and lays it on the bed.

She hears a clattering noise from downstairs and freezes. She stands absolutely still and listens, but can't hear anything now.

She can't think what the noise could have been.

Maybe the nail holding the framed photograph of her mother has given way?

Maybe the dishes in the sink have shifted position?

Valeria has invited Joona over tonight. They're going to have dinner together, and she's planning to cook spiced fillet of lamb with coriander, a recipe she found in Rex's new cookbook.

She hasn't told Joona he can stay the night, but she's made up the bed in the spare room just in case.

She goes over to the window and starts to lower the blind when she sees someone standing beside one of the greenhouses.

Instinctively she takes a step back and lets go of the cord, and the blind rolls back up noisily.

Valeria turns the bedside light off, covers her breasts with her hands and looks out again.

There's no one there, but she's pretty sure what she saw.

A thin man with a wrinkled face was standing very still between the narrow trunks of the deciduous trees, watching her.

Like a scarecrow on the edge of the dark forest.

It was a skeleton, her brain keeps telling her.

A skeleton in a green raincoat, clutching her old garden shears in one hand.

Now all she can see is the light glinting off the glass of the greenhouses, the trees, the yellowing grass and the rusty old wheelbarrow.

She lives alone in a house in the country, so she can't be scared of the dark.

Maybe it was a customer or a supplier who wanted to ask

something, then changed their mind when they saw her naked in the window.

She picks up her phone from the bedside table, but it's dead.

Joona should be here within the next hour. She needs to start cooking, but can't shake the feeling that she ought to go and check the garden.

Valeria pulls on her old bathrobe and goes downstairs, but stops before she reaches the bottom. There's a cold draught around her legs. She shivers when she sees that the front door is open.

'Hello?' she calls tentatively.

A few wet autumn leaves have blown onto the rug. Valeria pulls her boots on without bothering with socks, takes the flashlight from the coat-rack and leaves the house.

She goes down to the greenhouses and checks that the doors are all closed, then turns the flashlight on and looks inside them. Beads of condensation sparkle on the glass, and leaves pressed against the windows light up in the flashlight's beam, casting shadows into the greenhouses.

Valeria walks slowly towards the forest. The grass rustles beneath her boots and a small branch snaps when she steps on it.

'Can I help you with something?' she calls in a loud voice.

The pale bark of the willow looks like a geological formation in the light of the torch. The illuminated stems hide the darker ones behind them.

Valeria walks on towards the wheelbarrow, and looks at the brown flakes of rust, the holes in the porous metal, and realises that she's shaking with cold.

She moves cautiously to one side, points the flashlight up ahead and sees spiders' webs sparkle in the light.

There's no one there. The wild grasses don't seem to have been disturbed, but further in between the trees, just where the darkness takes over, is a grey blanket or old rug she hasn't seen before. She walks closer even though her pulse is starting to race.

The blanket seems to be covering something on the ground, something that looks like a thin body, a curled-up human form with no arms.